## ANN FEATHERSTONE

Ann Featherstone is Lecturer in Performance History at
Manchester University. She has written books and articles
about Victorian entertainment, including *The Victorian
Clown*, with Jacky Bratton. *Walking in Pimlico* is her first
novel.

Also by Ann Featherstone

*The Victorian Clown* (with Jacky Bratton)

*The Journals of Sydney Race 1892–1900*

# WALKING IN PIMLICO

## A Novel of Victorian Murder

◁◦▷

## ANN FEATHERSTONE

## JOHN MURRAY

First published in Great Britain in 2009 by John Murray (Publishers)
An Hachette UK Company

First published in paperback in 2010

1

© Ann Featherstone 2009

The right of Ann Featherstone to be identified as the Author of the
Work has been asserted by her in accordance with the Copyright,
Designs and Patents Act 1988.

A CIP catalogue record for this title is available from the British Library

ISBN 978-1-84854-174-0

Typeset in New Caledonia by Servis Filmsetting Ltd, Stockport, Cheshire

Printed and bound by Clays Ltd, St Ives plc

re⋯ ⋯able and
T⋯ ⋯ble forests.
⋯onform to
⋯in.

For my family

**To walk in Pimlico** *colloq.* to be handsomely dressed

*Murray's Dictionary of Slang, Cant and
Flash Words and Phrases*
(1857, 3rd edition)

## *Murderous Beginnings*

**Corney Sage – Whitechapel, London**

Here is a murder.

And here is yours truly, Corney Sage, comedian, clog-dancer, comic vocalist, actor and all-round funny fellow.

And though I never saw the murder, hardly knew the person what done it (not really), and only nodded to her what was done in, I was there at the beginning. And at the end too, though it cost me my health and reason, and still interrupts my sleep with bad dreams.

But stop me. I cannot tell the end before the start and, as per, I am going on ahead to put on my hat before my stocking. There is some business to be got through first before I can tell about the murder, so like the pro that I am, I thank you for your indulgence and trust to your good offices, and hope that nothing offends.

Or some such.

Now how I came to be doing my season at the Constellation Concert Rooms in Whitechapel is not of much importance, though if I was giving chapter and verse, as the parson utters, I should say that on this occasion I didn't get my shop through any advertisement in the *Era* newspaper (the Bible of the Acting Profession), but through the good offices of a young woman with whom I was acquainted, Miss Lucy Strong. No one, except the Gov, Mr Pickuls, would say that the Constellation was the best gaff in London, for it certainly was not, but I was short of a shop, and there was nothing else about, so I was glad to be set on to do a few turns on the platform. This was in the days when my dancing was something to behold. Dan Leno may offer to meet all comers and think he owns the world, but if he'd met me in my heyday there'd have been a different king on the throne! I don't blow my own horn as a rule, but it strikes me as rum when a man isn't give the credit for what he does best.

Anyhow, here are the dram. pers., as they give it in the theatre. Mr Pickuls, the Gov'nor, quiet-spoken, if full of himself, and his wife Mrs Gov, dark as the inside of a cow, and twice as mean. The Chinns, Mr on the piano and Mrs on the fiddle. (Not their proper names for they was from Roosher or some such far-off place, but their real moniker was such a tongue-binder that it was cut short – to Chinn.) And then there was the girls – a rum collection of Janes, Pollys, Nancys and Nells, but sweet-natured. Set on to do the poses plastiques which, when I first saw them, made me blush, so natural did those girls appear in their body-pink fleshings, standing stock-still on the stage and pretending to be marble figures of the Six Graces or what have you. There was not much of a stage, only a fiddling platform, and that barely off the floor and leaning to the right on account of the blocks having rotted away and being held up by house bricks. And a rag curtain what truly was a rag, so patched up was it (Mrs Pickuls's skill with the needle not being remarkable) and rings missing along the top. But it had been red plush (last century) and carried more gold than a Frenchman's breast pocket, so in a dim light it appeared to look the business.

'The Six Graces, Corney,' Gov says, with his chest puffed out, as the Chinns struck up and the girls held steady, some with their arms up, some down, and all of them gazing out to sea and like statues, as if they was made of stone.

2

But his judgement was to the mark, and no mistake, for the poses filled the Constellation to bursting with swells and City men and young rantans. There were bills up and down the High-street, and certain it was difficult to be ignorant of the 'startling and edifying display of classical statuary **IN THE LIFE!!!!**' so industrious were the bill-stickers with their paste and brushes. It all promised to be as rosy as the girls' cheeks, and I thought I should be settled there for a season, and had worked up a few pieces which brought me cheers of recognition when I stepped upon the stage. Just my dancing and some merry songs: 'The Industrious Flea', 'Alonzo the Brave' and the like, and borrowings from old pals, like Billy Ross, who I stood chummery with when he was at the Coal Hole. (But of him and his favour to me, more anon, as the story papers say.)

As I said, the Constellation was shining bright with success in its own firmament and would have continued until the appetite for the poses died, but one morning, of a sudden, the Gov decided upon a change. The poses were old sweat. The Judge and Jury was the thing. He had been on a convivial outing with his catering pals, and finished off at the Cyder Cellars in Maiden Lane where he saw performed his first judicial stunner, those naughty mockeries of mi'lords and mi'ladies, put up to inflame and amuse.

'I have expectations, Corney,' he croaked to me, looking pale and crusty, and with eyes like pips. 'My Constellation will be talked of all over the town.' He was much in earnest and so shabby from the night before, that I didn't have the heart to argue, and encouraged him, even as he was dragging the girls from their beds before noon and sending a special summons to the Chinns.

Bunting, the carpenter, was called up, to build a dock and bench (no need for plans, Bunting being very familiar with the inside of a courtroom), and Perlmann was given orders for the costumes. This Hebrew was not of the tailoring persuasion, of course, but in the 'Old Clo' business, having emporiums over three streets, and what

3

he could not provide in the overcoat line was not worth having. But judges' robes were a different matter, of course, and ladies' down-belows, neither finding their way to Petticoat-lane as a rule. And it was when old Perlmann started about me with his reckoning eye and his pencil stub and asking me whether I could muster a linen shirt, that I clocked that *I* was in line for the Bench too.

'In case you had forgot, Gov,' I reminded him, when he was taking a breather in the yard, 'I am only your comedian, with dancing – clogs and high boots – and comic songs as required. What I know about the Judge and Jury is like Nelly's drawers: too little to mention. And I am happy to say that I am also unacquainted with the law and the insides of a courtroom.'

But I might have saved my breath, for he had made his mind up. He patted me on the shoulder, mopped his brow, and said it would be in my interest if I conned a good few blue wheezes and read up on recent ripe goings-on in Battersea and Kilburn. Otherwise he'd heard Mr Jolliffe at the Salmon and Compasses in Pentonville was in need of a waiter. That marked it out for me clean as a penny. Either I sat on this Bench, or I could look for another shop, Pentonville way.

I wasn't the only one objecting, for some of the girls were rowdy about it too, but it was no use. He was like a man possessed, and would hear no argument. All he was bothered about was the show.

'What you must do,' he told us for the umpteenth time, 'is simple – make a mock of the swells and all their goings-on in the courts. It is very easy. Corney here is the Judge, and he will tell the case and introduce defenders and pleaders, and then you girls will act about a bit and make up this and that – Corney will tell you what. And the Jury will decide who's done right and who's done wrong – Corney will say. And that's that.'

It sounded to me like Corney was down for five years' hard labour. But no use arguing. Gov was so sure that his Constellation was set to be the Canterbury Hall of the East End that he went deaf, and then went out and bought new duds and a shiny watch and chain, and started wearing gloves and all, and peeling them off and putting them on again till everyone got sick of seeing them. He believed he was the Big Man about Whitechapel now, and no mistake, and if he wasn't fiddling with his gloves, he was whipping out his watch and chain (all going green of course), or waving his stick around.

He was quiet on the first evening, for there was only half a room full of locals, even though the bill-stickers had been hard at it for days, but after a very few weeks it was much better. And we were too, having grown accustomed to the business. Kitty and Lucy were mostly to the front, having the best figures and not shy, though it was me who did most of the speechifying, and that I gave with as much seriousness as I could muster, and tossed in a wheeze when I could, and would tip the audience a wink. After a few weeks, we were regular in the practice of Judge and Jurying. The Gov'nor would con the papers and come up with some new trial – how many there were, it was truly astonishing! – and we would quickly understand the meat of the argument and turn it into a jape in half an hour. After a few months we were a Judge and Jury what could hold their own, and the Gov said the 'Great Baron Richardson' had heard of us and meant to pay us a visit, which seemed to me unlikely, the 'Great Baron' having enough on with his own business. And, in truth, he never did come, though he was much looked for, if you know what I mean.

So after all this previousness, I have now arrived at the evening when my whole history, and that of others too, was stood upon its head.

Tuesday.

Not a packed room, but heavy enough with swells, who make a loud noise and cannot hold their drink. But they are heavy spenders and the Gov, who knew the Fancy all around, had put the word about that our Judge and Jury was worth a visit, and so this out-of-town party, half a dozen swells who was pretty much in their cups, took my notice as I was conning the crowd. They was frisky and handling the girls, though not roughly yet. Now I look out for our girls, although without a doubt they can look out for themselves, Kitty in particular, who had travelled the country with her father's boxing booth and has smacked a frisky swell more than once when he got over-playful. Not that the other girls were afraid of using elbows and knees when they was required, but it is a fact that swells turn powerful nasty of a sudden, unlike your working man who in general has a slower rise. So I had one eye upon our pack of swells, six or seven in number, who are noisy but not yet wild, and Gov is watching them too, though more concerned about his new tables and chairs, and the half-dozen mirrors he's put up around the walls only that afternoon.

We commence. Here is our courtroom, presided over by yours truly, a Learned Judge, with my wig and gown. Hammer in one hand, glass in the other, I Address the Assembly, what is the girls, some in gowns and some in breeches, trying to look like blokes, but not intending to do a good job of it!

'H-I shall co-mmence,' I always began, and rap my hammer on the block. 'Tonight we 'ave the case of Lord B and Lady C brought by Countess D who is much dis-tressed. Bring 'em on, Master Clerk.' And here Bessie, who is wearing a wig what slips over her eye and a clerk's gown over her down-belows, nips out to fetch Lady C and Countess D who are Kitty and Lucy, of course, dressed up like regular dames, only common, and showing a deal of leg and bosom. They parade up and down a bit and have the swells roaring so well that I have to bang about with my hammer again to get order.

'Well, Yeronner,' starts Kitty, trying to look aggrieved, 'I am much offended by the behaviour of my 'usband, Lord B. When we was married, 'e promised to keep me 'appy and attend to my every need. 'E said 'e would do anything 'e could to satisfy me.' (Here she winks – which was my idea – and starts the crowd laughing again.) ''E brought me into society, and let me 'ave a go at everything.' (Laughter.) 'And I did.' (More laughter.) ''E hintroduced me to Countess D.' (Here Lucy starts curtseying and showing plenty off.) 'She learned me a fing or two what I never knew before.' (And Lucy does a bit more.) 'And then, Yeronner, 'e took 'er off me.'

This always gets a good laugh, particularly when Kitty and Lucy embrace most passionately. It is here that I have to play the waiting game myself, using all my long experience to know just how long to let 'em embrace before I chime in. I have a long drink and light a pipe before I strike my hammer again and say, in my best Judge's voice, 'And what do you 'ave to say, Countess D? Is it true that 'er 'usband took you off 'er?'

Kitty looks about the room, and then gives Lucy one on the lips. Lucy appears much affected and is much inclined to attempt another embrace, but Kitty puts her off.

'Ho,' says Kitty, with much h-affectation, 'Lord B h-only wanted a bit of company. 'E is a gent much troubled by 'is h-affairs.' (Laughter.) 'Fings get very 'ard for 'im, and 'e yearns for relief. What h-I give 'im.' (Uproar.)

Lady C protests. 'You – flibbertigiblet!' (Laughter.) 'What about what you promised me? What about them bonnets what I give you? And them stockin's?'

I intervene. 'Yes,' says I, 'where is them bonnets? And them stockin's? Clerk. 'Ave these h-items been brung up as h-evidence?'

Bessie comes prancing in again, holding on her wig with one hand and carrying a small black bonnet and a pair of red stockings in the other.

'I've brung 'em, m'lord,' she squeaks. 'Do you want a glim?' (Not very clever, I know, but, my word, what roars of laughter it produces!)

And so we go on, with more of the same and, depending upon how enthusiastic the crowd is, we make it short or long. The Chinns play us on and off, and provide an interlude, and it is, as the Gov predicted, a belter. And it is good-humoured, also, with only one gent having a mardy, and Minter, the Gov's supporter, on hand to show him the way to the door. It is remarkable how poor the gentry are at holding their drink, though they have been brung up on it from the breast, as it were. But God's creation, as my old father, Mr Figgis, would say, is wonderful in its variety.

So, here am I, fit to burst (having a weakness in the bladder) and hastening out of the side door to relieve myself by the wall. And there, in the passageway between the house and the concert room is a swell and one of our girls, Bessie. He has her agin the wall and is belabouring her good and hard. And she, bless her sweet heart, is dead to the world. I enjoy my moment and breathe in the damp air and contemplate the blank, black wall, putting out of earshot the rasps and gasps of Mr Cocksure, for certain it is no business of mine. But Bessie I am fond of. She is only sixteen (though she looks older on account of her hard life), and I wonder whether this swell will give her what she is due, for he has handled her roughly and I hear her head smack the wall once or twice.

So I says quietly and without looking at either party, 'Wipe your-self off when you've done, Bessie, and get back sharpish,' and I nod towards the door, and then, turning my eyes away from the swell but letting him know I am addressing him, I say – 'Don't be too rough with her, sir. She's a good girl, and needs her looks.'

He is holding her by the shoulder, flat to the brickwork and her bare arms glow white in the darkness.

His lordship is aggravated by me. 'What business is it of yours?' he demands. 'You her pimp?'

I shake my head and open the door back into the hall, and for a moment all the fug and smoke and noise billows out into the yard in one great grey cloud. 'Not me, sir,' says I. 'But she's a good girl, and looks well. And deserves her dues, sir.'

He has released Bessie and she is all of a heap, half standing, half crouching against the wall and crying, I think. Or laughing. It is hard to say.

I call out to her, 'Bessie? You all right, gel?' and in reply she starts to sing.

'Here, Corney, listen to this:'

> *Johnny, John, what a lad*
> *Lips as smooth as a baby*
> *Hips so slim, cheeks so peachy*
> *Wouldn't you think he's a lady!*

I laugh, though it isn't so witty. But it touches Bessie, who shrieks with laughter.

'How much now then, my cocky? How much to keep Corney quiet when I've told him?'

'Tell me what?' I want to ask her, but her young swell is not amused, and kicks her hard when she cries out. I bite my tongue and debate what I should do, for though I do not like to stand by and see Bessie so ill-used, yet she *is* taunting him and riling him into a temper. Besides, I know that if I interfere and break the young devil's jaw (as I have a mind to) I will come off the worst, for he will lose me my shop. We both will lose our shops. So I try to hush Bessie, who is crying out that he has broke her leg, and I say to my lord, 'Since you have used her, sir, perhaps you should have a mind for her? She is a working girl and if you spoil her face, she must starve.'

But this touches a raw spot with him, and he makes a sudden rush at me, stumbling and lurching on the wet stones, and then sinks to his knees, cursing me for a pimp, which I much resent but leave to the night air.

There is no point trying to reason with a swell in his cups. That is what I told myself. And so concerned was I for my shop – my skin he could have any day – that I left him on his knees, and I know now of course that he was not saying his prayers.

When I got back inside, the Gov was in a rare old state, for our company of swells, having more coin than brains, had put a pile on the counter for another 'trial' and he was not inclined to refuse them. But Lucy had made herself scarce, Bessie also, and the Chinns were eating pork and cabbage across the way. So, as I was shutting the door behind me, and thinking of Bessie and her foolish song, Gov was upon me, plucking at my arm and smiling and demanding a favour of me – 'though I know you is only committed to two trials a night, Corney, but I will see you favourably obliged' – and, true to you, my wig was upon my head and my hammer in my hand before I could rightly tell him to go to heaven on a string. In fifteen minutes, we gave them Lady M who liked to dress as a boy, and the Mad Italian Countess and the Butler. It was a proper gaff-show, but as most of our audience was, as the hymn book says, beyond all comprehension, it was probably not of much account.

We finished sharpish – for we had been hard at the business some three hours, and even Mr Kean never went on that long – and once again my bladder was giving me a call, so I slipped out the side door and went to my usual post at the grating. The night was chill and damp, and when I put my hand upon the wall that peculiar London slime of soot and wet came off upon it like grease. It was a still night, too, even though we were situate almost direct upon the Whitechapel-road. But we might have been on Richmond Hill so still and silent was the air out the back. Like as if the walls held in the noise, and certain I was musing upon this after I had done relieving myself, when I was brung up with a start.

'Corney! Corney?'

It was Lucy. I could hear her, but I could not see her, and I looked about me and then saw her shadow by the yard gate.

'Lucy?' I cried. 'What you doin' out there in the Row?'

And when I walked over I saw it wasn't Lucy at all, but a gent also relieving himself (as I thought) by the wall, so I tipped my hat and asked his pardon and turned around.

'I'm here, Corney. Over here!'

I saw her then, in the shadows of the stable, her pale face staring out at me and her beckoning me over. And as I made to cross the yard, it was then that I saw something. A black shape, hard to make out, lying on the ground. I started to go up to it, but Lucy called again.

'No, Corney. Leave it. Come here. Quick.'

And in truth there was something rum about it that made me do as she said, and I skirted round the edge of the yard, keeping to the shadows, until Lucy grabbed my hand and pulled me into the stable. The smell of her body is what I remember, and how her lips, which were usually the sweetest part of her, were thin as poverty by the light of dark lantern.

I said, 'Now then, Lucy, you were missed, girl. You shouldn't nip off like that.'

I expected her to give me a mouthful, but she never, and I thundered on. 'You out here with company?'

She just shook her head and then she clung to me, as hard as ever she had. But it wasn't loving. Not at all. Here was a girl frightened.

'Ah, Corney,' she said, and her voice shook and her face was pale, like the moon. 'I have seen such – Oh my! Corney! What have I seen!'

And she begins to weep like she will never stop, but silently and heaving with fear and passion. I don't shake her hard or bend her ear, but hold her close to me, and continue to hold her until her tears have gone, when she looks up at me with lips trembling.

'That's Bessie dead, Corney. And I saw him what done it. The swell what was out here with her.'

She is breathing hard.

'I saw him do it, Corney. He hit her hard, like this' – and she raises her fists above her head and brings them down together – 'on her face. And when she tried to run away and fell to the ground, he kicked her hard. Over and over.'

My mouth goes dry.

'Corney, he was stamping on her. With the heel of his boot. He was stamping over and over.'

I have a lump in my throat as big as an egg as I look at that black heap lying across the yard, for I know I must go and see for myself. Not that I don't believe Lucy (for she is as truthful as any working girl), but I must see it. I leave her in the shadows and creep slowly out into the yard. There is a thin wind, the sort that scuffs up the leaves and rattles them around. And it is stirring, now, the edges of the shape which I see more clearly the closer I get. Bessie's hair, the poor threads of lace around her dress, moved by the cold wind.

I am standing over her and, as the moon comes out from behind the clouds it falls upon her face like a limelight. I push my fist into my mouth to stop myself crying out, and if I never sleep again it will be because I see that face, or no face, before me. So cruelly ruined, there are no eyes, nor cheeks, nor nose, but a terrible confusion of those features together, yet like a sad wheeze from a merry clown, they are framed about with her dark hair, which curls and tumbles like it was made to do. Even her poor hands have not escaped for they are broken and bloody too, and there are great wounds upon her arms and breast. When I feel that I will go mad if I gaze upon her any longer, I stumble back to Lucy, who has covered her face with her hands and started to cry again. I am trembling and feel a knot in my stomach to keep company with the lump in my throat.

But I put an arm about her shoulders and try to steer her back to the house, where a few lights are still burning.

'Come on, girl. You'll be all right. But we must tell someone, and get this swell caught and brung up.' And I give it her a dozen different ways, but no, she will have none of it. We stand in the stable, and it is nigh on a quarter of an hour before she can speak and longer before she can say anything sensible.

And then, with a great sigh, like she will never breathe again, she says in a whisper, 'Ah, Corney! He saw me! What shall I do? Heaven help me! He saw me!'

# 2

## *Constellation and Consternation*

**Corney Sage – Whitechapel, London**

There was such a commotion. The streets were packed and buzzing from morn till night for days on end. But, like I said, not that murder wasn't common enough. And death too. Here were starvations and death from want and cold – two a penny. Here were wives hit too hard by their masters, and pimps taking a chair leg to their girls. But Bessie's murder was different, for it was done by a swell, another theft from them who have nothing by them who have everything. And so there was a strength of feeling around the Whitechapel-road which might make *any* individual not directly of the area, so to speak, feel unwelcome. Hard words were said, and no doubt punches thrown, even at clerks and City men who strayed East on business, and as to the gawpers and holy Joes who flock around misfortune like flies to a privy, they were mostly shunned and ignored. And when all's said and done, who could blame us (for I count myself one of them)? Who could blame us for turning our backs upon the sneaking Jeremiahs and flash swells, or taking a poke at anyone who got too close? For Bessie might have been our daughter. Or sister. Or girl.

But I get ahead of myself. As per.

I shall put myself back to that night. Lucy and me crouched in the stable until we were both frozen, Lucy coming over stiff and staring. She hadn't fainted away, for her eyes were clear open and staring, but when I spoke to her about going inside and fetching the blue boys, she clutched my hand ever tighter and shook her head. It was like she was frozen up with the fear of what she had seen. I sat as long as I could, and, true, it was a terrible thing, out there in the gloomy stable and seeing the outline of Bessie's body, like a black stain on the yard, and knowing what horror the darkness covered up. But the cold was sinking deep into my bones and I was aching until I could have cried out with it, so miserable did it make me. Finally, I could bear it no longer and took Lucy by the hand, staggering myself in pain and stiffness, and steered us both back to the house. But she was most reluctant, and would have stayed hidden among the stinking straw and puddles all night if I had not insisted. Her fear, and she expressed it over and over like a charm, was that the villain had seen her, and was waiting to do for her in the same way.

'Oh, Corney,' she said, 'he has seen me! I looked into his face and him into mine! He knows me! He knows I saw what he did!'

And so piteous and low was her voice that my heart bled for her. I believe I caught some of her fear, for as we crossed the yard, past poor Bessie's body, and treading carefully around her (I made sure that we did not step in the blood which, though I could not see it, must have collected in the channels between the cobbles), I felt uneasy myself, all the time wondering if he was watching, perhaps lurking behind the wall or spying upon us from the dark, blank windows of one of the empty houses that looks into the back yard.

The moonlight came and went in the cloudy sky as we crept across the yard, but it was never really dark. And of course in the city it never *is* dark, like it never *is* silent. There is always a window lit or a lamp left burning, and always someone shouting or crying. Like on this night, where the yard was bright though there were great pools of darkness like blood, and there were noises of shifting and shuffling and the scraping of boots. Only I tried not to see or hear them. Just to hurry Lucy inside the house. And me also.

Of course, it was thick dark and quiet in there, everyone having gone home, and I closed the door, quiet as quiet, and stopped to get my eyes accustomed, Lucy hanging heavy on my arm. I could hear her breathing and smell her when she moved, salty and sour. We stood there, by the outside door, as I say, for some minutes trying to see through the darkness, when I heard someone behind us, outside in the yard, clear as a lark's song. A step and a turn like that person had stopped and perhaps looked across the yard. I know Lucy heard it, for I felt her hold her breath. I also knew that beyond the door, which I could touch with my very hand as I stood there, was whoever had done Bessie to death. Stood there breathing the same air as we had not a moment before. It came into my head what I should do if the door opened of a sudden and he should appear, knowing that he had seen us for certain. Not being a hero (though I have seen plenty on the stage), there would be no roaring about honour, but yours truly making haste across the floor and shouting for the Gov like my life depended upon it.

I have thought about it many times over, and have come to the notion that there must have been moon and clouds that night. For how else could the concert room be suddenly bright and then dark through the roof lights like it was? Tables and chairs, the black hole of the hatch into the bar, shapes in the mirrors, all of them coming into view and going again. Keeping to the sides of the room, I nudged my way along the wall, Lucy's cold hand in mine. In the public bar, the fire was still warm in the grate, hot embers rather than flames, but I parked her beside it, threw a rug about her shoulders and stirred it up, all the while whispering to her, 'You're all right, Lucy girl. You stay quiet here and get warm. I'm getting us a drink.'

She grabbed my arm hard, and I could feel her nails through my shirt.

'Don't leave me, Corney! My God, I'm so frightened!'

'You're safe now,' I says. 'Stay here by the fire. I'm only going into the bar.'

But it was a few minutes before I could get away from her, and all the time she was shaking and starting to cry again, till I was worried Gov would hear her. But suddenly she let go, like she'd given up, and I patted her shoulder and said I'd be back quick as quick.

I was more certain now that we would both benefit from a sniff of the Gov's brandy, and I struck out for the bar, a double-sided affair, opening into the public and with a useful hatch overlooking the concert room, where the waiters called for and collected their orders.

There was no good brandy on the shelf, of course. The Gov'nor was a mean-spirited man, and he took that description to heart, for he was mean *with* his spirits, and hid away his brandy inside the big pot he kept under the bar, which he said held the greatest evil in the world, and must never be opened. Bunting, our carpenter, said that it contained the slops from the Missus's jerry, emptied there by the maid and which, if true, certainly would be the greatest evil in the world. But I didn't believe any of it, having seen him with my own eyes, when he thought no one was looking, put in his paw and bring out a bottle of the best brandy. So I released the greatest evil in the world and filled our glasses, mine and Lucy's, and had a good snort first to steady me up.

All was quiet. Standing by the closed hatch, I listened, and the silence wrapped round me until I could hear it buzzing and swishing. Like it was singing in my ears. Like it was hissing. Like it was breathing.

Yes. Like it was breathing.

And then I realized that it *was* breathing. Someone was there, just around the corner, out of sight. Someone breathing hard down their nose, clenching up their teeth. Trying not to make a noise. Someone was standing on their toes, too, and they was in boots, for every now and then I could hear the leather creaking.

I knew who it was, would have put hard cash upon it. Here was poor Bessie's murderer come back to set about those who saw him do it, creeping about in the dark waiting for his moment. Lucy was his intended, I had no doubt, but he was not about to leave me to summon the hue and cry, so I was up for taking an earth-bath too.

Is there a right way of going about it? I cannot tell. I am no hero, as I have said before, and if I had truly followed my legs I would have been over the bar and out of the front door with all speed. But I did not, though I reckoned that he might be waiting there in the dark for his moment, and the thought of this set me trembling so hard that my hand shook best brandy all over my boots. In the theatre, heroes are always quick-thinking men, able to halt an engine or steer a runaway boat down a rapid like they was born to it. But I argue that most men cannot do these things, and are slow-witted and need time to work things out. If I had been a regular William Goodheart, no doubt I would have come up with something much stronger, but as I am only Corney Sage I did what I do best. I struck up a song. I took a deep breath, and bellowed out the first chorus that came into my head.

> *Do you know my Sally?*
> *Lives down Pleasure Row.*
> *She can strike my alley,*
> *With her what-d'y'-know.*
> *I asked if she'd wed me.*
> *She answered, 'Corney dear,*
> *You shouldn't have to ask me*
> *Just whisper in my ear . . . '*

And I clattered into the bar, glass in each hand and tripping a few steps around the table like I was doing my turn. Chorus now, two, three, four, and:

> Sal-ly. Sal-ly
> You're the one for me.
> Down in the alley
> Tickled my one-two-three.
> My pal Sal-ly. When will you agree
> Sal-ly. . .

Lucy's face, turned towards me in dim light, was a picture of amazement and fear, and she stood up and put a shaking finger to her lips like she was talking to a child. But it was too late. My little performance had woke up Gov who was even now charging downstairs with his candle in one hand and the Missus's gamp flapping in the other. And she herself followed, in her nightcap and a gown so wide it might have launched a fleet. Which was indeed a terrible sight. Together they stood like marvels in a freak show, while the little maidservant who had also been woke appeared from the kitchen, rubbing her eyes and, when she saw us all looking so queer, starting to cry. Always one to lend a comforting hand, Missus covered the floor in two and slapped the poor girl's head about the doorway for so long it became dull, when Gov was forced to step in and change the tune. Raising the gamp to me, he started his own rant, but I cut him short.

'Now, Gov,' I cried, 'don't you start on them what has done you a favour.'

He brought it down on my head with such vigour that the spokes flew out and the whole contraption opened up, almost blinding Missus, and allowing the maid to escape.

'You bloody little ruffian!' cried Pickuls, struggling with the gamp and his Missus and not winning with either. 'Waking up

19

the household with your drunken—' which was when he saw the brandy glasses and smelled it too. 'What have—'

But it was time to put him straight (and save any further abuse), and so I told him, with Lucy's help, what had happened. How Bessie had been done to death by the gent, how Lucy was afraid for her life, since he had seen her, and how, being concerned for my own skin also, I had heard him in the concert room. At this last, Missus and Lucy, and the little maid who had been listening from the scullery, screamed out, and it took the Gov shouting the odds at them all before they stopped.

'Is he there now?' Gov naturally asked and, since I couldn't tell him either way, we went into the concert room to investigate.

No, he was not there, but the outside door what I had closed was swinging open, and the cool night air filled the room. Gov got lamps all round, and shouted up the lad, and we went out into the yard, where I knew what we would find. The black mess of Bessie's poor body was still there, in the same place where me and Lucy had walked round it, and it was no less terrible now.

Gov had a good look and took some long breaths, for his shoulders raised and lowered a few times before he spoke.

'Go and get the police, Corney,' he said, 'but be quiet about it. This might bring us extra customers, or it might not. So play it careful until we get a scent of the chase.'

You're right if you think I felt disgusted with him, for I did, and was inclined to say so. But no good would have been done, and arguing over that girl's broken body. . . well. So I tripped out the back gate and into the Row.

Now here's a thing. And I will tell it how it happened, for I think about it often.

More than that, since I'm being confidential. It haunts me, and has me waking up in the night of a sweat, and has me avoiding dark places, and Rows especially.

For I stepped out, as I said, into the Row, and looked up and down it. Up towards the Whitechapel-road and the lamp what stood directly at the head of the Row, like a beacon. And down towards Club-row what cuts across, and Belvoir-street what goes beyond, and the lamp what stands at the junction. Standing in the gateway, I look down to Club-row and it's empty, and up to Whitechapel, and it's empty. And I step out. I shut the gate behind me, tugging hard on it for it's stiff. And I look down again. Down to the lamp at the junction.

And he's there.

He stands agin the wall with the lamp behind him.

He knows I see him.

For he begins to run, his boots cracking on the stones. Crack. Crack. I hear them in my sleep now.

And then I turn and run, thinking that if I can reach the road and the light I will be all right. So I run. I run without breathing. Like as if I've forgotten to breathe. And I don't look back, for I know he is there. Running after me, with his boots crack, cracking on the stones.

❧

So it was Constable Tegg I found in the bluebottles' nest, having his mug of char and a pipe by the fire. He saw me from the parlour and waved a halloo, and then I suppose realized something was up with me, for he came out. Tegg is like an undertaker's best pal, mute as a fish, and it was at that moment, when I knew I was safe with an honest Englishman, like Nelson would have been proud to intro-duce to his mother (as Mr Figgis used to say), at that moment I broke down completely. I am not ashamed to say I wept, which I did, and Tegg took me into the parlour and give me tea and a drop to warm it, and stood silent by me until I recovered myself.

Grown men cry. It is a fact, and I have seen it often. Hard men, who have seen some service and carried a sword or a gun, weep when a baby dies. Or when their best dog breathes his last. Or when Little Willie or Eliza goes to the angels in a Pavilion drama by Mr Trimmer. Englishmen are not wanting of emotion, for they will sing about England's glory and the true hearts of the sailor and soldier with a tear in their eye. And sure, when the soldier lads come a-marching by in their red coats, with the drum beating and the flag a-fluttering, many a hardened barrow-man or coal-heaver will cough and water his eyes, excusing himself to whoever wants to hear that it is the dust what has flown in.

So Tegg watched while I regained myself, and listened while I told what had happened. And listened again while I told it to Inspector Rudd, a reduced sort of nobbler, hardly tall enough to scratch his own head, but who spoke half-refined and with educa-tion. He rounded up Sergeant Bliss and Constable Fowkes, another bluebottle, and give them instructions to go with Tegg and me back to the Constellation, size it up and report back to him sharpish.

'You did right coming straight here,' he said, giving me a clap on the shoulder, 'and you have no need to fear. For Her Majesty's constabulary will protect you to the best of their strength.'

That made me feel warmer inside, and along with Tegg's tea and bracer I was ready to go back to the Row. When we got outside (and it is strange how clear certain things are in my head), there was a soft light in the sky, and I realized it was getting near dawn. Whitechapel-road was empty enough, a wagon rattling past with a driver fast asleep and horse who knew what was what. A lone swell, face bent close to the gutter, ready to take his pick or looking for his door key. Dogs on their way home, trotting with a purpose, and cats, already home, waiting on window sills. And in the doorways and passages, what might be heaps of rags thrown in, only an arm or a foot hanging out to show that they were men and women, with no home to go to. And here and there smaller bundles, wrapped tight, sometimes struggling. I knew them like I knew my own skin, for hadn't I been left like them, only wrapped in a theatre bill, and covered in ink. And shame, I suppose.

It was four of us, then, that arrived back at the Constellation, and I took them to the front door, and hammered hard to be let in, and soon we were standing in the public, where I been with Lucy, and then Gov and Missus, and looking through the bar to the hatch where the murderer had stood. Perhaps I appeared a bit shaken again, for Tegg touched my shoulder and nodded me to the seat by the fire (which had been raked and lit and was burning bright) where Lucy had sat a few hours ago. Gov stood everyone a drink (though I noticed it was not his best brandy) and made some brave remarks about the bluebottles being able to sniff out the murderer and no mistake. He could not hide, said Gov, even in this great city of ours. But no one was impressed, and indeed he started to look foolish, and would have carried on with the nonsense if the Sergeant hadn't said it was time they got on and did their duty, and he had better show them the business.

Gov fumbled with his keys, all fingers and thumbs, and trying not to show that he was afraid. But he was. We all was, I do believe, even Sergeant Bliss, who said he'd seen more dead bodies than had the bottom of the Newgate new drop. When Gov did open the door and we all trooped out into the yard, which was lighting up now with that greyish-pink light what picks out strange things – the edge of the stable door, I noticed, and the brick of the wall to the Row, all crusty – Gov hung back. The bluebottles went first, then me, but Gov stood in the doorway, turning the key over and over in his hand and licking his lips and getting his wipe out to dry them. Sergeant's face was pinched as a corpse as he looked out over the yard, and he cleared his throat and straightened his back and went over to where Bessie was still lying.

I stood by the door, but I could see her purple gown, one of Perlmann's best, spread out about her, and how pale her arm

looked against it, lying upon the stuff and her hand just hanging
there, like she was asleep. Her hair was let down, brown curls falling
out over her shoulder and face. Bliss stood for a while looking down
at her, and then walked around her, with his hand over his mouth.
Then he called young Fowkes over and said a few words and
pointed to the body, but being only a green constable, when he saw
it he was much affected, so that he was forced to pay a visit to the
very grate where I had stood the night before. It was Tegg who was
sent into the stable to fetch a blanket to cover Bessie, and then to
stand at the yard gate to keep out unwelcome visitors. For they were
beginning to crowd around, word travelling fast along Whitechapel,
and the Gov was eager to get back into his house and open the doors
and play the Big Man to all his neighbours and catering pals and
start making out as *he* found Bessie and chased off the murderer
and, no doubt, nearly caught him. Not a man to miss the opportunity of making a shilling over a penny, was our Gov.

Bliss scribbled in his little book and asked questions about times
and places, and who was here and there, and reminded Gov that we
would all have to be sent for when he made his report back at the
Station House. And he told him, in no uncertain terms and with
much wagging of his finger, not to touch Bessie's body.

'For,' says he, 'I know your sort. You'll try and make a penny out
of a poor girl's misfortune. If I catch you charging for even looking
over the wall, I'll have your licence, and your skin and all.'

Gov threw up his hands and swore nothing was further from his
mind (having already sent out for extra pies and brought in the
cellarman on his day off).

We trooped back into the house, where the Missus and Lucy
were up and sitting by the fire drinking tea and getting chummy.
Bliss was a charmer with the ladies, and they liked him too, for he
was a tall and handsome bluebottle and sported fine weepers and
curly locks, both of which he combed and oiled with great care. His

manner with the fair ones was always gentle and low, making them comfortable and listening hard to them like they knew something. So seeing Missus and Lucy, snug by the fire, he smoothed his weepers and tiptoed over to them, like they was fairies, and gave them his best (but not his fiercest) salute.

'Compliments, ladies,' said he. 'Sergeant Bliss, Whitechapel, C Division. And sympathies for the 'orrible tragedy what 'as 'appened in your midst.'

Pause while the ladies dabbed with their wipers and thanked him.

'If there is anythin' what you can tell me, anythin' at all, just you send for me. I want to catch this beggar – pardon me, ladies, but I feel strong about it – as I say, I want to catch 'im and string 'im up, and then we shall all feel safe in our beds.'

I thought he could have laid it on a bit thicker, having the weepers and hair to his advantage, not to mention the uniform to which many ladies are partial, but in the circumstances he did well enough, and Missus and Lucy promised they would follow his instructions to the point. With Tegg standing sentry-go at the back gate, Bliss and Fowkes departed for the station, reminding Gov not to touch Bessie's body, for they would be sending around a surgeon to sort it out. And indeed, a very few minutes later, Dr Gould arrived with his men and a flat cart and took her off, so that by dinner-time there was hardly any sign of her having been there at all, Pickuls directing the stable lad and the maidservant, with buckets of water, to wash away the worst of the blood. But he took care that the stain remained, foxy old devil that he was, haunting the yard and inspecting his new money-grabber. And within the week, in spite of what the Sergeant had warned him, payment of a penny would let you see the 'Site of the Whitechapel Horror!'. 'Come and See the Very Place where a Young Girl's Innocent Blood Was Spilt!'

The Judge and Jury, even the Poses, were put on one side for the duration of the Whitechapel Horror. Gov was enthusiastic for a show of some kind, and even brought in the Chinns to see what they could recommend. But they were God-fearing, of the Roman persuasion, and as well as doing a deal of jiggery-crossery about their faces and chests, and murmuring the while, they made it clear they was not going to be playing in-and-out overtures for Gov's exhibition. I think he was disappointed and surprised, expecting everyone to be of his ghoulish temperament, and when I told him to sling his hook also, he became frayed and annoyed.

The truth was that I was eager to get clear of that place. Lucy had started leaning on yours truly a bit more than he wanted. Not that I was unhappy about sharing a crib with her, for I could get accustomed to warm skin alongside. And she had pretty ways and a sweet nature, and always paid her way, which was no bother unless I considered how she came by the shillings she put on the table. But after a couple of weeks I got to feeling crowded and, the Constellation offering no prospects, I went round to Mr Tidyman's the Talbot Arms to have a look at the *Era*.

Nothing pleased me more on a warm autumn Sunday morning than to take my coffee, hot and strong, in Mr Tidyman's back room, with the sun lighting up the Classified columns for 'Wanted, for a respectable concert room'. Tilbury Docks (the cellarman, his actual name and no mistake) was within calling distance for words difficult to cipher and, for a penny, a letter written in a commercial hand. Here was a music hall, here a theatre, and here a circus. There were many shops for a man of my talents, and I was hopeful of a new berth. So when Lucy arrived with the sleep and injuries of the previous night on her face (for she had not been home), I did not let it bother me, but just shouted to the Docks for another cup. Lucy sat herself opposite me and picked away at her nails until she'd got her words right and ready what she wanted to say, and then let them all out together.

'I'm getting away from here, Corney, and quickly, for I fear he's looking for me, and I think he will find me if I'm here much longer. And if he finds me with you, he will do for the both of us. So I'm going.'

I wasn't surprised, for she talked all the time of her fears and was nervy as a thoroughbred, and true to her, if Bessie's killer thought she'd seen him, she was done for if he found her. And me too, though I tried not to dwell upon it. So I said the right things, that she must let me know when she got fixed up, and had she got the readies to see her by. But she was nodding and impatient, and interrupted me.

'See here, Corney, you've been a good pal to me, and that's all' (and I was relieved to hear it, too), 'but I need you to be a pal again. The best one ever.'

She put her hand inside her little jacket and brought out a packet wrapped up in oilskin and tied with string. Pushing it towards me she said, 'I want you to keep this for me, Corney. Keep it safe.'

Naturally I wanted to know what it was, although I have to say I had an inkling.

'It's about Bessie. And the swell what done her in. I've written it all down, Corney, in here, for I'm too scared to tell the police. I think *he'd* find out if I told the police, and he'd come and get me. I don't want to be trampled to death like poor Bessie.' And she put her hands over her eyes like she was trying to press the picture of it out of her head.

'I've written down what I know, Corney, and it's for your eyes. No one else's, until I'm a long way away, where he can't find me. You can read it now if you want, but let me get away first. And if you do nothing else with it, Corney, just keep it safe.'

For the first time, just about, I was stuck for words. If she'd asked me to wed her, I could not have been more stuck for words, but I nodded, and took the packet and put it in my coat pocket, and that seemed to pacify her, for she went quiet and sipped her coffee, and then quickly drank it off and, wiping her hand across her mouth, and rearranging her hair, she says, 'Mind your eye, Corney!' and she was gone.

It was a long time before I saw her again.

# An Introduction and a Murder

**James Yates – the Constellation, Whitechapel**

I arrived at the Constellation in good time, for the concert room was only half full, and I easily found a table towards the front. It was a good table from where I was able to watch the entertainment *and* the room. A waiter approached me, small and dapper, smelling of lime oil and with that tell-tale shine upon his hair.

'What will you have, sir?'

I ordered brandy, a bottle on the table, and water on the side, and tossed a dollar into the man's tray. He returned with bottle, jug and tumbler, trailing in his wake a pretty dark-haired girl, who had been watching me from behind the curtains in the corner where, I suppose, the performers were gathered. A gaggle of rosy faces peeked, not at all cautiously, around the shabby cloth. I knew they had been looking at me and, feeling suddenly self-conscious, I anxiously scrutinized my cuffs and my boot-tips the better to hide my blushes! All the same, it was gratifying that they recognized, without any introduction, the quality of which my appearance spoke, and their giggles and chatter were, no doubt, about who I might be, what I was good for, and who was bold enough – but they were working girls and needed little encouragement! – to approach me. The dark-haired girl dropped into a seat beside me and linked

29

her arm in mine with charming familiarity. I could smell her cheap perfume and the cheaper gin she drank, but her face was pretty, and she was amiable enough.

Her name was Bessie, I learned, and she was going to be a dancer. Her idol was Madame Taglioni, whom she had never seen but her coachman came in now and again. But this was simply prattle, for she was occupied in examining me most minutely. My cheek, my neck, my hair. The very fabric of my coat. She took my hand, ungloved, looked at it, then smiled and showed her teeth, which were shockingly black and brown, and said what fine hands the young gentleman had, such slender fingers. She touched my cheek. And neck. And traced her nail along my waistcoat, discovering the shirt opening which was when I caught her hand and stopped her.

She didn't protest but simply threw back her head and laughed with that brassy ring (too loud, too harsh, too revealing) I knew so well. I introduced myself, but all the time feeling as though I were playing a part and Bessie, while she was attentive and curious, played her part also, reciting those familiar lines from the whore's catechism. Charmin' gent. So 'andsome. Surely too young to be out so late and in such a place as this, and she pressed her hand against my breastpocket and looked at me keenly.

'You know, cocky,' she said confidentially, 'I didn't believe the other girls when they said, but it just shows 'ow you should listen to your friends, and take notice of them what know better.'

I was nonplussed, but laughed anyway, and she laughed with me.

'We was wondering when you'd show 'ere, for it's hot on the old turf for you now, isn't it? Not worried about knocking up your old pals, are you?'

I hadn't expected to be challenged so immediately and so directly that it took me by surprise, and I couldn't think of a clever rejoinder, but knew that I must quickly silence her, for she was running on and talking loudly about old pals and gaffs. I suggested a drink and reached into my pocket for money, but she quickly jumped up and planted herself in my lap, wrapping her scrawny legs around mine and thrusting her hips towards me. Her arms were around my neck and she pulled my face into her bosom, holding it tight to her damp skin, which smelled of sweat and cheap perfume, and the keen animal residue of many men.

'Are you old enough to be out on your own, ducky?' she said loudly, and looked around, but no one was listening. I tried in vain to hush her, but she shrugged off my remonstrations.

'Isn't it past your bedtime, Johnny?' she cried again, louder this time, and there were a few sniggers and nudges.

Then she threw back her head and sang, in a raucous voice of drunken abandon, '"Does your mother know you're out?"' which reached to the back and front of the room, and elicited a wholesale turning of heads and a roar of laughter and a scattered chorus of, '"Oh, oh, Johnny, does she, will she, can she?"' which she conducted with great relish, bouncing upon my lap and pretending not to see my embarrassment.

I pushed her away with an angry thrust, feeling assaulted by the stink of stale intimacies on her clothing and humiliated by her mockery and the ripples of laughter and comments around me. It was a mistake, I thought, coming here, and I made to leave. Perhaps the look on my face, my preparations to go alarmed her, for she was swiftly back at my side, stroking my cheek in a rough gesture of apology. But I was enormously, cruelly enraged, and this ironic show of affection – I could not believe she meant it – simply provoked me more. I wanted to strike her (and would have done so in a less public place), so affronted was I by her cheap mockery, but instead I turned away and clenched my fists until the pain of the nails digging into the flesh of my palms calmed me.

Bessie had seen it, though. And more. She could not, would not leave me and leaned towards me again, and began to croon:

> *Oh, Willie, does yer mother know,*
> *Does yer mother know,*
> *Does yer mother know,*
> *Oh, Willie, does yer mother know*
> *You're out, out, out.*

Or some such nonsensical song, which left her laughing uncontrollably, with her dark eyes wide and fixed upon me.

Suddenly (and mercifully), the doors were flung open and a rowdy crowd of young fellows appeared. They were well turned out, noisy, some pale-faced, some red-eyed, but all clearly very drunk, though not yet ready to fight about it. And they were immediately surrounded by a shrieking crowd of young women, who had evidently been waiting for them to arrive.

Heads turned again to look at them, mine included, and Bessie called out, 'Look out! We're 'ere! Over 'ere, girls!'

They steered the foot-shy assembly in our direction, tipping over chairs and tables on their way – which brought the landlord out of his hidey-hole behind the bar to keep an eye on proceedings – and deposited them with much noise and clamour. It was then, in that bevy of flushed faces, that I saw John Shovelton. Recognition was immediate, but believing my eyes took longer, and I looked once, twice, before I was convinced that it was he and then was momentarily panicked, and forced to turn my face away so that he should not see me. However, it was impossible to avoid the throng of fellows who were already taking their seats and helping themselves to my bottle of brandy and so I collected myself and smiled amiably and returned their salutes and even nodded to him. Bessie had forgotten me, and now had her arms about a small, fair-skinned, dark-haired young woman, who was wrapped in a gentleman's azure-blue cloak, and smiled fetchingly. A beautiful creature, Bessie called her Lucy, and naturally Lucy was the favourite of John Shovelton. When she had steered him towards a seat, he pulled her roughly on to his knee and, as she whispered in his ear, laughed and kissed her full upon her lips. I watched them, until Bessie's voice brought me up with a start.

'So, you like watchin' rather than playin', do you, ducky? Well, that's all right by me.'

I flung her an angry look, but she shrugged her shoulders and took a long drink of brandy and water before she cried, "Ere, Lucy, this gentleman 'ere is Mr Yates. *You* remember him, Lucy?'

But Lucy was either asleep or insensible. Her face was buried in Shovelton's neck, and the azure cloak, which had fallen open as she sat in his lap, revealed her naked arm and thigh, pale creamy ivory against the deep blue. I drank it in, but was a lone connoisseur, for no one else seemed to notice. They were all too busy shouting and jossing, sharing jokes and intimacies, and I realized, to my surprise, that I was one of that company, accepted by them, though I knew none of them.

Except John Shovelton.

I should not have been surprised to see him. It was hardly a coincidence, for the Constellation had the reputation as a popular place for young swells looking for low amusement and cheap women. All the same, though I was trying to appear unconcerned, I was anxious to make myself agreeable, for it was amusing to be one of the company, *his* company.

It wasn't difficult. The company hailed and hallooed me again and again, and because they were so drunk, they believed that they knew me. Not one of them wanted to admit that I was a stranger to him, and so all were jolly and amiable, and called me a fine fellow and shook my hand! Brandy was ordered, bottles of it, and when it was my turn I shouted for 'Brandy! The best!' which caused a great roar of laughter and I was slapped upon the back as though I had said something very amusing. I was particularly glad when John Shovelton cheered me, and put his arm across my shoulders, declaring that I was a regular good fellow and how fortunate he was to have come to this place to find me here. For a while I was the subject of drunken conversation, as fellows tried to recall how they knew me. From the Guards surely, one cried, or the City certainly, said another, or at Lord H's ball last season, or the race track or the Fancy. I agreed with everything, denied nothing. I made certain, however, that John Shovelton heard all, and he did appear to be listening intently, and at one point even suggested that he had seen me at Brighton.

'You have a memorable face,' he cried. 'I am sure, I *know*, I have seen you before!'

I demurred. I said that I was much in town and in Brighton and Bath, and any number of places and that, having many friends, went to many 'dos' (which made him laugh). The noise about us was intolerable, and it was impossible to hold a conversation, but he slapped my arm and asked if I knew Springwell in Derbyshire. He'd be there pretty soon. He'd enjoy my company for it was a dull place, but his sister was enamoured of it. She was gone from Town now, having extracted from him new gowns and bonnets and all manner of female foolishness, but they would be in Springwell very soon. They stayed at the George. I would be their guest, and relieve the tedium of the place, for it was full of ugly girls, with their mamas in tow, looking for husbands! Then he became animated and talked of a ratting ken in St Giles (which, of course, I already knew), and how he would meet me there and introduce me to some lively fellows.

'I like you, James,' he cried, smiling broadly. 'You have an honest face. Fresh as a . . .' but he could not find the word, brandy having overcome his tongue.

I could hardly contain my excitement, but tried to be moderate in my reply. I would cancel a planned visit to the country, although I was certain my hosts would be disappointed, but I should like to visit Springwell very much, and believed the waters there were . . . But he had already forgotten me, and was giving his full attention, once again, to Lucy. No matter, for I hugged myself in a glow of self-satisfaction, and I contemplated my success even as the room became louder and warmer and more crammed with people, all clamouring for seats and drink. Indeed it became so intolerably hot that the side door was opened and a welcome cooling breeze, but laced with the stink of stables and drains, surged in waves across the room.

The little stage was being set for the show. A well-made bench for the Judge, boxes for the witness and plaintiff, all built from wood and nails, rather than the paper and paint that are found in the theatre. There were tables and chairs arranged in front of the Bench, and even pen and paper set there for the clerk. All was supervised by a small fellow with carroty hair and bright eyes, who seemed to be everywhere at once. He pointed the shifters here and there, and made little adjustments himself. It was all very carefully done and I was so thoroughly distracted by the business that I did not notice the women getting up to leave, until Bessie, who had been sitting close, her thigh pressed hard against mine, took my hand and laid it upon her breast.

'Will you wait for me, cocky?' she said with mock sincerity, and her eyes were large and bright. 'I've to go and do the Judge-'n'-Jury, but I'll come back for *you*,' and she put her lips upon mine, soft and wet and tasting of gin and laudanum, and pushed her hand into my groin. I jumped, but only at the unexpectedness. She smiled and kissed me again.

'You *have* got lovely skin, cocky. Like a peach,' and she put her finger in her mouth, licked it and then placed it on my lips. The other women were gathered by the stage and called her raucously over the tumult. She kissed me again, and glanced provocatively over her shoulder at me as she picked her way through the crowd. A crude thrust of the hips was her parting gesture. It was a vulgar display, and I looked after her feeling amused and not a little excited.

I was roused suddenly by a shout and the crash of glass. A huge fellow towered over me, supporting himself upon the table and scattering chairs and bottles. His livid face was inches from mine and his hot, sweet breath fairly took mine away.

'Your dicky-bird has flown, old fellow! You should keep a tighter hold on her!' he roared.

I nodded and laughed. 'She's certainly flighty enough!' I rejoined, a feeble enough jest, but it caused the entire drunken company to hoot with laughter.

'She needs smarter attention!' cried one.

'Get soldier Dick out on parade!' bellowed another, and another thunderous guffaw filled the room.

'Didn't you know? Our Bessie's cock-smitten,' slurred the leering fellow into my face. 'She can't get enough of mine!'

'Or anyone's!' yelled another voice from the back.

There was more raucous laughter and a call for him to 'Sit down and hold your tongue!' but he continued in the same vein, and described in a loud voice and lurid terms what Bessie would do for a sixpence or a shilling, finally pushing his finger into my chest to punctuate his words.

'She's a filthy whore. The filthiest in all London. Have you asked her how many she's had today?' He shook his head in exaggerated seriousness. 'She can't count. Too many.'

I nodded and shook my head, by turn, hoping that agreement would pacify him. But he was slowly reaching the crisis of his rage.

'So she's saving the last job of the day for *me*. Not you.' He prodded his finger into my chest again, and from between clenched teeth, spat out, 'Not you. Not you.'

I was by now trembling at the prospect of the violence which I anticipated at every moment. A fist in my face, or a bottle at the very least. But drunk as the assembled crowd might be, they were not yet ready for a demonstration of fisticuffs, and there were cries of 'Leave him alone, Charlie!' and even 'Shame!' He was nevertheless determined to vent his drunken anger and made a stumbling lurch towards me, which was, thankfully, interrupted by a chord from the orchestra (a piano and violin) heralding the commencement of the entertainment and eager hands pulled him back to his seat, where he sat glowering at me over his glass.

I was very relieved when the show began, though I soon realized that it was little more than a crude, a very crude, burlesque on certain legal topics recently reported in the newspapers. The part of the Judge was taken by the carroty-haired man, in Judge's red robes and a large wig. He was witty and sharp, and kept the piece moving along with his own quips when the exchanges between the women began to flag, for it was quickly evident that the performers were young women selected more for their beauty than their histrionic talent, and accounted for why they struck a suggestive pose and stood perfectly motionless for some moments before continuing, the better to display their physical attributes. Some half of them were in male dress, tight breeches and open shirts, though they made no effort to conceal their true sex. All were much powdered and rouged, and some were clenching a cigarette between their teeth or sporting a large and flashy ring, the better to mock the class they were striving to represent.

My compatriots enjoyed it enormously, were inordinately amused, but the greatest roars of appreciation by far were for those Sapphic episodes (of which there were no small number), and the caresses exchanged by Lady C and Countess D were accompanied by constant calls of encouragement and offers of vulgar assistance, which the ladies acknowledged with many smiles and winks. Of course I watched Bessie with particular interest. She played the part of the Clerk and was required to trip back and forth across the stage, giving her ample opportunity to pause and strike, albeit briefly, a number of fetching poses to draw attention to her legs, bosom, arms and so on, which were revealed to within inches of decency. I was much taken by this and roared my approval. Like my comrades, I enjoyed it all thoroughly, the rawness of the parody, and the sensation of being, unequivocally if ironically, its object. I felt I was one of them.

The drink – I had a great quantity – filled me suddenly with rowdy confidence, and I looked around, feeling a surge of camaraderie and friendship with these fellows. Drink had taken hold of them as well. I noticed empty chairs, where a couple were forced to rush to the side door and relieve themselves in the rear yard. One was slumped across the table, another unconscious in his seat. Others were still drinking, their flushed faces turned towards the performers, wearing expressions of fierce amusement. John Shovelton was quiet, intent upon the stage. He met my glance, but I think he did not see me.

The show concluded and the performers left the stage, trooping off, after bows and curtseys, behind a green curtain where, I suppose, there were dressing rooms.

'Let's bring them back for one more!' said someone, and it seemed a wonderful idea.

'Pay up and they'll come back!' cried another. And suddenly the table was full of coins. I threw in a shilling, though I could barely afford it, and called, 'More drama!' A mistake on my part for I was immediately noticed by my earlier aggressor, who staggered over and began his assault once again.

'Oh, the cock-linnet wants another eyeful!' he roared.

'Who wouldn't want another eyeful of Bessie!' I returned with drunken confidence, but the room was beginning to swim and tip now, and I was alarmed when once again he loomed in front of me and pushed his face into mine.

'Big words for a boy!' he growled and reached out to touch my cheek.

I backed away, and though I laughed and affected unconcern, I desperately wanted to push him over, to see him stagger back and crash on to the floor. In my dreams he does. Sometimes I hit him squarely on the jaw with a smack, sometimes I carelessly thrust him aside. I favour the punch as much for the looks of amazement and admiration on the faces of the onlookers – and the drunken fellow – as for the crashing, lurching, reeling figure, plunging backward and away from me. He lies there and I stand over him, mutely inviting him to stand up and take another.

In my dreams, I say.

For in fact I stayed in my chair and was relieved when the other fellows took him by the elbow and, once again, sat him down, and plied him with brandy and a cigar. But I felt foolish, and angry too, for though I might have appeared to be a regular fellow, could drink and pay my way, and laugh at the bawdy jests, I looked like a boy, and I could not defend myself. I seethed for a moment, and took a long drink of brandy. A voice was at my ear. Shovelton.

'Don't mind Tiverton too much,' he slurred. 'He gets wild when he's had over the odds, and Bessie is a particular favourite of his.'

As if to prove this, when the girls trooped out from behind the green curtain and clustered around us like pretty moths about a flame, Bessie sat on the fellow's knee and allowed him such familiarities that I had to turn away, which she noticed and in which she seemed to take some pleasure. But they were not alone, for around them was a veritable orgy of lascivious behaviour, with all the fellows finding girls with whom to whisper and cavort.

All except me.

No one even approached me, and I was left sitting alone, feeling foolish and suddenly excluded, as though, having reached the threshold, the door was shut firmly in my face. It was time to leave. But just as I got unsteadily to my feet, Tiverton staggered to his, thrusting Bessie away from him with such a terrible ferocity that she crashed to the floor.

'You're a whore and a thief!' he cried, lashing out at her. 'You've given me the clap, now you're trying to steal my money!'

Bessie shrieked her defence and tried to get up, but the floor was slippery and Tiverton was advancing.

'The clap you can keep! I want the money you took from my pocket!'

Bessie protested loudly.

'Light-fingers and open legs!'

He kicked out at her and she squealed in pain as his boot struck her leg hard. He was a man in a passion and, though all around him frowned with concern, no one was anxious to intervene, for they clearly knew him and what he was capable of. We all watched and waited as Bessie backed away, begging her giant pursuer to 'Be kind, Charlie! Don't hurt me again!'

But here was, as they say in the theatre, the downer, for in the end there was no exciting denouement, and it was the caterer who came to her rescue. Or rather his supporter, a small, stocky, square-headed fellow who throughout stood, unmoved, at the bar and showed little interest. But chairs and tables were being toppled and glasses broken, and Mr Pickuls was understandably nervous of his mirrors, of which there were many ranged about the walls. A nod, and his supporter was despatched to quietly confront Tiverton, who was not at all subdued by the request and continued to kick out at the unfortunate Bessie. A swift glance at his employer, another nod from Mr Pickuls and the stocky individual laid a hand upon Tiverton's shoulder, who roared and, instead of Bessie, now treated this fellow to his repertoire of curses and followed it with a battery of flailing fists. But the man, Minter by name and a bruiser by calling, simply caught him neatly upon the chin and Tiverton crumpled, from shoulders to knees, into a heap. There was a moment's silence and then a laugh and a cheer, and Tiverton was unceremoniously bundled out of the room by the side door.

I helped Bessie to her feet, and she clung to me weeping and shaking, protesting that she never robbed him, that she was a good girl, and if she had sometimes done bad things, they weren't truly bad for she was sorry the moment she had done them. She was frightened and foolish, and I sat her down and called for gin to calm her spirits, at the same time filling my own glass to the brim.

'Ah, you understand, cocky,' she said, her lip trembling. '*You* know what a poor girl has to do to keep warm. These gents' – and she nodded towards the company, now subdued and chewing over Tiverton's bad character – 'they don't know how cold a doorway can be, do they? They don't know what it's like to have to oblige a gent when you have no inclination.'

Her eyes were clear and wide, and black as a gully.

'See, Mr Tiverton, he was a bad lot, cocky, but he paid well.' She sniffed hard, and wiped her hand across her mouth. 'He always handed over a shilling when the job was done, fair's fair. And he liked a soft bed, too. But now he's out for the night, so am I.'

She tossed off the gin, refilled the glass and made another tearful assault.

'He isn't a bad bloke when he's not in his cups, but he won't come here again. Mr Pickuls won't let him in. And Minter will have an eye open for him. So I've lost my bed and board, cocky. This time tomorrow some other poor girl'll be getting it rough, but at least she'll have a crib.'

I listened intently now, for I knew what was coming, though the conversation was difficult and tedious, and Bessie was almost insensible and much inclined to slide into a stupor. What kept her eyes open was that, as she reminded me more than once, 'the Gov' will not put up with no more 'slummin'' and if he found her sleeping under the tables again, she would be 'out of a shop'.

'I'll see you all right, Bessie,' I said, as brightly as I could.

'Too right you will, cocky, or I'll see you in quod.'

She threw me a knowing look and her voice was suddenly as hard as flint. She got to her feet and staggered a little, for I'd helped her drop the quietener in her drink, and been over-generous.

'Me and Mr cocky Jim are out for a breather,' she informed the rest of the company and grabbed my hand. But they were too far gone to take any interest and we reeled unhindered towards the door into the yard. On the stage, the carroty-haired man was dancing and singing, and watched us across the room and out of the door. When I looked back, he was still dancing energetically.

Outside the air was cool, though rank and Bessie's stale breath upon my face was a sore trial. But I pushed her roughly against the wall and kissed her hard. She laughed drunkenly, and drew the back of her hand across her lips.

'What you goin' to do now, cocky?' she whispered.

It was a good question. Drunk as I was, I was desperate to get Bessie and her free tongue out of the company before she could say any more, but out here in the yard, I was lost. I held her still against the wall, my hands pressed firmly on her shoulders. Her vulnerability was exciting.

However Bessie, for all her young years, was old in the game.

'Now then, cocky,' she whispered, 'you know what's o'clock. Ready now, pleasure later.'

I fumbled in my waistcoat pocket and pulled out a coin which she swiftly stowed. I touched her breast, I cupped it in my hand gently. She moaned softly. I felt her hair, which was soft and luxuriant, though stinking of smoke and sweat. I ran my fingers across her face and down her neck. Through the thin material of her fleshings, I felt her belly and explored her legs. I pushed myself upon her. I leaned upon her and felt her breasts flatten beneath me. I held her by the throat and kissed her roughly. She was not unresponsive and returned my kisses, and her tongue explored my lips and mouth. For all its over-use, her body was soft and yielding, and I was surprised when she gave little gasps of pleasure as I explored her bare leg and arse.

I was beginning to enjoy myself, even though the brandy had made my head swim and my mouth was dry and foul. But although I could not imagine how it would end, Bessie's young body had me unexpectedly hot and excited, and I barely noticed when the door to the concert room opened and closed. Moments later, someone was pissing against the wall, and I was aware of it trickling dully into the drain. He stopped and looked over, and though I could not see his face, I was suddenly self-conscious, and when he made some remark about not spoiling the girl's looks I was annoyed and provoked into responding. What business was it of his? I demanded. I've paid my money. Was he her pimp? Was there no one in this damned place who wasn't owned by another? Turning on him, I slipped and slid to my knees, and from that ignominious position realized he was the carroty-haired comedian. Bessie realized too, and seemed to think this was the right time to speak.

"Ere, Corney,' she mumbled, 'this gent is no gent.'

But I put my hand over her mouth, and pushed her roughly against the wall. Her head cracked the bricks and she moaned. The comedian said something more, but I didn't hear it, and he disappeared behind the door again. Bessie was becoming difficult now, and began to struggle, complaining that she was cold and wanted to go inside. I had to hold her hard.

'Listen,' I say, 'I've paid you, and I'll give you another five pounds. Five pounds. But you must promise to say nothing.'

Even as I am saying it, I know that five pounds will not buy her silence. Not five pounds, not fifty pounds, not five hundred. I will be buying her silence for ever. Or until she is dead. She seems to know this too, and begins to laugh loudly, a raucous whore's laugh which echoes around the yard, so I shake her and tell her to shut up, but it only urges her on, and she seems uncontrollable. I slap her hard with the flat of my hand and this seems to bring her to her senses, for she gasps and then pushes me away. But brandy has turned my legs to paper, so that even her feeble thrust makes me stumble backward and I fall and graze my hand. The pain is slight but my anger and irritation are not. I am enraged and cry out, and follow it with a mouthful of curses. Bessie is surprised and moment-arily silenced. But not for long, for she gains her composure, and, returning the compliments, we are locked in a scrap of words, fling-ing filth at each other, until she makes a last, desperate claim.

'I know you,' she pants. 'I know what you are and where you're from. And don't think five pounds or five hundred'll keep my mouth shut. Not for all the tin you promise. I'll settle you. You'll be back in jump-alley with the other soft-cocks and dry-cunnys before I've finished and—'

When I hit her, it is with a full fist, and a long draw, and it smashes into her cheek and knocks her to the ground. She cries out in pain and shock, and my knuckles sting, so I know I have, at least, broken the cheekbone or loosened her teeth. She is on her feet and clutching her face, all the time swearing on someone's life or soul that she knows who I am and when they find out, won't I be for it, and if I have spoiled her face these friends will spoil mine for good. But Bessie is scared also, backing away from me across the yard, stumbling over the rough stones as her legs buckle beneath her. Watching her fall, and rise, and fall again and, knowing the moment is mine, I am suddenly calm. The searing rage burns cold now, sits in my belly like a tight fist, and I take my time to stride over to her, enjoying the flood of composure. I possess the yard, even the foul red bricks with their greasy skin. I cover the ground, striking double time with my heels, and stand over her in moments.

In moments.

She is still cursing and babbling, but I am myself again.

She has fallen down, and is struggling to get to her knees. I make a prayer of my two fists and bring them down upon her hard, and she crumples, cracking her head upon the cobbles. I hold her down with my foot, and she groans, struggling and grasping my leg, but her other hand is under my foot, and I grind my heel into it, feeling the fingers snap. She releases her hold with an animal scream and turns her bloody face towards me, her mouth open like a child's.

I bring my foot down upon her face.

It yields.

There is a wet sound.

She is trying to cry out. I stamp again and again, feeling flesh and bone yield as my heel shatters her face, her mouth, her nose. She is trying to breathe in gasps which are choked on blood, and crawls a little way away. I let her go, watch her for a moment. Again I cover the ground and take my heel to her head and then her face again and feel it yield as I stamp and stamp.

I stamp and stamp, and grind my heel and have no sense of time. Only industry. I enjoy the rhythm, feel the flexing of muscle and sinew, and despite the brandy my head is clear and light, my shoulders loose.

Then I am aware of a cry, a long way distant, and I wonder, as I pound the pulpy mass beneath my foot, where it comes from, only slowly realizing that someone is standing in front of me, a woman with wild eyes, shouting. I know her. It is Lucy. She is both near and far, a face that presses into mine and then appears as a tiny white speck in the distance. I stop, fascinated, and realize that my leg is sore and that the muscles burn and tear with the exertion. Time slips, for suddenly I am opening the gate into the Row and, looking back, see a figure approaching. He shouts, and a voice shouts back and he starts towards me. I know him. The little comedian. Bessie's mild protector. I wait in the shadow, then pass through the gate into the narrow Row. The lights of the road are welcoming and I step out briskly. I stride it out, but do not run. Breathing the thin, cold air is exhilarating, and I cover the streets with great speed, reaching my lodgings in twenty minutes and then taking the stairs three at a time.

Only when I dropped on to my bed did I consider what had happened that evening. Tired as I was, sleep would not come, for as soon as I closed my eyes the room began to spin and lurch. Even worse, all the incidents of the evening started to repeat themselves to me, in particular the press of Bessie's soft body and the rough sweetness of her mouth, and I guiltily wondered what Helen would say if she knew that I had been unfaithful with a whore! I reached for the little portrait of her which I kept under my pillow and carried with me constantly. It is the dearest thing I own, my only reminder of Helen and our precious few weeks together. She had been unwilling to part with it, declaring that it was not hers to give, that it belonged to her brother, John, a gift from her to him on his birthday. She had even had it inscribed on the reverse. Encased in a thin gold frame, like a locket, on the back was the legend:

*For my dearest Brother on his birthday.*
*John Shovelton*
*From his affectionate Sister Helen*

But he was careless of it, and when I discovered it upon his dressing stand among his pins and links, I had no scruples about taking it for myself and keeping it without Helen's knowledge. Now I have held it so many times in my loneliness that I can conjure every contour, every scratch, even my poor attempt at defacing the inscription in a jealous rage. Like a primitive talisman, its familiarity was a comfort, and so as the waves of nausea coursed over me, I sought it out in the familiar depression under my pillow.

It was not there.

I searched again. And again.

And then I remembered that I had put it in my waistcoat pocket when I dressed. But even as I tried to sit up, I was struck with a terrible giddiness, and within moments saliva filled my mouth and the room lurched and spun. I found the bowl just in time and into it emptied the wretched contents of my stomach. However, the torment did not end there. Gasping for air between each convulsion and even as I tried to settle in my bed, images of the night's events paraded in front of me, and I watched over and over, and with maddening repulsion, the dissolution of Bessie's features as they merged with the black of the cobbles and murk of the yard. It seemed that as desperately as I needed to close my eyes, so that panorama of pictures was relit and rerun until I thought I should lose my mind. Only Helen and the image of her – dear, sweet, angelic Helen! – kept me from crying out.

As the nausea subsided and my stomach gnawed itself into a raw tightness, I searched in the watch pocket of my waistcoat (I was still dressed) for the picture of my dear girl. But it was empty, and though I searched repeatedly, I could not find it. I knelt on the floor and ran my hands over the bed and mattress, turning the sheets on to the floor, expecting every moment to hear a familiar clatter as it fell. Nothing. I lit a candle and tore the sheets, mattress, everything from the bed, hurling them across the room where they struck the table and tipped over the foul contents of the bowl. Inhaling again that acrid stink, I felt the familiar convulsion in my stomach, but the anxiety of the moment kept the nausea at bay, for I realized, searching the mattress and the sheets, my clothes, the floor around my bed, once, twice, three times in a mad frenzy, that Helen's picture was not there.

## Walking in Pimlico

I have read that in the midst of chaos there often comes a moment of clarity, an instant when time is shrunk to an image. And so it was for me. On my hands and knees in my own vomit, I had a sudden and minutely clear presentiment of Helen's image. *She* did not stand before me, but instead the little whore, Bessie, and I realized then – and in truth I very nearly laughed aloud – that I had been nibbled! How ironic that the light-fingered trollop had prigged the portrait from my pocket while she pretended to caress me! Hadn't Tiverton accused her of the same crime? Had charged her with stealing from him as well as giving him the clap? So I did not even pause to consider the best course of action, but stumbled back to Whitechapel in my befouled clothes, along quiet streets which were not empty but easy to negotiate, and arrived back in the Row within the hour. All was still dark in the yard as I opened the gate and, steadying myself by the wall, I held my breath and listened. There was not a sound.

Bessie was lying on her side where she had fallen. I tipped her over with my foot, and was startled by the wet sigh that escaped from her mouth, so I pushed her head around with the tip of my boot and for a moment wondered if she might still be alive. But it was soon clear that she was not, and so I set about searching her skirts and jacket. There was blood a-plenty, and my hands were sticky with it after a moment's work, but though I was thorough (indeed I was), I could not find the locket. Then I scuffed around the cobbles, thinking that she might have dropped it, but there was not enough light to see, and it could have rolled into any crack or pothole in the ground. A knot of panic began to form in my stomach, hardly distinguishable from the foul nausea that threatened to overwhelm me with every movement. If the picture was not on Bessie's body, not lying between the bricks of the yard, the only other place it could be was in the concert room.

The Constellation was in darkness, but I tried the door anyway and to my surprise found it opened easily. I took a few steps into the room, feeling my breath coming hard, stinging through my teeth and burning the back of my throat. My chances of negotiating a path between the tables and chairs without upsetting them and causing a noise were negligible in my unsteady state. And after all, how would I find the locket in the dark? It occurred to me that Bessie might not have stolen it. That I might have dropped it anywhere, at any time during the evening. One of the other women might have found it. Or the publican. Or the comedian. Anyone.

I closed the door quietly, stumbled across the yard and then into the Row. Once there, the gentle glow of the streetlamp was reassuring, and I walked towards it, keeping close to the wall. A clear head is what I desperately needed and in full measure now, but I was sick and dull and could not contemplate any further than that moment. The locket bearing Helen's portrait was not to be found. The darkness was too impenetrable, and the danger of alerting the publican and his family too great. But, though I regretted the loss of that reminder of my dear girl's face, it concerned me more that it might fall into the wrong hands. Better a drain or sewer than in the greasy hands of some slaughterman, or on the watch-chain of a clerk to be handed around and gawped at!

The Row was still and silent, and the noise from the road so faint that it might be a mile away rather than yards, and this is soothing, for my head is alternately light and heavy, and my tongue feels too big for my mouth. If I do not keep moving, I know I will sink irresistibly down against the wall on to the ground and be discovered by some light-fingered wanderer who will relieve me of everything I own and leave me naked. So I stumble away from the road, keeping close to the wall, towards the intersecting streets beyond, and the glow of another streetlamp, and am brought up by a noise beyond the wall. The opening of a door, a muffled call, a muttered curse. It comes as something of a shock, for I am so completely not myself that I have forgotten the horror that lies beyond this very wall which had seemed so comforting. It has not occurred to me to put distance between myself and the events of last evening. My hands are still sticky with the evidence and my fine new boots will not bear close inspection.

I realized, without panic, that soon the body must be discovered, and I cast my mind back (with some difficulty, it must be admitted) to recall the little comedian, who pissed against the wall close by. And another face. And a voice, which burst out of the darkness. I stop and try very hard to recall, but my head is too big, too heavy. Movement too is difficult. I close my eyes and lick my lips which are dry and flecked with vomit, and that sourness makes my gut lurch again. So I breathe deeply and try to keep the bile down and then, opening my eyes, it seems a face looms before me, so close that I am startled and slither a little on the greasy stones. It is shouting, but I cannot hear what it says, and its eyes are wide with horror. It recedes and then comes rushing out of the blackness again, and I believe I cry out.

I cannot tell whether it is real or a terrible dream.

I am standing with my back against the wall, feeling with the tips of my fingers the rough bricks, and thinking how fine it would be to sit, just for a moment, with my back against it. My head is pounding, and the bile is again rising, and though I try to swallow it back, my stomach will not tolerate it and I cough and gag as I jettison the foul effluvia at my feet. I long for cool water and the cold sheets of my bed, and as my knees begin to shake, I realize I am going to fall to the ground and with little prospect of being able to raise myself. So I struggle against the urgent desire to give way and as I do it seems that there is once again a figure before me, standing still in the Row. This time I am glad and stumble in his direction. I do not care who he is or what he knows. I will pay him, I decide, to guide me home. But my legs will hardly support me, and I know that if I lose momentum, I will fall, so I train my eyes upon him and begin to run. I run, and slip and trip, my boots cracking on the cobbles, and the figure that had seemed so substantial begins to melt away, and the more urgently I pursue it, the more certainly it retreats, until it has disappeared completely. When I reach the Whitechapel-road and stop, expecting to see it, the figure is nowhere, though I imagine I hear running footsteps in the far distance.

I am desperately tired.

I find the doorway to a shop and, supporting myself between the wall and the window, sink down and fall immediately into a strange sleep, in which dogs bark and voices come and go. Once or twice I try to rouse myself and see, indistinctly, legs and feet walk by me, and once someone lays a hand upon my shoulder and asks a question which I cannot answer.

# A Revelation

## Corney Sage – Springwell

It all started with the murder, and after the murder, it was like
everyone and everything closed up. People you had known for an
age cut you, looked at you different. Women in particular seemed
to close up, and took to wrapping themselves in shawls and blankets, and hurrying here and there without looking you in the face.
It was like they didn't want to be out longer than they had to and got
back inside their homes as quick as they could, though the houses
too looked different, with the windows shut tight as a nun's novelty,
and doors that had stood open for air and company were similarwise
shut on the world. Even the air smelled like it was old and had
been shut up and breathed in and out over and over, and when it
rained, which in general sparks up a London street, everything now
turned to grey and mud.

Constable Tegg was on sentry-go at the back gate of the
Constellation for the best part of a fortnight. From Hampstead to
Hackney, everyone came wanting to say they'd seen the yard, and
some looked for souvenirs. When the bricks started disappearing off
the yard wall, and Gov found a fellow selling them – dabbed in red
paint for the 'splashes of her very own blood' – he made a right stink
and threatened him with the papers (Fleet Street rather than Bow

Street). He didn't have to look far for ink-slingers and lawyer's narks were in great abundance, the first sniffing for a story, and the rest for a writ, and Gov was inclined to both persuasions. His ugly phiz was regular occupying the front pages of every picture paper in the land.

Lucy up and left. Mind your eye, she said, and that was her gone, and her stuff (not that there was much of it) with her. Only the dent in the pillow on my bed where her head had been the previous night showed she had ever been there. Where she went I had no notion at first, and I did wonder for a while if he, the murderer, had got to her after all. But I felt in my bones she was still alive, and true to you, she was, and doing all right for herself. For sure as death, one Sunday I came upon a square ad in the *Era*, the Postbox of the Profession, bottom of the column, back page:

NOTICE.

To Professor Moore [one of my professional names]. A note to Miss Bellwood, care of the *Era*, would be obliged and understood. Mind your eye, Corney.

I understood and obliged, letting her know that I was off to a nobby shop in the north, to Springwell, and that her packet was safe with me. I was fearful of it falling into the wrong hands – though whose they might be, I could not say – so it sat in my coat pocket, whether it was on or off my back. At first, I could feel it banging against my side while I was about my business, like it was reminding me it was there. Then I got so as I didn't notice it. It was always there, and I felt for it when I put my coat on, and sometimes wound the bit of string around my finger, and turned it about (for there was something hard and round inside). But I never thought to take it out. After some months, though, the edges started to get ratty where the oilcloth was worn, and I knew the string was down to threads, for I often caught my nail in them. When I reached in my pocket and found, not the accustomed shape, but one with flaps and edges and shapes quite different, I knew what had happened.

I was not inclined to open it. It had travelled with me around London as I looked for a shop, pressed against my side when I spent my only night in the House, and rode with me as I cadged a seat on an open cart heading northwards. I didn't take it out, for although I'm not superstitious (unlike some actors who won't say the name of this drama or that, and rub their noses with their thumb if someone does), it seemed to me that ignorance of what was under the oilcloth wrappings had seen me all right so far, and I wanted that state of things to continue. It might sound as though I am making light of the tragedy, and of course I am not. I was fond of Bessie and was much put out by what happened to her. But it is often my way to look sideways at life and ponder upon people and things that happen. Which is what I was doing in the Old Pitcher, Springwell, with my glass of Bunty's Best before me and my pipe, and the fire to myself. It was a while since the business in Whitechapel, the Constellation was now renamed the Tidy Woman, Gov had left and gone into the entertainment line on his own account, and everything was different. It was very different, and no mistake.

But men aren't always master of their fates, as Mr Figgis used to say to me, and certain he was very wise, for what happened was this. While I was waiting for Mr Flynn of the Old Pitcher to bring me a plate of bread and cheese, I went into the yard to wash away the dirt of the journey, and took off my coat and hung it on a hook by the door. It was my only coat, you should know, and though I had my bag with me, that was only to make me appear a respectable man, for it contained little more than a shirt and my notices. But I had clearly made an impression on Mr Flynn for he sent the girl with a stiff brush and cloth to dust off my coat, and when I turned round, with soap and water in my eyes, she was on her knees collecting the bits and pieces that she had turned out of my pockets on to the ground, and apologizing very sweetly all the while. The screw of bacca was there in its paper, a needle and a bit of thread in their tin (what Mrs Figgis had give me all them years ago and still with me, after all I've been through), and a lucky hen's tooth given to me by a genuine gypsy queen. Lucy's packet spilled out with everything else, so the bit of oilskin wrapping and the string and the bits of paper were all tumbled together in the girl's apron.

'I'm ever so sorry, Mester,' said she in her child's voice, for she could be no more than twelve years, 'they just fell out while I was brushing down your coat, like Mr Flynn told me. I think I've got 'em all,' she said, looking down into her apron, which had been white and now was all the dirty colours you could imagine.

I said it was not a whisker of trouble to me, and if I had a penny I would give it to her, but I hadn't.

'Oh,' says she, blushing, 'I'm sure you have,' and she looked hard into her apron again and then around her feet.

'I am sure I saw – yes, I did. I must have missed it.' She stooped down and picked up what did indeed appear to be a penny. And then she exclaimed, 'Oh, sir, it's not a penny, though it has a lady's head on it.'

She offered me the penny, and I saw that it wasn't a coin at all. I was about to say it wasn't mine and that someone must have dropped it, when I realized what it was.

It was that hard object in Lucy's packet.

The girl left, disappointed, I suppose, that I was speaking the truth, for I had not got a penny on me. And what I had in my hand was no penny but – well, I shall describe it. It was the size and shape of a penny, and appeared to be of the same dull metal. But on one side, where you might expect to find the face of our good Queen Victoria, there was a tiny portrait of a lady, set against a blue background. Here was an angel, surely, with tumbling curls about a face which wore a sweet expression, and was painted so very much 'to the life' as it were, that I felt I should know her immediately if I saw her. Her blue eyes smiled, her lips (the faintest pink) were parted, and there was good humour and sweetness there. It was a regular lady's face. And it was clear to me that the owner treasured this likeness, for it was covered with a piece of glass, cleverly held in place by tiny grips.

When I turned the coin over, the metal (gold probably) had been inscribed, though I had to peer hard at it to make out the words:

*For my dearest Brother on his birthday.*
*John Shovelton*
*From his affectionate Sister Helen*

It amazed me how so much writing could be inscribed upon so small an area, but more how someone might want to destroy what had been taken so much care over. For the writing had been scratched at with something sharp, and on purpose, as if a person wanted to score it out. It was ferociously done, and dug deep into the metal. I turned it around in my hand, and while the fire crackled and the clock ticked, and Mr Flynn's good ale stood warm in the glass, it occurred to me that perhaps I had in my hand something material in whatever had caused Lucy to flee and hide. And perhaps something material to the other business also.

I had restored the other bits and pieces to my pocket what the girl had tipped out, so it was but the work of a moment to rediscover them, and there, now wrapped roughly around by the piece of oil-cloth, were the papers that Lucy had entrusted to me. When I unwrapped them, I could see clearly where the coin had lain all these months, and its impression, which was quite dirty owing to the metal rubbing off on the paper. So I got them all out, all the bits that Lucy had put together and pushed across the table to me in Mr Tidyman's back room, me drinking my coffee and reading the *Era*.

There on Mr Flynn's table was everything in Lucy's packet. Two pieces of newspaper from the *Gazette* about the murder, and another with Gov's physog a-staring out like some gargoyle.

And there was another. Folded up very small, and yellow, not having been written on good paper to begin with. When I opened it up, the letters swum around before my eyes like tadpoles in a pond, so small and black were they. But, when Mr Flynn brung in a lamp and I was able to cast a good light upon it – well, things looked different. Everything looked different from what it did before, and I was obliged to sit still awhile and consider what I had read.

It was strange to see it all laid out before me. Words that I had only thought of, or that me and Lucy had spoke, were set out here, in Lucy's writing (like me, she is no scholar). But not just words, of course, but words that told about that night and the things that happened in it, which made me understand it all better because everything was now gathered up in one place, rather than in different people's mouths. Gov had talked about Bessie's murder (hadn't he just!), and Sergeant Bliss and I had seen her poor broken body with its marks of being stamped upon, but Lucy was there and saw him do it, the devil, and so wrote it down like she was in the yard watching it again. She saw the gent what did it, how he'd been in the concert room all that night, how he was knocking Bessie around and how she cried out and he saw her. No wonder she was frightened out of her mind, for she saw the horror what I saw, but more than that. 'I reach out and touch her hand and it's cold now,' her letter says. 'I stroke her fingers and I feel something hard between them. I think to myself, poor Bessie, all this for a sixpence, and I take it out of her hand. I wasn't stealing from her, but I know them as would.' Yes, girl, I think, so do I, and that sixpence is better in your pocket than in some others. I read the words over again and bite my lip, for it is like having her at my shoulder, leaning upon it and reading it with me. 'What a place to die,' it says. 'And I can't help but cry for

Bessie and me and all those like us and how wrong it is that poor girls should be used in such a way while the gents who use us so walk free.' I know she is right, and she has said it to me often enough. I have never read Mr Dickens's tales (not being able to get the letters in just the right order), but I am sure they can never give a notion of how he was speaking to a person in their ear, not in the same way as Lucy's words do.

I take myself and my glass to the window and look out upon the river and the trees, and peek up at the sky which is a nice shade of grey but going dark. There are a few ladies and gents out, taking the last of the air, hardy sorts, muffled, for the wind up here is a cutter. But it is a pleasant scene, and quiet. And think I am a lucky man in spite of all the knocks I have had. For here is Bessie, dead and cold in a yard, some mother's daughter, who had thought that one day she might see trees and sky, not brick walls, and feel the sun on her face, not a fist. It is not a fair world, and that's sure.

I drink off my Bunty's Best in one, and start folding up the bits and pieces on the table. It is when I am trying to get Lucy's letter back in its old shape that I notice something written on the bottom of the page, which I had missed. It is in different characters, but still Lucy's writing: 'Corney, if you read this do the right thing by Bessie and me. Here is the coin what I know is not a sixpence but something more.' I pick it up, the coin what Bessie had held on to, and turn it over in my hands and gaze upon the beautiful face.

Which is not Her Majesty.

By no means.

And I turn it over again and fiddle with the back, for it seems to me that it is loose. Which it is. And the whole business drops apart – glass, picture, gold back, lock of hair, tiny folded-up piece of paper. Another one.

It is as though it was written by fairy folk, so small is the writing. But it is round and clear, addressed to 'My dearest Helen' and finishing up 'Your Phyll'. I can make nothing of it, and feeling tired with the sadness of it all, I put the picture back in its case with the glass and hair and the tiny note.

∽⟨⟩∾

I am fond of shabby-nobby places like Springwell, but it is not often that a fellow like me can find a shop there for they are, as Gov reminded me when I asked him for a character, 'inclined towards the refined'. It is true there are some smart hotels, and rooms also (which will stretch a pocket), but mostly Springwell is not for the nobility, but their long-lost cousins. For pretty girls looking for a husband, and their mothers looking for money, and young men not minding over-much what they look for, as long as they have some fun. These are the same young men who, the week before, have been drinking and poking their nights away at the Constellation and places like it, have slept in shop doorways and alleys, and the next morning cannot even pass as a half-hour gentleman. There are many such in Springwell, and while I don't despise their sixpences and shillings, I do not want their company. But Mr Cashmore, the manager of the Springwell Pavilion, Pump Room and a couple of concert rooms does, and is of the opinion that a funny fellow with some funny songs will be just the encouragement they need. He it was who placed a 'Wanted' ad in the *Era* (the Bible of the Profession) for a comic singer, and who wrote by return to offer me a shop for the season – 'two turns every other eve., and a Grand Fashionable Night once a week' – when he had received my character from Gov and read my notices.

I was much pleased, for though I have worked such places before, it has always been 'on the road to somewhere else' as it were, a passing-through rather than a stopping-off. I might be a city concert-room man by habit, and appear to flourish in the hurly-burly world, but I am quiet by inclination. The concert room was my place of business, you might say, but like so many lawyers and City men, I liked to retire to the birdsong and bees, pulling up the draw-bridge, and putting out the 'Not at Home' notice. Springwell was that sort of place, and if I had to warble for my supper and be agree-able to young cubs with more money than sense, then I would if, in return, I could sit of a dinner-time in the Old Pitcher with my Bunty's Best and a plate of bread and cheese.

Mr Cashmore was a gloomy gent with a face much struck by misery (for it was a veritable criss-cross of lines and furrows all hoving downwards and with the expectation of no bright conclusion) and, though he claimed he was pleased to see me, it was not painted on his clock. I produced his letter and whipped out my notices (for I had sent him hand-copies), and another testimonial, all to prove that I was bon. fid., and he nodded and we agreed terms. He showed me his new pleasure punt on the river (asking if I would do boating seren-ades, which I declined, not having sea-legs). He told me of his ailing wife and the downturn in the bottled sauce trade, and even walked me around to Mr Flynn's the Old Pitcher and recommended me for a room. And that was that. Shop found, room found, friendly land-lord, quiet parlour. After Whitechapel, it was like taking a holiday.

I now had only one concern, and for them not in the business, it might seem a surprising one. I had not seen the orchestra yet and this played upon my mind somewhat. A comic singer is often anx-ious about his orchestra. I have known men who, on finding that their 'superior accompaniment' is nothing more than a chesty catgut scraper, have walked twenty miles and paid their own money to bring in a proper musician. Many caterers think it's of no impor-tance to have a band what can play *and* read music, and consider any old broken-down ivory-thumper will do.

But Mr Cashmore, for all he was a Jobanjeremiah about the phys, did not stint on his orchestra. Every morning when I attended on the Pavilion, here were four fiddlers, sober and ready, and with instru-ments so tuned they might play a jig along themselves! And a piano with its master, both of them polished and waiting. Here were men with proper sheets of music, covered in a black forest of dots and dabs, none of your scraps of paper with '2 bars agit, D major and wait while chorus'. I was comforted and impressed. Here was an elegant hall, with gas lamps (all working), a platform and curtain (no holes in either), a backcloth showing a street so full of horses and carriages and people and shops that to wander into it might be a positive danger, and out in the front a cheerful box-keeper, Mr Beeton, who shook me by the hand and told me that I was a particular favourite of his, and that my rendition of 'The Whistling Oyster' had lingered with him for many weeks. (I believe he was confusing me with some other fellow, and not wanting to take credit for another man's work, I obliged by including the 'Oyster' in my programme.)

Here was the shop I had longed for, then. Refined, in a country sort of way. Clean and tidy. Friendly associates, and the sort of respect to which I could become accustomed and indeed, after all these years in the profession, it was nothing but my due. In Springwell there was no 'Ho there, Corney Sage! Get yer arse in yer pants!' but a polite enquiry from Signor Frazerini as to whether Professor Moore (that's me, Professor Hugh Moore) was ready. And genteel applause all round, though more rorty when there were military about. Even so, there was not a man in his cups, not a woman bawling him out. There were no fights, no shouting matches.

And there were no murders.

Lucy's letter recalled to me that unpleasantness, for I had tried to put it out of my mind, good and sure. But to have it spread out on the table before me even when the parlour of the Old Pitcher was so warm and cosy, and Mr Flynn's beer drank sweet as a nut, well, it made me shiver some, especially when I thought of the dark Row and the footsteps tearing after me.

Lucy's packet sat in my pocket again, tied up with brown paper now and string, and I sometimes took it out to read her letter or the bits from the newspaper. Or look at the picture of the beautiful woman. Like I was on this particular evening. She was easy to look at, a regular angel, and whoever had caught her likeness had made a good job of it, anyone could see. I turned it round and round in my hand, and not for the first time thought how Bessie must have grabbed it in her struggle, and how she held on to it in all her agonies. And here I wiped my eye, and thought that I was a fond fellow for all my guff.

The door opened and the girl (whose name was Hope but was called Topsy on account of her clumsiness) fell in. I say *fell* for that was indeed what she did, knocking over a chair and rearranging a table on the way. The pot of beer she had brought me had watered the front of her apron and acquainted itself with the floor, but there was enough left to wash down the rest of my bread and cheese, and as she put it on the table I could see her eyes drawn to the picture, so I pushed it towards her.

'Now, Topsy,' says I, 'here is a beautiful lady who you would do well to imitate. Look at her fair skin and her golden hair. You have those features in abundance, and it would take only a pot of powder and a handful of pins for you to pass off as a lady yourself.'

Indeed, I flattered the poor child, for although she had indeed fair skin and golden hair, her other features were less striking, unless of course it was her two eyes, both of which were trained on the tip of her nose at the same time. She took up the picture in both hands like it was a jewel and gave it good scrutiny.

'If I was to ask the lady what powder she used, and how many pins, Mr Professor, would she tell me?'

I had to smile, for she was solemn in her fancy.

'I have no doubt, if you was to ask her in the proper way, polite and not forward, and did not spill anything on her good dress, nor knock her to the ground with your elbow, Topsy, I am sure she would tell you.'

She smiled. 'Then I shall go on my next day off with my friend Agnes, who is Mrs Garnett's scullery, and I shall be polite and not clumsy.'

'Where shall you go?' says I, thinking that, as well as all her other faults, the girl was soft also.

'To the George. She stays at the George, and walks out with the other lady, and a tall man. Very handsome. And as tall as a tree.' Topsy turned about and dashed a stool and the firedogs to the floor as she mopped up the spilled ale. 'I thought they was a family, two sisters and their brother. But Agnes says they are not, though they are very great friends, and sit with each other constantly. Shall I bring you another glass, sir?'

I think I nodded, though I am not sure, for my poor brain was considering Topsy's words. And it was still turning them over when she came back into the parlour, carrying a jug, and walking like there was glass or eggshells under her feet.

'So,' says I, trying to appear unconcerned, 'you say this lady is at the George?'

Oh yes, she was there. Didn't I know? Isn't that why I'd got the coin? She supposed I was a cousin, at least, though I didn't look at all like her, but then *she* didn't look like any of *her* cousins (which I could well understand). Her name? No, she didn't know that, but she could find out. Indeed, she would have to know that, wouldn't she, in order to call upon her and be introduced.

And her brother, I said, as though it didn't matter one jot, but holding my breath all the same, did she know *his* name?

She blushed again, and almost nudged my beer to the floor. She *did* know *his* name. Every girl knew the name of Mr Shovelton. And wasn't he the handsomest man in Springwell? So tall. So dark. Such blue eyes, such an elegant figure. He had noticed Mrs Garnett's girl, and she was not even a proper lady's maid. No, he was not in the military, though his bearing was so straight he might have been.

She had taken particular notice of him. Was that all, sir? Thank you, sir.

I turned the picture over and looked hard at the writing.

My room in the Old Pitcher was a simple affair, above the stables. Clean, yellow walls, an iron bedstead, a mattress without extras (the biting kind), and the friendly scent of four-footed companions shuffling and snorting below. I had lain there on my first night and stretched my bones till they cracked, and I felt all the hardness and difficulty of my life ease out and ebb away. I had woken up to birdsong not yawping, and the scent of stocks and sweet william rather than cat's meat and bones. Seated to my breakfast in Mr Flynn's parlour, his wife had brought creamy milk, still warm from the cow, and good thick slices of salty ham and white bread and flavoursome butter. I had found a berth here with which I could be content, and it occurred to me that I was tired of trouble and the hardness of city life. The clean air and bright sun, trees bursting with greenness, and the lapping river, all these simple things had been missing, and here they were in abundance.

But after Topsy had blushed her story out about the ladies and gent at the George, it seemed that a shadow was cast across me. When I reached my room, I locked the door, for the first time since I arrived in Springwell, and when I lay down on my bed, I felt as though all my bones were set agin each other. But it was an uncalled-for fear, I thought. Topsy was no great judge of features, surely? Here was a girl who was blind to tables and chairs when they was in familiar places! What chance that she should recognize this strange face as one she'd seen in the street? And how very strange it should be for this woman to be here! Out of all the women and all the places in this great country, how should *she* be in Springwell? And how should *this* picture, what I had now slipped under my pillow for safe-keeping, and its owner, and Bessie and Lucy and me, how should all this be threaded together?

I took off my boots and lay on my bed (which might have been in a corner of the Little Ease for all it gave me comfort) and thought about things.

I am no scholar. Mr Figgis (who brung me up, so not my father, but as good as) always said that I should use the bits of brains the good Lord gave me, rather than wonder about them what he didn't. Or something along that way. But it was beyond me to work out how I, not for the first time, was troubled by business that was not of my making. This picture of a young woman had found its way to me, just as surely as I found my way into the back yard of the Constellation and into the eyeline of the swell who did for Bessie, though it would take some clever Oxford fellow to explain how and why. And yet here they were, joined up like a Roman's rosary beads.

There was a bright moon and, wonder of wonders, shooting stars bursting across the sky. I leaned out of the little window and watched them make trails across the sky, and looked up and down the Parade, and I breathed in the clear air which I own I could not get enough of, after the stink of Whitechapel. It was all dark and quiet, only the distant rush of the water over the stones by the River Gardens. It was a perfect berth for me and no mistake, and felt like home. Whatever that might be.

I never knew my own mother, of course, though I understand she was a kindly, welcoming soul, and made comfortable any soldier or sailor who could find the coins to buy her a bed, and the appearance of yours truly was no inconvenience to her either, though perhaps something of a surprise. So surprising that she left me on the corn chandler's doorstep, wrapped in a large poster (torn from a hoarding) announcing a balloon ascent the following day, which she attended with a mulatto mariner. (I think this last bit about the mariner is not all the truth and, true to you, I don't know where it has come from. But it has become part of my story, so often have I told it.) The tale of finding me, the swaddling in which I was wrapped up like a parcel of fried potatoes and the search for my mother, was the sole subject of Mr Figgis's conversation for many weeks.

The Figgises had no kids of their own and were Baptists through and through, but they gave me a name – Cornelius, of course – and a home, clean as a whistle. But that life would never do for me, though, and I can see Mr F even now, looking heavenward for assistance. Kind as they were and never a thought for themselves, they were not the mother and father I knew had started me up, so to speak. When I was older, I quizzed them till Mr F lost his patience and Mrs F started to cry, and then I asked everyone from the turnkey to the tanner. But it was like looking for an honest man in a court of law. I never knew my mother and she never came to find me, though I searched the face of every small, red-haired woman (I fancied I had inherited her looks) who crossed my path. Even now I often thought of her, the mother who had wrapped me in the only thing she could find, and left me with only hope and charity as protection.

I fell to musing on this, and certain the mild night air and the bubble of the distant water was very pleasant. For though I sometimes felt sad that here was a mother I never knew and perhaps brothers and sisters also, Springwell was so comfortable a shop, so very mild and easy compared with what I had been accustomed to, I could generally bring myself about, and dwell upon more cheerful matters. And this I tried to do, sometimes with success, but other times, like tonight, to no avail, for what crept into my thoughts were darker memories. Cold nights in doorways. An empty belly and the pain that goes with it. Thoughts of murder and someone who might be connected with it sleeping in a bed only a few steps up the street. I could not help myself but lean out and look upon the windows of the George, some still lit, and wonder if the lady on Bessie's locket was in one of them. And whether the Mr Shovelton that Topsy was so struck by was indeed her brother. And how all these little things might drop together into something bigger.

And so I was considering the likelihood of these rags and trifles together, and feeling not a little careworn by them, when the sound of footsteps brought me up. Springwell was such a quiet, out-of-the-way place that anyone out after ten o'clock was probably up to no good. There was nowhere to go and nothing to do in Springwell when the night drew on, except sit by the fire or go to bed. But here was a gent striding out, heels striking the pavement like hammers and not caring who heard them, and stopping in front of the Old Pitcher, my little crib. I watched him cross the road and try the door, but Mr Flynn had turned down the lamps and turned himself into bed hours before and all was in darkness in the snug and parlour. His footsteps echoed around the side of the Old Pitcher and into the yard. My eye, I thought, he'll be for it if he discovers Mr Flynn's mastiff, and without thinking too much on it I leaned out of the window and cried out, not too loud so as to wake everyone, but enough to get the gent's attention.

'Hello, below!' I cried, and the clattering footsteps stopped. I couldn't see him owing to the deep darkness, and so I called out again, 'Hello, below there! Sir!' The footsteps turned themselves about and cracked across the cobbles, as I charged on, little thinking, desiring to be helpful.

I leaned out further from my nest and called, *piano*-like, 'What is it you want, sir? Can I help you?' He was as still as you like. I could almost hear him breathing. But, fool that I was, I kept at him. 'Are you lost, sir, or taken ill? Shall I call Mr Flynn, sir?' And then came again the sound of his boots, striking the stones like hammers and echoing around the yard. For he must have seen me, framed like a picture in the window, calling down to him. And I knew him. Or I knew his boots and their melody and their agony and what horrors they might create. It was as though I was back in Whitechapel, back in the Row behind the Constellation, back in my nightmare where he runs after me. The gent, Bessie's murderer, after me now, as Lucy said he would be.

I have no recollection of how long I stood at my little window looking down into the darkness, searching out the face that went with the sound of those footsteps and which I knew was looking up at me from the shadows. Searching it out, but not finding it. It might have been minutes or hours, but something decided me that the only thing I could do was, like a rabbit bolting into its hole, to slam the window and secure the catch, and then check the bar on the door, and put my chair against it also.

# 5

## *Matters Better then Worse*

**Corney Sage – Springwell**

I spent a bad night, the first one ever in Springwell, and got up the next day feeling very cheap. It was Friday, and a Grand Fashionable Night at the Pavilion, and Mr Cashmore, being an exacting man, liked to 'give patrons a taste of the Metroplis', as he put it – and charge 'em Metropolis prices. No one minded. It was the only entertainment to be had and Grand or Fashionable or not, people bought their tickets and looked forward to it.

I attended business as per, talking myself up and feeling sunnier as I stepped out upon the Parade, and tipped my hat here and there, and was greeted most cordially by Mr Beeton, the box-keeper who, as far as I could see, never left his box, but lived there entirely. Indeed, inside the box, which was no more than a cupboard, he had everything a man could want. As it were, a home in miniature. A pail of water in the corner, covered by a towel, for washing. A small stove on which he heated water for his tea. Mr Kean, his dog, and Mrs Malibran, his cat, both settled in their places, one sleeping always at his feet and the other on the top of his ledgers on a high shelf where she kept down the spider population. An old hat box stood duty as a container for clean collars and handkercher, hair oil and toothpicks, and a small, round-headed punisher, for dealing with difficult patrons. His meals (which he sent out for and which were brought round regularly by a crippled boy called Nidd) he ate in the box, so that there was always the lingering smell of mutton and greens to greet visitors. (But Mr Cashmore didn't seem to mind, which surprised me for in every other way he was a to-the-letter man.)

Mr Beeton was, as I said, eager to greet me, and came out of his box (which he did so infrequently that he had to pause and adjust his pins and look up into the sky with an expression of wonder) and pumped my hand up and down like he was drawing water.

'Professor Moore,' he said in a high and whistling voice, 'I've been looking forward to this occasion. Will you take a turn with me, sir?'

I was surprised and began to excuse myself, for I was due in the hall for a half past ten call, and do not like to keep musicians waiting.

'Just five minutes, sir,' he pleaded, 'knowing your duties are onerous and time so precious, but feeling confident of your good nature. . .'

I had to give in. How could I not? At which he laid his hand upon my arm in a confidential way and we walked a few steps back and forth in front of the box.

'It is a pleasure to me, Professor Moore, to talk to an educated man. Many persons pass by my window, sir, but few have a university education. From which university did you gain your degree, sir?'

Here was a puzzle and a dilemma. It was a surprise to discover that Mr Beeton was not wise to the world of the concert room. If he had been, he might know that most every comic fellow was a Professor or Doctor or Monsieur, and that these were adopted titles for the stage, and not signifying anything. But here was a man in earnest, with his hand upon my sleeve and a smile upon his lips, not at all anxious to hear that I was found on a doorstep in Portsmouth and educated at the Ragged School, but rather that I was the son of a respectable clergyman, and that I had been to the best (the only) university I had heard of, so I said, with as careless an air as I could muster, 'Oh, Cambridge, sir, but I got tired of all the talking and the reading, so I tried the stage instead.'

His earnest face lit up like a lamp. 'Did you really, sir? Well! And what a thing to do! Get tired of reading books all day? And of educating young gentlemen in the philosophy and the Greek? Why, I can't count the pleasure I have in my little library, sir. Every day I take down a volume and open it up, just so, and here is Homer, sir, and the letters of Pliny, sir, and the *Lives of the Emperors*, which are my favourites.'

I nodded sagely and said I was partial to the *Lives* myself, though I liked a letter or two if they had plenty of moment to them, and weren't too much occupied with politics, which I couldn't abide. He looked at me curiously, and then laid his hand across his mouth and laughed for all he was worth. Indeed, the tears rolled out of his eyes and down his cheeks in a way I have never seen before in a man.

'Droll, Professor Moore,' says he, wiping his eye with a handkercher, 'which a man can be with a education such as yours. Could I ask you, would it be a great imposition to invite you into the box to look at my little library?'

I had already begun to shake my head, but he whistled on.

'I would deem it such an honour, sir, such a privilege to have your opinion and perhaps, though I should not impose but feel emboldened to do so, perhaps your recommendations. A bookseller in Plymouth sends me them cheap, if they are deficient by a page or two.'

He was so earnest and desirous of my attention that I could do no more than follow him into the box (and we were tight and cosy in there) and fix my eyes upon the twenty or so volumes ranged upon a shelf above the window. Mrs Malibran, who I believe saw through me immediately and was merely waiting on her moment to denounce me to her master and to the world as a fraud, looked down at me from the shelf above, though Mr Kean, as usual sleeping under the table, was in no way interested in my dilemma. I scratched my chin and cocked my head this way and that (as I've seen men do outside booksellers), and I made murmuring noises (as above), while Mr Beeton looked anxiously on.

'Well, Professor Moore?'

'Mr Beeton,' says I in my most serious tones, 'here you have a very fine library.'

He was looking hard at me, and attending to my every word, and nodding too.

'Yes indeed, and, confidentially' – I inclined my head and he drew and, I believe, held his breath – 'I consider this as good a library as the one I used to use for my studies.'

'At Cambridge?' said he, looking surprised. 'Have they only twenty-three books in the library of that great university?'

'Only twenty-three worth reading, sir,' said I gravely. 'And you have 'em all.'

He thought for a moment, and then clapped his hands. 'Ah, Professor Moore, you are surely a great credit to the University of Cambridge! Tell me, was that where you became acquainted with Mr Shovelton?'

Shovelton.

I had not thought to hear that name spoken. No, allow me to correct myself. I had not *wanted* to hear that name, but now here was Mr Beeton obliging me with it and expecting a smile and a nod, no doubt. For some moments all I could think of was Topsy and the merry way in which that name tripped off her tongue. So, true to you Miss Topsy, I thought, you was correct. That is his name. The very same and no doubt residing, as she declared, at the George.

Mr Beeton was raising his eyebrows and licking his lips, still waiting for the smile and nod, and indeed Mrs Malibran trained her yellow eyes upon me and even Mr Kean raised his head to hear my answer.

But, 'Mr Shovelton?' was all I could muster.

'He has enquired for you, sir. Wishing to renew your friendship, I expect. I told him he could find you here tonight, and he was delighted to be sure, and said he looked forward to it.'

Mr Beeton, I believe, was now waiting for a hearty college story. One that might have concerned youthful pranks and glasses of the best ale, while I was still hopeful that there had been some unfortunate error on the part of Topsy. And indeed on the part of Mr Shovelton, who surely was seeking out a different Professor Moore, one from Cambridge University, a gentleman who read many books of letters and lives, and who had never been so unfortunate as to have seen a murderer. So I played the donkey.

'Shovelton?' I says again. 'No, I don't believe I recall Mr Shovelton. Mr *Castleton* was certainly a good friend of mine. And Mr Middleton also. I remember lending money to a Mr Partleton, though I don't begrudge it, since he was a Presbyterian. But Shovelton?' Here I scratched my chin and my head and stared hard at Mr Beeton's bookshelf. 'No,' I said, 'he does not come to mind. Do you think he might have confused me with someone else, Mr Beeton?'

The box-keeper didn't think so, saying that Mr Shovelton was most insistent on paying his compliments, and had already bought tickets for the entertainment that evening.

Tickets?

Three. For himself and his sister and her friend. He had knocked upon the door of the box today and enquired of Professor Moore in the most earnest terms. Indeed, I had missed him by minutes, and if I hurried along the Parade, I might even catch him up.

No, I had my call and I was already late, which Mr Beeton understood.

'Ah, you professionals, if I might be so bold! Always at work and to the mark, and never time to indulge yourselves in ordinary pleasures! Professor Moore' – and he took my hand – 'it has been a pleasure and an education, sir. I salute you, sir, as you go to your task. As the esteemed Seneca put it, *ars longa, vita brevis.*'

I resisted the inclination to make something of this, and hurried away to the hall where I was already ten minutes late. The orchestra, having tuned and scaled up and down, were well advanced with Madame Laurie and her selection of Scottish melodies, so I sat at the back of the hall and thought on what Mr Beeton had said, for I was sure now – though not glad about it – that if this Mr Shovelton was who I thought he was, a close acquaintance with him was not desirable.

In the days before I left, the police in Whitechapel were still searching for poor Bessie's murderer though the trail was, as Tegg told me one night in a ratting ken, 'cold for want of 'eat' – and no likely customers apart from a gent who had been hauled in and given a roasting, but then let go. There were posters reminding anyone who had been in the colonies or in quod of the awful murder of an innocent girl and calling for witnesses and anyone with information, but I knew that the very girl and the very bloke who could say much – Lucy and me – were too scared and, as I thought, one of us too far away.

But this gent, this Shovelton. Well, was he the one, the cove that I saw in the yard of the Constellation? Who Lucy saw stamping the life out of poor Bessie Spooner? And if it was him who had stood there in the yard at the Old Pitcher, and let me know that he knew me and where I was... Well, true to you, Corney Sage was not a safe man. For if he had done Bessie in, sure as sure, Mr Shovelton had not come upon Springwell by accident, nor for the air and the water. If he had followed me here, it was a different matter. A different complexion, as they say, and one not so rosy.

Signor Frazerini was in a poor temper that morning, having lost a fiddler to a neighbouring town and being forced to bring in a bass player whose instrument had been so knocked about in transportation that it had the appearance of something fit only for kindling. His hair was a positive explosion, no doubt where he'd been tearing at it all night, and he was snappy, though still polite enough.

'Professor Moore,' cried he, 'will you join us on the stage, or do you prefer to perform from the rear of the hall?'

'Signor,' says I, making my way down the aisle, and not wishing to inflame him, 'I am at your service. I would rather have you in my eye than on my back!'

The fiddlers sniggered and shuffled their music.

'So, sir, now you have found a moment to give us your attention, which piece shall you offer this evening? Shall it be' – and he sniffed and sorted through my pieces – '"Alonzo the Brave" or "The Spider and the Fly", or perhaps that old favourite of yours "The Ratcatcher's Daughter"?'

But I had other plans.

*§*

The Pavilion was packed with the great and the good, top to bottom. Mr Beeton had sold every ticket, and had a list as well. From half past six, carriages were drawing up and the little River Walk was so crowded with folks hanging about waiting to get in that Mr Cashmore was forced to open up the refreshment bar for fear that someone might end up in the water! He opened the Pump Room too, and could be seen, leaning into the job like it was a strong wind, with his bunch of keys, opening doors, raising hatches and putting out chairs. The orchestra was rounded up before their due hour and persuaded to 'play on' like they was enjoying the extra work, and the Signor, who was smiling but tetchy, played everything, in his agitation, double time, so we were all of a hot fluster by the time eight o'clock come round, and Madame Laurie, the first on, took to the stage.

Standing in the wings, with my eye to the curtain, I trained it over the assembly, while Madame started with her 'Bonnie Braes'. By the time she'd worked through her 'Annie Laurie' and her 'Blue Bell of Scotland', and commenced her finale, the grand 'Loch Lomond', I had ranged across almost every row and gangway (extra chairs being placed there) from back to front, and was commencing upon the front chairs. Here were three rows of the military, all red coats and red cheeks! They was well-behaved, though chatty, and it was only Madame Laurie's powerful vocals and steely eye, both of which might have stilled the waves one way or another, that kept them down. When she finished there was loud applause, and she looked somewhat startled, thinking that a ribbing might follow, but Frazerini, who knew the military of old, just give a nod and struck up 'Old Ling Sign' or whatever it is, and had them all sing along, not in a free-and-easy way of course, but refined with Madame as lead horse. I took my medicine – Cream of the Valley to open up the chords – and, holding it in my mouth, looked through the curtain again.

Which, you will anticipate, is when I saw her. The very image of the woman in the picture, even now, lying in my coat pocket alongside its paper and wrappings. With the face of an angel, with golden hair and skin like a chinee doll, the artist had not done her any disservice. She was quite as beautiful in life as she was in paint. She was dodging around, trying to see alongside a soldier with a wide head, and leaning into her neighbour who, by the smile on his face, didn't object to her attentions at all. And those attentions were slight enough. A little smile or a word, a nod of the head, the flutter of her fan (for the room was hot despite Mr C's best attentions to the windows). Now at any other time, I would have willingly got a cold-in-the-eye from training it through the glory-hole, just to take in this young lady, but it was the gent on her other side who I was eager to see and his face was blocked out by the square shoulders and massive napper of another military, a sergeant-at-arms, a one-man barricade. Whatever rank he filled, he also filled the seat like there were three of him, and I felt sorry for the parties behind him who would see nothing of the platform and everything of his collar and the lime oil in his hair.

I was also annoyed, for though I could see the angelic lady on his right and the pleasant dark-haired lady on his left (who leaned to talk to him and so was surely acquainted with him), I could see only his arm, try as I might. And so occupied was I in trying to get even half an eyeful of Mr Shovelton that I very nearly missed my spot. Madame finished, and there was the usual roaring and stamping that the military believe shows appreciation, and I was introduced with one of Frazerini's jaunty medleys.

The stage is my home. It is where I am most comfortable. Under the gaslights it is warm when the weather is stormy without, and the sun always shines on a backdrop street. When I step out and Professor Hugh Moore comes along with me, we make the wooden world our own and though no one regards me in the street and I eat in the back parlour of a public or a coffee room, on the stage I am the king of all I survey, and all eyes are upon me. I have been at this job so long that I am easy with myself. I know some artistes get the back-door trots regular, even though they've been at the job twenty years, but me, I do it like it was a natural thing. I feel safe behind the floats. To me they are the wooden walls of old England, excusing the pun, for they keep us apart, the monster with the many mouths and me.

So when I stepped out on to the Pavilion stage that evening, and felt the warm hiss of the gas and the waft of oil and lavender that comes from a well-heeled audience, I knew once again that I was

# Walking in Pimlico

King. Frazerini stood in the orchestra with his arms up and hair to attention, and 'Alonzo the Brave' broke out at a merry lick. Then 'The Industrious Flea' and a couple of Sammy Cowell's tunes (passed on to me by that gentleman). But when we got to the point where I usually took off my jacket and put on my clogs (too heavy and thumping to walk around in) I changed my mind. Not of a sudden. I had thought it round like a clever fellow. I shook my head at Frazerini who was ready to give the medley of Olde Englishe melodies to which I capered, and I walked over to the wings and instead of my clogs, I brought out a wooden-backed chair and placed it carefully, dead centre, with its back to the audience.

Not a sound. Not a movement. Even Frazerini was still.

I unbuttoned my shirt and coat, and let it slouch off one shoulder. I gave my hair a ruffling. And I walked around the stage, slowly, with my hands in my pockets, and my shoulders down, like I was a man on his last legs. Then I sat astride the chair, and cast my eyes about the audience, slowly, from one side to the other, like I was considering.

I've seen my pal Bill Ross do it a hundred times in the Cellars. He walks on to the platform, and the waiters shout 'Mr Ross is about to sing!' and 'Take your seats! Mr Ross will sing this moment!' and the whole of London, it seems, crowds in and falls silent to hear one little man sing one song, even though they've heard it countless times before. And I am often one of them, standing in the wings, holding a glass of Bill's Cream of the Valley (which is where I picked up the habit) and waiting while the quiet settles on the audience like a door closing. He'd keep 'em waiting, Bill, for he could, and times I've thought he kept 'em too long, but no, it was like they was all holding their breath, every one of them. And then he'd begin, and I would feel my skin crawl with the fear and the power of him. And the song.

I've never sung it myself, even though Bill said I might. Out of

London, of course, and I have sometimes thought I should try it out, in my own way, for I am taller than Bill, and with a voice what is lighter. I did not have about me Bill's props – his clay pipe and his tattered clothes. But that didn't matter.

I began. With my voice as low as a guardsman's box, I started quiet and slow.

> *My name it is Sam Hall, is Sam Hall,*
> *Oh, my name it is Sam Hall, is Sam Hall,*
> *My name it is Sam Hall,*
> *And I hates you one and all . . .*

Here I paused and looked around.

> *You're a gang of mockers all,*
> *Damn yer eyes.*

A few ladies gasped, and I conned Mr Cashmore in the wings ready to fly on. But Frazerini held him up, and I carried on.

> *I killed a girl they said, so they said,*
> *I killed a girl they said, so they said . . .*

I knew why Bill Ross loved this song, for it spoke out fiercely of the rotten lives of poor men and women, like Bessie and Lucy, trampled and done over by the likes of them sitting out front, with open mouths and full bellies. And one in particular.

> *I hit her on the head with my fist like it was lead,*
> *And I left her there for dead, damn her eyes!*

There was a bit of a buzz now, and some of the ladies were look-ing troubled, but I knew how it should be done, for I had seen Bill do it many a time (though not with so many fine ladies present, I admit). I got up off my chair and walked around, and Frazerini, who had shifted the cove off the piano, struck up with a solemn march to pace me out. When I got back to the chair, I gripped it hard, and stared out, but not meeting anyone's eye.

> *She lay there dead and still, dead and still,*
> *She lay there dead and still, dead and still . . .*

And I took a breath, and looked swift and hard at where I judged he was sitting.

> *Bessie lay there dead and still,*
> *But I hadn't had my fill,*
> *So I trampled her some more,*
> *Damn her eyes!*

It didn't rhyme, but I didn't care for I felt someone was looking hard at me now, and for a moment my mouth dried up like a witch's cunny, and Frazerini stopped his piano-playing and he too looked at me. There was a longish pause before I started up again.

> *They will catch me, like a rat, in a trap,*
> *Oh, they'll catch me like a rat in a trap,*
> *Ah, they'll catch me like a rat,*
> *And I ain't no dandiprat*
> *Nor a bloomin' aristocrat, damn their eyes.*

Frazerini was in his element, stomping away on the ivories, and even Mr Cashmore had forgotten where he was and seemed to be taken up by the power of the song. The hall was dark, and even more inky from the stage, where it is difficult to see beyond the front row, so I might have been fixing on quite the wrong place, but it seemed like there was no one else in that place except me and him, and as I stand there, with everyone seeming to hold their breath, I hear his steps after me, snap, snapping on the stones, and smell the piss and sweat in the yard.

It was hot under the floats, and the sweat stood out upon my brow like drops of rain and ran into my eyes. I drew my handkercher from my pocket to wipe it, and carried on.

> Oh, the hangman he draws near, he draws near,
> Oh, the hangman he draws near, he draws near,
> Oh, the hangman he draws near,
> And I don't shed a bloody tear,
> I don't know the taste of fear, damn yer eyes.

Of course, if he had seen and recognized me, then my card was marked from that moment. This raced through my head and nudged me hard, but before I could decide what to do, me and Billy Ross had already took him on, and mocked him out.

> So this shall be my knell, be my knell,
> So this shall be my knell, be my knell.
> This is my funeral knell,
> And I'll see you all in hell
> And I hope that you roasts well, damn yer eyes.

And I showed the air and the ladies and gents my fist, just as I'd seen Bill do. There was dead silence and then – what a commotion! But don't think that ladies fainted and gentlemen had to be held back from clocking me. Or that there was outrage and a-calling for the police. Not on your life! Here was applause like Professor Hugh Moore had never heard before, lifting the roof and making the windows rattle. The military a-stamping and a-roaring like they was on a battlefield. Gents smacking their hands together and 'Hurroo-ing!' till you could hardly get your breath. Then I sat on the back of the chair and waited, just as I'd seen Billy Ross do. I looked grim and held my face in both my fists, like I was looking death in the face.

I am not a brave fellow. I have moments when the spirit of Waterloo taps me on the shoulder, but they are rare visitors, and I knew as soon as I got to the wings that I had done a foolish thing.

# Walking in Pimlico

Mr Cashmore was beside himself, of course, and offered to raise my fee by two shillings and as much Cream of the Valley as my throat needed to repeat Billy's song each night. It's true that afterwards, 'The Cobbler's Awl' seemed tame, and 'The Ratcatcher's Daughter', though I'd heard old Sam Cowell's pipes around it many a night, was as flat as a nun's chest. The audience was restless and buzzing, and couldn't settle, so I abandoned 'The Spider and the Fly' and gave them some riddles and a soft shoe dance, and I could do nothing wrong.

I had no chance to bask, though. Mr Cashmore, hearing the roars, greeted me again, this time like a long-lost friend, and shook my hand with a vigour that was painful, and desired to treat me after the entertainment, to which I agreed, though I knew he would be drinking alone. I held up with Mr Beeton in his box – how honoured he was to have Professor Moore's company once again! – and then, paying my dues and picking up my bag, I took the river path to the end of the Parade and jumped upon the first cart I saw.

⁂

No, I am not a brave fellow, but I knew what I ought to do. The cart took me to the station, and the train took me back to London, and shanks's pony took me to my old ratting mate Constable Tegg. I found him out in the Marquis of Granby, sat in the corner with himself for company. (It is a lonely life being a copper, and no mistake, and I think I would rather starve than be so shunned by the rest of humanity.) His physog lit up a bit when I hove into view, but soon sobered down when I told him about my errand. I had thought hard about what I should do, though I was certain that I should bring out Lucy's letter and the picture. I let Tegg read it, and then I showed him the picture, and turned it over to let him see the writing on the back.

He considered it slowly, and took some pulls on his beer before he said, 'You should've brung this before.'

I said I couldn't. I was under obligation, but here it was now. It struck me that since Bessie had got hold of the picture – thinking it was a sixpence – and was holding it till her dying breath, and since the picture, not a sixpence at all, belonged to 'Shovelton', the name what was there, written on the back of it, here were more facts than even the bluebottles needed to point a finger at the devil. Tegg said he thought I was probably right, but he would have to hand it all over to Inspector Gould, who was still in charge of the case.

Which he did. And I spent the best part of two days drinking Inspector Gould's tea and sitting in his chairs, and chewing over that strange evening.

Until he said, 'Mr Sage, I think we can say, with certainty, that we have our Whitechapel Murderer.'

(He was a great one for the drama, was Gould, and I do believe he was represented on the London stage, perhaps at the New East London or the great Britannia itself. There was no doubt he had a great sense of himself, and would pace about and do stuff with his hands like a magician. Only not producing an egg, of course.)

Some of what happened next, as they say, I know only through the papers, in particular the *Illustrated Police News*, to which I am very partial on account of its educational pictures. Mr Shovelton was gone for at his lodgings, with a full turnout of bluebottles and a Black Maria to boot. He was recently arrived from the country (don't I know it!), and they call upon him at his London place, a good house in Canterbury-square, but his beautiful sister is not on hand. This causes a sensation, for when he is charged the papers want to see the beautiful sister, and are only half interested in him. But she is disappeared back to the country or Brighton. In the courtroom, I am brought out to talk about it, for, try as they will, they cannot find Lucy and I do not blame her for lying low.

It is a strange thing how judges and juries, and the sight and smell of justice, makes me feel like I'm being crawled upon. Here I stand, wearing my best shirt and collar, and boots what I've borrowed (too small), and gloves what I've borrowed (too large), and the worst hat ever to have come out of Gov's back room, and I want nothing more than to run away and hide. For I am asked question after question, and the cove in the greasy wig and dusty gown is not looking at me at all, anywhere but. It is as if he does not want to meet my eyes in case I stare him down. I answer all his questions, though, and tell again what happened on that night at the Constellation when young Bessie was done to death. And when the greasy wig asks me to look at the prisoner and say whether it was him what I saw a-doing Bessie agin the wall, and making off after squashing her head, I have to stare hard at the gent. Shovelton. Certain, he was one of the party on the grape in the Constellation. But was he the gent in the yard? I couldn't say for sure. It might be him, I say. Certain? No, it was dark. But certain enough? Not really. Was the height correct? Yes. The build? Yes, just about. Did he speak? Yes. They ask the gent to read something. A column from a newspaper about distemper in dogs. It seemed all right at the time, but now it's comical.

Was it him, says the wig, now that I have heard his voice?

Could be, says I.

Was it him?

Possibly, says I.

Was it?

Yes, says I.

No, cries Shovelton.

And that is that. It might seem that I am making light of this business. But in truth, I want it over. Here is a gent who *probably* did kill Bessie, and, who knows, he might have done it to others. Poor working girls, trying to scrape a penny, are always fair game to gents who have never known a cold night in their lives. It was probably him. And I hurry away as fast as I might, thinking that it is a bad job badly done, but over with now.

I have told this quickly, though I could have said plenty, for the courtroom and police and sessions at the Station House with Tegg and Gould were lively enough, and gave me plenty to relate when I fancied an audience and a pot. But at the time, I wanted nothing more than to pack up and leave London and all of it behind. So, when my part in it was over with, I took myself off sharpish to Mr Tidyman's back room at the Talbot and once again consulted the *Era*. Another nice little shop, quiet, was what I most desired, and I thought regretfully about what I had left behind at Springwell, for I had grown fond of my room at the Old Pitcher and even Mr Beeton and his high notions of my education. It was a pleasant place, to be sure, and I could have found myself quite at ease there.

But, as Mr Figgis used to say, we are not put on this earth to tread the primrose path, but to take the steep and thorny way. A jolly chap was my adopted father! So I ran my finger down the column of 'Wanteds' and found many called and few chosen, but a Mr Blitz of the Harmony Concert Rooms, Birmingham ('refined entertainments, no acrobats, thank you'), seemed to fit the bill. And I did something I have never done before, in all my professional life, so eager was I to breathe different air.

I went on spec.

# 6

## *James Yates, Introduced at Last*

### Miss Marweather – Whitechapel

When I first put on a pair of gentleman's breeches I was eleven years old. In the back yard of my father's tavern, deep within the Old Nichol, where policemen (if they were ever seen) patrolled in twos and threes. Yes, in the back yard of my father's tavern, I found, in a sack, a pair of gentleman's breeches! They were destined for an ancient Hebrew, who dealt, of course, in 'old clo'', but other goods as well. He was a close confederate of my father, though what their business was I knew better than to ask. The sacks, which appeared in the yard periodically, constituted part of *that business*, and the persons who accompanied them were in *that business*. I knew this instinctively, and the cuffs and blows I regularly received were a signal reminder. This sack, like the others, had been left just inside the gate but, unusually, it had fallen open and, tumbling out on to the cobbles were not only breeches, but an entire gentleman's costume, all of the finest quality. Boots, a shirt, a coat. And the scent that arose from the sack and with which the clothes were saturated also spoke to me of 'gentleman', for every night in my father's tavern that same scent would rise above the stink of sweat of working bodies like a fragrant mist. As I swept the floor or collected pots, I moved in the aroma of the gentleman!

And these *were* gentlemen, for all they were swells and the other ugly words my father and his confederates used to describe them. Dukes and earls, titled men, powerful men, somehow they lounged in the saloon bar, though for everyone else there was barely room to sit upright! And they swaggered through the crush of the dancing saloon, where the other occupants were forced to push and shove. Their voices cut through the din of the drunken Saturday night crowd, and though they might be in their cups and could be found spewing and sometimes brawling in the street, there was still a marvellous distinction about them.

My father was a Big Man in the Nichol. There were few men who would stand against him, for he held sway in the ring and the pit, and the Fancy flocked to our door. And the police. But there were gentlemen whom my father would not cross and to whom he deferred, even while he bit his lip and clenched his teeth. Lord This and the Earl of That. Men who barked or soothed their way, but who got their way because of that power which they wore like a second skin.

I watched them very closely whenever I could, which was easy enough. As a girl (never a pretty nor a striking girl), I might have been invisible for all they were aware of me. Collecting pots and wiping tables, carrying coals and sweeping the floors, I watched and learned. I saw how they behaved, how even turning upon a heel or holding a stick gave them that elegant authority that made my father look like a fumbling clod in spite of his size and reputation. Only once was I espied in my observations.

The table around which my father and his supporters, along with a handful of the Fancy, were congregated one evening was in our parlour, a title that dignified a mean room at the back of the house, reserved for private business. It was small and low-ceilinged, and blistering hot from the roaring fire, so the windows had been thrown open to the night air. I was in the yard and, looking through the window, was much struck by a new face at the table. I even remembered his name. The Viscount Mountgarrett, Earl of Kilrush – tall, lean and more darkly handsome than any man I had ever seen. He arrived late, the table was already crowded, but room was found, a chair and a brimming pot placed before him. He smiled around that table, reserving personal greetings for a favoured few, and those men swelled and shuffled in their seats. His eye was bright, his lips full and red, and when he walked out into the yard with my father, I thought he was the most fascinating of men. He paced about as they talked, his boots striking the cobbles with a rasping clatter and, as he turned, I dipped behind the shadow of a water barrel, fearing to be seen. Their conversation lasted some minutes and when it seemed to be at an end and I thought they had both returned to the house, I emerged from my hiding place. Only Mountgarrett stood before me, with that easy elegance of bearing I so admired but, at this moment, feared.

Indeed, I was much inclined to run away, but he caught my dirty hand in his and held me fast.

'Hello! What do we have here? Aren't you Banks's sprat?' His voice was as richly potent as the aroma of spice and sandalwood that seemed to exude from him.

I told him my name, all the time looking anxiously about me.

'I think you are spying on us, miss. What did you hear? Perhaps I should call your father.'

I begged him not to do that, knowing that my father would beat me and lock me in the cellar with the rats. I protested that I was not spying, merely – and then I was overcome with embarrassment. He was amused.

'Ah, then I must have an admirer! How flattering! And one so young!'

He was laughing at me, mocking! But I didn't care, for as long as he held me, even at arm's length, I could observe him closely. Could smell that heady odour of quality, of money, of power.

But he was urging me on, shaking me, demanding a reply, and so, because I was too overcome to invent an excuse, it all tumbled out. I confessed that I much admired him, his appearance and, in particular, his – boots. They were such fine, soft leather. They must have cost a deal of money. I had never seen such beautiful boots in all my life. I think he was surprised, was perhaps expecting me to rhapsodize over his handsome face, for he dropped my hand and took a step back, looking hard at me as though I were an imbecile.

'My boots?' he exclaimed. 'Ye gods! Now I've heard everything. Banks! Banks! Get yourself out here, you idle dog!'

My father emerged from the parlour like a rat from a trap, followed by a pack of his cronies, though seeing me and Mountgarrett all were comically arrested in their tracks. He looked quizzically at both of us.

'Banks,' said the noble Viscount, with only a trace of irony, 'this child says she admires my boots,' and, looking down at my bare feet, he shook his head, extracted coins from his pocket and pressed them into my grubby hand. 'For God's sake, man, get her some!'

He strode away across the yard, leaving behind him in the night air a trail of sandalwood and benevolence which, sadly, was not sustained by my father who swiftly removed the coins and reminded me of my station by caressing me with his own, much mended boot! But I could not forget Mountgarrett, though not for his generosity since I saw none of it. He remained in my imagination a talisman of elegance and breeding and power. When I thought of him, I saw my father's face, a picture of anxiety and eagerness to please. A Big Man brought down. I pictured the scenes in our tavern, when Mountgarrett and men like him ruled the company with that easy authority that we instinctively understood. How women fawned when encouraged, but knew to keep out of the way at other times. How men knew their place and kept to it. Only the fighters, the champions, men with flattened noses and bruised faces, might argue or take a marquis by the elbow. It was, to my young eyes, all in the bearing, for my father ruled by brutishness and a hard fist, yet Mountgarrett, smaller and slighter than he, had only to stroll into a room to command deference as well as obedience.

That unprepossessing sack, then, with its contents spewing out on to the yard, I knew was one of the keys, so I secreted it behind a stall in the stable, and brought out the contents, one by one, to my little eyrie room at the top of the house, where I carefully stowed them beneath the floorboards, wrapped in sacking or newspaper. Early one morning, before anyone in the house was stirring, I took them all out and laid them upon my bed. Breeches, shirt, waistcoat, short coat, boots. They were mightily rough now from being rolled and stowed in that narrow place, and as I unfolded it I noticed for the first time a brown stain upon the back of the shirt and a ragged rent in the fabric. But that was old business and not mine, and I was eager now to try on this finery. For it had been my growing idea, not planned but maturing over the weeks, to see how it felt to wear these clothes, even to walk around in them. I had no mirror, but I needed none. I simply wanted to put them on.

Of course, everything was too big and hung on me ridiculously. The previous owner had been a tall man and broad-shouldered, had worn his sleeves long, his breeches cut close. This was evident as I examined myself in the oversized garments. But though the coat trailed and the boots came over my knee, even to my thigh, I still enjoyed the sensation of linen against my skin and the subtle bouquet of leather. Pulling on the breeches, feeling the material coarse between my legs, produced in me a powerful sensation. In my body, of course, but there was also something else, more potent. And the coat, with its stiff shoulders: I had never worn anything so thick, so bristling with layers and materials. I strode about, struck poses (how ridiculous I must have appeared!) and determined, at that moment, that I would have a suit of my own. Would have boots and breeches, and would take to the

London streets and be generous to young girls and buy them shoes, and be important and respectable and powerful!

It was an immature dream and a long time coming – and, indeed, another story altogether. One that took me from pot-girl to the Fancy, and from penny theatres to prison. But at the end of it I had amassed enough to *buy* my suit. The first time I put on a pair of gentleman's breeches, ones that fitted me like a skin, I felt naked. But then nothing could have prepared me for wearing my *own* breeches, made for me at my instruction. Before a long glass, I examined myself from every point of view. I felt like an artist, assessing and appraising his work, considering every line and every aspect. Here were my legs, and all that stood between them and the air was a single covering of cloth, and this so close that every contour of thigh and buttock was as defined as if it were deliberately drawn!

The tailor, a Mr Ziter, had done an excellent job. He asked no questions (he was well paid, of course) when we met in my room in a dingy lodging house in Theatre-court, near to Drury-lane, and he solemnly unfolded breeches, coat, shirt, waistcoat from a package of brown paper and then waited outside the door while I put them on. My hair was cropped as short as I dared and it gave me exquisite pleasure to run my fingers through it as I had seen men do, without thinking, time and again. Those many freedoms that men take for granted! At other times, I wore many hairpieces, secured with quantities of pins, and which, at first, took an age to arrange but, as I became more practised, I could apply swiftly and expertly.

I scrutinized myself in the glass. The trousers were dark and fitted me, as I have said, like a second skin. The shirt and waistcoat, white linen and a subdued olive-green satin, felt soft and light. The great-coat with its wide shoulders and nipped waist was the pinnacle of my transformation. Even as I thrust my arms in and pulled the lapels into line, I felt myself transformed. My shoulders rose then settled, my spine straightened. Here I stood, without prompting, legs apart, my weight slightly on one hip, my hands hanging loosely. I felt as if I had put on someone else!

But though in the mirror I looked well enough, I needed to go out into the street. So I laced up the small brown boots of soft leather with their metal studs on heel and toe and took turn upon turn about the room until they were eased and I felt confident. The landlord rapped on the door and asked me what I thought I was doing. He was driven half mad by my clattering and pacing. If I wanted to walk a mile, he cried, I should wear out the pavement and not his floorboards and the patience of his guests!

I took a last inventory in the glass. My shoulders were square, the breeches hugged my thighs which were slim but defined. I had a waist, but not too much. My chest swelled under the elaborate waistcoat, but it *was* indeed a chest. I gave myself a sidelong glance, and caught sight of the hat sitting jauntily on the back of my head, and the short curls of my dark hair tumbling over my forehead. I found myself smiling, and enjoying that smile. I liked who I saw! He would be a good friend! A sound fellow!

The keeper rattled the door again. Who was in there? If I didn't show myself, he would go to the police.

I retorted that he could go to the D—! I was paying good money for the use of his miserable quarters, and if he didn't like it, I would take myself elsewhere!

I talked to the door as though I had swaggered through half the regiments in the land! Here was my voice suddenly become, I thought, deeper, though I wonder now if it wasn't the effect of the cigarettes I had been smoking. But it gave me confidence and I stamped my foot and kicked the door in my temper.

There was a silence outside. He asked if 'Miss' was in there, and hoped she had not come to harm. I retorted that he was blind or mad or both, and that there was not, there never had been any 'Miss'.

There was an apologetic cough. Begging the gentleman's pardon, but with his own eyes he had seen the young lady enter the building not two hours previous and—

I stamped my foot again and flung open the door. The keeper was crouched at the keyhole (as I had suspected), and shuffled back on his haunches as I advanced. His amazement was palpable, and he peered past me into the room, evidently seeking out the 'Miss' who had entered it. There was nothing to be seen, of course, my female attire having been packed away in the trunk behind the door.

'I could have sworn . . .' said the man, with such pitiful perplexity that I almost felt sorry for him. 'It was but two hours ago, the missus said, and I saw the lady mount the stairs, though I didn't take her up myself. She said she could find her own way, but—'

Here he stopped and looked hard at me and then at the open doorway.

'Did you see the lady?' he said. 'Did she pass you, or perhaps she did business with you? I have to say, sir, that I don't encourage it regular, like, but seeing as it's you . . .'

I frowned hard at him. 'Do I look as though I'm hungry for Cock Alley?'

Clearly I did, for the man was unable to answer, and gaped at me open-mouthed. This took me by surprise, but I rode it out.

'Your eyes did not deceive you,' I said, quickly inventing a tale. 'Yes, there *was* a Miss here, but she's gone now. You might see her again, however, and if you do you will be kind to her and not treat her like a cheap ladybird. She's not. She's a lady of quality and refinement.'

That covered it. I paused dramatically.

'She merely happens to be a whore!'

He took it all in, nodding his way around the landing, promising to be a good fellow and looking forward to the reward I promised him. I watched him down the stairs, and he watched me.

I closed the door quietly, turned the key in the lock, and then carefully stuffed it with paper. I realized that I had passed the first part of the test, though I was hardly surprised. It seemed to me to be a natural instinct. I felt I had released a creature within me that relished breathing air and freedom, and those brief moments on the landing were proof enough that, should I wish to, I could take him out into the world and he would be perfectly, completely and utterly safe.

And so I did. Day after day, night after night, James Yates (a name I adopted naturally as though it had been given to me at birth), gentleman, late of the Hussars, son of Mrs Yates of Christbridge, a thoroughly decent fellow, explored the great metropolis with an assurance that startled even me. Over two weeks I attended St James's Hall and relished Mr and Mrs German Reed's entertainments. I visited the Egyptian Hall and admired Haydon's massy renditions of natural catastrophe. I doted upon Miss Keller, adored Mademoiselle Roselle, made love to Miss Montague (indeed I did!). I dined well in restaurant and coffee-house, was recommended to three clubs by five fellows who swore I was first-rate, and I drank excessively and expensively everywhere.

When the attractions of the respectable halls of Terpsichore and Choryphee palled, I struck out to East, to the haunts of the Fancy (which I knew well from childhood, of course), and revisited ratting kens and low gaffs, even my dead father's. There are so many of these foul places, sunk low in cellars and tunnels, and announced by sign and whisper to the fraternity, that with my good looks and easy manner I could choose where I slummed from any number. At first, I arrived alone and drew curious glances from the hardened element of thieves and murderers, but I drank and swore and gambled.

And won.

That was an important introduction, for my luck was another

token of credibility, and it wasn't long before I was an accredited member of that set of drunken wastrels, comrades who leaned upon my shoulder and laughed at my smooth cheeks and girlish mouth. And among them – I could hardly believe my run of good fortune – was John Shovelton. Tall, elegant, with the same handsome whore permanently attached to his arm, he was that frequenter who absented himself – always on 'family business' – but rejoined the fraternity again as though he had never left it.

Yates's first 'costume' had cost me dear, and drained my purse to its very dust and thread, and so of course I took advantage of invitations to country houses and estates, to weekends in town at someone's expense, to suppers and parties, but I was still living, as they say, up to the door. The money that supported the life of an independent fellow who drank and gambled and generally put himself about, came from my old profession. I was unwilling to attach myself to a 'house' and a madam, though, and hand over hard-earned coins for the privilege, so I exploited those resources that had served me well in the past, and in particular that pretence to modesty which men found very appealing in the ambient setting of Walhalla or the Cremorne. It is curious how much gentlemen relish the bonnet and gown and canezou which, in the audience, cover every inch of the female form, while ogling nakedness on display only feet away! But it was all to the good. My skirts might be shabby around the hem, but the gentlemen with whom I was briefly acquainted each afternoon and evening had little regard for frayed satin.

And James Yates was worth every desperate pawing, every shabby union. For with him, though I breathed the familiar old London air, stale and much used, trapped between the streets and the thick fug of autumn days, I strode out. James Yates and I were true companions. We sat inside each other, as if we had always been.

# Walking in Pimlico

One autumn evening, wearing my very new suit, I shake off the couplings of the day, and claim the streets. With each stride and rasp of heel upon stone, Yates emerges, and I leave my other self behind. I feel his energy, as though I grow flesh and sinew, and with it a confidence that stands me upon tiptoe. I round the corner and sidestep a gaggle of girls, who look after me and whisper to one another. I don't hear what they say, but I do hear their laughter, and I know they are talking about me. They watch me admiringly as I stride on, a little aloof and very much pleased. I am well turned-out. My wardrobe now is small but of the best quality I can afford. In the past I have practised economy and bought shirts of inferior quality, but they chafe my skin, particularly at my neck where I am unused to having a tight collar. But now, having softer linens, though they cost me dear, makes a deal of difference, and I am hardly aware of the collar other than to make me hold my head erect. Likewise, I find I must have my boots well made and the leather soft, otherwise I cannot stride out as I want, and this, almost above anything else, gives me the greatest pleasure.

I relish my possession of the streets! No more downcast eyes, no more hurrying and scurrying, no more yearning to dawdle by a shop window or watch a handsome carriage and its occupants go by but not daring to. I long ago realized – how quickly I realized! – that James Yates could spend five minutes or five hours on a street corner and no one but whores and beggars would remark him. Freedom has become an addiction, and I indulge myself and protect it fiercely, for it has been hard won. I stride the streets. I ensure that my boots are heeled and capped with steel so that I can hear myself, rasping across the cobbles or snapping sharply on granite. I measure my pace, and drag my heels so that I beat double-time. I tip my hat and incline my head, and I know that gentlemen imagine that they know me, and ladies wish that they did!

I am making my way to the Constellation Concert Rooms in

Whitechapel where, I am told, there are to be seen bawdy representations of what Baron Nicholson called 'Sapphic amorosa'. I have heard that the Baron himself might attend, though I find that hard to believe, since he is rarely seen abroad these days, and certainly not in Whitechapel. I am striding out – I use that word because it seems to me to summon up all I feel when I am taking the streets – and the streets are wet. I sidestep rubbish, for I do not wish to have my new boots dirtied. I could, of course, take a cab, but I am in the mood for walking.

I ponder this as I traverse the streets, stepping out at a brisk pace, and allowing my stick to beat time as I go. I take such intense pleasure in this simple activity! So intense that I frequently recount it to myself as I lie in my frowsy bed in Guests's or Moses's or whatever lodging house I am currently staying in. (I change house frequently. Whoring raises suspicions, and keepers of lodging houses are notoriously inquisitive, and have no compunction about breaking into a room and ransacking possessions.) It often seems like some fantastic enterprise or expedition when I am lying in a thin, cold bed, but when I am, as now, in the place, in the street, with James Yates, it is as real as this policeman or that city clerk.

It is a strange thing, but I find my thoughts and the routes which they take are quite different when my legs are in breeches and boots. I demand rather than request. I am altogether more forthright. And I am happy to have James Yates's company. We enjoy the sights and sounds of London in her evening gown, dressed for the supper room, or in the shape of the late clerk wearily trudging home. We sniff the rich scent of dinners plated and served, and observe, if we care to halt awhile, white-aproned waiters balancing aloft plates of potatoes and rich pies or chops, running with gravy, eagerly awaited by the hungry diners. We can pause and peer into windows and watch and capture the scene. We can *taste* the scene, relish the moment. We can, above all, stop and stare. I understand now the terrible liberation of men! Their absolute freedom to observe and contemplate! I stand, we stand, James Yates and I, watching, drinking in moments of companionship in supper rooms and ordinaries, the little intimacies of friendship between men on a street corner or an omnibus. We absorb the intervals of handshaking and back-slapping, of thumb-squeezing and hugging, relics of masculine intimacy of which we were unaware. We store them up.

We have the leisure to watch and understand in the street and through the window.

We are watchers and lookers.

We are mesmerized.

## Reunion and Disappointment

**Miss Marweather – Springwell**

*Steppingstones*
*Northamptonshire*

*Dearest dearest Phyll*

 *The place is Springwell in Derbyshire. I am to travel*
*up with a servant as far as Reading and John is to meet*
*me there. And then on to Springwell where we stay at the*
*George, I think. For three weeks. Mama says that the waters*
*are beneficial – and John is convinced that the air will relieve*
*me of my melancholy.*

 *I am so longing to see you, my best, my dearest friend, for*
*I have dresses to show you, and gossip to tell you about the*
*Miss G—— and Mr W—— which you will simply die to hear.*
*They will be in Springwell I am sure, and it will be such fun.*
*Perhaps we will both have husbands by the end of the season!*

 *With love and love and more love*

  *Your*

   *Helen*

Here was the much looked-for note that summoned me to
Springwell, a sleepy spa, 'a veritable place of pilgrimage', where

Helen would soon be. Having lost her portrait (that precious memento and its lock of golden hair and its silly note), the thought of not seeing her again or, even worse, catching a glimpse of her in a London street and being unable to approach her, forced my resolve to settle for a few weeks in Springwell. And, I may as well confess it, I had formed a strong attachment for Helen (perhaps born out of our separation) that occupied my imagination ferociously. I thought of her constantly, with an ardour and a desire that were quite new to me. Let me be frank, I loved her passionately, dwelt upon her image, preserved it in my imagination, retraced our conversations and pondered, with obsessive attention, upon what was said. I contemplated concealed meanings, and conjured up intimate moments in an attempt to descry the deeper connection that I was sure Helen also felt.

Her arm through mine, a kiss upon the cheek, a whispered confidence I wove into a fantastical romance, in which Helen had been signalling her devotion to me, and I, all innocence, had been unaware! Only now, as I read and re-read her letters and dwelt upon our conversations, did I fathom her true meaning. She was in love with me, was attempting in her girlish way to have me understand and return those expressions of affection. And up to now I had failed completely. The more I contemplated our conversations and scoured her notes, the more convinced I was. And the more determined that I must see her and let her know I now realized that my feelings were in accord with hers. Where this fine romance would end I did not care. I would journey to the ends of the earth with Helen Shovelton, would endure hardships and privations and still count myself fortunate to be with the woman I loved! This and much more I was eager to disclose to her, if only she would come to me.

In my darker moments, waking early in the morning to a damp, grey dawn, I convinced myself that Helen would not come, and I began to open her letters with a trembling hand. If all my efforts to remove to Springwell had been in vain – this was an agony I could not contemplate. For I deserved my reward! In London, I had lifted my skirts ten, twenty times each day, and was in danger of becoming known as a common trollop rather than a lady of liberated inclinations! My skin was looking dull, and it was an effort to be constantly amusing. More troubling was that I had begun to hear talk of James Yates. In corners of Leicester-square, in the dark walks of the Cremorne, his name was frequently mentioned, and whispers also of who was he? What was he? His girlish looks – certainly, this was how he was described – were noticed, though never criticized. But he was a phenomenon, a fad, and it was a good thing that he had dipped out of gay society for a season. I heard stories that he was out of town. He was in the country. His mother was ill and needed her boy at her bedside. (This latter was approved of, and did much for his reputation as a gentle and devoted son.)

So, after weeks of late nights and shabby mornings, my purse was at last full for I demanded more than a penny from *my* gentlemen for their pleasures. I packed a trunk, hired a dour-featured woman called Gifford, who had been the gate-keeper at Walhalla in Leicester-square, as general factotum and to complete the appearance of refinement, and took a room at the George in Springwell, a down-at-heel though genteel house overlooking the Parade and the river. Springwell was shabby and dull, a fourth-rate watering hole squeezed in at the bottom of a lofty gorge. Along the length of the Parade were crowded countless lodgings from which mamas and their single or ailing daughters hunted for husbands or took the waters. Here were military families and minor clergy, widowed mothers and their children, all respectable but not wealthy. In their thin muslins and home-trimmed bonnets, the daughters of dead clergymen and career soldiers affected disinterest in the sons of factory owners and merchants, while their mothers consulted one another and drank tea.

# Walking in Pimlico

When I could contain my anxiety about seeing Helen, it was a relief to sit quietly and observe the comings and goings on the Parade. Slender girls with their stately mamas, bristling soldiers resplendent in their crimson uniforms, the drab doctor, the invalid, the governess and companion, all passed before me. I thought I was quite adept at discerning not only class and occupation but also disposition and inclination simply from a gentleman's walk or the way a lady carried her sunshade. As days ran by, I amused myself by noticing the changes in Captain Boldstride – from his arrival in Springwell, the bold swagger, chest pouting, head thrown back – to a less bullish demeanour, and finally reduced to a sinking, slack-shouldered fellow, given to spending hours watching river fowl, or leaving the Old Pitcher tavern by its back door. What caused this change? He was unlucky in love I hazarded, or at the races, or simply suffered under the thrust and pull of Springwell society, a reflection in miniature of the larger world beyond. Thankfully (otherwise the view from my window would prove too depressing), the reverse in fortune also occurred, little scenes in which the drab daughters of distressed clergymen's widows, slight, mouse-like creatures, with downturned eyes and smiles that hardly dared creep on to their lips, were suddenly transformed, and on the arm of a poor but upright bank clerk became gay and frivolous, whence their laughter rose to my window like lark-song.

From my vantage-point, as I scoured the comings and goings of Springwell's transient population, seeking out Helen's face, I conned another language. For if dress and bearing spoke loudly of rank and wealth, then glances and secret smiles whispered of love and longing. In less than a week I was fluent in the language of the heart. I could translate the love affair, dalliance, the promised couple, but also the intrigues, those who hid their desires from overbearing guardians and arranged covert liaisons. I could detect the briefest of amorous glances and the slightest and seemingly innocuous touch. Here displayed on a public stage for all to see, if they would, was forbidden love. Helen and I were not alone! Not that I observed any romances quite like ours (though perhaps the loving looks that passed between a pair of lady's maids were telling), but there were many moments of secret passion that gave me heart.

Neither were the energies and inclinations of James Yates excluded from the satisfying panorama of humanity daily displayed on the Parade, though I confess it was with more mixed emotions that I contemplated the young men in all their varieties. It was the assurance of the officers that I envied most, but the swells, as fashionable as this dull place could muster, were also in evidence, particularly when the sun shone and they displayed themselves to their best advantage. While I still envied their poise and elegance, most of all I craved their freedom. Not only did they possess the street with their long strides and square shoulders, but the street bowed to them. It was not just their swagger, nor their privilege to bellow at servants and tradesmen, or stroke the cheeks of a chubby maid. Neither was it simply their costume, which I always admired, the brilliant uniform, tight breeches, soft leather boots. It was what these separate and collective elements embodied – freedom and authority. And, of course, with James Yates, I had tasted this heady wine.

One morning, having sent Mrs Gifford out on an errand that I hoped would take her all day, and left to my own company, my attention was taken by a gaggle of young women, and their coquettish encouragement of the strikingly turned-out militia, all shining boots and buttons. They were a noisy company, for the periodic bellow of male laughter penetrated even to my window seat in the George, and I wondered what had amused them. But the moment's dullness was suddenly, startlingly relieved when, the group of young women parting, I saw her.

Helen.

She was standing directly in front of the hotel, looking up at the window, and she met my eyes with a directness that was as breathtaking as it was familiar. We stood in each other's gaze and I did not want to move just in case that movement should be misunderstood and she went away. I had to go to her and so, holding my breath and telling myself that this silly act would keep her there, I dashed outside.

As I came out of the hotel, she was looking earnestly down the Parade, and I was glad, for had I met her eyes again I am sure I would have cried out her name. As it was, I crossed the road, sedately under the circumstances, and was able, for the benefit of anyone watching, to maintain some façade of decorum. She was far more adept at concealment than I, for she betrayed no sign that she had seen me at the window, and instead would have convinced the most acute observer that she was surprised. This was all the more remarkable given that our letters had been preparing for this meeting for weeks. But how glad I was that I had conned the secret language of love, otherwise I would have missed, in the ordinary pleasantries we exchanged, the true meaning of these expressions.

'Miss Shovelton.' (Helen.)

'Miss Marweather.' (Phyll. How glad am I that you are here!)

'How unexpected.' (I hoped you would come, Helen! Oh, how I have longed to see you!)

'You look very well.' (Phyll, how glad I am that you are here!)

'Is your brother here?' (I have read your letters over and over, Helen.)

'Yes. He's just greeting some old friends.' (Letters are a poor substitute.)

We sat together in an ecstasy of pleasure! Just to be beside her again, to inhale the subtle scent of her body, to feel the warmth of her knee pressing against mine, was so affecting that I could hardly bear it! The busyness of the Parade was silenced, and there was no one in the world but we two.

She took my hand – hers was so tiny, encased in a white glove – and looked into my eyes, saying, 'Where are you staying?' (I have imagined this moment – and more.)

'At the George.' (I can hardly bear to be so close to you.)

She gasped. 'Here? How splendid!' She looked down at our two hands and smiled.

I thought it was a knowing smile, and I understood completely.

'What a happy coincidence. I did hope you might be able to, but rooms are so difficult to find.' She clapped her hands – just like a child. 'What fun! Just think, Phyll. We can be such close friends once more,' and – I hardly dare write it! – she licked her lips, and then parted them in such a provocative way that I hardly knew whether to laugh, or kiss her pretty mouth there and then! Fortunately, the arrival of John Shovelton saved me from the dilemma. So tall, elegant, amiable. Every mother of an eligible daughter counted him as their closest acquaintance. He was a doting brother, though I am sure mothers and daughters envied Helen unreservedly, but since they also knew that Mrs Shovelton was an invalid and could not leave the family home and that John regarded it his duty to ensure that Helen enjoyed all the social pleasures to which she was entitled, he simply rose higher in general estimation. During the season the Shoveltons visited Scarborough and Lytham, and their house in London, and out of season they came to the spas, quieter places such as Springwell. In between (and, I think, whenever invitations were extended), they were to be seen, the most attractive brother and sister, at minor country houses. This is where I had first met them, at the country house of Lord and Lady Sanders.

I had passed, for a while, as the orphaned daughter of Lord Ardagh and Clonmacnois. (There were so many supposedly Irish landlords among the floating aristocracy that I thought one more dead lord would never be questioned, and in fact he served me well for almost a year.) I lived by moving between houses and palaces, by invitation, and appealed most strongly to those fatherly nobles whose ancient lusts were satisfied by a sad face and a pale bosom across the breakfast table. I had enjoyed Lord Sanders's hospitality (and his none too furtive gropings) for six weeks before Helen arrived, which was when my world was changed for ever. There was an instant understanding between Helen and I. Our eyes met across the dinner table, our fingers touched at cards, and we both knew. We conversed, kissed briefly (on the cheek), linked arms and held hands. And all under the noses of twenty-three house guests and a watchful brother! Of course we also walked up hill and down (the Sanderses were energetic walkers) and sang silly songs and acted as nymphs in a little entertainment. But the closer we grew, the more adventurous we became in the subtle arts of deception. Indeed, the necessary secrecy of our liaison was both frustrating and exciting. We came to enjoy it.

One afternoon, secluded on a window seat, while the rain beat down and the other guests were reading and dozing and playing some interminable game of cards (we both hated cards), Helen begged me to recount some little incidents in my early life. This shook me with its suddenness and, as if to encourage me, the little pet told me of her own schooldays with an ugly governess and the music teacher who would lay his hand upon her knee while she played a fugue. What could I tell her? My mind raced as she chattered on about parties and acquaintances, of idyllic summers and cosy winters with friends, cousins, aunts and uncles. What could I say? Tales of the Nichol, perhaps. Stories of ratting and dog-fights, cuffs and kicks, of 'uncles' whose intimacies did not stop at a kiss upon the cheek or a hand upon the knee. Of sweltering summers and freezing winters, of blue jack cholera and scarlet fever. If I told her how I had clawed my way out of my childhood, she would not have understood even if she had believed me, and what then would have become of our perfect friendship?

So, almost without thinking at all, I wove a tapestry of tales remembered from books and penny papers. Not the cheap and inky 'bloods' which I rescued from the sacks in my father's yard or stole from under the counter of Mr Dalby's shop in the Mount, for my first primers were of thieves and cut-throats, and my fairy tales of Spring-Heeled Jack and Dick Turpin. No, I was selective, if sensational, and Helen smiled encouragingly as I described my first kiss, a lingering and passionate one, bestowed upon Margaret, our cook's daughter (and the object of my first passion), when I was nine years old – recited, almost word for word, from *Mallora, the Witch of the Dark Vale*. And as I gained confidence I told her how I explored the sleeping body of my cousin, Jane, who moaned in slumbering delight under my caresses (loosely adapted from *The Wretch of the Far Dark Mountains; or, Lust and Greed*); my first moment of exquisite passion (Helen's eyes lit up at this) when I was twelve, riding *à deux* with Isabella, an Italian neighbour, who, on feeling me tremble behind her, stopped the horse, turned around and kissed me full and long, and bit my lip so that it bled, calling me her *bambina sangua* (stolen from *The Wicked Girls of the West* and *Diamond Fanny and her Ruby*).

I was clever at describing this world of forbidden pleasures and, from the expression on Helen's face, utterly believable. She was entranced by my 'confessions', begged me to tell her more and of course, because I wanted to keep her close to me, I obliged. Stories of intrigue with the kitchen girls of our country house, with my French governess, my dressmaker (all decanted from those vile books) stirred Helen's feelings and produced blushes in her cheeks. She held my hand and prompted me when I hesitated.

I too was struck by the novelty. Those stories, which had only aroused my curiosity and kept me amused as a child, now pricked my imagination, particularly if I substituted Helen's face and body, and began to imagine the milky whiteness of her skin, her voluptuous curves and contours (she was no skinny whippet of a girl!) in the shape of governess or housemaid. The abandon that these fictional women exhibited I thought I recognized in Helen, for could she not be reckless and wild? What pent-up emotion was simmering beneath the composed girl who casually took my arm, and kissed my cheek?

We were in constant danger of detection, though this, of course, was an added sensation. The servants, I am sure, were suspicious (servants always are). And Helen was never discreet in her demonstrations of affection for me. John Shovelton doubtless believed that we were merely silly girls, who walked arm in arm, and sat close together whispering and giggling – as all girls do. Certainly, he regarded me as a sister, playfully attending to my whims, and indulging both of us with his gay wit. He took my hand and called me his 'other sister' and was so happy in our society that he included me in as many of their visits and excursions as was possible, much to the irritation of the mothers and daughters who harboured designs upon this handsome, eligible young man.

Of course, when the Shoveltons announced their intention to remove to their family home, my heart broke, only to be mended the instant I was told that I might accompany them. There followed Arcadian weeks in which Helen and I discovered our true and undying love. Days full of sunshine and warmth, days spent walking in the woods and evenings by the fire. It seemed as if they would never cease, that I had found, at last, the place where I was perfectly happy.

The crisis came sooner than I had expected (though from a perfectly predictable quarter), when I was surprised by the kitchen girl suddenly entering my room and locking the door. She had the momentary advantage and, grasping me by the shoulders, pressed me against the wall, pushed her face into mine, and declared that she 'knew Old Nichol-street and Mr Banks and his "spit" [myself]', and unless she had ten shillings in her hand within the hour, my word, wouldn't she tell some tales! It was as surprising as it was galling, for though it was unlikely that our paths had crossed (we were, after all, in deepest Northamptonshire), her white skin and lank hair, her dog's breath and rough hands did give her that unmistakable stink of the Nichol, and those few details she volunteered confirmed to me, a native of that region, her origins.

But I would not simply bow to her demands, and so when she confronted me an hour later with a sly smile and an open hand, I allowed myself the full vent of my feelings, noisily expressed, and in terms she well understood. And, as if she needed it, a fierce blow across her silly face with the flat of my hand was a reminder that I was in earnest. She gasped and was inclined to yell, but another blow, which sent her reeling, brought her to her senses. I reminded her that, since I came from the sewers, I knew very well how to deal with sewer rats. That if she opened her mouth and my name was upon her tongue, I would serve her out. And that if she truly believed I *was* a child of the Nichol she would know what that might entail.

She seemed cowed after my threats and cuffs, and, after all, she had been well schooled in St Giles's lessons! But this over-stuffed dumpling had more guile than I gave her credit for, and in spite of my efforts she tattled to the kitchen maid, who gossiped to the cook, who ran to the housekeeper, who bent the ear of Mrs Shovelton, who called me to her bedside – and gave me notice to remove myself from her house immediately.

I protested. I denied everything. I said that it was a kitchen maid's spite and invented reasons why she might malign me so.

Mrs Shovelton listened and then put her finger to her lips.

'Please, please, no more. Let us have no more of this. And certainly no more pleading.'

She motioned me closer and I obeyed, reluctantly.

'Miss Marweather, if that is indeed your name, you will leave my house, the town and the county by this time tomorrow,' she said, in a voice low and pleasant, as though she were giving the cook her orders for dinner. 'If I find you within twenty miles of this house, I will inform the magistrate and have you arrested. As a thief. Or a harlot. Or anything I choose. You have, I think, credentials in these occupations, so I could select any. Or all.'

When she looked up at me, her eyes were cold and blue.

'I do hope I make myself clear. Even before I knew such of your history as I do now, I was aware that you are not what you pretend to be. What you imagine you are. You have a certain refinement, but it has been acquired by observation and not breeding. That will not do. I think you are probably digging for gold. But not in my house, and with my daughter. You have also upset my household. You have abused my servants and, I think, taken pleasure in it.'

She paused.

'Yes, please do consider the many occasions on which you have cuffed a servant or ill-used my maid. *I* have noticed them, if my daughter has not. I wonder what she would say? And what explanation you would give? Something picturesque you endured yourself, no doubt? In your interesting past?'

I was taken aback by her perceptiveness, and wondered when she had had the opportunity to see me enjoy those secret torments, for I could not deny the pleasure I took in abusing those whose existence depended upon their silence, and I had never stopped to consider why. But evidently Mrs Shovelton had.

'I have heard what the girl has said, and have made enquiries about you, and while I cannot but admire your tenacity in attempting to drag yourself out of the mire into which you were born, I reiterate, you will not use my house and my family to do so.'

I tried to protest, but she interrupted me very swiftly with a dismissive wave of her hand.

'Do not think you can manage me as you do the others. You are less of an adversary for imagining that you can. You're a cunning young woman,' she added. 'I might have grown to like you had you not contemplated fingering my daughter.'

She continued, unsmiling.

'No, I won't reveal any of this conversation to Helen or John, and my housekeeper is the emblem of loyalty. You have probably suffered and I am not quite the monster you imagine me to be. Unless you force my hand. And then, believe me, I will send you back to whatever rat's nest you came from.'

She had the floor. Even from her bed, the old woman owned the moment, and I was like a mouse before her. Once again, birth and privilege and power held sway! She rang a bell and I was ushered swiftly and firmly from the room and, by the stroke of noon, from the house.

So there was no tearful parting from Helen. It had been arranged – how skilfully Mrs Shovelton manoeuvred her troops! – that her daughter should visit neighbours and not return until the evening. Even so, I was able to leave her a brief note, excusing my sudden departure, and desiring that she should write to me soon, and often. Her first letter reached London – 'care of Post Office, Bow' – before I did, and what a dear letter it was, full of love and regret and how she missed our conversations! Oh, how eagerly I anticipated her letters with their insinuations of tenderness! For no one but we two would guess, so artfully did she write. And so it was through our correspondence that we arranged to be in Springwell together. How she managed the subterfuge under the very nose of her mother I never discovered. But here was Helen at last! Our history, our love, stood between us, secret yet thriving like a hot-house flower. I knew that she felt it also, for she placed her hand upon my leg and squeezed.

'Ah, Phyll' (her affectionate name for me), 'I have so much to tell you. But we must be entirely alone and secret. No one must overhear.'

She laughed and laughed, her cheeks growing rosy and her sweet breath pouring like perfume upon me. I was about to call her my kitten or some such childish thing (which always made her smile so beautifully and made me feel grand and powerful) when her brother interrupted. Heads turned, girlish laughter rose like a charm of birdsong.

'Miss Marweather,' said he with an infectious amiability, 'Phyllida, how good it is to see you here! And what a happy coincidence! Springwell would not be high on *anyone's* list of diverting places to visit, and yet here you are!'

Was there sarcasm in this? I am not sure. He smiled into my eyes, took my hand, and kissed it briefly, while Helen jumped up and leaned upon his arm.

'I was hoping,' said he, 'that we might also be joined by a friend. A young man from town.'

Helen wrinkled her adorable nose and tried to be stern. 'Oh, John, not another of those awful fellows who hang upon you! They might be agreeable company in a concert room or on a racecourse, but anywhere else they are so very uncivilized. All they want to do is strut about and behave very stupidly towards us ladies.'

John took his sister's hand and looked and spoke earnestly. 'Dearest sister, I can assure you that Mr Yates is perfectly agreeable. Not in the least stupid, in fact a rather serious fellow. I think you will like him, as will Miss Marweather.'

I was forced to turn away and hide the smile that threatened, while he continued.

'He is elegant, well-connected, not least in the tailoring department.'

'I am glad to hear it,' rejoined Helen, who was still, I think, unconvinced. 'I would not like to keep company with a – a rag-tail.'

It was so unexpected and funny that John and I were reduced to silence before laughter overtook us.

And for her part, Helen was wide-eyed and completely nonplussed, and after several moments looking from one of us to the other, she tossed her head and cried, 'Is he not the best brother anyone could have?'

He shook his head and laughed.

'Yes, you are, John, you know you are. I am so fortunate! And look, Phyll, what my silly, doting brother has bought for me,' and she produced from under her wrap a tiny brown dog.

'This is Tippy. My little dolly-dog,' she cried in a voice more suited to a four-year-old than a grown woman, thrusting the creature towards me for closer inspection. Its face was crumpled, as though it had too much skin, and it snorted and snuffled through a tiny flat nose. Its body was surprisingly firm, though, like a tiny barrel, and it struggled in my arms with some energy. Helen giggled and, taking the little dog back, allowed it to take tiny biscuits from between her lips, which it ate with relish.

'Oh, Tippy-dog, you are so clever!' she cooed, and kissed it until it snorted for breath.

I was both amused and horrified, but she was completely enamoured of it and would not give it up to the Boots, but insisted on walking with it along the Parade, where the dog tottered at her side like a child's toy. Its velvet collar and tiny silver leash simply added to the comical effect. We had hardly gone a few yards before she scooped it up again and wrapped it in her shawl, and insisted that 'Tippy is a tired baby-dog and wants Mama to carry him!' So we walked and she divided her chatter between the dog and us, John Shovelton amiably sauntering between us and offering me his arm.

'John insisted that I had a completely new wardrobe for Springwell. I have gowns and shoes, and the dearest bonnets you could imagine!'

'Then I will appear very shabby,' I replied ruefully.

'No! No!' cried my girl, looking so winningly and playfully into my eyes that I had to look away. 'You shall have any of my things, shan't she, John? Anything at all. For you are my sister, Phyll. And what is mine, is yours.'

And gave Tippy another torrent of kisses.

'Aren't I right, John?' she said.

And John, with a shake of his head and great guffaw of laughter which echoed around the gorge and made everyone look at us, agreed.

'I know, Phyll,' she cried, 'you must come back to the George and look at my new things, and then we shall see what you desire.'

She took my hand in hers and was so bold that I thought she must give us away. But John said nothing, happy (as he said more than once) to parade before the great and good with a fair rose on either arm. It was difficult not to be entranced by this handsome brother and sister, and we made very slow progress as we stopped to receive compliments and attention from the society that lingered by each bench and tree. Miss Shovelton was admired, Mr Shovelton was admired, even Miss Marweather was attended upon and Tippy, of course, was adored by one and all! Helen, the newcomer and a fresh face in Springwell, was surrounded by military and country in all their shapes and hues, scraping the ground with their silly bows and making fools of themselves. John pretended to be only mildly interested, but I think he took great pleasure in Helen's amiability, and smiled indulgently at every soldierly breast that hove into view.

So it was with some relief that we returned to the George to take tea and discuss the amusement to be had in Springwell. When he learned of an entertainment at the Pavilion the following evening, John insisted on going there himself and purchasing tickets. This left Helen and me alone for a precious hour, in which we renewed our friendship and I was quite certain that we loved each other as much as ever we did.

Helen was excited less about the entertainment than showing off her London finery in this provincial backwater, and I was amused to see her little exertions, the fussing which attends any girlish excursion. When she finally emerged, dressed and ready to go (I was ready a full hour in advance of her!), I fell in love with her again, so radiant was she! Her eyes shone, her cheeks were flushed, and when John announced that she was the toast of Springwell, that already she had been noticed by Major Tripp and Mr Shepherd, her lip trembled. My pretty Helen! So modest! Even a compliment her could make her weep!

It was advertised as a 'Grand Fashionable Night', but in reality was a dull succession of amateur vocalists from the neighbouring town, leavened by a couple of professionals – a mountainous singer of Scottish melodies, Madame Laurie, and a comic who called himself Professor Hugh Moore (it had to be explained to Helen over and over before she finally understood!). The room was at first chilly, the seats hard and twin guardsman giants, each full seven feet tall and as square as two turrets, sat directly in front of us, so that John, sitting behind them and between Helen and me, had but a partial view of the platform, and that achieved only by squirming this way and that. It meant, of course, that Helen and I were not as close as I would have liked, but it was enough for me to know that she was near, to hear her silly laugh and her low whispers to John, and it allowed me the opportunity to look about me and study our fellow sufferers.

Half a company of military men of various hues, officers mostly, were in attendance, noticeable by the creaking of their boots and the odour of dubbin and lime oil which lingered about them. They were eager for amusement, and determined to find everything in the programme delightful. Madame Laurie, resplendent in plaid and wearing a brooch the size of a dinner plate upon her breast, was the first performer and gave powerful renditions of songs about bonnie braes and 'Prince Cherly', and had the rapt audience stamping their feet and clapping their hands with great fervour. The orchestra played selections from Balfe and then a jaunty tune which introduced Professor Hugh Moore, comedian and champion dancer.

Apart from Helen, this little man was the reason I was foxholed in Springwell, for he was, of course, the comedian who was an accidental witness to James Yates's exploits in Whitechapel. It took very few enquiries in the vicinity of the Constellation on behalf of Yates (who had temporarily gone to ground) to quickly reveal that the comedian and erstwhile Judge of the concert-room entertainment had secured himself an engagement – in Springwell. I felt a compulsion and more than a little curiosity, like a dog returning to its vomit, to track him down. Happy coincidence? Perhaps. But I learned that a veritable procession of middling entertainers, songsters, musicians and balladeers would make their way out of London to watering-holes such as Springwell. And indeed this unprepossessing backwater was a veritable candle-flame to these shabby moths. Of course, had the comedian not selected Springwell, I would have been forced to make a choice but perhaps, given my present preoccupation with Helen Shovelton, there would have been no choice at all!

He was immediately noticeable in the street, for the Professor carried with him his London ways – that darting, suspicious look and busy step. A curious fellow, solitary in his walks along the Parade or sitting outside the Old Pitcher where he lodged, in the sunshine, with a glass of ale in his hand and the landlord's mastiff at his feet, it was difficult to reconcile him with the forthright individual who had remonstrated with Yates in the yard of the Constellation. But how much he knew or guessed or even recognized was a different and pressing matter. The solution lay with Yates, and since it was difficult to keep him confined indefinitely, and particularly since I had carefully stowed in my trunk a set of his clothes, he took a night excursion to try the resources of Professor Moore.

Springwell was a sleepy place even in the season. That night the Parade was empty. Only a lone fox scurried across my path as Yates strode the streets, beating double time. The Old Pitcher was in darkness, but I espied my quarry at the window, taking the night air, and made enough noise to draw his attention. Did he recognize Yates? I could not tell and short of breaking into the house and cornering the fellow, there was no opportunity to try him. But I believe I read fear in his face, like a rabbit caught in a trap, and this was enough to persuade me that plans were needed to prevent Professor Moore revealing what he thought he might have seen that night in the Constellation yard.

In the Pavilion, the Professor struggled to amuse at first, and in any other venue would probably have come to grief. He seemed ill at ease, but gradually warmed to the task and sang a few low songs about fleas and bold bandits, just the recipe to amuse a military audience. An unpleasant song about a murderer going to his death created a small stir and, although I perhaps give him credit for more invention than he actually possessed, I do believe he sang it purposely, to throw down the gauntlet, as it were, to Yates, for his eyes roamed anxiously about the audience and seemed to be searching out a face. Confirmation, if any were needed, that he might pose a difficulty.

That audience, however, was ready to ignore his shortcomings and allow him any liberty, so determined were they to be amused. Even John Shovelton, who was trying in vain to obtain a glimpse of the Professor around the guardsmen ramparts, gave him rapt attention. I, however, was more keenly aware of Helen, and I wondered how she, with her delicate feelings, would contend with the strong subject matter being played before us. She, of course, had covered her face with her handkerchief and, I first thought, was turning away from the unpleasantness, but now, I realized with some alarm, that it was towards her next neighbour, a youngish, darkish man, who, smiling broadly, showed a very full mouth of teeth and an inclination to guffaw. I craned forward, trying to catch Helen's eye and reassure her, but her shoulders were towards me and all I could see – it was a small enough gesture, but it is burned into my memory – was his hand offering to her – I am not sure, but I think! – I am positive! – it was a bonbon in a tiny box, such as is to be found in trinket shops, and in which the French keep tiny cachous used to sweeten the breath.

These moments ran slowly, as though time itself was stilled in order that I might explore each gesture for its own particular exquisite pain.

In fact all I could see was the open palm of the gentleman's hand and the tiny, gold box, for it was Helen who leaned forward to obscure my view. Helen, whose shoulders, creamy and smooth, were lit by the flickering lights. Helen, her neck glistening in the heat, and little tendrils of fair hair lying sticky upon her skin. And as I consumed her and excluded all else around me for want of her, she slowly turned around and, seeing that I was watching, turned away, laughing into her neighbour's face. Then, as if to add insult, the minx looked back at me again and, seeing me still staring, laid a hand upon his arm, which he covered, for a moment, with his own!

On the stage, the comedian was still enthralling the audience with his miserable little song in its minor key, which seemed to last an eternity. The hall was silent, except for a few gasps of horror from the ladies and harrumphs of disapproval from the gentlemen. But my attention was still drawn to Helen and the flirtation – it was nothing less! – that was taking place under my very nose. One to which she gave, suddenly, it seemed, all her concentration.

No, not all, for she reserved a little, a very little, for me, and that she threw like crumbs to a starving bird. Indeed, she was completely aware of the effect upon me, and made sure that I could see the exchanges between herself and Mr Stranger. Indeed I believe she exaggerated them to cause me even more pain. And between us, completely oblivious to these agonies of love and jealousy, John Shovelton shuffled and shifted in his efforts to descry a mediocre performer, while the sweat from the necks of the two heaving guardsmen in front showered upon us every time they moved.

Professor Moore ended his performance to thunderous applause, many in the audience on their feet and clapping the fellow vigorously from the stage, after which they settled again, the entertainment continued, the vocalists resumed their poorly disguised torture – and I heard nothing, so preoccupied was I by Helen's performance and her betrayal. With her brother between us, it was difficult to seek out her face, and I was left with the glimpse of her hands, composed in her lap or, worse, on the arm of Mr Stranger – and reeking of infidelity! The interval arrived, though I waited in a snare of nerves, when I knew I should have the opportunity of exchanging some words with her, and I composed carefully my remonstration, even including a harmless witticism about her neighbour's jawful of teeth, which I knew would amuse her, and perhaps win for me her little smile of encouragement. But how all occasions informed against me! Mr Stranger, with complete disregard for propriety, it seemed, offered her his arm – and Helen took it, leaving me to trail in their wake, like some pensioned chaperone to be ignored and even avoided!

Did I tread upon Mrs B's toes, or elbow Mr D in the ribs? I do not know, for despite my best efforts in the crush of the vestibule I lost sight of them. Helen's fair head disappeared in the throng, and I was unable to reach her. Turning and turning about, I was searching desperately through the crowd, and on the point of shrieking out her name, when her brother suddenly appeared at my shoulder. I know I was distracted and must have appeared as one on the brink of madness, casting about me and standing a-tiptoe. But John was calmness personified, and kept a firm grip upon my arm, steering me away from the mêlée and into the less populated regions of the hall.

'My dear Miss M,' he said, with amusement playing upon his lips, 'please, please be calm. My sister is in no danger. See! There she is on the balcony with Mr Newman.'

'Mr Newman?'

'Our neighbour. In the Pavilion.'

Indeed, there they were, framed by an organza rose bush and a pot of ferns, my girl smiling and inclining her head – and piercing my heart.

'Mrs Gifford is standing sentry,' he added with a smile. 'The citadel is in safe hands!'

I was dumbstruck by his levity, and my expression must have registered – what? My disapproval? Disappointment? Despair? I am not sure. Nevertheless, he retained hold of my arm and led me towards the opposite door.

'I suggest,' he continued, taking my hand and placing it upon his arm, 'that we take in the River Walk, and the cooling breezes. You look rather pale.'

Pale, perhaps, but seething with a jealous fury I could hardly contain. We walked for only ten minutes, elbowed by half the population of the town, along that narrow path. Even Professor Moore hurried past us, his head down and his bag slung across his shoulder, never to be seen again in Springwell. I watched him go, torn for a moment by concern to keep him under my eye. But Helen claimed my attention more, and John Shovelton was distracting and amusing, and quickly forced me to smile at his witty parody of Springwell's Guide to the Venetian Carnival, the wonders of the enchanted grotto and fairy dell! Indeed, I soon forgot Professor Moore and succumbed to the charms of this amiable man. But when we returned, refreshed, to the Pavilion, the old anxieties returned. Helen and Mr Newman – plump, moneyed, vacuous, as well as toothsome – were where we had left them, still deep in conversation, and this dampened my cheer and increased my irritation.

There is no need to describe the agonies that followed. For the remainder of the performance I was intent upon Helen and her partner, and upon convincing myself that it was, after all, merely flirtation. I should be cross with her tomorrow, but would forgive her for her amiability, her simply being affable. But my resolution was soon shattered when, at the end of the evening, Helen left on the arm of Mr Newman, and walked ahead of us, while her brother and I, trailed by Mrs Gifford, sauntered in the rear. I was eager to draw level with them, and hear what they were saying, but John Shovelton showed no inclination to do so, and indeed seemed determined to remain at a distance. On arriving at the George, I was informed – by Helen of course – that Mr Newman was invited to join our party the following day, the prospect of which clearly delighted him, and further encouraged his expressions of admiration for Miss Shovelton!

I was in a turmoil of anger and jealousy – and forced to disguise these emotions under a façade of polite interest. And worse, Helen was unreachable. She might have been upon some distant continent for all I could talk to her, or even catch her eye. She seemed determined not to see me, and even moved out of my reach, so that my whispered words could not, did not find her ear. So we stood in the doorway of the George, Mr Newman bowing and smirking, and patting Helen's hand with a familiarity that I thought would drive me mad. At last, he left amid fulsome farewells and I saw my chance to speak to her.

But as we reached the foot of the stairs she tripped swiftly away from me, and, on reaching her room, was calling for Tippy who bounded out and on whom more affection was bestowed in that moment than I had ever received in all the hours we spent together! There was the swiftest goodnight, the door was closed, and she was gone, and though I tapped and called to her over and over (despite Gifford's shaking head signalling that my persistence was becoming noticed), Helen ignored me, and there was nothing for it but to retire.

Had I known what the next few weeks held in store for me, perhaps I would not have slumbered so easily! For after that wretched entertainment and the intrusion of Mr Newman into our society, I enjoyed only inconsequential smiles and everyday familiarities from Helen and nothing more. The more I tried to be alone with her, the more she seemed intent on avoiding me. Only in my imagination now did we spend afternoons, under the dozing eye of Mrs Gifford, confiding our love and exchanging kisses. Only in my dreams did I steal barefoot across the corridor to burrow comfortably into Helen's bed, where she would call me her 'rabbit' (as I imagined), and curl close to me. No more of our walks, our confidences, our secret times together, since now we were in the company of gentlemen almost continuously. Cousins might have been more intimate than we! The most annoying – and persistent – of all the gentlemen, the ubiquitous Mr Newman, showed no sign of ever departing. Indeed, although he had explained in tedious detail that he had appointments in manufactories the length and breadth of the land, there to do business with magnates of unimaginable importance (at which Helen's eyes grew large), they mysteriously shifted to 'Oh!, next week!' and 'Ah!, a fortnight Friday!' when a new walking excursion or amusement was projected.

It was difficult to believe that the love my girl once professed for me had changed so much. And so soon. Cast again upon my own resources and with no confessor, I examined my soul, my behaviour, towards her, for any little way in which I might have offended. I was certain there must be an explanation for her sudden change of heart, her cooling towards me, her disinclination to continue those fond exchanges that we had both so eagerly anticipated.

There was an explanation, of course, which I quickly formulated – it was all the fault of her amiable brother, who was so anxious for her happiness and amusement that he encouraged the attentions of young men, whether rich or poor, dull or fascinating, to compensate for their dreary life at home. Hence the steady procession of callers at the George, eager to make the acquaintance of Miss Shovelton. And John himself was not without admirers. Certainly the matrons temporarily resident in Springwell were happy indeed to discover a young man, independent, unattached and unaffected, who was inclined to look upon the attention of their gaggle of silly daughters without the least hint of irritation. Consequently they pursued him relentlessly. When we took a turn upon the River Walk or the Parade, he was accosted by mothers of all ages and dispositions with 'Good day to you, Mr Shovelton,' and 'How does this fine weather suit you, Mr Shovelton?' while their doe-eyed daughters simpered or stared!

I, too, had my happy band of followers. From the moment that Helen received (if not encouraged) Mr Newman's attentions, I too was pursued by a succession of young men – the dashing Captain Witney of the Lancers, Mr Devine of the West Indies, Mr Carmikael, who claimed to be something of a scholar and wrote brief and enigmatic essays for the local newspaper, and the pale and sickly Mr Tennant, a member of the Church of England and, as

John wittily put it, soon to be a partaker of Life Everlasting! These and many others made their way to the George or the Pump Room or the Pavilion during our weeks at Springwell, so many in fact that it seemed the entire unattached male population of the country had hired a horse and hat and presented themselves for our inspection! Mr Treverrick, a Cornish gentleman accompanied by an elderly mother and two rosy sisters, paid me constant attention, and wherever I went his florid face and bushy side whiskers were somewhere in attendance! John Shovelton made quite a joke of it, calling him my Cornish pisky, after the mythical folk of that county!

I recall these incidents now with some amusement and irony, but was less distracted by Mr Treverrick, or any of our admirers, than I was by Helen, and the relish with which she appeared to entertain their attentions. It seemed to me a betrayal of our love and our friendship that she was unable to look upon me now with the same affection that she did of old. Suddenly, all that we had promised to each other, even if said in the heat of girlish passion (which triteness it never was on my part), was held as nothing, and I watched her with a heavy and jealous heart as she smiled upon Captain No-chin and Mr Red-nose as she had once smiled upon me.

I have many faults, but self-deception is not one of them. Years of thwarted desires have forged in me stoical acceptance, but also painful self-knowledge. I have survived, I have sometimes thrived, but I have always understood my own heart. However, Helen's sudden withdrawal left a greater void than I could have imagined possible. It was not merely the want of her physical presence, but her easy companionship and gay-heartedness. She shone in dark days like a bright star in the night sky, and her mild temperament, so fond, so easily amused, was my constant pleasure! I loved her with such a simple fervour that if I could have devoted to her my every waking moment, I would have done so gladly, and to have had her smile upon me now would have been a reward treasured above anything else! She was a perfect star in my universe! Nay, she was the *only* star in my universe!

Now, empty days stretched before me, days empty of Helen. We had been all and everything to each other – or so I believed. And now there was only an abyss of longing. I saw her, but could not possess her. Could not even reach her. Suddenly, it seemed, she was remote, a mere acquaintance. And if I am honest, that pained me with such an intensity that it was difficult to bear. Her indifference induced in me a wretchedness I had never known before and her cold politeness was torture. When she smiled upon Mr Newman, and nodded to Mr Evans, and flirted with Captain Ellis, my whole being was consumed with a raging agony of despair and misery.

This, in its turn, was gradually replaced by dull resentment and anger. Helen's little ways that were once so delightful now irritated me to the point of fury. Her once charming laugh, with which she punctuated all her conversations with Mr Newman, now seemed false and shrill. Her childish ways – putting her finger between her lips, pouting, and that wide-eyed stare that she thought so alluring – simply enraged me. And when she nursed Tippy, and called it her baby, her pug-dog, her Tippy-dog, I had to walk away, fearing that I might scream at her or the dog, or the attendant gentlemen, all of whom smiled and simpered and found her 'so charming'.

The final event of the month was a ball. Handbills and tastefully printed notices were evident throughout the town and, of course, everyone would attend. There was the promise not only of dancing, but of fireworks, a Venetian gala upon the river, and a cold supper. Helen was in raptures of excitement, and each day brought with it a new crisis – this gown was old-fashioned, that had a torn hem, these slippers rubbed her feet. She was a fright! She could not go!

How quickly feelings change when they are abused! I could have adored her tantrums once. And indeed, seeing her stamp her foot and grow red-faced and hot, I still felt a trace of that affection that only weeks ago would have made me want to fling my arms about her, distract her, and make her laugh! It should have been an easy matter to stroke her cheek and command Mrs Gifford to repair the injuries to her dress. Yes, once it was, but now that affection was short-lived, and her display of temper simply the outburst of a spoiled child, for, constantly excused and indulged, she was liable to lash out at any offending object or person. On the very morning of the ball she was still stamping her foot and declaiming in a shrill voice that her pink gown was quite the most unfashionable rag, the white made her appear ill, the hem of the blue was ragged and torn, and how could she be expected to go looking as though she could not afford a decent gown! Even her brother, usually amiable and even-tempered, excused himself from the excesses of her demands. It seemed a good notion – to escape – and I offered my own apologies and invented an errand.

'Then go!' She turned upon me. 'Why bother to tell me? Why should I be the least interested in anything *you* do? Go! Don't hurry back! Stay away as long as you wish!'

Startled, and much inclined to remonstrate, I bit my lip, and perhaps she saw this tiny sign of weakness, for it was enough to inflame her temper even more.

'What are you waiting for? For goodness sake go! Go!'

She paced about, pale and ugly, picking up a gown and throwing it down again, kicking her shoes across the room, all the while her childish temper rising.

'I do hope you weren't contemplating coming tonight, Phyll, for then I shan't have to talk to you. Indeed I *won't* talk to you. As I am going with the Evanses, and as you haven't been introduced, I'm afraid you'll be all alone.'

I was taken by surprise. It had never occurred to me that Helen would 'cut' me, could be so thoroughly cruel. But, then, I reflected as she ranted on, she is her mother's daughter.

'Have you seen my card? It is already full,' she was raging. 'Every dance. I'm sure you don't even have a card, Phyll.'

It was true. I had relied upon the Sheveltons. For the first time in my life, I had fallen upon the generosity of others, thinking that they might introduce me to their acquaintances as the dear friend of Helen Shovelton of Steppingstones, —— shire, and Canterbury-square, London. I imagined I was clever enough to vault those chasms of class and family and discover a new path to respectability and wealth. My appearance, my pretensions to refinement and the carefully plotted history, much rehearsed, were my passport. But here was Helen destroying my dreams as completely as she was rending to pieces the bonnet she had snatched from the table.

'All my partners are wealthy and handsome. Mr Newman will partner me for four dances. And he is *very* wealthy. And Captain Harker. He is *very* handsome. I shall probably marry one of them, though I can't decide which.'

She paused for breath, and I sense the approaching hiatus.

'I can't bear to look at you, Phyll, you ugly creature. You're so – plain. Your skin is coarse, and your hands are rough, and I hate your hair. You think no one notices your hairpieces, but *I* do. I know you have to wear five or six, and they don't match. And the pins show.'

I instinctively put my hand to my hair. I wanted to remind her of our afternoons of pleasure when she whispered that she would never leave me, and we had planned that she would disguise herself as a boy-servant and we would sail to the Indies or the Americas where no one would know us, and live together happily for ever. I wanted to remind her, but I didn't. It would have been of no use.

Helen continued in the same vein, a veritable tirade of venom, her pale face beginning to show the ugly red marks of fierce passion as she paced the room.

'You've never told me anything about your family! Daughter of an Irish lord?' Her laughter was hard and broke my heart. 'How preposterous! I know *that* was a story and so were the others. French governesses and dressmakers! Ha! Your family are probably butchers or – or—' (The poor thing struggled to imagine an occupation of which she had no comprehension!) 'Or omnibus drivers! Or you don't even know who they are. I expect you're an orphan or a charity child or something worse.'

I instinctively reached for her, but this inflamed her foul temper even further and she stamped her foot and clenched her little fists and screamed as though she were in agony.

'Leave me alone! You watch me continually. Everywhere I turn, you are there. I hate your moonish face and the way you grab my hand all the time. Get away from me!' she screeched. 'Leave me alone! I hate you!'

She was quite beside herself, and I really thought she would dash her head against the wall or break something, so passionate was she. Gifford appeared, standing open-mouthed in the doorway, as Helen, in a final paroxysm of rage, rushed at me and would have slapped my face had I not caught her wrists. She struggled like a fly in a web, all the while protesting and calling for John. But I was stronger than she, and reluctant to let her go for fear of feeling her nails in my face, yet not really knowing how to resolve the situation. Eventually her passion subsided and a simmering mutinous scowl took its place. I released her and noted with alarm the deep red marks left by my fingers upon her wrists. But though the storm had lessened, there was still an ugly squall; Helen had not finished yet, and stepped back the better to look at me.

'I had thought we could be friends, perhaps for ever, and that you would be at my wedding, like a real sister. But I know that can never be. I've seen you talking to the servants, even the pot-boy, and sometimes you use words that are low, and there are other things that make me hate you. John thinks so too.'

She pushed her own pale and twisted features into mine.

'I never want to see you again! If you ever speak to me, just one word, I will tell everyone who you really are!'

Before I could speak, she had stamped out of the room, pushing Gifford out of the way and slamming the door hard enough to send a picture hurtling from the wall. Gifford mutely gathered it up and with a look I could not decipher – though it was certainly not pity – left me to my misery. Perhaps I should have known, ever since our first afternoon together in Springwell, that I could only be simply an amusement and that she no longer loved me, if indeed she ever had. But even though they were said in a temper by a spoiled child, her jibes and insults pierced my usually impenetrable armour. I had thought myself impervious to the assaults of this world, but here was a new and terrible pain, and I felt it so exquisitely that I almost cried out.

The room, with the scent of Helen lingering in the air, was oppressive and stifling, so I fled outside, intending to walk myself into calmness. The pock-faced Boots, a dead-eyed youth of thirteen or so, was standing at the door of the hotel, contemplating with a grim countenance the lowering sky, while on its silver leash Tippy tugged at his arm, eager to be out. It was doubtless the Boots's least favourite duty, his daily trial – walking the ugly little creature upon the Parade, where he would suffer the taunts of his fellows and the smirk of any passing maidservant or below-stairs girl. Many times I had watched him taking the route around the back of the hotel, in order to perform the hated task without running that gauntlet of derision, so when I pressed a shilling into his hand, took the leash and told him to 'foot it', he wasted no time in scuttling away. Tippy was also in a hurry, and tugged valiantly, hoping to reinspect the scents and puddles it regularly visited when, on its walks with the Boots, it was allowed to be a dog rather than a doll. But I steered us in the opposite direction, away from the shops, hotels and lodging houses, heading out of the town, and, though it was unfamiliar territory, the dog still bounded along at my side with touching excitement. Approaching walkers obliged me to scoop it up and I tucked it under my cape, where its body wriggled and squirmed to be released, but when I crossed the river by the ironwork bridge and plunged into the wilderness, I released it, and Tippy was once more sniffing eagerly and darting in and out of shrubs and grass.

I was not sure exactly where I was going, but the cold fire that seethed in my chest and stomach and the pain of Helen's stinging words told me what I wanted to do. Tippy and I made brisk progress along the river path, until, following a scent, the dog pursued a fork, a narrow track, and I followed after it. I would let it do the work. Here was not entirely unfamiliar territory, for we traversed paths that had been pointed out to me on one of our companionable walks. Companionable! These were occasions on which Helen took the opportunity to flaunt at me her admirers, always glancing over her shoulder to ensure that I was watching or listening, and taking pleasure in my agony. It was along here that Helen had allowed Mr Newman to catch her about the waist, and when that same gentleman had presented her with a sprig of forget-me-not, which she wore pinned to her breast until it had quite withered.

Now the dog was rushing here and there as we went deeper into the woodland, past standing pools and outcrops of rocks, and as the canopy of trees closed in the air grew cooler and damp, and even the birdsong seemed hushed. But we tramped on, Tippy and I, until a pool came into view, black, still and overgrown. The dog was consumed with curiosity, for I am certain it had never in its short life been exposed to such a variety of scents, and it ran back and forth, snuffling and snorting at every turn, with its pink tongue hanging out of its mouth. It was thirsty, and tottered to the edge of the pool and began to drink with little gurgles and laps.

I stood behind it and, as it turned to look at me, I pushed the dog into the water with the tip of my boot. Perhaps it had never swum before, for it seemed to gasp and panic and flailed before me, all legs and mouth, desperately paddling. Its puckered face was thrust above the water's surface, and for minutes it thrashed around, now and then disappearing and then reappearing with a snort. But the creature laboured towards the edge and then struggled to haul itself out, slipping back over and over and having to begin the struggle again. The grass was wet and the sides of the pool steep and muddy, but it eventually found a gentler slope and, with a tremendous effort (for it was tired), almost pulled itself out. Almost, for I waited until the dog had its forefeet upon the grass, and then pushed it back in again. It dipped under the water for so long that I thought it had drowned when suddenly it strained to the surface, gasping and choking. Its eyes were black and fixed, but it paddled to the edge of the pool where I allowed it to almost save itself again, before I nudged it back. The creature's tenacity was surprising, for although its strength was failing, and each time its struggle to dry land was more arduous and I thought it must soon give up, over and over it dragged itself back, clinging to life. Finally, however, the battle was lost and it legs seemed to freeze in motion. The struggle ceased and it fixed its liquid eyes upon me. I am not completely without pity and thought, for a brief moment, that I might, I should save it. And then, like a bad taste, Helen's words came back to me.

I turned about and walked away.

Helen was inconsolable when Tippy was discovered missing. The Boots was summoned by the manager, was harangued, given no opportunity to explain, and dismissed. Apparently, he had appealed to me – 'Miss knows. She took it.' – but no one listened to him, and I was never questioned. Various of Helen's gentlemen were sent out looking for the dog, and could be seen combing the back streets of Springwell and calling for it. 'Lost' notices were pinned everywhere, with a fulsome description and the promise of a reward of five pounds 'for the safe return of a much loved companion, Tippy'.

Days later, early morning walkers discovered the animal, floating in the pool, and its body was brought back to the hotel.

Helen grieved, but would not look at the remains. She had the velvet collar washed and perfumed, and this she preserved in a box inlaid with mother-of-pearl, presented to her by one of her gentlemen. She was miserable and red-eyed and laid so low by the death of the little dog that I almost pitied her. But the rage was still dull and aching within me and I wanted her to suffer.

# 8

## *A Reunion*

**Miss Marweather – a journey**

Though there was the immediate satisfaction of revenge, it could hardly be sustained when the object of my anger was absent. Helen, having summoned an aunt for the sake of decency, left one morning for some dismal north Derbyshire town, and did not return. Gifford, through her connections, learned that it was Mr Newman's invitation that had been accepted and that Helen had repaired to the hills and the rain to mourn her dog and, I supposed, be courted by the rich manufacturer. She left no note of farewell, no letter of explanation, no communication at all. We might have been strangers. And indeed I might have been a stranger to the entire family, for John Shovelton had already left, a hurried departure one evening, which I only realized when I saw him, astride a horse, with his bags in a cart following, on top of which his manservant was uncomfortably perched. I was taking the air before the damp evening closed in, and lamps were lit along the length of the Parade.

A week later, on that same walk, Gifford panted up behind me waving a newspaper in one hand and an envelope in the other. The latter I had anticipated for some days – a bill, 'to be settled immediately', from the manager of the George. He had been trying to catch me and I had managed to avoid him, for I had no means of paying. Every pound was spent and all that remained in my purse were a few shillings. But more interesting was the newspaper. Gifford indicated a long column entitled 'Whitechapel murderer – latest news', under which the sterling efforts of C Division, headed by Inspector Gould, to apprehend and bring to trial the brutal murderer of Bessie Spooner were detailed. But what stopped me in my tracks and forced me to sit and study the article was the announcement that 'John William Henry Shovelton, of Canterbury-square, eldest son of the late Mr John Archibald Shovelton and Mrs Henrietta Shovelton, was arrested yesterday afternoon at half past two o'clock, and taken to the C Division Station House for questioning.'

I almost cried out! Here was revenge sweeter than any drowned lap-dog! How exquisite! And it roused me from the lethargy that was ready to engulf me.

Now there was business to be done.

'Start packing our bags,' I told Gifford. 'But leave the trunk. I'll deal with that.'

She wanted to know where and how we were going and when I would not say, stormed back to the George with many a sullen backward glance. I carried on with my walk, needing that activity and interval in order to think. Pausing by the river, I sat and re-read the article, but soon realized that it revealed very little, that arresting Shovelton was probably a last resort and a sop to those East End agitators who had been increasingly noisy as the passing months produced no culprit, no arrest and no conviction. And I pondered the connection between this latest development and the sudden disappearance of Professor Moore. It was a coincidence, certainly, and perhaps something more, a consequence of Yates's midnight excursion and that comedian's natural instincts, but not yet a pressing concern.

Knowing now of John's arrest, I longed to see the farrago, and though I wanted to see him disgraced, I wanted more to see Helen brought down, for the degradation of the brother was also the humiliation of the sister! How smitten would Mr Newman be when he discovered that she was the sister of a suspected murderer? Even as the spits of rain now whipped my face, that charming industrialist might be at breakfast reading this very account and contemplating the cancellation of an evening's game of whist with the now not-so-charming Miss Shovelton! And how much I should like to sit in the courtroom and hear John Shovelton's respectability publicly rent apart, and with that bring down his superior mother in her Northamptonshire bed of disdain! For surely Shovelton could not escape the public accounting, much relished by prosecuting lawyers, of every lascivious misdemeanour, every adolescent fumbling he had ever enjoyed. It made me smile to contemplate his discomfort as his tumblings with every whore in London were itemized, and witnesses called who could testify to his violent outbursts. Indeed, there were many women who made a tidy living out of just such tales, embellished with a black eye or swollen lip (courtesy of their bully). And, of course, Yates was witness to his taste for ratting and dog-fights.

Yes, Yates.

He, too, might enjoy a seat in the public gallery of the Bailey. Or even in the stand. I was comforted by the thought of that young man.

But my walk back to the George was again interrupted by Gifford, emerging hurriedly from a narrow street, this time with two bags in her hand and a rug over her arm. Taking my elbow, she steered me in the opposite direction.

'Don't go back there, miss. The clerk's on the lookout for you, and the manager has called the constable.'

I was horrified. 'For an unpaid bill?'

She gave me a hard stare. 'For goings-on, miss. I did tell you not to use the back stairs on account of the unfriendly staff, but you wouldn't listen.'

It was true. In my effort to keep us in bread and tea, I had entertained gentlemen in the afternoons and had advised them to use the back stairs, which seemed to me the least public route. But unsympathetic servants, naïvely, I had not anticipated. Gifford shoved me along the back streets until, rather out of breath, we emerged at the far end of the town.

'There's a carrier goes into Buckton in half an hour. It will cost a shilling.'

There were only three shillings left in my purse and a handful of pennies. She read my mind.

'It's too far to walk.'

'And the trunk?' I had left it strapped and locked since James Yates's last excursion.

'I've had it taken to the carriers. They will hold it until you send word. Under my name. You owe me sixpence.'

'You'll have your sixpence when we get to London.'

Her face brightened. Gifford was no country-dweller, and apart from her excursions to Buckton (from which she often returned late and quite drunk) I thought she was probably very miserable. The city and city ways suited her and she was positively amiable when the carrier arrived, and joyful when we reached Buckton. But it was not an easy matter to buy a ticket to London with only two shillings. In fact it was impossible, and we faced the prospect of being stranded and penniless in a cold, bleak Midland town, populated only by factory hands and stray dogs.

As the sun disappeared, we stood shivering on the windy Market Place and were just considering which of the mean-looking public houses might accommodate two ladies for the night, when there was a 'Halloo! Miss Marweather, I think? Halloo there!' and a beaming Mr Treverrick peered out from a covered carriage drawn by two handsome horses.

'My dear ladies,' cried the Cornish pisky, darting from within and hastening across the road, 'what are you doing? Here? At this time of day? Alone? Unchaperoned? May I help you? Please, I beg of you.'

And so it went on. Questions, questions like a battery of friendly fire. I made an excuse about reaching an ailing relative in London with which Gifford quickly agreed and, indeed, embellished. With the anxious Treverrick fussing and offering us his carriage and driver and the hospitality of his houses in Buckton and Tavistock and Richmond (and others too numerous to mention), we arranged transport there and then. Within two hours we were warmly fed (at Mr Treverrick's expense) and within three, though the hour was late, we were on our way, promising to send word about the condition of the invalid immediately. Was my conscience at all pricked when I gave him a false address in London? And, having eaten his food and allowed him to transport me, and promised him letters and return visits which I never intended to fulfil, did I not feel just a little guilty? Not at all, for he was rich and foolish and had nothing to do in the world but amuse himself. Whereas I had only two shillings in my purse and the wide world to struggle against.

When we reached Abbotswelford, some twenty miles from London, I dismissed the driver and carriage, with the excuse that I was tired, would stay with friends and arrange my own forward transport to London. Gifford was none too pleased, of course, having a taste for what she prosaically termed 'the high life', but at the same time was eager to be back on her home ground. London was within a day's reach, and one more night away might be tolerated. But I had no intention of reaching London within the day or the week, and Abbotswelford was no more a casual berth than Springwell might have appeared, for I had a quarry to locate here on behalf of my friend Yates! And I might as well sniff her out sooner rather than later.

Lucy, whose creamy skin set against the azure cloth was still a potent memory, whose wild face and piercing cries still rang in my ears, was here, somewhere in this unremarkable town. She was easily discovered. In the guise of Lucy's wealthy, Christian sister, I had sought out Mrs Pickuls, the wife of the proprietor at the Constellation, and she quickly revealed everything I needed to know. How women will chatter! And how freely, when their correspondent wears a decent sober gown and reeks of goodwill and good deeds. My story, invented as we sat in Mrs Pickuls's crowded parlour, was that I wanted to offer a home, a respectable home, to my wayward sister. A home in the country, where church and charity would direct her inclinations, rather than gin and passion, and where the guidance of myself and my curate husband would ensure that Lucy was a woman of God rather than a woman of the streets.

Eager nods of assent from the severe Mrs Pickuls, and a fulsome account of her last conversation with Lucy, shot through with lurid detail and righteous indignation. A bad girl, but brought down lower by the appetites of wicked men! She had tried to set her on the right path, had suggested she left London and went to somewhere decent like Hull (her aunt lived in Hull and she had heard that it was a very refined place). But it was no use. The bad influences kept her bad, and after the murder – had I heard about it? In her very back yard, not feet away from where we were sitting! – she dropped even lower. She arrived at the Constellation one day to collect some few things she had left behind, and said she was going away but wouldn't say where. Would send for letters ('Who would write letters to a girl like that? I thought'). But her sister, Kitty, was more forthcoming when she called. Was going up north to fetch a baby from a farm, and was to bring it to Abbotswelford and Lucy. Abbotswelford, I repeated, and Mrs Pickuls affirmed, adding that Kitty was most anxious that she told no one, for Lucy would be mightily put out. And Mrs Pickuls had kept her word, only mentioning it to a very few.

So here was Lucy and here was I, to see after her and what she was about. Lack of coin was an immediate concern, but I had strong legs and back, and a stronger sense of business, and since Lucy had recommended this town which most people would pass through rather than settle in, whoring seemed an obvious course. Fine whoring pays well, but takes time to commence. Anyone with a decent gown and a ready smile can do business on a street corner, but there is no rushing a town to embrace a new, refined face. On the next fine evening I inspected the likely areas around the theatre and Corn Market, and sure enough there were girls doing business. But I was not a street corner whore and it took a few days for me to discover the dancing salon (in reality, little more than a platform but with pretensions to grandeur) and to gain some introductions. After that, and a brief argument with a woman who desired to be my 'mother' (and would take sixpence a day for that privilege), I became Mrs Collette, a lady lately arrived from France, who could speak that language and was adept in many of the more interesting French customs.

I found better rooms the following week, where gentlemen were tolerated (on payment) and I was not forced to wear out my shoes tramping the so-called 'salon'. Every day, while waiting for callers, I could once again indulge my pastime of watching the comings and goings from my window which, if it was not as wide as that in Springwell and did not command such an attractive prospect, still offered the view of a busy street, and trees and seats. On this particular afternoon, quite mild and sunny, I was struck by a young woman with an infant in her arms. Indeed, it was the child I noticed first: a bonny, blooming child, with delicately pink cheeks and golden curls peeping from her bonnet. The tree under which they sat was beginning to shed its leaves, and the infant reached out for each golden leaf as it fell. Even as I watched, the tiny fingers yearned to grasp, clutching at the air as the leaf fluttered past. She was a merry soul, and laughed with an abandon that turned the head of every passer-by. Mothers smiled indulgently, their daughters cooed, and for half an hour the child was the focus of adoring attention, until the warmth of the sun began to wane and she grew tired and fretful. Then the woman (her dress told that she was not a servant) wrapped her into a bundle of warm blankets and bore her off, and the street was deserted.

The following afternoon, a little sunnier than the previous day, found me again in my window seat, taking in the scene below. And again, I found myself entranced by the appearance of the woman and baby, which was today royally clad in a tartan dress and bonnet and grasping a miniature Union flag in her hand. Certainly the costume was a draw. And certainly the babe was not averse to the attention, for she laughed as a tiny poodle trotted past, and reached out hopefully for the whiskers of a cooing military man! Yes, a charming scene, with much variety and interest and, as Yates later remarked, with a familiar cast.

Yes.

It was not until the next day that, Gifford's chatter at the grocer's shop bearing fruit, she informed me, with great pride, that the young woman was something of a celebrity, and that afternoon she directed our steps towards the Orangery in the grandly named Botanical Gardens where, apparently, Lucy Fitch, wife of Captain Fitch of the Flintshire Rifles, and mother of Caroline Emma Victoria, aged two years, was often to be found. And sure enough, when we had picked our way between the palm trees and fruit vines to a little clearing of decorative seats, there she sat. The gospel according to Gifford was that her husband was a soldier serving abroad, lost for the past three months. All of Abbotswelford knew that she was ailing and had only a short time left, though quite what disease afflicted her was unclear. So much and so little was known of Mrs Fitch that when I first saw her, with the baby in her arms, surrounded by ladies and gentlemen alike, I did not immediately recognize her.

Only when I had the leisure and distance to study her, did I realize that here was my quarry, presented to me like a surprising gift! Her powers of metamorphosis were clearly remarkable. Although her languorous beauty was evident at our first meeting, across the table in the Constellation (and certainly was fixed in my memory), now all the varieties of wholesome attraction and merriment, quite different to those I had seen before, seemed concentrated upon her, and she was disposed to share them with everyone. She laughed and smiled, listened attentively, bent her head and nodded as if every word said to her was of the utmost importance. From the highest landowner to the humblest servant, she treated them all to her extraordinary joy of life.

Why she should be so simply joyous was difficult to fathom. Her husband of only three years was missing, believed captured or dead; she and her sister were orphaned (or abandoned, but certainly parentless). The most touching tale, the one guaranteed to elicit tears from matron and clerk, was that her little daughter, who had never seen her father, would shortly be orphaned herself, for the delicate, the merry, the captivating Lucy Fitch was dying of consumption.

Tragedy clung to her slender figure, and that ever present melancholy made her merriment all the more poignant. But I suspected (rightly, as I discovered) that the tragic history was not all hers, or rather was not from her mouth. She never spoke of her illness. Or her dead parents. Her heroic husband was always in the present tense of 'keeping well', 'fighting for the Empire', 'is such a brave fellow, that's why I married him'. The truth was that people liked to believe in tragedy once-removed, and heartbreak close to one so beautiful simply added frisson. So her misfortunes were, ironically, her fortune, and as a consequence her every excursion, even to the Orangery, was a public event. For everyone knew her, and everyone wanted to greet her, and press her hand. She was celebrated: her movements were published by word of mouth, and her engagements known in advance. I watched her pale face and tremulous hands, the lustrous hair (it was her fashion not to bind it up, but have it tumbling about her shoulders) and bright bird-like eyes, as soldier and merchant, great and small, paid their little homages. She was ever gracious, nodding, smiling radiantly, listening attentively. And then, appearing listless and weary, she would signal to her attendant, a dour and watchful woman, Mrs Strong, and they would slowly (even regally!) depart. Sometimes a carriage would be provided by a wealthy admirer (I think they *were* admirers, one and all), and she would ride in grand style, a tiny figure among the rugs and paraphernalia.

I was less inclined to join in the mêlée, though eager to meet her, and so wrote a brief note, expressing my desire to visit her in her lodgings, with a novel that I thought she might find amusing. But the reply was not as immediate as politeness generally requires. In fact, four days elapsed before a hastily written note on inferior paper was delivered, with the somewhat peremptory instruction to attend upon her at a half past two o'clock.

At a rather down-at-heel lodgings in a shabby street, I was greeted at the door by the tall, the imposing Mrs Strong. She nodded me in and announced, with little grace and ceremony, that although Mrs Fitch would see me now, she could spare only twenty minutes. Captain Hawker was arriving at three o'clock, and Mr and Mrs Collins at half past. In the sitting room, overheated and with the curtains already drawn, Lucy Fitch was reclining on a couch, a shawl about her shoulders and a rug over her knees. Beside her, on a little table, was a tray containing a collection of phials and bottles (her medicines, I assumed), and a wine glass, half full. She turned her radiant smile upon me, and begged me, in a low voice, to sit. I made the usual enquiries – how she was keeping, whether she had everything she needed, whether she had found amusement. All of which she answered unenthusiastically in the affirmative, nodding her head, and every now and then coughing delicately, covering her mouth with a white, embroidered cloth, which she kept tucked under her rug. I produced the book.

'In my note, I promised you a novel,' I said. 'I hope you find this amusing.'

She took it and glanced carelessly at it, while Mrs Strong hovered and, as the wine glass was drained, she re-filled it. The invalid looked up sharply.

'Surely it's time for my medicine, Mrs Strong?'

The good lady shook her head. 'Another two hours, madam.'

'I believe you are in error,' replied Mrs Fitch quickly, and with more than a trace of an east London accent. 'Indeed, I am quite sure that I should have my medicine now,' and a look of petulance and irritation passed across the beautiful face.

But the servant was adamant. Mrs Fitch's medicine was her duty, and if *she* didn't know what o'clock it should be administered, well, Mrs Fitch had better let her go now.

It was of no use. Mrs Fitch insisted. Pleaded. Cajoled. Demanded. Mrs Strong was equally resolute. An impasse arose between the two women, during which both appeared to forget my presence and continued to bicker in the most common way. I might have felt extraordinarily embarrassed if I had not been so engrossed. Eventually, Mrs Strong was dismissed, and left with reluctance, while Mrs Fitch appeared to have forgotten about me for she was momentarily puzzled, and looked at me for some time before saying, softly, and almost to herself, 'Oh! You still here!'

I was hot and uncomfortable and inclined to take my leave. I had seen enough for the present, and at close quarters also. But Mrs Fitch would have none of it.

'Don't mind Mrs Strong. She gets above herself and I have to put her in her place. We regular have tiffs like this.'

Her lapse was amusing and I held back a smile, but she seemed quite unaware of it.

'Mrs Co-llette, I wonder if you would do me a kindness and refill my glass. Since no one else will.' This latter given with volume to reach the servant's ears.

A bottle of very ordinary Madeira wine stood on the dresser. I filled her glass and, turning to replace it, caught a look of childlike cunning pass across her face. She licked her teeth and with them pulled the stopper from a tiny phial, swiftly tipping the contents into the glass. It was such a telling performance, so adept and knowing, that I was inclined to applaud, but instead I pretended not to notice and, carefully restoring the wine bottle to its tray, resumed my seat. Lucy drained the glass in one and settled back into the cushions as languorous as a cat. When she spoke again, her voice was soft and drowsy.

'My medicine,' she whispered. 'I must have it. It's what keeps me alive. For you should know, Mrs Co-llette, that I am dyin'.'

That much was already clear to me. I was far more curious about other matters. I nodded and sympathized and then wondered where her child might be. She frowned.

'Your child. Your baby.'

She laughed softly, and her words were slurred. 'I'll tell you a secret, Mrs C, since we're both in the same business.' She frowned, almost defiantly. 'Pretending, Mrs C. Pretending to be what we ain't.'

It was my turn to be nonplussed, but she would have none of it.

'Oh, come on, Mrs C. I know about you. You're no more a Frenchy than I am.'

I kept silent on that matter. 'And the child?' I said.

''S not mine. 'Course it's not.'

I tried not to smile. What had made her so suddenly disclose such a very important secret? I knew the child was not hers, of course, but it was even more enthralling to hear it from her lips. So I silently blessed her 'medicine', and feigned surprise to her face. Not hers? Surely it was! It was impossible to believe otherwise! Was she taken in by me? I couldn't tell, and at that moment I wondered if I had underestimated Lucy Fitch (or whatever her name was).

'Look, it's powerful dull here and I get tired of the game,' she was saying, and inclined her head, her usually bright eyes sleepy and dull. 'So it's nice not to 'ave to put it on all the time. *You* know how it's done. The kid's from a baby farm. Near Wakefield, or some-where,' and she waved vaguely to indicate. 'I had one before but it died on me. It started coughing like the devil and looked like it was ready to cock its little toes up.' She stared hard at me, with a drunken defiance in her face. 'And no one wants to see a dying baby, do they?'

'They want to see a dying woman,' I replied.

There was a telling silence, during which she was stupidly fixed upon the linnet in its cage.

'Dying woman, yes. True to you, Mrs Co-llette.' Our eyes met, though she was forced to stare hard, and struggled to focus. Her lips and mouth were sticky, and she wiped them with the back of her hand. If the almost imperceptible tremor in her voice was part of the performance, it was clever and effective. But I wanted to bring her back to our subject. The dying woman.

'Yes. Dying woman,' she said, after a moment. 'Of course, that's different to dying kiddies. Dying kiddies are just tragic. But a dying woman is a powerful strong sight, especially to men. They like all that weakness and lying about and panting and struggling.'

She lay back, stroking her breast and gasping delicately, her eyes half closed, her lips parted. Then she smiled, and raised herself on one elbow.

'They're *very* fond of that. And it makes them generous.'

'So you're not really dying?'

'I don't know. What do *you* think?'

I was so struck by her audacity and her naïve willingness to take me into her confidence, that I began to doubt my own judgement. Who was the hunter, who was the hunted here? She was reprehensible, I said with some humour, and it was surely against some law. The baby, the feigned illness, accepting gifts. But even as I said it, I knew this display of piety was unconvincing, and she saw through the pretence immediately, and took my hand in her hot one and looked drunkenly into my eyes.

'Now, my dear Mrs Co-llette, you know what it is. It is business. That is all.'

A sudden knock came at the door, and Mrs Strong was its originator, announcing the arrival of Captain Hawker. But before he could be admitted, the redoubtable woman pounced upon her mistress, rearranging her hair and setting to rights the rug over her legs. It was soon done; Lucy was sleepy again and stupidly co-operative, dozing for a moment only to awaken and look around her in confusion, and then, seeing me, was about to speak only to be overcome by stupor.

Of course, I was now not inclined to leave, and as there was no one to insist that I did, I remained where I was. After straightening a chair and smoothing her apron, Mrs Strong surveyed the room and her mistress with a critical eye and, apparently satisfied, enquired if miss wanted the baby.

Mrs Fitch roused herself enough to sigh, 'Only if it won't cry, Mrs Strong. I cannot bear it if the brat whimpers. If it does, you must come and get it straight.'

Mrs Strong was unsympathetic. 'The mite is asleep, so it's very likely she will cry if you awaken her.'

Lucy sighed again. 'If anyone else were hanging around I'd let it alone, but you know Captain Hawker dotes on it, and last week he gave me five guineas. The kid's got to earn its keep, like the rest of us.'

Mrs Strong was stoical but inclined to remonstrate, and the scene seemed likely to fall into bickering again. However, Lucy was adamant.

'Oh, bring it in! But give it some cordial first to keep it quiet. And don't look at me in that way, Mrs Strong. It's *my* kid, and I'll do what I like with it.'

Lucy smiled disarmingly.

'Oh come on, Mrs Co-llette – or whatever your proper name is. Like I said, it's business. There's no point in getting sentimental.'

My silence she read as an affirmative, and nodded to herself.

'Now, where's the kid? And Captain Deep-pockets.'

I was entranced by her assurance, her consummate skill in slipping into the part of dying mother, orphan, widow. It was a pretence so purely motivated by gain, and further amplified by the arrival of the said Captain, who was (to my amusement) genuinely distressed by her predicament. Here was a *mise en scène* that I longed to memorialize, so expertly was it engineered, and I felt nothing but admiration for Lucy. The child, which was fractious even though mildly stupefied, she held lovingly in her arms, uttering, over and over, fond endearments – 'Mama's little angel' – and mild chastisements – 'Hush, Caroline! What would Papa say!' – until the poor Captain, a young man who displayed his emotions without embarrassment, was close to tears. They spoke of her husband – a portrait of a young man in uniform stood on the table beside her – and her difficulties. Her sister, though presently reliant upon Lucy, had every intention of becoming a governess and making her way in the world.

'For neither of us, Captain Hawker, want to be a burden upon anyone. Even little Caroline here,' and she gave the dozing baby a surreptitious shake (none too gently), at which she whimpered pitifully. The Captain reached over and stroked the baby's cheek, clucking affectionately and repeating her name. Looking over his

147

shoulder, Lucy Fitch's eyes met mine, wide and shining now that the immediate effects of her 'medicine' had subsided.

'Captain Hawker,' she whispered, smiling radiantly and, at the same time, bringing out her white embroidered handkerchief, 'would you be kind enough to hold Caroline. I fear I cannot. . .' as the cloth was raised to her lips and she coughed.

It was a bold ploy. The young man took the child, inexpertly but gently and, after an initial struggle, she settled into his arms, blue eyes gazing steadily at him, and a smile upon her baby lips. Lucy, meanwhile, settled back into the cushions and watched, calculating, no doubt, how deep the young Captain's pockets were today! A fascinating little scenario.

She was, I reflected on my walk back home, a decided challenge.

Following this interview, I kept company with Lucy Fitch many times, and though I enjoyed the notion that I could betray her, I didn't. Not even to Mrs Gifford. It was amusing to be party to such a grand deception, for people *were* deceived, but their gullibility never diminished the power of Lucy's impersonation, which was really alarmingly convincing, and a far better impersonation than I could ever have imagined. It seemed to me that she *became* the unfortunate creature desiring to spend the last days of her mortal existence in Abbotswelford among gentle friends and in comfort. Her little child was all innocence and, had it been schooled in its part, it could not have played it to better effect. Mrs Strong (who, I discovered from Mrs Gifford, was in fact Lucy's mother) was dour, but attentive, with lips permanently sealed to her daughter's scheme, and a countenance as impenetrable as her daughter's personation.

As inexorably as I was drawn into the subterfuge, I was also drawn into Lucy's daily life and found myself not only on errands to the wine shop and butcher, but also embroidering that fictional

existence in which Lucy moved, and with an adeptness that
astonished even me. One morning in Agate's Bazaar I described in
terrific detail to a rapt audience the moment when Lucy and her
sister Charlotte were orphaned, their poor parents drowning in
their desperate efforts to rescue their children. My mind was running on – rescue them from what? A capsized pleasure boat at
Ramsgate? A flooded Scottish fishing village? A remote Welsh cottage caught up in a conflagration on a biblical scale? It could have
been anything I fancied, for the field was open to me to fabricate as
extravagantly as I wished. Consistency was never at issue. The fic-
tion that Lucy – and others – wove around her was unsubtle and
endlessly varying, and no one seemed perturbed by it, least of all
Lucy herself. So I mused as, here in her rooms, I sat one dark afternoon, mesmerized by her audacity, as she held court.

'Oh, my dear Mrs Fitch,' the handsome young curate, Mr
Freelove, was saying breathlessly, taking Lucy's hand in his, 'I was
so moved to learn of your tragic loss.'

Lucy smiled, and her eyes filled with tears. Baby Caroline
gurgled and grasped the curate's finger in a chubby hand.

'Were the bodies of your brothers and sisters ever discovered?'

Lucy dabbed her eyes and her lips trembled.

'A tidal wave took them, I understand.'

'H-oh yes,' she quivered, 'h-I believe they was washed up round
India. But,' she added quietly, for dramatic effect, 'without no
'eads.'

One day, when Lucy and I were alone, I broached the subject of
her missing sister, the one who had been so helpful in disclosing
their whereabouts to Mrs Pickuls.

She sniffed. 'Oh, her! I tell you, Mrs Co-llette, that girl has
nearly cost me everything, and it is only my hard work what
has turned it around. For starts, we settled that it was her job to go
and arrange for Baby. I had plans to come out with another pal,

Bessie Spooner, but she was—' Lucy stopped for a moment and bit her lip. 'She had other business, so I took Kitty on instead. It was a mistake from the start. I should have known. Anyhow, we left London in a bit of a rush, but as I'd my eye on this line for a little while and as I'd found the kid . . . All Kitty had to do was collect Baby. She should've brung it to me straight away, but, no, she took it to her mother's first.'

*Her* mother's? So they weren't sisters at all?

'She had this notion that the kid was hers. And she was taken up awful strong by it and wanted to keep it herself.'

I asked how that could be a bad thing. Lucy's glass was empty and she filled it to the brim and added a few drops of 'medicine'.

'Look,' she said, 'I paid up for that kid and had my eye out for it from when it was first brung. It was me not her who give the missis at the Farm extra to keep it healthy. For if the kid's not in good health, Mrs Co-llette, the business is no good neither.'

I understood completely. Baby Caroline was plump and sweetly alert, and much given to chuckling and babbling in a most endearing way, which pleased men and women alike. Also, Lucy confided, a healthy child might be more readily 'subdued' with cordial when necessary, without the inconvenience of accidental death, which was easy if a child was 'nought but a bit of stick and gristle'.

'So Kitty disappeared,' she continued, 'and I was worried my business would be shot. But then she turned up with baby well and good, though *she* isn't right at all.'

She frowned hard into the glass.

'She's always piping her eye which puts people off. Anyway,' Lucy said, filling the glass again, 'I've sent her on to make arrangements for us in the next place.'

I was taken off guard, I admit, and showed it. The next place? Why contemplate moving when people were so fond, so interested? She was loved and fêted and, from what I could judge, was making a good enough living. Surely it would be madness to move while she was in such demand?

'Mrs Co-llette,' she said patiently, as though she were explaining it to a child, 'there are two great things to know in this business – when to turn up and when to disappear, and the last one is the most important. For you see, the longer you stay, the greater your chance of getting tumbled. You have to leave while everyone's still fascinated but not asking questions. That way no one's disappointed.'

I had, then, foolishly imagined she might stay, might 'die' in Abbotswelford, even. In fact, it had crossed my mind a number of times (and not in an altogether disinterested way). Surely her death would bring about a sensational flood of interest. She laughed lazily, for her 'medicine' was having its accustomed effect, and she gestured to me to sit beside her. Her warm body was soon heavy against mine, and she threw one of her naked legs across my lap.

'You *are* a green goose, aren't you! Look, if I died, what then? What would they bury, eh? And how would we manage the kid? Where would we go next?' She smiled, closing her eyes, as if she were dreaming out the perfection of her business. 'What we must do is disappear. Flit. Everyone is buzzing the following day, but by the end of the week they're interested in something else. Besides, if you're very clever you'll arrange another story, an ending, and they'll hang on to that.'

Was that what she was going to do? I asked.

'Probably. But better for us you don't know too much, for I've already told you more than I should so don't you peach on me, Mrs C. I shall know if you do, mark my words.' She closed her eyes and soon appeared to be sleeping, though I knew she was watching me.

But I was not about to betray her. I was fascinated by Lucy Fitch, by her complete lack of morality, her apparent indifference. I was charmed by her beauty (more than a little, for those naked limbs and that sleepy languor were most affecting!), which was extraordinary, and which she exploited so skilfully. I judged she was not a danger. Not to me, nor to James Yates. Not for the moment.

And so we went on, for little more than a week, and Lucy did not mention our conversation again. Perhaps she had changed her opinion of me. Or perhaps she had changed her plans. One afternoon, when she was noisily entertaining a bevy of young soldiers, I sat with Mrs Strong in her parlour. The baby lay in her cradle, the linnet chirruped in its cage, the curtains were drawn against the dark and the rain, the lamp lit. We were cosy and confidential, which is doubtless what prompted me to probe the reserve of the taciturn Mrs Strong.

'Lucy tells me she intends to leave Abbotswelford soon?'

The lady was surprised and stared at me for some moments, as if deciding whether she should invest in me the trust that her daughter shared. Eventually she shrugged her shoulders resignedly.

'You know Lucy, Mrs C. If she has her mind made up, she will do it, whatever anyone says. We just follow along with her. Follow along.'

The baby let out a gurgle of delight as I tickled its tiny foot.

'Where will you go?'

Mrs Strong considered. I sensed that she had her own opinion of where their destination *should* be, but that Lucy Fitch would have her own way regardless.

'Lucy has made arrangements for us to go to the country, Mrs C, and has sent Kitty on ahead. A notice in the *Era*, the Organ of the Profession, solicited upwards of twenty replies from various establishments. All genteel, of course,' she continued. 'No sea ports, and no mining towns. I believe she has secured a concert-hall engagement for her and Kitty.'

'And yourself?'

'I shall go to my sister's in Walthamstow for a while. The Blue Dog, a quiet place with rooms to be had by the night. Or my other sister in Birmingham. Her man is a hard worker and wouldn't see me out of a shop.'

'So no more Mrs Fitch?'

She shook her head.

'And baby Caroline?'

'Oh, back to the Farm. She was never bound for anything else, poor little mite.'

And as if she knew and understood, Caroline's baby delight stopped suddenly, and she gazed with unfathomable and serious blue eyes into mine.

'Well, you preserve a – a professional distance,' I replied, vainly searching for the appropriate words to describe her attitude, which seemed to me to be devoid of feeling.

'I have to, Mrs C, or I'd be good for nothing. Now Mrs Skinner, the Missis up at the Farm, is as hard as a charity, for it is all business to her. Children, babies mostly, just come and go and disappear if their parents want them to. Or if the money stops. It goes both ways, you see. Buying babes. Keeping them alive. Letting them go.'

I was amazed. 'So Caroline?'

She shook her head again and regarded the child with a face that moved between impassivity and strong emotion.

'This one was hand-picked, poor little mite. Lucy went out to the Farm and picked her out not long after the last one died. She knew what she wanted and so did the Missis. Now I've heard that there are some that go in for child stealing, but Missis is a cut above that. This one come in, and Lucy went up, at her own expense, and said she'd do, but was a tad too young, so they agreed five shillings a week, and Missis would keep her and feed her up until she was ready.'

Like fattening a goose for Christmas!

'Then they both went, Lucy and Kitty, to have a look at her and make the arrangements.'

She rocked the cradle, idly, with her foot.

'Kitty was in an odd way when they came back. Girls get hungry for a baby, Mrs C, and once the hunger's there, there's but one way to satisfy it.'

The child murmured contentedly, and Mrs Strong regarded her with a faint smile.

'It'll be a wrench for me too, this time, for this 'un's a little angel. And so quiet and loving. I'm fond of babbies. I lost three of my own, and wet-nursed two.'

We sat in companionable silence for a while, and when I left baby Caroline that afternoon I had no presentiment that it was for the last time. That night (I assume it was during the night), they left Abbotswelford, and I never saw the child again.

As Lucy had said, it was all business.

And she was perfectly accurate in her calculations. The inhabitants of the town were at first shocked and concerned at her disappearance and I, regarded as one of her confidantes, was the object of repeated questioning as to her circumstances and whereabouts. But I was unwilling to be further embroiled in her scheme, and with no instructions regarding what I should say, I simply confessed my utter ignorance. Nevertheless, within hours the rumour-mongers had been at work: Lucy Fitch had taken a turn for the worse, was losing her grip on life as each hour passed, and had taken herself and her child to the Convent of the Holy Name, some sixty miles distant, where she might receive care and the last rites, and the charitable Sisters would assume guardianship of her child. Sensational, sentimental, it was, nevertheless, a suitable conclusion to Lucy's story. The young ladies shed tears when her name was mentioned, and for a while her unbraided hair was adopted as the *nouveau style* in Abbotswelford. Mothers looked admiringly and a little sadly at visiting young officers, and the *Abbotswelford Looker-On,* while it never mentioned her by name, spoke in glowing terms of the 'sacrifices made at home by the wives and children of our soldier-heroes'.

# 9

## *The Sisters Bellwood*

### Mrs Collette – Abbotswelford to Burdon Oaks

Bent over a bowl, sick and aching, with Mrs Gifford's stern eye upon me, I was presented with a difficulty. I was pregnant. In my eagerness to accumulate funds in Springwell, or in entertaining officers to sustain my stay in Abbotswelford, I had been less rigorous than usual in taking precautionary measures. The effects came upon me shortly after Lucy Fitch left, and though Gifford attempted to remove it with the usual methods, the child clung to my belly like a limpet. Every morning and evening my face grew pale, my hands shook, and I had neither the energy nor the inclination to move from my window seat except to hang over a bowl. Gifford was so full of herself that, as common folk say, she was quite empty! She dealt with callers, brought me tea and dry toast and made as sympathetic a noise as she could muster. And one morning she claimed, with a note of triumph in her voice, that she had the solution to my problem, that our passage was booked, and we were shortly to retire to an uncle's house in London where, for the duration, I could be 'properly taken care of'. Bustling about the room like my lady's keeper, she was bursting with self-righteousness, in no doubt that I had *her* to thank for this good fortune, for who knows how I would have managed otherwise. Indeed, if it was not for her, I would be looking at the workhouse gates or worse! She was always thinking of me, she said, always putting my wants before her own.

If she was expecting gratitude, then she was disappointed, for I was beside myself with fury. Who did she think she was to assume responsibility for my affairs? I demanded. Writing to whosoever? Disclosing my business? And this 'uncle'? I had no 'uncle'.

I knew, of course, the answer to this last enquiry, for the accommodation she had arranged was with no doting relative. The 'uncle' to whom she had written – who had replied and was expecting me, for I had made it my business to read her letters – this 'uncle', who was so solicitous for my welfare, was a dealer in exotic prints in Holywell-street with houses in other parts of London, and had a particular liking for pregnant women. These he took in and subjected, over the ensuing months, to varieties of intimate scrutiny, thereby satisfying a gross and inexplicable fascination in the physical process. There was no doubt in my mind that he intended to keep me as a living specimen in his domestic prison (Gifford destined to assume the role of gaoler and how she would enjoy that position!), always available to him for close inspection and whatever else took his fancy as my condition advanced. His interest in me would doubtless disappear immediately the child was born, when he would have no conscience in ejecting us both. A despicable man, who preyed upon children as well as young and unfortunate girls, he and his abominable practices were well known among streetwomen.

Gifford, I knew, would profit well by my incarceration, and the thought that I had been sold into slavery by my own servant enraged me, but I coolly let her know this sunny morning that I was, as they say, 'up bright and early' to her game. To her pale and astonished face, I reminded her that it was I who paid her and put up with her and, yes, put her up, whether it was in the George or, latterly, in Pugh's Lodging House. And that if it was not for my tolerance and good nature, I was not the only one who might find herself in very poor circumstances.

But Gifford was not yet ready to concede defeat, and retaliated with her own brand of pious indignation, one that allowed her to vent her hypocritical self-righteousness while at the same time keeping a tight hold on self-interest. How Uncle was a good man and a generous man, how he might settle on me an allowance (he had done so for other young women) and would never turn me out until I had a place to go to. Of course, it would be necessary for me to do as he bade me, down to the last letter if I wanted to avoid unpleasantness and keep him amiable, and a mite of shame and contrition would not go amiss. If I would only be guided by people who knew better. People like Uncle. And her. For I wasn't, she said with a parting smirk she made no effort to disguise, half as clever as I considered myself to be.

No, I thought grimly, but I am twice as clever as you! The spiteful pinches I endured when she was supposedly helping me to dress and her undisguised smugness were irritants, but I consoled myself with the knowledge that I had seen through her deception and allowed her to have a taste of triumph before I announced, with some relish, that I would not be going to Uncle's, nor to London, and that she had lost her ten guineas, and her situation, for I did not want her. Her face, frozen into the image of some gawping fish, was almost comical.

'But, miss,' she cried, when she had come to her senses, 'you cannot – you must not – in your condition – contemplate – living alone? Where will you go? How will you live?'

She gazed pitifully upon me with moist eyes, as if it were she who was cast adrift upon the hostile world. But I knew that look of old! The Gifford look that she hoped would melt my heart and bend me to her desires. And whether she feared Uncle's wrath or for her own uncertain situation, she was also struck by fits of weeping which came on as soon as she looked upon me. More troubling were the letters (so easily intercepted that my suspicions were aroused) flying more frequently now between Abbotswelford and London, and which signalled that, since I was not about to take up my new residence voluntarily, 'other arrangements' were being made. I knew force and abduction were possible and that, despite my increasingly heavy condition, it would be in my best interests to make my escape. Soon.

I was not idle, therefore. Indisposition brings with it the opportunity for reflection and I reflected much on the whispered conversation I had had with Mrs Strong on the last occasion I had sat with her. When she and Lucy were 'settled', Mrs S promised, she would send word to me. I waited with mounting impatience, and was soon rewarded when, returning from an afternoon walk, there was a letter from Mrs Strong. Lucy, she wrote, was about to give up the pretence of widowhood. She had been obliged to continue temporarily the tragic life of a military widow (the generosity of a 'clerical gentleman' was the inducement) but someone acquainted with Abbotswelford had 'clocked her' and they were forced to remove 'sharpish'. Lucy's resourcefulness was never wasted and she had quickly 'called up one of those parties' who had responded to her professional advertisement, and now they were comfortably accommodated in Burdon Oaks, and I was invited to call upon them whenever I wished. Lucy's precocious talents were matched with Kitty's looks and so, as the Sisters Bellwood, they were 'powerful lively girls' and gents were 'much struck by them'. Lucy was anxious to see me, and for her part, Mrs Strong believed that no one had such a thoroughly good and steady influence upon her daughter as Mrs Collette!

I sent a note of thanks to Mrs Strong by return, and in it enclosed a letter for Lucy, congratulating her on her new enterprise, and acquainting her with my own situation, and the difficulties in which

I found myself. Lucy's letter similarly arrived by return, as I had half hoped, half expected.

*Dear Mrs C*

*You poor dear thing! What beasts men are, an't they, to use wimen so! When you say you don't want no help, well I should take it if it were offered. You must know how hard it is for a womun to be on her own with a kid. Your proberly thinking of how I managed and that I don't do too bad. Its true, I had a fair living, but it wasn't always so, and some towns were terrible hard and no one come to see me or parted with so much as a penny. I don't recimend that line of work at all, Mrs C. Besides you need someone you can trust alongside of you. I've got Mrs Strong, who is also my mother, and she is powerful good. But you have no one.*

*You should write to the gent who has got you in pod and skin him good. It's the only way.*

*Mrs Strong says you are without a shop. If that is so, come to us, Mrs C. Don't dispare. We are your frends and shall look out for you.*

*Afestshionately*
*Lucy Fitch (Miss)*

*Apoligs for want of spelling. I am no skoler, but a hard working girl.*

In my mind, it was settled, and I was glad to know that I could soon leave, for Gifford hung after me like a bad smell, uncertain of her position, and in receipt of some unpleasant communications from Uncle. No doubt he was unwilling to excuse her from the duties they had agreed upon, for though I was harsh and unpleasant towards her, she declared would not believe that I no longer required her services. Finally she tearfully admitted that, so

attached to me had she become and so bereft would she be if I dismissed her, she would consider it a duty and a privilege to attend
upon me until the child was born. Now I was even more suspicious
of her intentions, and even more alert! But in my present condition
she was useful, and so I grudgingly allowed her to accompany me to
Burdon Oaks, prompted by another letter from Lucy Fitch.

> *Dearest Mrs C*
>    *This is to let you no that me and Mrs S will expect you in*
> *Burdin Oaks at yore convynens. We are at the Live and Let*
> *Live, and have room for you.*
>    *But Dear Mrs C, how are you? I have wondered if you*
> *was keeping well. And not to sick with the mornings which is*
> *a terrible thing. Kitty is with us, but I should like to drop her*
> *as she is slack.*
>    *Hopin this finds you well.*
>       *Affecshunotley*
>          *Lucy Bellwood (Miss)*
>
> *Mrs C you will see that I have changed my name for the derashun*
> *of bein in Burdin Oaks. But I am still your frend Lucy Fitch*
> *whatsomever.*

Rather than accept her invitation to lodge at the Live and Let
Live, however, I decided to take a cottage. (Lucy was completely
understanding, opining that 'no matter how clean it pretended to
be, a tavern is still a tavern, and no place for a babby'.) It was a small,
a very small cottage at the end of the village, with its back into hillside and its front looking down a short dirt track to the road into
Burdon Oaks. It was secluded but not isolated, spare, warm, and
contained everything I could possibly need. It was called Jasmine
Cottage – ill-named, for I found no trace of jasmine – and clung to
a hillside on which the only living creatures were sheep. It had been

in former times the home of a farm labourer and his family, but now belonged to a medical man in Castledon, who leased it at a modest rent. It was, after all, a modest house, with a single room and scullery on the ground floor, and a single bedroom and boxroom upstairs. The walls were thick, the roof sturdy, rebuffing the constant winds that howled up the valley with mellow Shropshire stone and hard Welsh slate, and when the storms rolled in – and there were many that winter and spring – there was nothing to do but lock the doors, draw the curtains and keep the fires burning brightly. We lit the lamps after our midday meal some days, as the darkness and wild weather closed in around us.

I say 'we' for Mrs Gifford would not be separated from me, and this, I was convinced, was entirely due to Uncle. Her spirits lifted as soon as we were installed, and I noticed the little gifts – the pots of jelly and boxes of sweets – that began to arrive each week. Angered though he was, my distant benefactor was not yet prepared to give me up, and would rather have Gifford close by than have me cared for by a local woman. She strove to keep her irritability at bay and in particular her daily complaints about the discomfort and cold which attended upon her accommodation on a truckle bed in a tiny cupboard room, but as her aches and pains grew so did those needling grouches, until one morning I could endure it no longer.

'We are two women alone in a cottage,' I cried, 'which seems to be at the end of the world. Here we are and must remain, more or less, for the next three months. If that time is to be at all tolerable, you must learn to accept the situation and not constantly complain to me about the conditions. You can go as soon as you like, you know. I can manage perfectly well on my own. I did not ask you to remain here with me. Unless,' I added as dryly as I could muster, 'you wish me to write to our 'uncle' and ask that you be relieved of your duties. And that I will do most gladly.'

She was shocked into silence, and for the rest of the day spoke not a word. But the following morning, as we sat at breakfast, she enquired after my nausea, and offered to fetch me a mixture from the pharmacist when she next visited Castledon. It seemed that although our relationship was now never likely to be friendly, she had resolved to make it at least amicable. She sat with me most afternoons, and then we chatted more agreeably than I had ever known, while we sewed tiny clothes and edged blankets and sheets. I did not trust her, but she was, at least, company.

⌘

We dragged through the winter months, each tolerating the other, the tedium lifted by my visits to Lucy and Mrs Strong at the Live and Let Live and Gifford's to Castledon, where I had no doubt she posted and collected her communications with Uncle. But one visit to Lucy, on a bright and chilly day, when the cries of the sheep on the hills echoed around the hilly market square, confirmed my growing unease. When I informed her of my intentions, Gifford was more than usually attentive, a veritable shadow, eager to dissuade me from my little excursion. Bad weather threatened to leave me stranded, she claimed my colour was poor and she thought I seemed breathless, and there were countless things to be done in preparation for the birth. She was so urgent and anxious that I was even more suspicious, and when she watched me from the gate as I walked along the path to join the road for Burdon Oaks, I was convinced. She had never been so protective, usually glad to see me out of the house so that she could drink gin all day and retire early. But today she had been altogether more resolute, hiding my shoes, my purse and at one point holding me by the arm. I was never so relieved to see her dark figure disappear from view around the bend in the road, and so glad to see Lucy and Mrs Strong.

I told them my fears, even mentioning the threat of Uncle and Gifford's unholy alliance with him, and of course they were insistent

163

that I should stay with them at the Live and Let Live. I sent a note to Gifford immediately saying that I had been taken ill and begging her to send me the few things I needed – and my trunk. A room was secured for me, Mrs Strong promising to 'look out' for my health, and while Lucy and Kitty (a silent, morose creature, with dark eyes, who burst into feverish animation every evening) performed their songs in the concert room, I sat in the parlour warming my constantly frozen feet and reading penny novels, and during the day wandered the streets of the village, my arm comfortably linked through Lucy's.

And now I hurry to an episode that takes no time at all to tell, but which altered the course of everything that happened subsequently. I once heard a story from China, or perhaps from the Indies, about a child who tossed a pebble in a lake, the ripples from which so multiplied in number and strength that they eventually overwhelmed a village, crushing all before them and drowning the inhabitants. Nothing and no one could be saved, and the entire landscape, the lives and futures of the village residents were utterly changed by that single insignificant action performed unthinkingly by an innocent child. And such a catastrophic incident, so simple, so unassuming, happened one day to me, as if it had been awaiting its proper moment.

James Yates had been away for weeks and months, but he was never far from my thoughts. Even as my waist began to thicken and I became clumsy and slow, I recalled with clear delight those heady moments when we possessed the street, and enjoyed the devouring glances of the girls, the slap on the back from other men. The races, the ratting kens, the pleasure gardens, John Shovelton – 'You're a good fellow, Yates. I like you' – and again the sound of heel upon cobblestone and the dark, dank night.

One afternoon at the end of the week, having resolved that today I must go back to Jasmine Cottage and prepare for my confinement

– Mrs Gifford is alerted, and has sent word that all is ready for my return – I am crouching on the floor of my room in the Live and Let Live. It is quiet and still, for everyone is out, and I take the opportunity (the first time in many months, and the last time for the foreseeable future) to drag my trunk out from under the bed and empty it of Yates's suit and shirt, his boots and stockings, his lime oil and sandalwood balm, spread out around me. I am once again caught up in the aroma, now slightly stale, which returns me not only to the immediate past, but to my childhood, to Mountgarrett and the yard of my father's tavern. I have Yates's fine linen shirt around my shoulders and I am, once again, inspecting the pockets of the waistcoat for Helen's picture. So absorbed am I in this that I do not hear the approaching footsteps. The door opens suddenly and, before I can move, Lucy Fitch is framed there, beaming merrily, and carrying a cage, shaped like a miniature pagoda, in which flutters a tiny bird.

'Mrs C,' she cries. 'Look what I bought to keep you company instead of me! Another songbird, but prettier!'

In motions slowed down to their moments, she turns, holding the birdcage aloft. I see the tiny creature flutter in a blur of colour. I see Lucy's face, as she sees me, and then the clothes scattered across the floor. I see her register, by the second, the waistcoat with its heavy embroidery across my knee, the kid leather gloves, the silk handkerchief, the creamy white shirt in folds about my shoulders. I have beside me Yates's boots which have been wrapped in a cloth since that night at the Constellation, uncleaned, still greasy. She sees them too. She gazes at me again, unwraps me, and I realize that she is looking at my hair.

My hair.

For I have taken off the hairpieces, five or six of them, and they lie in an untidy mess on the bed. I have oiled my cropped hair, slicking it close to my head, teasing out a curl or two across my brow. I have tried to get close to Yates again.

For once, I am struck dumb but know that I must speak. My mouth is stopped up, as they say, and as I look at her, though I struggle, I can think of no excuse except the most banal and transparent lie.

'My brother's clothes.'

She is like a statue, transfixed by my face. My hair.

Anyone else, I have thought afterwards, would have said, 'What are you up to, Mrs C?' or 'Those aren't your clothes, Mrs C. Where did you find them?' or would have walked over and, out of curiosity, picked up a boot or the shirt and said, lightly, 'Dressing up, Mrs C?' But not Lucy Fitch. She has no need to ask questions, understands more and immediately. The moments drag themselves into pools of stillness, as she now shifts her gaze, looking from me to the trunk to the clothes to my face, my hair. Her face is blanked of all emotion, and though I try, I cannot tell what she thinks or what she will do. But I hear in the silence, like a faint echo, a hiss of fear.

Now she stares fixedly, not at me, but at Yates's clothes, taking them in piece by piece. Her eyes range across them, consuming every thread, every crease and fold, until – and this comes upon me with surprising swiftness – I am restless with indignation and, at the same time, increasingly afraid. My instinct is to thrust her from the room, and I struggle to my feet, clinging to the bed for support. In so doing I drag Yates's little wooden box containing his rings and other jewellery from the counterpane. It falls to the floor with a clatter, and the rings skitter under the bed and the chest of drawers. Lucy puts down the cage. She bends to pick up the rings and, as she turns, our eyes meet.

'My brother's,' I say again. 'He died.'

I don't attempt to elaborate, for in my heart I know it will be inadequate, but I take the rings from her hand and once again feel her eyes upon me in a last, careful scrutiny, for moments later she is gone and I hear her footsteps retreating along the passage.

In a fever of industry, I replace my hairpieces, jabbing the pins into my head and scratching enough to draw blood in my haste. I repack the trunk, carefully and quickly folding and stowing, at the same time enacting in my imagination conversations I will have with Lucy Fitch. And then, weary, I sit by the fire, trying them out, listening, in my fancy, to the direction they take. Lucy is always friendly, pleased to see me, affectionate even and, though I have no desire to possess her, I find her caresses and spontaneous intimacy very appealing when we have sat together on the sofa, and she has laid her drowsy head upon my shoulder, holding my hand in hers. Then would often follow a dreamy hour, whilst her 'medicine' does its work and she is inclined to chatter – about men and babies and business. I try to recall the names: Captain Harker, Mr Newman (the self-same), the Lloyds, the Trenshams, the Peabodies. Not a mention of John Shovelton. Or James Yates. Not the Constellation, nor Whitechapel. Nor a murder. Not yet. But it will happen. For here, in this room, with the evidence of his life (and crimes) strewn over bed and floor, James Yates has presented himself to Lucy as certainly as if he had, once again, stood in the yard of the Constellation with Bessie Spooner at his feet.

After this, I know I can only wait for the moment, for I know it will come, when recognition suddenly overcomes reserve, and Lucy will say, in that flat, slow voice, much dulled by 'medicine', 'You know what, Mrs C, I know you, don't I? You're the bloke that did for Bessie. Only you're not a bloke, are you?' She will laugh, and wipe a hand across her mouth. 'You're no more a bloke than a Frenchy, are you? 'Course you're not.'

And I am perfectly certain now that I must attend to Lucy.

My thoughts were interrupted by a knock on the door and the appearance of Mrs Strong. I wondered if Lucy had revealed anything to her of what she had seen but, if she had, Mrs Strong was staying true to her name. She shut the door very carefully behind her, but advanced not a dozen paces, and when she spoke it was in her customary measured tones.

'I won't linger, or I shall be missed,' she said. 'But you should know, miss, that we are leaving for Birmingham. Today. We've had – well, Lucy has had – a communication. About a better shop starting next week.'

She shook her head as if she did not believe the suddenness herself. She continued, 'So I shall be going with them. My sister will find us lodgings, I'm sure. I'm very sorry, miss. We were rubbing along handsomely, and Lucy is terrible fond of you.'

Silence hung heavily while Mrs Strong searched for her words.

'They are still the Sisters Bellwood, Lucy and Kitty. She believes the name has brought them luck.

'Mrs Collette, I'm sorry to say goodbye to you so soon,' she said after another pause in which we both stared at our feet. 'You're a young woman all alone, and I dare say you believe you can get along well enough, and perhaps your pretty face will do you a favour. But it is hard to be alone in the world, and easy to trip and fall.'

She was struggling now and, in spite of everything, I felt sorry for her, so I began to say as much, but she stopped me.

'No, miss, I shall not go on beyond what I should. Except to say, if you and your babby are ever in trouble, then we should count ourselves fortunate to be able to help you.'

She handed me a scrap of paper from her pocket.

'Our address. You might look for us in the *Era* also. The Sisters Bellwood are often mentioned in the provincial reviews.'

Reaching the door, she dipped into her pocket again, took out some coins and placed them in a little pile upon the table.

'For Lucy's medicine. I know you've been generous to her and I like to settle our accounts. We owe no one anything then, miss.'

Little more than an hour later, noises downstairs alerted me to the departure of Lucy and her little entourage. She was standing anxiously upon the pavement, looking up and down the street for the trap that was to take them to Trensham Junction and then on to Birmingham. When she saw me, she struggled to maintain her composure, and Kitty also seemed drawn and pale. Only Mrs Strong, sitting stoically by their baskets, appeared unmoved. We exchanged tense farewells, Lucy tearful and tremulous, but I stood and waved them off, and as the trap turned the corner with a last dark flutter of Lucy's cloak, I felt relief drop from me.

With their departure, there was no longer any reason for me to delay mine, so I instructed the pot-boy, the prosaically named Prithy Taverner, to bring the trap around, packed my own few belongings, and made ready to return to the cottage.

It was still a fine, clear day, and skylarks sang high above the wide fields. My heart was light, and I was determined to return to the cottage in cheerful spirits, to show Mrs Gifford that my mutiny had brought about good effects. So I instructed Prithy Taverner to drive back the longer route, along the Bliss Valley, and then up and over Bliss Hill, approaching our cottage from above and behind, rather than traversing the length of the village. The journey would take longer but, I argued, I was better able to prepare myself and enjoy the precious solitude (Gifford would now haunt my every move!), for Prithy was a gentle companion, never speaking a word, but constantly solicitous of my comfort.

We had just rounded the hill and I looked with pleasure out over the valley spread like a green patchwork before me, and Jasmine Cottage below, with its smoking chimney and – I clutched Prithy's arm in horror, hardly believing what I saw. Before the house stood a carriage, black and enclosed, and two people, one a hugely fat man in a pale coat, leaning nonchalantly against the cottage wall and the second a woman dressed in an institutional dark blue dress and white apron (the detail is fixed in my memory), beside him, their backs towards me, looking intently along the village road. The road

I would have taken had I not determined to enjoy this last taste of freedom.

How long we sat before I commanded Prithy to turn the trap very quietly about and return to the Live and Let Live, I cannot tell. Without question and without any spoken commands to the horse, he did so, while I gazed with mounting fearfulness at the little group below, joined now, I saw, by the tall figure of Mrs Gifford. She too was fixed upon the road, but I knew it could only be moments before she turned around to look up the valley and saw the trap – and me. What she was doing, who the other figures were and the purpose of the enclosed carriage, I could only guess, but I feared that Uncle had lost patience and sent for me.

I looked back constantly, at every turn expecting to see the dark carriage and its sinister attendants pursuing me at rapid pace, and my heart thudded in my breast as I fought with the rising terror of what I should do. To run and hide in my present condition was unthinkable and impossible, and yet I could not imagine submitting meekly to Uncle and incarceration. Suddenly the fields and hills upon which I had looked so fondly seemed menacing, and I scoured the little tracks and narrow lanes leading to out-of-the-way farms and shepherds' huts for the thundering black carriage. But all was as still and quiet as before, and we returned upon the same lonely roads, meeting no one and seeing nothing until we reached the Live and Let Live.

I was not safe, though. My thoughts raced as we approached the hotel, for what protection could it offer me? Could I hide? No. There was nowhere in this tiny place, and I was suddenly filled with despair and terror. Mrs Gifford knew well enough where I was staying. It was only a matter of time before the black carriage and its attendants arrived in Burdon Oaks. Even now, I thought, they are on the road, and within the quarter-hour will be here and I shall be discovered.

Prithy Taverner stood by the trap, my belongings still stowed, my rug at hand. He looked at me curiously.

'You feeling bad again, miss?'

'I am,' I replied wearily. 'But I must go to the station. I want you to take me to Trensham Junction, Prithy, with all speed.'

I had an address to add to the notice I had recently torn from Lucy's *Era* newspaper in my pocket and, by the time he handed me on to the train at Trensham Junction bound for the nearest large town, a hastily scribbled note (addressed 'care of' Chittick's Circus in the city of Birmingham) for my eager pot-boy to take to the Post Office.

# 10

## Chittick's Circus and Mrs Marsh

### Corney Sage – Birmingham

Cities is rather like women. The more you know about them, the less comfortable you feel.

When you first make the acquaintance of a city or a woman, you're inclined to be struck by their beauty or their conversation. You feel proud walking down their streets, or having them on your arm. You cast your eyes about at this shop and that carriage, and she looks like she's just walked out of Mr Robertson's drawing room. And you think, What a grand chap I am! Living in this place and walking out with this finery. You think you're heading for Swell-street and no mistake, and you start looking out for yourself. Cleaning your boots and slapping lime-and-litharge on your hairy lip of a Sunday to get it nice and black. You think you might take in a park or an exhibition, or hear this and that great man speak upon a subject about which you know nothing and care even less.

Then, before you know it, everything goes cock-eyed. You are cornered by the landlord, who was at first so obliging. Now he shows you his fist and wants his money up front. And now there are shifty coves at the gate, and more appear on the corner. And the lady is more inclined to eel pie than potted shrimps. You find yourself getting into city ways, and clucking and nodding, too. All as if you've never done anything else. That you've been brought up to it. But it's a bit like wearing a new pair o' boots what pinch, and remind you of how uncomfortable you are. So you've to walk about like you got somewhere to go even though you have blisters like sovereigns. Put your head down and mind your own business. Be one of the mobility, as Lucy used to say, and disappear.

I was doing just that – disappearing – in the crowd outside the station, and waiting for a train, also. (But of that, more anon, as the parson said to the dairymaid.) It was one of my favourite places, for I always liked stations and watching people coming and going. Families going visiting. Theatricals, always good for a laugh with all their airs and graces, but might tip a barney and sing a song or give a few steps if they thought anyone was looking. Wives and husbands saying their tearful farewells. Mothers and sons meeting up after years and years apart. The son all spruced and doing well for himself, with a flower in his buttonhole. And gloves. The train arrives and the mother looking fearful and a bit confused, 'cos she's well on in years now, having been looking for him since he was just a baby when she give him up. Now she's seen him and he takes her up in his strong arms and she's weeping with joy, for she's found him and can die happy. (This is one of my particular favourites, a story I tell myself made up of sights I've seen while hanging about, for I have a notion of how I might one day come upon my own mother and how it will be.)

My train came in and I waited while two more emptied, looking for a familiar face, or for someone to approach with a clap on the shoulder and a 'Corney Sage! There you are!' But no one did, and though I hung about until the porters started giving me the evil (thinking I was up to no good), still no one did. So I didn't notice this woman at all till I got outside, feeling not a little disappointed with the world. Now if I'd been of the thieving persuasion, I thought (and I was not in a sunny temper), I would have made straight for her. Given her a nudge, since she looked none too steady, and have made off with her bag and purse before she knew what had happened.

Hello, I thought, there she goes. And the woman sinks down on cue, as it were, upon the bench. She was very pale, with great black shadows under her eyes and splashes of mud on her travelling coat, and I could see she had a little black purse on a string round her wrist, which was easy pickings. And no doubt she had a trunk too. I watched her for a while, and thought, Corney Sage, you're getting city ways. You're starting to think like a city cove. And I was in certain. I thought that if I didn't look sharp and give her a friendly hand, someone else would guide her ever so carefully to the refreshment rooms, jostle her to the floor, and rob her blind.

So there was I, strolling across the road, avoiding the horses, chaffing the cabmen, and straightening my everyday, with this lady in my sights, when suddenly there's a whistle and a shout: 'Hoi! Corney Sage! H-over 'ere!'

I was, as the song says, 'Somewhat inclined to give him the bird' and continue on my errand. But – well, Mr Chittick, my new Gov'nor, had sent me out with orders what I couldn't very well ignore. Round the back they was just unloading three great rolls of canvas from Mr Griffin in Bolton, and it was all for me. So I gave the lady a good looking at and told her, under my breath like, to stay where she was until I got back. And the fact was, I said to myself, giving her one last look over my shoulder, she didn't look much as if she was going anywhere soon.

I hauled the handcart round and promised old Loudmouth (who was still shouting to me, and gave his haitches to everything what didn't need them) a free pass to the show if he would help me stow the goods. The job was too big for one man, and Chittick might have sent a couple of others at least. But that was the trouble with some circus men. Mean-spirited. Not like your theatricals who look out for each other and offer a helping hand when they can. Circus men are hard-hearted. Everyone knows they think more of their animals than their fellow men.

Of course, when I joined Chittick's Mammoth establishment I was glad for the shop. What with that bad business in the other place, I was eager to jump the next wagon (not having the readies) and was pleased to find myself in the great city of Birmingham. On spec. The truth was, I should have been much relieved to find myself in Timbuctoo, so eager was I to be out of trouble, but I have never gone to any shop in the blind, so to speak, and the only thing I knew about Birmingham was what Lucy and her mother, Mrs Strong, had told me, for that lady had a sister living here who might take in lodgers.

But I looked like a hay-seed, my clothes were shabby, my clogs didn't tell and even the 'Flea' and 'Alonzo the Brave' refused to go. Most of the city concert rooms were huffish, but finally I talked up Mr Blitz of the Harmony in Reed-street (the very same as I found in the *Era*), and he offered me a shop. Which I took for one night only. I think about it with shame now, for I must have looked a proper wall creeper. I was the first man on the platform (which I would never accept in the usual way of things), and gave them a round of clogs, two improving recitations about working hard and keeping on the right side of the law, and finished up with a motto song about caring for your mother before it's too late. A tidy little programme, I thought, and well received, though the company was dull. But when Mr Blitz, a real dismal Jimmy, without a nod, give me notice to change my coat and wait on tables for the rest of the evening, I was struck to my liver and back again. This was something I have never done! Will never do, unless I am starving.

I've told this tale to several parties since, but for all the telling it is as close as a cuss is to damnation to what I said to Mr Blitz when I dropped my apron at his feet. He said not a word, and of course he profited by my indignation for I got not a penny from him, having told him that he and his concert room might go and roast in another place. For I was straight away out of the door, and now without a shop or ready or lodgings. And I was wondering whether to pay a call upon Mrs Strong's sister and appeal to her goodwill.

But fortune smiles on those who don't press her too hard, and one of my daily trips was down to the railway station (carrying bags and hailing cabs will put a sixpence in a man's hand), where I was forced to pass the circus in the Cattle Market. It was not the great wooden building itself that stopped me, though I'd often peeped in and breathed that aroma you don't get anywhere else. A regular mix of smells – tan, what is sharp to the nose, and animals and their sweet sweat, and human sweat too, which is never sweet. Not to mention the orange peel and damp shoe leather and the oats and straw wafting up from where the horses are bedded. I get quite lyrical about it, but I maintain that the smell of the circus is like nothing else. You couldn't bottle it if you tried.

But what usually halted me was what was going on in the yard where they were exercising or walking the animals. I regular stopped to admire the fine physic of the strong man – and get an eyeful of the physic of the sawdust ladies while I was at it! By and by I got on chatting terms with everyone, and they would hail me as I went past. Then one day there were wagons in the yard, and everyone busy painting and carpentering. And, according to Herr Klein, the strong man, they were soon to leave for a tenting season in the country. As luck would have it they were in need of a funny man.

'Some of your good fresh air. No?' says Herr Klein who, by the way, was brung up in Builth Wells, but had talked in the foreign way for so long he couldn't help himself and talked like it by habit now! I was quickly conscripted into the company. The previous talking clown had disappeared (to another circus company, Mr Chittick believed), and anyway his jokes were old and dry. A bit like him. They wanted some fresh blood and new wheezes for the tenting season, and although I protested that I was no horseman, and had never tumbled in my life (except when I was on the lush), the Gov'nor would have none of it. I was transformed there and then into Funny Foodle with an orange wig (until my own grew) and white paint, and made my sawdust debut that very night.

They made me as welcome as they could any mummer, for 'ne'er shall sawdust-men and mummers meet', said Mrs Chittick when I found her alone on the steps of her living wagon. I made bold to ask if that applied to sawdust-women as well, and she smiled, and said that all joeys were alike. But she smiled at me again afterwards, and caught my eye a few times when her husband wasn't looking.

So I felt not all out of shape. I had found a shop, made myself useful and agreeable, and would warm my feet on the Gov'nor's wife at the first opportunity.

But back to my train and this interesting lady. The one sinking low outside the station? One thing at a time. I arrive at the circus as usual this morning and have Mr Chittick's instructions to collect some rolls of canvas, ordered from Glasgow, for the new tilt (that is the roof), in readiness for our going a-tenting. I am listening to these instructions for the umpteenth time, when Mrs comes wafting across the yard (a fragrant lady, and no mistake) waving an envelope and crying, "Ere, Foodle, it's for you!'

Me? I have only ever had two letters in my whole life. One to say that Mr Figgis, my dear old father (only not my true father), had died and the other from Mrs Figgis, telling me I am left his Bible and a drawful of stiff collars if I would like to collect them. But here is a letter with my name upon it, 'Corney Sage (Prof. Moore)', and 'care of Chitticks Circus, Birmingham'.

'Chittick's Mammoth Circus,' the Gov puts in. 'They've left out Mammoth.'

No one pays him any attention, for they are all waiting on me to open it. But inside is just an untidy note, requesting me to meet a train at a certain time on a certain day (today) and signed – but none of us can make it out. There is no 'to your advantage', no 'you will learn something interesting'. Not even, 'where you will receive a hundred pounds'. Just a day and a time and a train and a scribbled name that not even Mrs can read, and she is a scholar. From my circus pals, there is much advice offered, mostly to ignore it, for it can only mean trouble. Probably, says one of the grooms, I was going to be jumped at the station, and robbed of everything, which alarms Chittick no end. I am to guard those rolls of canvas with my life, he cries, and if any are missing he will turn my brains to butter. So off I go with the letter in my pocket and a frown upon my countenance.

Which did not lift, for the train came, and another, and the one after it, and there was no one to meet and no reward to claim, and no doubt some prankster in Wheezetown having a chortle at my expense. But there is no point weeping over an upturned churn (as Mr Figgis would say), so I turned my sights upon the interesting lady a-sitting on the bench.

As I hauled the handcart round the corner, I made a point of looking her up. She was still there, a bit brighter, but not much. And when she stood up, I conned what was going on with her, for in a few more weeks she'd be increasing the population by one.

She seemed to know I had her in my eye, and stared me down.

'Afternoon, missis,' says I cheerily, tipping my hat. 'Can I assist?'

'A cup of water, if you'd be so kind,' she replied, and I could see her tongue was fairly cleaved to her mouth, and her lips were dry as dry. All about us were the crowds coming and going to the railway, and whistles hooting and cabmen shouting, and everyone giving her the curious stare but not wanting to enquire. (That is what I have found about city people. How they enjoy looking and will halt in the middle of the roadway if something takes their eye, and before you can turn about there is a crowd. That's how crowds are made, I believe, from one person's eye-wagging. But that is all they wish to do. Eye-wag. And would not think to lend a hand.) So there was plenty of people, but not so many cups of water, and I said so to anyone who would hear, and that turned the army on to its back foot. But, says I to the lady, if she could step across the way there is the refreshment room in the Railway Hotel what isn't nobby, but has water a-plenty. I thought she smiled to herself, a little smile that made her look away and draw her hand across her face.

'You're very kind,' she says. 'I will go directly to the Railway Hotel.'

And she got up, heavy like, and weary, and I wondered if she would get across the road without having to have another sit down, so bad did she look. But here was a how-d'ye-do as well, for I was encumbered with my cart and the great rolls of canvas sticking out and poking people, and causing cabmen to give me language, and here was an ailing woman, whose purse was hanging loose about her wrist, and who was not likely to cross the street without coming to injury. So I hailed old Loudmouth, who himself had come to get an eyeful of what was going on, and promised him a glass of Felkin's Particular if he would take my cart back to the railway yard, when I would collect it later on. He gave me a selection of haitches again and attached some of them to his own variety of laughter ('Haah!' 'Ha-aah!' he goes, in a fashion I've never heard by any other mortal), but he took the cart and left me with two free arms to guide the lady across the road and into the Railway Hotel.

Now it is not a plush place, the Railway, and even though it calls itself a hotel I have never met anyone what has stayed there, nor has wanted to stay there. The Station Hotel is a different matter, having all manner of rooms and saloons, and a superior cove on the door what would knock your hat off in the street if he didn't like the time on your clock. I have had fighting words with this cove before, when he showed me his Oliver with the tattoo on each knuckle. So the Railway Hotel it was, and Rudd, the landlord (a decent bloke also with a tattoo but on his back, and this of a ship in full sail, which he will reveal for a penny, and a fine bit of artwork it is too), wiping his hands on his apron, kindly showing us into his parlour round the back and bringing the glass of water for her and the glass of neck-oil for me, while she insisted on coughing up for it. She was in the only comfortable chair in the whole house, what Rudd has dragged out and dusted off, and she has fallen dead asleep straight away, not minding that the room is chilly and dusty. Rudd's wife (a mulatto and the most handsome woman I have seen in all my days) came in and took a look at her and fetched a rug to cover her up, then draws the curtains and shushes us out.

So, not knowing what else to do, I sit in the public with Rudd, and watch the clock and listen to the flies and take a glass, until Mrs Rudd goes into the parlour with a cup of tea and some bread and butter and comes out with a quizzical look on her face.

'She wants you,' she says, and I am regular put about by this woman's beauty, which is considerable. (I do not know how she happened to get stuck with Rudd who, apart from his tattoo, which is artistic in the extreme, is horrible to behold. If I could have got to the Americas before him, I would have snapped her up right as right, but being a sea-William, I would never have the chance.)

Anyhow, I goes in to her, and she's sitting up with the rug over her and the fire lit now.

'Thank you. Thank you for looking after me.'

I said it was nothing. That any Christian man or woman would have done the same. But she wasn't listening, for a look of panic was struck upon her face and she grabbed my coat sleeve and give me this piece of paper. I recognized it, for it was torn from the Professional's Bible, the weekly *Era* edited by the esteemed Mr

Ledger (who I don't know personally but believe to be a gentle-man). Here it is.

'The Pets of the Men'
SISTERS BELLWOOD
Lucy and Kitty
Dashing Duettists and Dancers
Great success at MINTON'S PALACE and
GREAT TURK (Lower Marlpool-street)
Every evening from Monday next
'Oh you Bhoys!!!'

'Can you – will you – help me please? I don't know you but I think you are a good man and would help a lady in desperate need. And I am desperate, sir. For there are people coming who want to take me. But here are friends' – and she pointed at the piece of paper – 'good friends, and they will make sure that I am safe. But I'm a stranger here, sir. A stranger.' I believe she began to cry, though she turned away.

I looked at it, and then at her, and then at it again, for those names presented themselves like old friends, and I was inclined to say as much. Only I didn't. For though she seemed respectable, I didn't know this lady or why she should claim friendship with Lucy and Kitty. And, even stranger to me, was that she intended visiting Minton's Palace and the Great Turk, for these places (the Great Turk in particular) were not elegant establishments. (And indeed I was disappointed that Lucy had not found a better shop, though I expect it was only for a few weeks.) So, I debated quickly what I should say, and elected to be unhelpful.

'I can't say where they are, miss, not being a native-like. I don't know streets 'cept those around the circus where is my place of work.'

'Please,' she said. 'I can pay you. Only take me to my friends. That is all I ask.'

Her eyes were pleading, and her face like an angel's. And a catch in her voice that made your heart melt clean away. Besides, she did mention money.

But I told her I couldn't take her there, and I was telling the truth, for I had to be back and doing my work in the ring. Besides, I said, they could have moved on and might be anywhere now. And I was still wondering how she knew Lucy, for it surely could not be that they were rubbing shoulders together, she being regularly ladylike and Lucy – not.

While I was thinking about this, the lady was shaking her head at me and saying yes, she was entirely sure that the Sisters Bellwood would still be there, for wasn't this a recent card? Where were these places? Could she get a cart to take her? Oh, indeed, it was very important that she found them, for she had no other friends. No one at all on whom she might depend.

I replied, yes she could get a cart, but—

Then that was what she would do, and she started to get up, pushing away the rug and wiping her brow with a handkercher. And then she put her hand to her face and covered her eyes and sat down again and began to weep.

'Look here, miss,' says I, all at once (for I hate to see women cry), 'it seems to me you're not feeling tip-top. It seems to me you might be better placed to gather your strength and go tomorrow, when you can hire a cab and do it at your leisure. For if these *are* professional ladies' – I nearly smiled when I said it, for at the Great Turk they mostly *was* professional ladies, if you know what I mean – 'they will be having their cup of tea and bread and butter and a bit of shut-eye before their night's work, and will not take kindly to being disturbed.'

The truth was, the more I sat with her, the more I felt she might persuade me to take her to Lower Marlpool-street or, indeed, wherever she wanted to go. For she was powerful affecting with her pale face and her dark eyes. And yet. How can I describe it? I had a feeling about it. About her. That it was, she was, not quite the thing. Not quite right. You will understand when I explain more. But not yet.

I tried another tack.

'You might fancy putting up here. Or at the Station Hotel. A much more genteel establishment.'

She shook her head, and I looked at the mud on her skirt, which was worn about the edges, and I wondered if money might be at the bottom of it, so I plunged on.

'Well, I know a lodging house, miss, Mr Halls's, where I feel certain there are rooms. Cleanish. Just for the night. While you get your strength back.'

Here, what brass Corney Sage has! *How* should she, *why* should she agree to such an offer? I might have been a murderer or some low nibbler who would take advantage of a lady (whether she's respectable or not is a different matter) what is down on her luck. But it was getting late to start travelling around a strange city, and she was done in and no mistake, and looked as though another step might kill her. We must have thought similar. Or she had no sense at all. But she stopped crying and her shoulders sunk down like she had given up.

'That would probably be a very sensible solution, Mr . . . ?'

'Mr Corney Sage, at your service, miss – madam,' I stuttered, for I did not know what to call her.

'Mrs Marsh.'

She looked hard at me with those dark-shadowed eyes in that pale face.

'Mr Sage. I hold you to your honour as a gentleman *not* to betray me or do me harm.'

Out of the blue this came, but she said it with such earnestness, and such a ring to her voice, and she was looking at me with a face like an angel. But it was one of Mr Doré's that I once remarked in a book (and got scared of) a long time ago.

I will not tell how I first came upon Halls's establishment (for there, as they say, lies another tale and one that would take much telling). It was in the back of a back-street neighbourhood of the town, not far from the canal and within a spit of the Cattle Market. I fancy it had been, in the springtime of its youth, an elegant gentleman's residence, for its marble floors and twisty stairposts and handsome decorations could still be seen. But it had fallen upon hard times, and no mistake, and now there were cracked panes in the windows and weeds in the garden, and a houseful of Irish labourers next door. How Halls acquired it I cannot tell, but he'd been there a while, for his marks were all over it, mostly dirty marks along the walls where his hands and shoulders had rubbed, and around the keyholes where he pressed his eye (which consequently was always on the water). But for all its shabbiness, here were rooms with a single bed, not dormitories where you were closely acquainted with your fellow man and all *his* acquaintances. And here were curtains to draw, and doors to close (and support with a chair if you'd a mind to), and a washstand and a fire in the grate, if you bought your own coals. In cert, it had no comparison with my little cot at the Old Pitcher; there was no lapping river, nor quiet dark sky. But neither was there a murderer looking out for me.

And how we got to Halls's Lodgings, Paradise-court, I won't trouble to tell either (there being enough minuteness already). I delivered the canvas to our circus (Chittick was curious, and came out to have a look – my lady, Mrs Marsh, was sitting on a bale of straw and Mrs C had given her a cup of tea), and then we made for the lodgings. I had half a dozen words with Halls while she stood in the front, but after looking her over, he needed no more persuasion. Indeed, it was dreadful the way he carried on, fawning and creeping like he ran a nobby establishment. He had a nice room for her, he said, first floor, but he hoped there weren't too many steps. Would she have a cup of tea in his parlour? Should he make her up a fire? Open the window?

She was quiet and steady, of course. Yes, she would take the room and paid up in coins. No, she needed nothing more. When we'd stowed her trunk (which I'd brung on the handcart) and Halls had offered to open it up – 'to get your stuff aired, missis' – and which she had firmly refused, she shut the door, saying she wanted a lie down.

Halls was very struck by her. He stood outside the door for a while, and I wondered whether or not he was going to chance his eye at the keyhole. But he thought better of it, and came down the stairs like a shadow against the wall, for he was dreadful thin, and breathing hard, though whether through exertion or the weight of the coins in his pocket I could not say. He quizzed me about the lady within an inch of my life, but I had precious little to tell, and when he was satisfied he got the bottle out and two cups, and poked up a fire. We heard her moving about above.

'She's ripe, Corney,' Halls said in a whisper. 'Now then, how shall we manage her? Rush her? Or wait till she goes out?'

He had it all thought out and told me so, for he had a 'quick mind'. And she was, after all, prime. A lady who could not shift for herself and pretty much at sea. With a decent trunk, heavy, and a purse, even if it was on the light side. He had three shillings in his pocket and there was more.

But even as he was wheezing on, and I was nodding to keep him sweet, I had one ear on my lady upstairs. The creaking floorboards made it impossible for her to move about without a sound, and I could hear her go to and fro, opening the window and so on. And the more I listened to the sound of her, the more I thought that there was something about her. And it wasn't her pale skin and the way she spoke, which had impressed Halls mightily, and in certain had drawn me at first. It wasn't just that. It was the way she had with her. Like she was play-acting, but very good at it. The way she talked refined, quiet, beautiful-sounding, like she might break into a song, but all put on. And what lady, in her condition, I asked myself, would be travelling alone? And how come she tagged along with me, a stranger, so quickly? Why, I could have done her over, robbed her blind. She must have banked on – something – that I wouldn't treat her so.

I put my hand in my pocket and felt the folded-up paper with the address on it, what I hadn't told Halls about. And I let it be. For he was pursuing his own line.

'Get her out of here tomorrer, and I'll do over the trunk,' Halls goes in his low voice. 'Whatever, we'll split it two ways,' and he tapped the side of his nose, like one of your music hall funny men. 'There'll be jewellery – I'll get rid of that. Books, too, by the weight of the trunk. You can have them, Corney.'

I let him know that books were no good to me, and that if anyone ought to have the stones it should be yours truly, seeing as how I found the party. He smiled at me, and spoke agreeably enough.

'You drive a hard bargain. And I'm a poor man as you know. I can't work 'cos of me lung.'

Now he told everyone he only had one lung. According to Halls, he was born like it, his mother having been scared by a hot-air balloon exploding in the pleasure gardens. Call me hard-hearted, but I think he told more lies than an egg, for I've heard him sprint upstairs like a child when he thought a lodger was trying to flit without paying. And with my own eyes I've seen him leg it down the road after a Chinee who walked in on spec and run out with a hatstand! He could also water his plants better than any mummer, so I didn't feel bad sticking him out, and, after a while, he shrugged and said maybe she wasn't as flush as she appeared to be. And then he said what I'd been thinking.

'Anyhow, what's a respectable woman doing walking around fit to drop any moment? No ring on her finger.' He scratched his chin and filled his cup – but not mine – and fell to musing again.

'Happen she's rich, a duchess from somewhere? On the run with the family jewels? She'd pay a bit to keep us quiet.'

I said I thought a duchess might have a bit more baggage about her. And why would a duchess run off when she's up the spout? Anyway, I said, it was time for me to get to the circus and earn some *honest* money. Indeed, it was half past six and I had barely an hour to transform myself into Funny Foodle. But when I reached the door, there was the young woman herself, standing with her bonnet and coat on, for so set were Halls and I in our conversation that neither of us had heard her come downstairs, loose floorboards or not, and it did cross my mind to wonder how long she had been standing there, and whether she had heard what we'd been saying about her. But, whatever she might have overhead, she gave me a pleasant enough smile, and nodded over my shoulder to Mr Halls. I explained what I was about, that I was in a rush.

'For,' I said, 'if I'm not in the circle sharpish at half past seven, then Mr Chittick will remind me with his stick across my back. He is not a forgiving man, is Mr Chittick.'

She nodded seriously. 'I'm very grateful to you, Mr Sage, for your kindness, and for recommending this accommodation. I am sure I will be very comfortable here, but I do need to find my friends as soon as possible as they are expecting me. I have a mind to walk into the city now. I am happy to do so. Please don't be concerned.'

No matter what had gone before, I was still bothered by this proposition, and I said so. It wasn't the time of night to be walking out alone in streets where she was a stranger. And especially Lower Marlpool-street, which was most undesirable.

She looked sharpish at me. 'Oh, but I understood you were unfamiliar with that neighbourhood, Mr Sage.'

She had caught me out, and knew it, and the flicker of a smile played around her lips for a moment until she possessed herself once again. I was silent as we walked along together, but had the feeling of Halls watching us down the street and, no doubt, putting on his coat and muffler and trailing us a little, one lung or no. She was chatty as we walked, enquiring now and then about churches and who lived here and there, and was there a concert room to this public house or no. She was pleasant company and a fine figure (although heavy), and though we drew curious glances along the way, she seemed not to notice and I pretended not to. When we got to the circus, she looked tired.

'Here, miss,' I said of a sudden, 'why don't I give you a free order to the show? You can sit down for a bit and' – for she was shaking her head – 'on my word of honour, I will find your friends tomorrow. If they are to be found,' I added, just in case.

She took a little persuading, protesting that she must be about her business, looking for her friends. But I think her plates were bothering her, and certainly her face was pale as chalk, and her beautiful eyes were ringed with dark bruises.

Mrs Chittick took a look at her and without me saying a word passed her through and found her a seat by the end of a row.

'What have you been up to then, Corney?' she says, giving me the eye. 'She's a bit above the sawdust, wouldn't you say?'

But I felt uncommonly protective towards my lady, and didn't feel inclined for banter, so I passed round the back of the circle, keeping her in my sights all the time, and though the place was filling up nicely, felt comforted that I could see her figure on the end of the row.

⚬⚬⚬⚬

People often wonder what a circus is like behind the curtain. Most think it's an orderly kind of world, with people standing quietly in lines, and animals behaving themselves, chewing on carrots and straw until they're needed. But it is not like this at all. By no means. Behind the ring curtains is pretty much like Bedlam. Horses stamping and coughing, and grooms (if they're sober) hanging on to maybe four bridles at a time, trying to keep 'em still and quiet. Tumblers stretching and pulling their legs up and over till you can't hardly look at 'em for feeling your own tackle tighten up. And lady riders rigged out in spangles and costumes hardly covering their dignity, and the band getting ready, shining up their brass, and combing their hair, for bandsmen are notoriously vain. (Worst of all is the band leader. We had Mr Peabody, the size of a barrel, always short of breath, and more attached to his moustache – the biggest, by arrangement, in the band – than to his instrument.)

As I passed through to the sheds at the back where I put on my whitening and rescued my costume from the damp, my heart sank to my boots as I heard the familiar sound of Chittick belabouring one of the grooms with his stick. His favourite – and today's victim – was Joe, the Negro. Joe never made a murmur, for he was mute, his tongue having been taken while he was in slavery, so we were told, though how anyone could know it I never found out since Joe himself couldn't tell it. I felt sorry for the poor devil, who toiled longer and harder than any of us, and earned nothing but regular thrashings for his efforts, and I let Chittick know it once. It did no good, and I too got the end of his stick for my pains, so I let it be. But the thud of his stick on Joe's back set us all silent and there were looks and rumblings among us, for circus people stick together and hate injustice.

Chittick's red face appeared around the doorway, and it was clear as water that he was too drunk to see a hole in a ladder, if you get my drift. His eyes were pink and his face was lit up like an oven. It always being the best policy never to have truck with him when he was in his cups, I took no notice and having whitened up my face and put on my tunic and frills, all I had to do was arrange my hair into its accustomed peak and collect my oversize wooden spoon, the property with which I had become associated. But he *would* have words with me. You can imagine him speaking, with his tongue too big for his mouth and dry as an old tart. He points the finger at me.

'You, Duke o' York' – it was his name for me since I was such a talker – 'soldiers in tonight. From the barracks. Give a good night. None of yer fancy double-talking. Plain blue and no sweeteners.'

I saluted him, but he wasn't in the mood.

'There's good custom in the promenade,' he slurred. 'Gents from London and all. So none of yer wheezes about gents. Or sojers.'

I bowed, and then saluted again. I had some nice wheezes given me by a clown retiring from the business. Wheezes that were insulting of both gents and military, some of whom would laugh like good 'uns within the building but then wait for me outside, and give me a black eye to go with my white face. But tonight these gents and red herrings were regulars, the sort that treated the company and stabled their horses in the stalls, so Chittick wanted to keep 'em sweet. I had my orders: no insults, no fancy talk, just a bit of blue and watch the Fancy. Pity the ladies then. And I thought with alarm about my lady, on the end of the row, and what she might think of me.

The band had begun the overture, a rousing march, and the bell had rung, signalling the whole company to assemble for the opening parade. Mr Humphrey, our ringmaster, at the head of the line, marched smartly out, followed by some of the ladies on their horses, and Herr Klein with his dog, Hector, a natty little procession around the ring with a good rousing tune and the audience a-clapping in time. Of course the military can be wild, and whistle at the ladies and cat-call as well, and Chittick stood at the curtain watching up to the promenade, for if there's trouble in a circus you have to be on to it sharpish. As I come out of the ring, breathing hard, I hear a crack, like a gun going off, which sets some of the ladies screaming, while the military roars with laughter and gives up more calls and more whistles. We carry on into the circle, doing our second circuit, when another crack follows, then a third, and then a cloud of thick smoke starts to drift from upstairs. Then there is a whole bagful of bangs and cracks, like a company of rifles letting off, and the smoke that goes with them covers the balcony and drops down into the crowd below. Someone shouts, 'Fire! The place is on fire!' and then it is hell's delight, for everyone panics.

Now a panic in a theatre or a circus is worse than a battle, for there soldiers look out for their fellows and sacrifice themselves. In a panic, each man thinks only of himself and would trample wife, mother and the Queen to save his own skin. Children are thrown down or abandoned, men elbow their sisters out of the way, and everyone rushes for the doors, climbing over chairs and benches – and bodies, if they are in the way.

Ours was an old circus, a wooden building built twenty years before, when fires, though they happened regular enough, were still not considered important. The doorways were narrow, the passage-ways even narrower. There were no attendants or constables, and consequently there was nothing but a crush. The parade in the circle stopped, and Mr Humphrey called for order and rang the bell, but he couldn't be heard above the din. For as people screamed and shouted, and flung themselves towards the doors, the soldiers (who were the cause of the panic) let off more firecrackers (that is indeed what the bangs were) and created more smoke. Those of us in the ring when the cracks began tried to spy out the culprits, but by the time we got up into the balcony the panic was well under way, and no amount of chiding would stop the drunken military for whom it was all a lark. Herr Klein selected a couple of the ring-leaders and cracked their skulls, and Mr Humphrey was up there as well, laying into them with a whip as well as his fists.

But my thought was for my lady, Mrs Marsh. When I looked to where I knew she should be, I could not see her, and I feared greatly that she had been trampled – or worse. I went back through the ring curtains and around the building, where the horses were tethered, and neighing in agitation and fear. Had there been a fire, they would have been rescued first, for circus people value their animals, but now the grooms were calming them and fetching water, and called anxiously after me.

'Ho, Corney! What's to do? What's the show?'

But I was intent on getting outside and seeing what could be done. The yard was full of people, hurrying to be clear of the building, shouting to each other, and then of course standing back to view the calamity – if there was going to be one. The streets around the circus were lined with people, arms folded, watching for the flames and bodies being brung out, burned to a cinder. Crowds again. There is no accounting for them in my book. But my lady was nowhere to be seen and, when I enquired, no one had seen her. And nobody cared neither. I went back round and into the ring again, where people were still pushing to get out, but fewer now and the smoke was clearing.

It was a scene of destruction, Mr Chittick said the following day. I don't know about that. I saw some seats smashed up, and someone had nibbled the curtains from across the doorways. Also the cushions from the best seats, and Mr Humphrey's shiny hat which he'd dropped in the ring. I wandered around, expecting to find the poor woman dead on the ground, but there was no one, not even a child. Out in the yard, I wondered what I should do, when I noticed a commotion over by one of the living wagons. A small crowd had gathered and were making up for their evening's lost entertainment by having a good eyeful of someone else's misfortune.

It was her of course. My lady. Mrs Marsh. She was on the steps of the wagon and something was going on. I pushed my way through the crowd, who were tightly packed, I might add, and not inclined to let me pass, lest I spoil their view and enjoyment of the scene. But I elbowed some in the ribs, and trod heavily on some toes, and got to the lady just as she was letting out a groan. She didn't recognize me at first, for she shrank back as I approached, and then she must have seen past the whitening and the tunic, for she grasped my hand hard. Someone in the crowd shouted words that a lady shouldn't hear, and it caused a swell of laughter around her that gave her alarm, so I opened the door of the wagon (it was an empty one, having belonged to the clown who had recently done a flit), and assisted her inside. No easy matter, for she was, I realized, about to do the business.

I made her comfortable as I could – there was a cupboard bed and some blankets – and I lit the lamp and drew the curtains, for them outside was climbing over each other to peer in. It was a bare enough place, clean, though not lived in for some weeks. A rug on the floor, and a few pans and dishes on shelves and in cupboards. A man's wagon. Just enough to keep himself, and no more. It seemed a sorry place to bring a baby into the world. But it could have been worse.

She was quiet now that I had got her into the bed and covered her over. But I had to go and fetch one of the women. Or a doctor. And I told her so.

'Mrs Chittick'll know what to do. She's had six of her own, and all in a wagon.'

She would have none of it, and began to cry.

'I beg of you, Mr Sage, do not leave me. I am so afraid. I think—' But she had no chance to tell me, for her face screwed up in pain, and she let out a howl which was terrible to hear. She bent upwards, and laid her two hands on her belly, clutching it and wailing, while big tears rolled down her face. When it was over, she lay back, her shoulders shaking and her face wet with crying. I was distracted myself, and for all the world might have fled from the wagon had she not grabbed hold of my hand again.

'Please, miss,' I said, 'let me go and find help, for *I* cannot do anything.'

But, no. She would not let go of my hand, even though she closed her eyes and appeared to be asleep. As I moved to go, her grip tightened, and her face once again was twisted in suffering. She groaned and moaned and filled the wagon with her cries until I wanted to stop up my ears.

It sounds poetical, but it wasn't. I wouldn't have been there for all the world if I could have escaped, and that's a fact. The lamp flickered and sputtered, and it struck me that darkness might be a blessing, for at least then I wouldn't have to *see* her misery! Then, as she sank back again into the pillow, the door opened and through the sea of faces, still assembled for the show, came Joe the Negro climbing into the wagon and closing the door quietly behind him. He smelled of horses and smoke, but he took her little hand in his as gentle as gentle. She opened her eyes and shivered, and then seemed to know, for she let go of mine. He laid his other hand upon her belly and she never flinched. And then he turned to me.

'Mr Corney, sir,' he said, 'I will need your help.'

My mouth must have hit my boots in surprise. I couldn't help but say, 'Joe? I thought you was dumb? I thought you had your tongue ripped out for answering back on the Plantation or somewheres?'

'Nope,' he says, 'I'm not dumb, just looking out for myself. But right now, Mr Corney, I'm looking out for this lady, whose baby is coming.'

Mrs Chittick and all the other ladies of the circus had disappeared, he said, taken themselves off to their lodgings. There was no one else to help my lady 'cept him and me, so that was what he proposed to do.

'Mr Corney, I would like for you to fetch some hot water in a can.

And some spirit. But not gin, sir. And maybe some more blankets. It's chilly in here.'

And this is how it all begins, I thought to myself as I crossed the yard and closed the gates. The crowd had gone home, and so had the company. There was nothing and no one about the place, 'cept Mr Toplady, the keeper, who watched the horses, and kept a light burning in the back. He was in the building, raking the tan and tidying round as best he could, to sweeten the Gov'nor's temper in the morning. As I opened the door, he looked up concerned, and then surprised.

'You still here, Corney? What's what? Fancy a tip?'

His was a lonely life and he was an old man, keeping company with horses and an empty ring full of shadders and spirits. But whereas some other time I would have shared a glass with him, this night I had urgent business, and I made my excuses and hurried into the backs on my errand. There were blankets a-plenty but none for my lady, still less to wrap a baby in. Horse blankets were coarse and filthy, and saddle pads no better. Then I thought of Herr Klein, the strong man, and his bed, a makeshift affair of sacks, but covered with gaily coloured blankets. They were cleanish, and smelled of liniment and oils, but soft, and I folded them quickly under my arm.

Mr Toplady had pulled out the coke braziers (which warmed the building) into the yard for fear of fire, and I revived them and placed pans full of water from the pump on top. As I struggled with the buckets I looked over to the wagon, where the yellow light of the lantern glowed, and Joe's shadow moved about. Her cries were muffled, but *I* could hear them. More than once – as the water slopped over my feet and then hissed as I heaved the pans on to the brazier – more than once I resolved to run away. It would be the work of a moment to step across the yard, unhook the gate, and take myself off to Halls's, or anywhere I chose, anywhere to be free of what seemed to be drawing me in. I am not a fanciful man, and I like to think that I know my own mind, but here, with the thin wind picking up and catching the coals, and the stars twisting and flickering above – well, I felt more alone than I had ever done in my whole life.

I'm not one to feel sorry for myself. I was always told I have much to be grateful for, and I wouldn't argue. My father and my mother, though they weren't blood kin to me, took me in out of their charity and because they were Baptists and didn't have kids of their own. Me, what had been wrapped in paper and laid on their doorstep like a fishmonger's parcel. My father told that story over and over. I was like Moses found a-floating in the bulrushes. Even so I was brought up to be grateful, and certain the thought of the black stones of my parents' doorstep warmed my back many a time. (It is strange how I keep a particular horror of the cold to this day.) But once I left them I resolved never to return. I did not want to look again upon the shame of my birth – a cold doorstep, a wet and windy night, and a scullery-maid hurrying home and seeing me a-lying there in all my nakedness, the ink of the paper staining my hands and filling my mouth.

Now here was another one, another life brought bawling into the world, raising its fists at the hardness of it all. Though its mother was gentle and her voice was low, how many blows would *it* suffer, how many curses would *it* endure, this scrap of humanity, born in a circus wagon with strangers looking on?

# A Baby

**Corney Sage – Chittick's Circus, Birmingham**

It's my belief that the poor woman would have cried herself hoarse had the baby not come when it did. As it was she was well nigh beyond her own strength and using up someone else's by the time the morning came and with it the child. And when Joe opened the door and let me in for a moment, I was more put out by the sight of her lovely face all strained and white by the long effort she had been through than – but more of that.

She opened her eyes and took my hand in her own, which was cold and damp, and I wondered if she knew me at all, it took her so long to speak. But speak she did, in a low, faint voice, and with a sour breath, so that I had to hold mine.

'Mr Sage, Joe tells me that you have waited all night.'

I could not tell a lie. It was a cold vigil, on the steps of the wagon, and though I fetched a blanket from one of the horses, and pulled up the brazier, I still felt closer to the icy stars than the warm earth. But I could not say to her what I really thought: that I would rather sit out under the sky for a month than be in that wagon for a night. So I just nodded.

'You are both true gentlemen and true friends. How I will ever repay you I don't know.'

I looked over at Joe who was sitting on the steps. His face was like a stone statue, not that I've seen many statues of men of colour, though I've seen some waxwork and he was fairly like that. Still, and no inclination to blink or move his eyes about. I wished he would say something. But perhaps he too was worn out.

I had done everything he asked. I took orders from a black fellow, and I never struggled once. I got blankets, I found cleanish towels, I heated water in the pans. Just as he said. And when all that was done, I knocked on the wagon door. When he opened it, I could so smell the pain within that it shot me back down the steps, and I was standing on the ground like some fool, looking up at him. I came closer, with one foot on the first step, and I could just see past him, and the dark shape of the lady in the cupboard bed. I gazed and gazed, and suddenly – oh horror! I thought the sight would blind me – she turned her face towards me, her mouth drawn open in a scream, what had no sound to it. And it went on and on until I thought I should go to Bedlam.

'For God's sake, Joe!' I cried. 'Let me go for a doctor!'

But he shook his head, and she screamed, 'No! No doctors! No doctors here!' And then in a small voice, that was full of tears and misery, she said, 'Only Helen! Let Helen come!'

We didn't know any Helen, but I heard Joe saying she'd been sent for, and she fell to weeping again. I stood there in the yard for some while, looking at that old door to the wagon, and thinking how it needed a coat of paint, and how I would do it a nice bright red, like I'd seen some of the other wagons, and with flowers creeping up the sides. It would be a pleasant task, and I would take satisfaction in it, for I'm a man who likes to be busy. And then suddenly there was another awful cry from within, like there was an animal in there just trying to get out and though I knew it was that lady, I ran inside the circus like every devil was after me.

I found myself a stall with a nice, quiet mare – Beauty, in fact, as gentle as gentle – and pushed myself into a corner and covered myself over with straw for my shame. Now I fell asleep, I can't hardly say how, for when I lay down I was cold, and shaking, and strung up like a fiddle. But perhaps the warm straw and the breathing of the horses round me, and the sweet smell of their bodies, were like a drug to me. For when I awoke I was calm, and everything around me was still, and the lamp on the post was burning low. Outside the sky was dark, but coming light around the edges, and too early yet for birds singing, but as I stepped quietly across the yard, there was a sound – it was like the low moaning from the wagon had never ceased all that time. And as I came closer, Joe must have heard me, for he opened the door and I could see from his face, how it was strained and tired. There was blood on his hands, too, and stripes of it down his shirt.

He said quietly, 'She's very bad, Mr Corney, and only the Lord knows if she will survive. And as for the child, well, I reckon you should say some prayers.'

I protested that I didn't know any (which is not true), and Joe said that he thought the Lord God wouldn't mind what I said as long as I meant it. But I'm not a believing man, so I said nothing, and I often wonder if I *had* said a word or two whether things would have taken a different direction. So, when I should have been praying I was sitting out on the steps of the wagon, with the dead embers in the brazier before me, and Beauty's blanket about my shoulder, watching the night sky melt into day, and stopping up my ears with my two fingers when her cries got bad, and wondering how such things come about.

My old master used to talk about the 'fetch 'n' carry of life', how you fetch your own fortune and carry it with you till the right time comes up and then you put it down. How there was no reason to it, and a man might wonder till he fell to dust but he could never bottom it. I wondered for a while, watching the sky pink up over the chimneys, how it was that I plucked this woman, whose name I didn't know, from all those around the station, and how it was that I was a-sitting on these hard steps instead of lying warm in my bed, listening to her cries, rather than Mr Halls's snores. I felt like I was watching myself. Over my own hunched shoulder.

Suddenly, the terrible cries from within reached a pitch that I can't hardly describe (and don't want to recall) and, of all the people in the wide world, they greeted Chittick as he come around the corner and opened the gate. It was like a drama what you see in a poor theatre. One of those where bad things are always happening to the good characters, and those bad things are spied out by the bad characters, who use it agin the good, and cause all the trouble. Chittick covered the yard with a great speed, and was about to push me aside and go into the wagon when the lady let out a cry that stopped him in his shoes, and instead he set upon me, cracking me across the shins with his stick.

'What's all this, Duke? Is this a circus or a lying-in ward?'

I was much taken by his observation, though I quickly realized that he might have a pretty broad knowledge of childbearing, having six of his own. I explained briefly, and made much of the panic of the previous evening, even suggesting that things might have been 'brought on' by the crush and the alarm of the fire-crackers. I added that she was a respectable woman, and would no doubt feel obliged to recompense (a good word) him for the use of his wagon when she was in the way of moving about again.

I believe he was about to turn all sides of this inside out when the door opened and Joe, wiping his hands, filled the doorway. Now if Chittick had been inclined to vent his meanness on Joe – and I believe it crossed his mind – he very quickly thought again. Here was the Negro, with bloody hands and sweating like a horse, and asking – silently, for he was mute again – for a drink of water, and one for the lady, and giving Chittick such a look as stopped up his mouth then and there.

And so it was the Gov'nor who returned with a can of water, and who directed me to get the fire lit and coffee made. Who peered around Joe's legs at the figure in the cupboard bed and the bundle in the drawer next to it, and shook his head and shambled off into the building. Which was when I saw her lovely face and went and took her hand, and sat with her till Joe came and touched my shoulder. She was asleep, and it was like her beauty had been strained from her. It was still there, but pulled thin and pale.

Joe had washed his hands and covered his bloody shirt, and was drinking coffee from a tin. The child – I assumed that was what was in the drawer – was still. Dead, I thought, which was sad after all that pain and crying. But that was that. So it was in the quiet, as we sat alongside each other at the top of the wagon step, that I couldn't help a curious look or two at Joe. I had discovered things about him that night which I would never have thought in a donkey's age. Here was a Negro who was mute, but not, and who knew about things that most men, black or white, did not. And who was not afraid.

'My master was a physician,' he said, and I was took aback again, for he seemed to be able to read minds too. 'Since I was a very little child I was with him, and he showed me things, and taught me about the body and how it works. He gave me the skill, taught me how to open up a man and stitch him again, to give him medicines that will take away pain or make him forget.'

'Why?' I said, not entirely believing him. 'Why should he show you? I expect you were a slave.'

'True. But my master suffered a seizure, and his hands became slow. His speech was like a drunkard's, but his mind was still sharp. He taught me, and I was his hands. He directed me, and I was his machine.'

That took some thinking about, and we were silent for a while.

'I have brought many children into the world, though none quite as difficult as this. I had no way of relieving her pain. Which was very great. There was much bleeding. The child was—'

He stopped and looked very hard at me.

'She does not realize. She does not know. When she knows, I think she will die.'

Know what? He stood up slowly and went into the wagon and, picking up the bundle, and looking keenly at the sleeping woman, stepped carefully back out again. He cradled it in his arms, and I thought (as I often do when I remember him) how powerful those arms were and how slight that bundle. He pulled the towels apart and looked intently at the child.

'Mr Sage, sir, it cannot live. It will surely die.'

Now I am not a fanciful man. I have seen the world (some of it), its wonders (few) and its horrors (many). If there is a God, he does not know me, and I do not choose to know him. I can do without him, and he won't miss me. But, as Joe handed me the child, there I was, saying something my father, Mr Figgis, had taught me many years ago.

> *Little child, remember, in God's sight*
> *Thou are more precious than sunlight,*
> *More treasured than the pearls and gold*
> *Of emperors and kings of old.*
> *Sweet babe, thou art the work of God—*

Here, as I gazed upon the babe, the words froze up in my mouth.

It was a very tiny creature. Indeed, the cloths in which it was wrapped weighed more, and when it lay in my hand, there was no more weight to it than a feather. I parted the cloths, and looked inside. Its body looked like that of a baby bird. Too much skin and bone, and arms and legs, thin as wisps of straw, jerking and shuddering. And all of it covered with hair, which was long and fine. A head too great for its body, and traced all over with blue threads. And though its eyes were tight shut, its mouth was wide open and sending out a noise, from the back of its throat, which I still hear. It was raw and dry, like the call of a hungry creature, casting around for food.

I nearly dropped it. I wonder now if I should have dashed its brains out upon the steps and – but, no. Joe took it from me and pulled the towel about it.

'The poor creature has come before its time. It needs milk, which she cannot provide. She is too weak. I think she will die.'

'Then *it'll* die, Joe, and a good thing too.'

He shook his head and frowned. 'It's a life, Mr Corney, and we must preserve it. What milk do we have?'

Only the mare, Cora, whose foal had died. The poor creature was milk-bound and suffered agonies each day while hard-handed grooms relieved her.

And so, as its mother slept, never stirring, hardly seeing day or night, her child lay in Joe's arms and supped on mare's milk.

⟞⟨◦⟩⟝

Until this time I was mostly lined up. I had my berth in the circus, and an eye on Mrs Chittick, who was tipping me the nod and letting me know she was not disinclined herself. There was steady work to get the show ready for the tenting and the prospect of employment for as-long-as, and I didn't mind the clowning now I had some wheezes in my pocket and wasn't all the time being kicked by the horses or the Gov'nor. I had a comfortable shop in the Mammoth establishment, and no cause to complain.

But the fetch-and-carry of life changed all that and no mistake. Here was a sick woman and a sick baby, and neither one of them looked likely to see Christmas. The lady said her name was Marsh (but I know now that it was a false one) and she was fairly wrung out, and slept so long I thought she would never wake. Maybe it would have been better if she *had* just slipped off in her sleep, for then she wouldn't have had the world of troubles that she faced when she woke up.

It was the day after the child was born when she started very sick, and Joe, who was already fagged, was looking out for her again. Mrs Chittick looked into the wagon once and pronounced 'childbed fever' and made haste away. The fever was on her, red-hot, so that she knew no one and saw visions that sent her shouting and thrashing about. Then she complained of pains and how they hurt so much she could not bear to move so much as a finger. And the smell was like she was rotting from inside. Indeed, it hung about the wagon fearfully, for Joe would have the door and window open, saying (to me) that there needed to be clean air about her. And he had buckets of water and soap to scrub the floors, and had all the bed-linen burned and fresh brought (Mrs Chittick sent her third best).

We were burning sulphur candles, of course, for Joe said they was the only thing. But Chittick was afeard the stink would drive away customers, and having the wagon in the yard and Joe in attendance did cause some interest of the wrong sort. Mrs Marsh was in a poor way, her fever showing no sign of letting up, even after three days, and Joe all the time by her side, and Chittick getting impatient. The truth was that he was anxious to leave, there being only a children's audience these days, which made a deal of mess and trouble. So the wagons were brung out, and mornings were spent painting and oiling, and repairing rotten bottoms. Bills had been printed, announcing 'Last Week of the Season' in black letters which shouted about 'specials' and 'benefits' which, of course, never come about. Not like the theatre, where benefits are the marker for the end of the season, and all the company hopes to put a bit extra in their pocket by a good turnout. Chittick was not of that mould, and what he took in the box he was inclined to keep. Not a man who had charitable thoughts, wasn't Chittick, but a man of business on account of having pulled himself up, as he often reminded me. I knew he was on the lookout for me, and had avoided him, being more nimble of foot than he, but he caught me one evening after the show had finished, when I was sat on an upturned bucket taking a breather.

'You, Duke o' York,' he cried, 'when's your Mrs What's-her-name-beyond going to be out of my wagon? I aren't no Chittick's Mammoth Charity, unless you didn't know.'

I could see he was pleased with his clever remark, for he was puffing and huffing himself about, and waiting for me to laugh. But I was in no mood. Truth to tell, the last few days had made me think again and my thoughts were that I might clock out of the clowning business, having taken one too many cuffs from the Gov'nor, not to mention a decided coldness on the part of Mrs Chittick. Pleasant though some of it was, there was not enough money in the circus life to make it worth enduring the thumps and cusses I regular received, and a cold cot to boot rendered it hardly comfortable.

The Gov was in full flow now, fairly bursting with funniosities.

'She does nowt but wail,' he was complaining in a feigned northern accent. I heard tell he was from Putney, which is south, and also Easington-lane, which is north, but my view is that he was from nowhere at all, born on the road. The point being, of course, that he believed he knew all men and tongues.

'She stinks the place out, and Mrs says there have been complaints from our neighbours.'

Who were, on one side, a glue factory, and on the other a brewery: complainants who knew a good stink when they nosed one, I reminded him.

But *he* was the only man making wheezes, and I ducked under his fist as he made to cuff me.

'*I* keep you, and don't you forget it!' he said with that nasty curl to his mouth. '*I'm* master around here. *I'm* the one who's pulled himself up, and *I'll* say what's what. *She* goes.'

I had half expected it. He knew a good trap when he saw one.

'Now,' he says, 'we are moving shortly, and if you wants to keep your shop, you'll get rid of her.'

I protested. How could I do such a thing? She was sick and likely to die. And where would she go? He was not inclined to listen, he said. It was not his business. No more was it mine. She had outstayed her welcome. And indeed, he had been more than generous in allowing her to lay her head in his caravan which, though it no more belonged to him than to me, was a-setting on land for which he was paying rent. Therefore – and how he did enjoy holding forth like a lawyer's clerk! – no court in this great land would deny him his right to turn her off as soon as he liked.

I blame myself for what happened next, for I should have been more careful. It was like this. Joe and I had some talks (at a distance from the circus, of course) about Mrs Marsh and her kiddie. Joe was of the opinion (and I had no cause to doubt him, since he'd been on the spot up to now), that she was not long under the stars. Only days, he said, and certain she looked in a very bad way. Indeed, worse than her child, which though it was a terrible creature to look upon and no mistake, seemed not against supping mare's milk and rallying. And while its mother sweated and turned about in her bed, it lay still and calm, with eyes as big as balloons, and arms and legs all the time grasping and kicking against thin air like a spider's. The hair what covered it when it was born still remained, like cobwebs, and long too. And when it cried – oh, my life! Not loud, but unnatural, dry and thin in the back of its throat. Not like a baby at all.

Joe undertook to care for both of them, as well as his grooming and sweeping. Some days he couldn't hardly support himself on his two feet, and I felt bad for him and would have helped only – I cannot tell a lie – I had a horror of the child and would rather sit out

206

upon the road than sit within and know it was a-lying there in its box in the corner. I think Joe understood for he never pressed me, but just seemed glad of my company whether I was within or without. So we were odd pals, and many in the circus made comment, if not about Joe, then about the ailing woman what most of them had never seen. And truth to say, it *was* a strange thing for though circus folk are generous to their own, they are not always welcoming of outsiders. They are, so to speak, wary of them, and even I was still looked upon without favour by some. Equestriennes in particular. When they slipped into their St Giles's Greek, these ladies abused you something terrible, Joe told me, and never held back, so you felt like you was in a foreign land in your own country when you stepped past them and they began jabbering and nodding to each other.

They were curious about Mrs Marsh, and rightly so, for most mothers want to show off their babby even if they're not feeling too spry. But we were 'closed up' and babby was not for view, naturally, so they were feeling put out and suspicious. It was only a matter of time, though, before the true state of play was known and it happened almost by accident. Miss Rosa (Daisy Birkin to her mother) was passing by the caravan, saw the door open and unguarded, and went in sharpish. Simple as soap. But she come out all of a-shake, and it took no time at all for her to do the rounds of the other horse-ladies and for them all to come out and stare at the wagon. Then out comes Mrs Chittick and they bend her ear, and then the Gov, puffing and huffing and grizzly, for he's been brung out of the public before his time, and he comes bursting forward and elbows himself past me, who is a-sitting on the steps and trying not to be noticed, and into the wagon, where there's Joe and Mrs Marsh and babby.

He comes out a deal quieter than he went in, and takes Mrs to one side, and she – I suppose she thought he was boozy – digs him hard and goes in herself to verify. And *she* comes out, with Joe, who is wiping his hands and looking ready for a fight. But there is no fight, and everyone goes back to their business, and I get ready for the show, and Joe, after giving the world the dark eye, shuts the door tight.

If the Gov knew something about babbies and childbearing, he also knew something about exhibiting, for, no doubt about it, he had words with Mrs and stared at the bottom of a few glasses and, red as a boiled lobster, caught me by the sleeve as I was crossing the yard. I will not attempt to describe the many rambles he went through to find his way to his finish, but it turned out something like this.

'She goes. Babby stays.'

I protested. She was the babby's mother, and it was not Christian, not human, not right to separate them. Gov shook his head like it would fall off into his lap.

'Babby will make bags of shiners, if it's given out properly, and who knows better than me, Chittick, how to do that.' And he puffs himself up and waves his arm in the direction of the caravan where, because it's getting dark, Joe has drawn the little curtains and put a friendly lamp in the window. Gov is in full flow of his own importance. 'It's all in the telling, Corney. You know, a good showman can make a flatfish a whale, and turn water into best ale if he knows how to talk them up. And here' – and he waves again at the caravan with a triumphant, know-it-all look on his face – 'here is the Fairy Child what I, Chittick, will talk up.'

I had no doubt at all that the Gov was as good as his claims and could make something of the babby, for in truth it had a good start, being a monster to begin with. But I couldn't in my conscience forget Mrs Marsh, whose pale face and terrible cries haunted me by day and night. I wondered if it was time to get out that piece of paper she had given me weeks ago and seek those friends of hers (and mine, of course) in Lower Marlpool-street. I resolved to do so, and showed the paper to Joe, and told him what Chittick planned and what I planned: to go to the Great Turk and see if they were still there. But I kept it close that I knew Lucy, for I still had a worry, like an itch I couldn't reach, and I didn't know what it was. Joe was all for the plan.

'I think that is all we can do for her, Mr Corney. We should find her friends and beg them to care for her and the child.'

Which is what we did the following day, leaving the poor lady sweating and only half herself, and the child lying in its box.

# 12

## *The Sisters Bellwood, Again*

### Corney Sage – Brummagem streets

Joe and I set off, tidy and licked, with a notion that our errand would be soon crossed off, that Mrs Marsh and her kid had the prospect of kind friends and a brighter future, and that afterwards we might look after ourselves. The prospect of tenting around the country, building up and pulling down the tent every day, with Chittick nasty and tight as a Jew's pocket, had bothered me for a while, and not being one to stand about and wait for the situation to slap me around the face, I had already consulted the Organ of the Profession and found myself a nobby little shop (so I hoped) in a town I had never heard of, but whose name suggested country and quiet. I was thinking on this and how I ought to look out my little book of wheezes and songs and write out a few notes for the bandsmen as we traversed the Brummagem streets.

We had walked ourselves into a street close by the railway station and the public squares, a street full of shops of every kind (what street in Brummagem isn't!). Some had uniforms hanging outside, pressed and clean, or stained and drab, all the buttons gone west with the braid. Some showed tins and pans, crate-loads of forks and spoons, pots sitting up in wobbly towers, and strewn about with straw. Great baskets of cups and saucers, stew pots and jars, along-

210

side candles and lamps. And in between these busy places, the black hole of an empty shop, the plate windows covered up with white paint and a square for a peep-hole cut in, and outside a drum and an Irishman got up in a skirt, shouting to all comers, 'Here it is! About to start! Listen here now! The show's about to start!'

But that was not all, and Joe too had stopped, mid-track, as it were, and laid his black hand upon my arm. We were not mistaken, for it was indeed a pile of tripes and guts laying in the middle of the pavement, buzzing with flies and starting to dull off in the sun. Being in the performing line, we were naturally brought up to wonder at this and with Joe still hanging on to my coat sleeve – though he didn't need to stop me – we waited outside the blacked-out shop in company with the Irishman and the drum and a gang of Brummagems of all ages to see what wonder might emerge from the doorway.

We were not disappointed! As a youth with a wasted arm laboured away on the drum, a fellow in a tidy suit and shiny hat strides out of the shop and, seeing us, stopped in his tracks. I say 'seeing us', but only after he had seen every single body in the street, every likely bearer of a penny, even down to a little girl without teeth and a milk-can in her hand, and a drayman watering his horse. He was a real showman, eyes everywhere, taking in the opportunities, weighing them up, throwing out the halt and the lame, and calculating profit and loss while he picked his teeth and kicked the pot-boy. He circled the tripes, being careful not to step in the puddle of blood and muck that was creeping out from underneath them, and looked up and down the street again, all the whiles, so it seemed, looking at us.

I had seen his kind before (though never at such close quarters), so that when he met my eye, it seemed to me we were brothers somewhat.

'Just about to begin, gentlemen,' he said in a southern tongue.

'Step inside, why don't you!' and I liked the way he licked his lips, and ran the edge of his finger along his moustache, to neaten it up I thought. There was a cockiness about him, like he owned that bit of Brummagem street and God-help-anyone-who-tried-to-take-it-off-him!

I was all for seeing what was inside the shop, for it seemed to me there was a-roaring and a-yelling in there that wanted investigating, but Joe held back, murmuring that we needed to be on our errand. Besides which, a crowd was gathering, and it became noticeable, to us and the showman, that some were looking at his show, and some were looking at Joe. I should say (for I believe I have omitted this in my haste) that Joe was unusual in his own way, being small of stature, though perfectly formed, he assured me, in every other way. Now I am no longshanks, but Joe looked my belly-button fully in the eye, and no higher. So we made a curious pair, with my carroty hair and his short legs, and folks might have thought we were part of the show. Indeed, before we had decided to move on, the showman had made certain of it and we was standing square to the tripes and guts whiles he was talking up a crowd.

'Now, my dear friends, you see before you a mere taste of the delights within. Look here upon Little Snowball, the smallest Negro you will ever see. Arrived only today from deepest Mississippia, and come straight here. His mother was the most beautiful woman, and she went with the missionaries, taking the Bible to the deepest jungles and the most ignorant of natives. People who never covered themselves, nor washed, nor had never heard of our Queen Victoria nor good Bass ale. And it was while she was about this good work that she was captured by these natives, and taken roughly in a boat down the river to their village. And the chief of all of them, when he saw her, found that she was the most beautiful creature he had ever seen . . .'

Me, Joe, the crowd, we were all open-mouthed, hanging upon every word he said. Even the boy on the drum stopped his beating and leaned upon it, like there was nowhere more comfortable in the whole place. And even though the flies were settling and rising up, and that pile of tripes and guts was starting to make itself known in another way, the crowd grew by the moment, people pressing and elbowing and telling each other to quiet up, so they could hear the story.

'. . . her hair a-falling down her back like a stream of gold. And this native chief, he has never before seen such a thing, for all *his* native women have black hair, which is as rough as a donkey's back. So he decides he will have her for his thirty-second wife.'

Gasps all round!

'She declines!' cried the showman, who has warmed up so much that he has taken off his shiny hat, revealing his own golden hair underneath. 'She refuses, ladies and gentlemen! "As I am a Christian woman," she exclaims, "I cannot agree, though you torture me!"'

Another gasp from the crowd, and the young lad drops his drumstick.

'"Ah," says the chief, "I will not torture *you*. But, for every day you refuse to marry me, I will kill one of your people." For he had captured the missionaries as well. And there and then he brought out one of them, and laid his head on a block of wood and prepared to smash it with a rock! The very block of wood, the very rock are displayed within for your enlightenment, ladies and gentlemen!'

Some of the women screamed in horror, and that sent a cloud of flies buzzing up again. But no one shifted, not an inch. In fact, everyone appeared more determined to hear the end of the story. When they had settled down – and not until – the showman commenced his story again.

'"Stop!" demanded the golden-haired angel. "I will not sacrifice one of these good people for my honour. I am only a poor Christian woman bringing the Bible to the ignorant savage, and I cannot let these people die. Marry me if you will!" And so he did, that very day. And there was a great feast, and crocodiles were hunted down and roasted, for they were a great delicacy. And the skins of these very creatures can be seen within on payment of one penny. Now Little Snowball's mother was a good woman . . .'

Everyone turned to look at Joe who, if he had been able to, would have blushed.

'. . . and she made the chief promise to let all the missionaries go, so as they could do their good work somewhere else along the river, while she stayed behind. So they went and left her behind, among the savages, where her clothes soon ran to rags and her shoes fell to pieces in the jungle heat. The chief was good to her, but the other thirty-one wives were jealous, and had a tendency to pick on her and make her miserable. Because she was such a new wife, she was given the worst of tasks, which meant she had to tend the heads cut from the enemies of the chief.' (More shrieks.) 'These heads were boiled in great pots of herbs and magic roots upon a fire in the middle of the village. Heads that bobbed around in the great stew pots, so that they grew smaller and smaller, to the size of taters, yet all the features remained, and were then hung up all round the village to frighten off any intruders. She had to tend them. To make sure that the pots never boiled dry. And when they were cooked, she had to pick 'em out and hang 'em up to dry! These can be seen within. The very heads, with hair and teeth, ladies and gentlemen, what she picked out of the pots!'

The crowd buzzed as loud as the flies, and the showman took a pause and looked hard at me and Joe, as if to say, 'Don't you move!' But we weren't thinking of moving. We wanted to know what happened to Joe's ma!

He began again and the crowd fell silent.

'So one night, thinking that she could bear no longer the attentions of the village chief and the boiling and hanging up of the heads, she escaped, stealing out of the village and taking one of the boats, which she was skilful enough to manage. She sailed up the river, all the time expecting to see the chief coming after her.

214

For she knew that if he caught her, she too would end up in one of the pots, with all her golden hair a-streaming out!'

The crowd was enormous now, spilling out into the road, and pressing harder and harder towards the shop, so that the only space was around the tripes and around us.

'When she reached civilization, ladies and gentlemen, she found a good English family what took her in and looked after her, gave her clothes and shoes, and fed her on good English tea and white bread and butter.' (Murmurs of approval.) 'And soon after she produced Little Snowball, here,' gesturing at Joe, who looked surprised and then uncomfortable. 'But imagine her horror when she realized that her child had taken on some of the characteristics of that terrible task she was forced to endure by her savage master! That his poor body had shrunk like the heads she had watched, bobbing in those pots every day! Is it any wonder, though? Breathing in those foul fumes? Being splashed by the poisonous stew?'

Everyone in the crowd stared hard at Joe, and I swear all you could hear was the buzzing of the flies. And the showman let them look a good long time, while Joe, if he could have shrunk any more, would have done so to escape their attentions.

'But poor Little Snowball's mother died.' (Gasp.) 'The agonies she endured I cannot describe, and even the attentions of an English doctor brought from London by the good English family could not save her. She died in a foreign land, and is buried there, in a corner of the graveyard under a good English oak tree. Little Snowball was happy for a time, but then the good English family left, and he was given to be cared for by a family who sold him into slavery. A little child! Friendless! Abandoned! But that is another story, ladies and gentlemen! Now, now is the time to enter Soloman's Great Eastern Emporium and see for yourself the shrunk-up heads, the crocodiles, the execution block and the bloody stone! Only a penny to enter! Commencing now!'

With that, the showman gave the boy and his drum an urgent look, though it took the boy some moments before he could drag himself out of the jungle and apply himself to beating. And in fact he was hardly needed. Everyone in the crowd, it seemed, wanted to step around and about the pile of tripes and guts and pay their penny to see the crocodiles, and the heads, and the wooden block and bloody stone as promised. They had another good long look at Joe as they queued to go in, and Joe, though he was acting like his britches was full of fleas, let them have a last eyeful. Of course, they had an eyeful for nothing, and we knew it, and wondered what the showman would do, for I could see by the look of him that he had something in mind. Moving us along the shop – but not away from it – he produced some coins which he pressed into Joe's hand.

'That's to show to you that I'm an honest man and I pay what's fair and deserving,' he said.

He was right too. We could have legged it, off down the street, and then there would have been no Little Snowball and no crocodiles. (Though I've often wondered since how he could have known we would come along. We were a stroke of luck and no mistake!)

Joe took the coins and nodded, but all the while eager to get away.

The showman turned to me. 'Your friend has been a booster to my business. Where do you live? *How* do you live?'

*I* wanted to ask the questions, and know how he came to be able to string out a tale like he did! And were there really crocodiles within, for I had a powerful fancy for them! But I kept it short.

'We're circus men,' I said eventually. 'With Chittick.'

The showman nodded. 'I know Chittick. A hard man. *All* circus men are hard. It's the way of the business.'

'The money's on the drum each Friday,' I replied, though I didn't disagree with him. 'He's sure.'

I couldn't help myself, I had to ask him about Joe – and Snowball

– and the heads; and the bloody rock. Where did he find them? And the heads? Had he got all of them? So many questions. The showman's face was as serious as my questions, and he rubbed his moustache thoughtfully.

'True to you,' he said in a low voice, 'people mostly want to believe what you tell 'em. But you must give 'em a reason. Stand this young man' – and he put his hand upon Joe's shoulder – 'in a church or a chapel, tell the congregation that his mother was a missionary and died at the hands of the heathen, and they will cry 'Hallelujah' and shake his hand and *perhaps* put their coppers in the collecting plate. But round them up with plenty of noise, show them a nobby flash and a smart individual' – I believe he was referring to himself – 'give them the smell of the jungle, tell them they will see a bloody stone and shrunken heads, and as many marvels as you want to create in their heads, and I tell you they will pay their pennies over and over for that privilege.'

It sounded flash, but I was not convinced, and must have betrayed myself by the look upon my face, for the showman pointed to the boy with the wasted arm, who had given up on the drum, and was now staring down a gang of street kids who were trying to sneak into the shop for free.

'That's Freddy McHenry. His mother, while he was still in the womb, witnessed a terrible accident in which a boy lost his arm to a steam-threshing engine on a farm in Devon. All was well until he reached the age of eight years, but from that age onward Freddy McHenry's arm was liable, at any moment, to shrink and shrivel up so that only his fingers could be seen, and those half the size they should be. When I first came across him, the shrivelling and the shrinking was so severe that it had almost reached his shoulder, and had I not treated him there and then, I very much fear that his arm would have disappeared altogether.'

He shook his head and looked me straight in the eye.

'Even now, Mr Merryman, even now, that arm begins to reduce if exposed to excessive sunlight. Or the noise of a steam-thresher.'

I gazed in wonder at the youth who had no idea that he was being talked of, and was getting himself ready to charge the kids and lay about them with his drumstick. The showman also gave him a long eyeballing.

'What would you say if I told you that Freddy McHenry's arm, which you see before you, can be restored by the application of a specially prepared salve?'

'I should say, let me see it work, and I will believe you,' said I, quickly falling into this line of thinking.

He smiled. 'Then I will show you,' and he called to the lad to roll up his shirtsleeve. His arm was certainly short and thin, little more than a bone with the skin hanging upon it, though the sun was glaring and I was forced to shade my eyes.

'Soloman's Sure Salve is applied,' announced the showman, and the lad produced a pot from his pocket, took a good dollop of the stuff and rubbed it vigorously, like a washerwoman, into his arm which I swear began to grow before my eyes. Where there were just stubs for fingers, big ones appeared and in length that arm grew inches and, I do believe, had another dollop of the salve found its way there, would have produced an arm rather too long than too short. I remarked that the showman ought to guard his recipe very carefully, for there were those who would stop at nothing to lay their hands upon medicine so miraculous, and indeed if he had a pot to spare, I would gladly purchase one. Joe shook his head and turned away from me, and I felt a little put out by his manner. The showman was not at all bothered, and produced a small, gaily coloured jar, covered with shooting stars and grinning imps, and 'Soloman's Sure Salve' exploding out of a cloud in fiery letters.

'A gift,' he said, and I was ready to argue with him, and at least offer him a penny or two, but he took off the lid and begged me to smell the compound. I took a noseful, and wanted to say goose fat, and on the turn, but feared offending him. It did have all the appearance of goose fat, being thick and greasy and grey, and the pong was not difficult to place, but I knew it could not be, for this, according to the label, and the showman, and Freddy McHenry's lengthening arm, was Soloman's Sure Salve.

Joe grabbed the jar, sniffed it and quickly handed it back.

'Goose fat,' he said, and the showman smiled.

'True to you, young Snowball.'

I wanted to argue, but Joe tugged my arm with urgency now.

'Remember,' said the showman, 'that folks *want* to believe. If I say this is Soloman's Sure Salve, then it's true, if you want it to be. Why should you not? Why should you *not* believe your eyes? Why should goose fat *not* cure a wizened arm, or anything else, if you want it to? And if *I* tell you it can.'

Why not indeed!

'It is the very essence of showmanship!' he said, smoothing his moustache, and making it sound so deep, so full of meaning, that it might have dropped from the lips of a parson in a pulpit.

Joe again pulled hard at my elbow, and I lifted my hat and made a polite farewell. The showman did likewise.

'If you're ever in need of a shop, come and see me. I have other shows hereabouts and I can always use two good men. Particularly young Snowball here,' and he nodded towards Joe, who nodded back. 'The name's Roscius Soloman, the Bountiful Beauty, the Emperor of the East.' And with that he disappeared into the shop like a rabbit into a wizard's hat, pushing his way through the crowds of people eager to sample the crocodiles and heads. I would have gone in myself, but for Joe's urgent tugs.

He was silent for most of our journey, while I was still considering the Sure Salve and the wizened arm and heads shrunk down to taters, but after half an hour's walking he took my arm again and directed me into an alleyway full of nothing but mossy cobblestones where the sun never lit them, and dead cats what crept there to die. We stood in the shadows looking down that dim and narrow gap between Godkins's horsemeat shop and an empty building, occupied by rats and tramps. It was quiet and damp, though the sunny street, full of people about their business, was only a step or two away.

'What's up, Joe?' I said, for I had a sense of his unease.

Joe rubbed his knees: they pained him, he often said, on account of his short legs being set oddly and his feet being on the large side. When he walked any distance, he did so with a roll, and that roll became greater as he got more tired and so his knees pained him. He crouched down and gave a sigh, and I perched on a burst sack of straw, scattering mice underneath me.

'Mr Corney, sir,' he said in his deep voice. 'We must decide what is best for the lady. And the child. If we don't then others will, and they will decide what is best, what is profitable, for *them*. We have a duty to care for those who cannot care for themselves, but we, you and I, we cannot look after Mrs Marsh. So we must find these ladies, the Misses Bellwood, as Mrs Marsh asks us to, and urge them to take her in. I think you must say to them that, if they will not take their friend in and give her a home, she will die. I think you must say this to them in a way that they understand.'

I wanted to ask him about the child, and he looked into my head before I had the chance.

'If the child remains here alone,' says he, rubbing his poor knees, 'it will die. If the child goes with its mother, it will die. But it is better that it dies in the arms of its mother than alone and with strangers.'

Easy to say, Joe, returns I, but how to do it? We knew what Chittick had in mind for the child. Always with an eye on making a quid, he planned to exhibit it. Buy up a nice painting of a child with a head as big as Wales (two a penny if you knew where to look), work up a little stage with curtains, find a female to hold the kid and a talkative cove to tell the tale and there's a tidy earner. At a penny a throw, before the main show and all day until the kid died, it was an easy blow-off. And, though he didn't have the style of Soloman, Chittick was a showman and knew how to do it.

Joe agreed.

'And another thing, Mr Corney, although it is right that we save the child, we must also save ourselves. Mr Chittick will regard himself as a cheated man. He will be angry, and if he finds out what we have done, he will blame us. He will think that he could have earned plenty of money with this poor baby, and we – his clown and his groom – have deprived him. Yes, I think he will be very angry!'

I thought Joe had about put his moniker on it right enough. Chittick's anger was not something I wanted to dwell upon, having often had a sample of it. But I was out of the circus line soon enough anyway, having found that tidy berth from the *Era*, and thinking about that reminded me of the scrap of paper torn from that very Organ of the Profession which was even now in my pocket. The one given to me at the Railway Hotel by Mrs Marsh. I brought it out, intending to look again at the card for the Sisters Bellwood and flattened it upon my knee. I thought I had put it more carefully into my pocket, for the paper was curled around the edges, so I turned it over the better to straighten it out.

> feat of throwing a double somersault. They have a large troupe of vaulters.
>
> BIRMINGHAM
> Chittick's Mammoth Equestrian hippodrome and zoological circus are still amusing this town. The novelties produced at this establishment are beyond the average expectancy of its

numerous visitors. Miss Martinetti on the tightrope is a most
competent little artiste, and an act of horsemanship by Mr
Martinetti, entitled 'The Wild Indian' was portrayed in a
most daring and intrepid style. The various clowns are droll
and witty, a new addition, Mr Corney Sage (Funny Foodle),
in particular. We also witnessed the clever feats of a highly
trained camel conducted by Mr Crockett.

I read it. Then I read it again, for I was taken by surprise to see
my own name sat large as life before me in such a respected newspaper. And I turned it over and there on the back were the Sisters
Bellwood, a little crumpled. And then I turned it back and there was
yours truly. Here in my other hand was an address for the Sisters
Bellwood. And all these pieces of paper were handed to me by a
lady (of sorts) who even as we sat in the alleyway was sweating her
life away, and who said Lucy and Kitty were her friends. The same
friends as me. I could not see how this could be, but it was. A coincidence multiplying over and over.

Now I have to interrupt here to say something that I have mused
over, for I am brought to mind of a story that my old master used to
tell about the time an old dog rushed out of a chandler's shop and
bit him on the leg. The wound was very great, almost to the bone,
and my old master was much inconvenienced by the injury which
took him from his work for nigh on a fortnight. But that old dog,
who was still rushing out of the same chandler's shop and doing
injuries to other innocent passers-by, was the means by which a very
great change came over my master. For it was while he was laid up
with the wound that my master came to know that his wife was
enjoying the lodger's bed, and the lodger too, who was a city clerk
and quite twenty years younger than she. My old master was unsus-
pecting, as they say, and so the discovery was a great shock to him.
That wound, he would say, given to him by the chandler's dog, left

a scar upon his leg, but also a scar upon his memory. For when that old scar pained him, it recalled his wife and the city clerk and the unhappy discovery he made.

So, like my old master, I cannot now turn the pages of the *Era* and see 'Birmingham' written in bold letters without recalling that moment when I turned over a scrap torn from it and saw my own name.

But Joe was still talking, in that slow, steady way he had, talking in rhythm with the rubbing of his poor bent legs.

'I wonder,' he was saying, 'if we might lay the blame for the disappearance of Mrs Marsh and her baby upon your landlord, Mr Halls. Perhaps we might suggest that she has been hidden away by Halls. Or got away. At least for a short time. It will be a distraction for Mr Chittick, and it will give us the opportunity to get ourselves away. But we must tread very carefully. From what I have heard, Mr Halls might also be a dangerous man.'

Clever Joe. He'd been thinking along practical lines while I was wondering about something else altogether. I had forgot about Halls and the difficulties that might entail whether he was in the plan or out of it. Like Joe said, he was a mean devil, and cunning with it, and I did not want to cross him. And in truth, I could not have forgot him even if I had wanted to (which I did), for Halls and his lung had been haunting the circus like a spirit for days, looking for me and Mrs Marsh, and asking everyone he come across where we was. Circus folk, as you know, are tight-lipped with strangers and were not about to tell him anything, even though he wheezed and held on to his chest and looked pitiful. Not that they are hardhearted. Far from it. But they can spy a mongrel when he creeps up to them, so they spun him a yarn, and Joe (who knew about Halls and how fond he was of Mrs Marsh and her trunk) had been spinning him a regular three-piecer. In mute language, of course. Yes, he'd seen missis a week ago hereabouts; no, Corney Sage he hadn't.

No, didn't know where he'd gone to. Yes, missis might have gone with him. No, he wasn't certain. Yes, possible. Yes, likely. All this fairly turned Halls about, and Joe said he couldn't hardly hold back his anger, turning red to white like a barber's pole, and no doubt thinking that he had been regular done over by one and all.

But, said Joe, that didn't knock him on the head, for he was still poking his face about and upsetting the animals and women. 'He is dangerous,' said Joe, 'like a nasty dog that licks your hand and then bites it.'

Dogs again.

All things considered, as we watched the flies buzzing around the horsemeat shop, we were in a pretty dilemma, though better off than we had been when we'd set out. Joe examined the coins what the showman had give him and found they amounted to three six-pences – the price of a cart to take Mrs Marsh and baby to her friends in Lower Marlpool-street, he said.

## 13

*Lucy Fitch*

**Corney Sage – Lower Marlpool-street**

Lower Marlpool-street was not a bad street. It was not a good street, either, being short and close-packed, with the railway yard at one end, and the other end opening out on to Upper Marlpool-street. The Great Turk was nowhere near as grand as it pretended to be, and Minton's Palace – named after the landlord, Hector Lysander Minton – was the building round the back. A concert room in cert, newly built, with its own door, indicating that Minton and his establishment was on the up. But we did not linger on the outside, having a considerable thirst, which only Felkin's Particular would serve and, as Joe reminded me, a tall order of a day's work to complete before the evening.

Within the Great Turk all was tidy and clean, and the maid (who was quite a stunner for such a back-of-the-way sort of place) was not against chatter dressed up with flattery. So, trying my hand at the showman lark of telling a good tale, I made out I was the long-lost brother of two sisters who I had traced from my home in Africa, where I owned a score of gold mines, and six hundred slaves (Joe being a sample), and as I had come into cash and was of a generous spirit, I wanted to lighten my load by 'handing over a corn-siderble amount to my dear sisters, what I had not seen since we was separated

225

as children'. I gave this tale plenty of colour, while Joe assumed his 'slavish' air – where he said nothing, looked nowhere and breathed quiet. The girl was much took, and in certain, Mr Soloman, the show-man, was to the mark when he said that people want to believe what's told them no matter how out-of-the-way or uncommon. For so took was she that she gave us house-free glasses, and twisted her curls about her finger and lifted her skirt (to show a pretty ankle) and alto-gether let me know how agreeable she might be. I was inspired.

'So you see, Tilly,' I was saying, stroking her hand (which was none too soft, and red around the knuckles), 'I am in 'aste to see my sisters, for I must be back to Africa to make sure the gold is dug out right. I cannot trust these darkies to do the job.' I give Joe a good hard stare, which he ignored. 'They would dig out the rock and leave the gold, so stupid are they!'

At this, Joe glanced at me, and I wondered if I had gone too far, but it was too late.

'H-oh yes,' gives Tilly, with a giggle and another curl of hair, 'I have 'eard that darkies have no sense at all, and are so stupid that when they are 'ungry instead of buying a pie or spud off the 'ot potato man, they eat each other!'

I was stuck for what to say, but Joe, tired of insults, looked hard at Tilly and let a great smile creep across his face, showing his white teeth, which he champed, and then smacked his lips together, and licked them round and round, and mumbled some nonsense under his breath, and started to get up. Tilly squeaked and put her hand to her mouth and it was all I could do to stop her fetching the land-lord to save her from being eaten. Instead, I put my arms about her and whispered how I would protect her and how Joe was too cowed to defy me. And to bolster this I said some nonsense to Joe which he pretended to hear with alarm. All the while, Tilly's gratitude was making itself very clear, and she crept alongside me and allowed her hands to explore the insides of my coat.

'Here,' I says, trying to make light of it, 'what are you about?'

'Why,' says she, 'I'm digging for gold.'

I won't record the rest of our conversation, it being of a low character and me promising all kinds of things (which made her and me blush) if she would tell me about my sisters. Which she did.

'Oh,' says she, 'you mean the Bonnie Sisters Bellwood. Lucy and Kitty.'

And then she frowned.

'Well, it *must* be a long time since you saw them,' says she archly. 'Don't you know them? Why, they're over there!' And she pointed to a snug corner where sat two young and sprightly girls, with a follower each hanging on their shoulders, who were having a rare time of it, laughing a lot and loudly. Fine, rorty girls, as Mr Vance would say, with pink cheeks and full lips, and a deal of bosom uncovered and knowing about it. Those followers (who also knew about it) were nicely hotted up by the girls, and putting their hands in their pockets in a regular way to keep the water of life flowing and everyone amiable. It was stunning to see how clever they performed, for they were girls who could hold any amount of drink whiles men bought them, said men getting drunk as pipers and then later, oh-ho, how their pockets are eased of coin!

And here were more dilemmas, which were mounting up like an honest man's debts, for coming here to find the Sisters Bellwood I had thought to see my pal Lucy once more. Indeed, the address upon the scrap of paper had led me to believe so and the notice from the *Era*, both the property of Mrs Marsh, she much in need of her old pals. And certain here was Kitty, sleepy and beautiful as ever, but whoever sat alongside her was not Lucy. Not Lucy Fitch. Lucy was dark and this young woman was fair. Lucy's milky skin and brown eyes, and her front ivories slightly over her bottom lip (which gave much sweetness to her appearance), and her very nature which was childlike and womanly at the very same time – all these

227

were missing in the thin and shabby girl sitting alongside Kitty, for all she laughed and tossed her head. I had almost made my mind up that here was a mistake or, even simpler, that the Sisters Bellwood had got a new sister and that Lucy was off on her own account when the door of the public opened and in walked Mrs Strong, Lucy's mother. Now that was a rum thing, for where Lucy was, there in certain within two streets was her mother, who was known to be most careful with her daughter.

So I was struck silent and was pondering this, and wondering how to explain it all to Joe. All of it, for I was thinking I should take him into my confidence, since though he might be short on his pins, his brain-box was a monster and in prime working order.

'Joe,' I mused, keeping Mrs Strong's figure in view and feeling a dryness about my mouth and throat, 'though it is said that this great world is so full of people that we can't hardly comprehend it, it can't be so big. For I have come from one bad shop a long way, so I thought, and it has trailed after and found me. Likewise, I have left faces behind and look, here they are again.'

I am afraid my eloquence was lost on Joe, so I had to spell it out for him.

'I know these girls, Joe. The Sisters Bellwood. Or I thought I did. They was with me in a previous shop, and a bad shop it was, and all kinds of miseries went with it. So I don't know how it is that they are here and I am here, and why our Mrs Marsh should know them. Or why one of them is missing, but her ma is here.'

Joe turned his glass round and round, and for once was not inclined to fire questions.

'Reckon it's what they call a co-in-cidence, Mr Corney,' he said, but he didn't seem too bothered by it.

I was bothered, though, so bothered that I turned upon my heel and found the door and, finding it, made acquaintance with the street, and with the next and the one after it. I had my hands in my pockets and my head down and if I wasn't running I was doing a close measure. Joe was in difficulty to keep up with me and I could hear his breath coming on like a steam train behind. After a time I slowed up and he caught my arm and pulled me on to the steps of a chapel where we sat, with him panting from his exertions.

'Mr Corney,' says he, between gasps and grunts, 'if you know these Sisters Bellwood why are you running away from them? And if they are friends of Mrs Marsh, then surely they will want to help her. And her baby.'

True to you, Joe, I thought. All correct and ship-shape. Here was a lady in need, here were people who she said were her friends. But on the other side of the road was a respectable lady, and here were the Sisters Bellwood, and they were chalk and cheese. Besides, one of them was missing, though her name, Lucy, was still alive. And I knew *her* very well. I knew *her* from the Constellation Concert Room, Whitechapel, and I carried a bit of her around with me, still in my pocket. The portrait of the beauty I had seen in Springwell Pavilion, the sister of John Shovelton, the man brought up for the murder of Bessie Spooner.

How was it then that the dog's bite brought back Lucy and me? Which bit of that paper, the *Era*, the Organ of the Profession, had Mrs Marsh torn out? Was it the Sisters Bellwood?

Or was it me? Mr Corney Sage (Funny Foodle), droll and witty and to be found every night in Chittock's Mammoth Circus, Birmingham? And how was it that whichever way I turned it around, there was Bessie Spooner and Lucy Fitch and Mrs Marsh?

We sat on the steps for some little while, chewing over the ins and outs of the story, which Joe pinched from me, a bit at a time, like fleas from a dog. And I believe he was much taken with it, for instead of giving me his opinion in an instant, he was quiet and thoughtful, and even gave over rubbing his knees. The steps were warm, Felkin's Particular had half done its work, and I put my back against the knotty door and let the sun warm my face. I was so comfortable I could have snoozed and perhaps did so for a moment or two, but the sound of footsteps close by made me open my eyes. Across the street, just passing a stationary horse and cart, was Mrs Strong. She was walking, head down, like she was in a hurry, not stopping to look in the shop windows, nor moving out of the way for oncomers. I nudged Joe, and we crossed over and kept within a few yards of her, for I wanted to see where she would go.

Now then, all this mystery! Like we was two regular 'tecs on the force trailing a desperate shady fellow, rather than a widow-woman with a basket and dirty boots. So we strolled along like we were meant to be there, and followed her down one street and then another, then in at a court, across a yard and a door shut behind her. It was a warm day, and the court was neighbourly. There were women sitting on doorsteps chatting and watching children playing with hoops and kicking a rag, and an old woman dozing on her chair, all in the bright sunshine. We stood at the entrance and looked around the square, and Joe wandered over to the tap and took a drink. It was like the Queen had suddenly stopped off for tea! All eyes were on Joe, and some of the children ran to their mas, much inclined to pipe their eyes. But, when he was inclined to it, Joe could be a regular charmer, and it wasn't long before those kids who had toddled off in terror were clinging to his knees, or touching his black face and woolly head. And though their mas were wary at first, soon they too wanted to have a closer look at Joe's dusky skin. It was the right moment, then, to knock upon the door behind which Mrs Strong had disappeared – and for certain that was Joe's purpose, for he tipped me the eye as the kids fell upon him.

It was a small court of two-storey houses of the poor-but-respectable brigade, and the door I was interested in was no different to any of the others. Outside sat an old woman, an invalid by the looks of her, wrapped about in shawls and blankets, no matter that the sun was hot and bright. But, 'the old feel the cold, no sin, skin's thin': that's a rhyme told me by the great Harry Henry, the oldest clog-dancer in all England and a man reputed (by himself, it has to be said) to be ninety-nine years old and who laid much store by mufflers. (And true to you, I have indeed begun to feel the benefit of a blanket about my shoulders, which often pain me, of an evening.) As I tipped my hat to her and made to knock upon the door, at that very moment it opened and Mrs Strong, almost stepping upon my toes, came out, a cup in one hand, a rag in the other. She gave me a moment's glance, and then bent over the old woman, adjusting the shawl around her head.

'I wondered if *you* might turn up, when I heard you were with the circus. You've taken your time.'

She was a sharp-tongued female always, and her temper had not improved. But caring for elderly relatives, I reflected, was probably not inclined to assist, and if Lucy was carrying on in the military widow line of business, no doubt Mrs Strong was left to shift for herself. I wondered how to bring up the subject of Mrs Marsh and her baby, though that lady's difficulties now seemed something on a par with Mrs Strong's. But perhaps Lucy might lend a hand. Or Kitty. So I launched into it, and gave her the full story and some more, for I felt she needed heavy persuading, so hard-set was her face. She let me run on without moving a feature, and indeed she might have been formed of wax or marble, so still was she. Finally, when I had run out of Mrs Marsh's miseries to share and was about to commence upon my own account, she allowed herself a shake of the head.

'I'm very sorry to hear of Mrs Marsh's difficulties,' she said, 'I am indeed. And I did say that we – I – would assist if we – I – could. She was a Mrs Collette when we knew her, of course, but a lady and no mistake.'

The old woman shifted in her chair, and a keening sound, half-way between a song and a moan, rose from the blankets. Mrs Strong laid her hand upon the old 'un, in a soothing kind of way.

'Hush, my dear.'

She looked hard at me.

'As you can see, Mr Sage, I have other duties now. She takes up a full day – and more, if there was such a thing. For she can do nothing for herself, and we would be in a workhouse or hospital if it wasn't for Kitty. Now there's a good girl for you. Never complains, but works most days in the milliner's and nights at the Turk until she can't hardly stand. And keeps me and Lucy with never a thought for herself. So I'm sure I would like to help Mrs Marsh – and I know I promised, God will forgive me – but my Lucy occupies me day and night.'

Lucy? Like a comic fool, I looked around for her. Across the court, into the sunlight where Joe was still surrounded by his admirers. And back at Mrs Strong who was wiping her brow and staring across the yard at Joe. But there was no Lucy that I could see. And then, as I glanced down at the old woman's feet, I saw, poking out from under her drab dress, a dainty pair of pink slippers. And then I took in the hands lying in her lap, which were soft and plump where they should have been scrawny. And the eyes that looked into mine were wide and brown, and with a fringe of dark lashes. Even the hair was dark and thick and curled about her shoulders and face, but that face, though it was the Lucy I knew, was still *not* the Lucy I recognized. For this mouth was half open and these lips were wet and bubbles of slaver were forming which Mrs Strong mopped up with a rag, and then set straight this head, which lolled awkwardly like a rag doll's.

I was struck dumb. I recall Mr Figgis once telling me about the man, a Bible character, whose tongue cleaved to his mouth, like it was stuck there and set, and could never be freed. And in certain, that was the state of my mouth when I realized that the woman I thought was an old woman, an invalid, was Lucy Fitch.

Mrs Strong had turned her eyes upon me in between mopping Lucy's mouth and giving her a drink of water from a cup – no easy business, for she could not drink like you and I, and was moving her mouth about and making mewing noises.

'Mrs Strong,' says I, when I had recovered enough to speak, 'what has happened to her? For mercy's sake, was it an accident?'

I confess I was much moved, and was fighting hard to keep back my tears. And I do believe Lucy knew this for she mewed pitifully, and her poor hands twitched in her lap. Mrs Strong wiped her mouth gently and I think found the grief difficult herself, for though her lips were drawn in a line as straight as a Methody's, her voice was all of a tremble.

'I don't know, Mr Sage, and that's a fact, and perhaps it wouldn't do much good to know. It wouldn't do *her* any good. When we left our last shop at Burdon Oaks, she was full of life. When we got the temporary diggings at the Turk, she was full of life. That night she complained of a pain in her head and how her arms felt frozen, and she went to bed. It was Kitty who heard her cry in the night, and gave her the medicine. But – I don't know. It seemed to make her worse, and she started coughing like she couldn't get her breath. Kitty fetched me and I put some camphor in the fire to air the room and sat with her. But she got worse and in the morning Mr Minton come round and sent for his doctor. She had lost her speech by then. And her legs . . .'

At this she started to weep and was unable to continue for some moments. And all the while, in the bright sunshine, were the sounds of children's merry voices, and the laughter of their mothers.

'Her poor hands – her voice – I am certain she understands, for her eyes speak though her sweet voice . . .'

It was again too much, and we both wept, until Lucy got too

restless and Mrs Strong said we should take her indoors. I was ready
to help, but she would have none of it and with her two arms picked
her up easily, like she was just a baby, and carried her to a chair by
the fireside. I was much struck by this, for though wasted, Lucy was
no babe-in-arms, but mothers do things for their children, so I'm
told, that pass all understanding and this was one of them. When we
were settled inside sharing the cup that cheers, she told me how
Lucy had suffered an apoplexy so great, the doctor said, that few
could survive it, let alone recover a bit. I was stunned for, as I said
to Mrs Strong, she's hardly out of smocks and bonnets, and apoplexy
was surely the complaint of the old and infirm. What had brought
it on?

'The doctor couldn't say, though I wonder if it was her medicine.
She always had a mighty appetite for her drops, and would have
twenty-odd a day and more, no matter what I said. But since this
happened, she won't take any.'

Lucy lurched about like an excited child, and Mrs Strong took
her hand and stroked it gently, all the time looking into her face, but
talking to me.

'You remember, Corney. Once upon a time she couldn't do without it,' she said, 'but now she can't abide it. If she even sees the
bottle, she makes her noises and throws her hands about. When she
was first took bad, we thought it was just her way of being eager for
it, and we give it her on a spoon or through a babby-tit, and I can't
help think it made her worse. But I don't know,' she said, smoothing
Lucy's hair, and then frowning, 'now she's a bit better, she turns her
head away, like she doesn't want it.'

Lucy groaned and gurgled, and I think now she was agreeing
with her mother.

'And will she recover more?' I asked, though I knew what she
would say, and sure enough Mrs Strong shook her head, and the
tears welled up so that she could hardly utter a word.

'The doctor says the apoplexy has taken away her voice and her legs and she can't hardly hold a cup, let alone drink from it.'

I looked at Lucy, sitting in the chair by the dead fire, and thought on the time when her head had made that hollow in my pillow, and how the smell of her clung to my bedclothes. I thought of the letter she wrote about Bessie and the murder and how many times I had read it and heard her voice, which I would never hear again. I put my hand in my pocket and pulled out from the corner, where it lodged in the lining, the picture of the beautiful young woman that Lucy took from Bessie's hand as she lay in the yard of the Constellation. I held it out for Mrs Strong to see, and to discover how much Lucy had told her about that terrible business.

'It's strange,' I said, 'how these things just carry on. For I had believed that when the Shovelton fellow was arrested, poor Bessie Spooner would be laid to rest. But no. Everywhere I go I am reminded of the Constellation and what happened to her.'

I do believe that Lucy Fitch understood every word I said for she mewed and groaned and her poor hands twitched and even her little slippered feet kicked a bit. Mrs Strong was obliged to take one of her twisted hands again and stroke it, and wipe her mouth, and altogether calm her. When she came to the table, she picked up the portrait and gazed at it keenly.

'True to you, Corney, she's a pretty creature. But what had she to do with Bessie Spooner? Or did Bessie lift it from someone? Not wanting to speak ill of the dead, but she was a light-fingered girl.'

Had Lucy talked of her? Of this locket? Of what she saw? Oh yes, Mrs Strong knew all about that business.

'Lucy took it from Bessie's hand as she lay in the yard, thinking it was a sixpence,' I said, speaking no more than the truth. 'What sends me dizzy is how such a beauty can have a brother what would trample a poor girl to death. Why, looking upon a face like this you would think that she kept company with angels, not murderers.'

'But he wasn't convicted, wasn't Mr Shovelton,' Mrs Strong said with surprise in her voice, and Lucy seemed to agree, gurgling and rolling her eyes and kicking her feet. 'Didn't you know? He was set free. No case to bring against him. No evidence to convict him.'

'But I was at the trial . . .'

'And didn't hang about either, or you would have seen *us*. She told me everything, didn't you Luce, and you didn't want to go, but I made her. We owed it to Bessie, I said. So we went back, and we went to the trial. Sat there in the court with judges and wigs all pointing their fingers and trying to twist her words about.' She paused and frowned hard at me. 'The gent in the dock, who you saw and they accused, it wasn't *him*, was it, Lucy? Mr Shovelton wasn't the brute who murdered your pal.'

So I *had* been right to wonder if that gent was the same one I saw, for darkness and fatigue and the clothes he had on (which all gents wore), was trying. But I'd been pushed hard, and nodded my head when I ought to have shook it. And I said so to Lucy who, anyone could tell, understood me, for she was so agitated it took Mrs Strong all her strength to keep her from falling from the chair and had to strap her in with a belt, which brought tears to my eyes again.

'He's been good to us has Mr Shovelton,' said Mrs Strong. 'How do you think we live so comfortable? For you know he was fond of Lucy, and when she was took bad I wrote to him, care of the address in the papers, and he came here straight away.' She stroked Lucy's hand gently. 'He wanted to take Lucy off and have her properly looked after, so he said, but I wouldn't have it. Looked after by strangers when she has her mother! So he says, I'll send you some money, to keep her decent and get her good food, and true to you he did, and we bought a few nice things, didn't we, Luce? But it's not regular, so I'm looking out for us. And Kitty.'

I hardly heard the last of what she said. So Shovelton was not the brute who did for Bessie? And all the time I thought it was, because of his clothes and the way he looked, but also the picture and the writing on the back and the name that kept turning up like a bad penny. I turned that picture over and over and fiddled with it while Mrs Strong put the kettle on the fire. One of the clips had broken off and another was loose, through being so long in my pocket, I suppose, and the back was sliding out. Inside was the tiny note which I had seen before and quite forgotten. I unfolded it and spread it on the table and when I looked up, Lucy had her eyes fixed on me, and she had stopped mouthing.

'What is it, Lucy?' I say, for I feel she is trying to tell me something.

But whatever it is she cannot get it out, though she tries, looking hard at me and then hard at the picture.

Mrs Strong takes her hand and pats it.

'We talked about it, didn't we, Luce, because Lucy knows who did it. She said to the judge when we went to court, "Mr Shovelton didn't do it. It was that *young* man, the one who had a fight. The one who took young Bessie outside. It was him." But they didn't listen to her. "Young," she told them over and over, "a boy almost."'

Yes, I knew that Lucy had seen him. She told me, and she wrote it down.

And for the first time I knew him too.

In my mind's eye, I could see him clear as water. Smooth-faced, small features, elegant. Well turned-out. A young swell trying hard.

Familiar, I thought, though I couldn't say why.

'Did they arrest him?'

'Not him. He was long gone. Doing over some other poor girl I should think.'

I collected up the note, but my stubby fingers found it hard to press it into the back of the picture, so Mrs Strong lent a hand. It was she who took the note to the window.

'Remarkable what people will say to each other. This doesn't look like a note from a brother, does it? More like a girl's writing.'

I had never noticed. In fact, apart from the occasion when I first found it, when the girl Topsy turned it out with the rest of my stuff at the Old Pitcher, I had never looked at it. For you don't. Things get carried around and become part of you, and you never once think to look close. But now I did.

I read it again, then Mrs Strong. And we said nothing to each other for a while, while we considered it. Lucy's cries brought us up and the poor girl wagged her head about and drummed her little feet until Mrs Strong said, 'She wants to hear it too, don't you, Luce?' and she read it out to her.

*My dearest Helen*

*Time passes so slowly when we are not together. I long for your gentle touch and your sweet, sweet kisses. My dearest, sweetest Helen! My own fair mistress! Shall I come and find you one night like we said? Shall I scale the ivy as I promised and leap, like Don Juan, into your room and into your bed? Oh, how I shall love you! I shall put on my breeches and shirt and pull off these silly pieces and let you see me as I am with my boy's hair, just as I've told you in my stories.*

*Dear Helen! Sweetest girl! My love!*

*Your Phyll*

We talked about it long and long, for we are wanderers in the world and hear of such things as women's affections for each other and how powerful they are. I am of the live-and-let-live persuasion, and Mrs Strong of much the same mind, and Lucy too had her opinions which she voiced in her own way.

'What is more rum, Mrs S,' says I, getting ready to shift myself, 'is how the young gent got hold of it. And what a co-in-ci-dence, as

Joe would say, that Mr Shovelton's name is written upon it. I do recall his sister, for I saw her clear as clear from the stage of the Pavilion at Springwell. She was there with her brother who I didn't see, and . . . '

Now there's another rum thing to make the trinity, as they say, for it seems to me I see the row of faces and the square battlements of the military gents, and the angel face of Miss Shovelton (not difficult to place from the excellent likeness) a-peeping around those battlements. Yes, and another face, which I cannot remember to the letter. Perhaps it was turned away. Perhaps this was the Phyll who wrote the letter, I said to Mrs S. Who knows, says she, taking up the locket and putting it carefully in Lucy's hand to pacify her, it is past all understanding and that's a fact. I shivered, though the day was warm and there was sunshine coming through the window. It was time to go, and I took Lucy's poor hands in mine and kissed them, and there were tears in her beautiful eyes which fell upon her cheek, and her poor mouth was red and trembling.

'I'll come again before I leave the circus,' I said, knowing that I probably wouldn't, and because I knew it, I said, 'And, look, if you need a bit of cheering up or want me at all, here is where I'm going. A nobby little shop, I think, and no trouble.'

I wrote 'The Vine Concert Hall, New Clay' on a scrap of paper. Then added my name, just in case it got lost. And our little joke, 'Mind your eye', which would make Lucy laugh when she read it. I stuck it up on the mantelshelf, alongside Her Majesty's left ear where Lucy could see it.

'I'm sorry I can't help your Mrs Marsh,' said Mrs Strong, opening the door. 'She was a good soul, and we enjoyed her company in our last shop, didn't we, Luce?'

Lucy rolled her head from side to side and worked her mouth about and drummed her feet until Mrs Strong had to go and calm her down with stroking and gentle words. I closed the door as quietly as I might and struck off across the court, but hadn't got so far when Mrs Strong's voice stopped me. She was holding the locket in her hand.

'Keep it,' I cried. 'It's not brought me a shred of good fortune.'

'I will do that,' she returned, 'for Lucy seems taken with it. I'll put it on a chain for her to wear around her neck. She still has a fancy for pretty things. Trinkets and such like.'

I collected Joe from his sun spot. His novelty had quickly worn off, and he was sitting, quite Tom-all-alone, with his back to the wall and his black face turned to the sky. As we walked back to the circus, I thought how fine it would be to have no worries, no ailing women and monstrous babies to fret about, no friends done down and sad. But just to sit, peaceful and quiet, and warm my bones in the sun.

# 14

## A Return

**Miss Marweather – Birmingham – Halls's Lodging House, Paradise-court**

When Mr Corney Sage related the details of his visit to Lucy Fitch (a story much embellished with sentiment) I was disappointed to discover that I had misjudged the strength of her medicine. I had anticipated that she would have been insensible, then quite dead very soon after taking it, but what I learned was quite the reverse. However, although it was not an entirely satisfactory outcome, I did take some pleasure in the horrible piquancy of her 'living death'. And those coins left on the table by Mrs Strong for her daughter's 'medicine' – forty pieces of silver! What exquisite irony in that gesture – the mother unwittingly paying for the child's destruction! Particularly as, only moments later, I made those very arrangements via the excellent if dim-witted Prithy Taverner.

It was his regular duty to visit the chemist's shop on behalf of his adored mistress to collect her 'medicine' but, having once or twice made an error in describing the prescription, Lucy had taken to writing a note in which she indicated the strength and quantity of what she required. I had Prithy come to me after he had received his orders from Lucy and, to make his errand less complicated, copied Lucy's instruction on to a note with mine (a simple preparation to relieve nausea). But I made sure that, in transferring Lucy's orders, the strength was much increased, a simple alteration which I calculated would not be queried. And indeed it was not. A few coins in Prithy Taverner's grubby hand and the business was concluded.

No, not entirely concluded, for I needed to see for myself the wild-haired creature who had confronted Yates in the Constellation yard now tamed, and indeed Sage's description of Lucy's present condition was so surprising that I could not be satisfied with his account. Feeling much stronger than I appeared to the world, I once again relished contemplation of my handiwork and, with the aid of James Yates, it would prove a simple enough exercise. It necessitated, of course, the return to Halls's lodging house to recover Yates's clothes, which were still (I hoped) in my trunk. I was, in truth, quite excited at the prospect – not merely the opportunity to put on those breeches and boots and to take the streets, instead of borrowing them as a woman does. No, it was not just the pleasure of the putting on, but also the danger involved. I was hungry for Yates's excitement. It was a long time since the smell of sandalwood and lime oil had not just been stale odours on his shirt and collar, but pungent and real on my hair and skin.

However, I hadn't anticipated having to keep company with the odious Mr Halls, who I had glimpsed skulking about the circus precincts and who had surprised me as I stepped into the street. He had been anxiously looking out for me for some days, he said, and cupped his hand under my elbow the better to firmly propel me along. I offered no resistance, although more than once I wondered if I should cry for help (for effect as well as entertainment) but, anxious to secure James Yates's belongings and my own plans, I was compliant and allowed him to steer me to Paradise-court and his gloomy back sitting room. He closed the door and supported it with a chair (because it was liable to swing open he said), and produced a bottle and two cups, though he filled only one. He came to the point quickly after enjoying half a cupful and refilling it.

'Your babby, miss. I have heard a whisper about it,' he said confidentially. 'I have an interest in it – and you. So I have approached an acquaintance, a man in the exhibition line, and he is also interested in it. I will introduce you to him I will cut you in at a shilling a day. You'll have your room here, all found. I'll see to it, don't you worry.'

He coughed horribly, and spat a ball of thick mucus into the grate, where it bounced and sizzled. And then – it was comical to observe – he suddenly realised that the 'asset' about which he was so concerned was absent. He consulted the floor and my lap, and it was all I could do not to smile.

'Where is it, the babby? Sick? Not dead?'

'No, not dead, Mr Halls. Taking the air with a friend.' (It was in fact in the capable hands of Blind Sally from the workhouse, whose baby had died but whose milk was still plentiful.)

'Well, I want to see it before I part with a copper,' he growled, and then realized what he had said. 'Not that I don't trust you, miss.'

'What makes you think that I haven't already made arrangements, Mr Halls? In fact, I am perfectly satisfied, being well provided for and quite comfortable in Mr Chittick's company,' I returned, though it was a lie.

'Ah, now you might *think* that you have an arrangement with Chittick, miss,' he said, with an air of knowledge and confidence, 'but there I do have the advantage of you, for I know better. Chittick don't figure. Don't come into it. Not for a moment.'

He licked his lips in a most unpleasant fashion, and drank gin from the chipped cup, all the while regarding me with proprietorial fixity. The clock ticked and the poor coal on the fire spat and crackled as we sat for some moments in silence.

'Ah, miss,' he whined eventually, 'I am sure that we can accommodate each other. We are, don't you know, of similar dispositions? Both trying to make our way in the world what is agin us? This is the way I see it, miss, and you will correct me if I am wide of the mark. You have an infant what is remarkable. I am interested in said infant. You might want to reconsider my offer – one shilling a day. All found.'

Picking up the poker, I nudged the coals and watched the flames lick and tremble into life.

Mr Halls sighed at my silence. And scratched his head, watching me carefully as I continued to stir the fire.

'Of course,' he said, with a hint of irritation in his voice, 'I might make it easy on myself. I might just take the child. I know where it is. Who would stop me? You? Chittick? Nah! I have friends. You won't get in my way.'

He had played a poor hand, resorting to threats, and from that moment he was no adversary, no opponent at all. Just another greedy little man with one foot in the gutter. He takes another cup of gin. I see that his hand shakes.

'So, let's get back to our business.'

'No, Mr Halls,' I say, and he starts, 'let us not. I have made my position clear. There are no considerations. There will be no cutting in.'

He frowns, and the cup which is halfway to his lips freezes there momentarily, whilst he considers – and he lets me know how seriously he considers – by squinting his eyes and pursing his lips.

I continue. 'I shall be removing my belongings from your establishment imminently. I have no further need of your services, Mr Halls.' I put two shillings on the table, and keep my fingers upon them. 'This, I think, will clear any misunderstandings.'

He looks at me. He looks at the coins. He raises his eyebrows, and a hiss struggles from between his lips.

'I hardly think so, miss,' says he in a whisper, 'I hardly think so, since I've been so put out on your behalf. Perhaps we should have a little talk about that.'

I wait. I want to hear what he thinks he knows.

'You see, I thought you wasn't coming back, miss.' He is almost intimate. 'I heard that you was awful sick with your kid, and since there was no hide or hair of you, I thought you was dead, miss. But, what about her family? thought I. What about her dear sister? Won't she want to know where her dear loving girl is?'

He stops dramatically, and a thin smile tightens his lips.

'I thought, I must open her trunk,' says he, leaning towards me, and laying the tips of his fingers across mine, 'and take a look inside. It is my public duty, for I want to find your relatives. A letter perhaps, with an address to which I can write and communicate the sad news. And I found one. I found many. Interesting reading, miss. Kept me awake at nights, they did. So I've a letter prepared for Miss – what's-'er-name? – Shovelton, I do believe. Ah, dearest, sweetest, *ripest* Helen! Like the feel of soft flesh, do you, miss? Fancy them soft golden curls and them sweet lips? And other parts. Very h-eloquent, miss. Touching. Gets a man hot round the edges, if you take my meaning. And I take it you like dressing the part too, miss? All yer fine breeches and so on.'

So he had been through James Yates's belongings! I feel a familiar surge of anger.

'But, miss,' he continues, warming to his theme, 'explain to me, for I am an ignorant man, how you got this kid of yours? Not by playing with the girls, did you? With Miss Helen. But perhaps you lost your appetite. Well, I'm not particular,' he says, and his face is so close to mine that I am breathing his breath. 'A man like me doesn't get much for free.'

That breath, the only thing I can hear, is whistling in my face now, and the mucus rattles and crackles in his throat.

'And afterwards,' he says, 'we can talk about your kid. And Helen.'

He has turned away to drain the cup and refill it. The poker, with its hot and knotty head, is still in my hand. As he turns towards me again, I swing it back, then forward and it meets the side of Halls's head with a soft thud. He looks at me with opened-mouthed amazement, and I swing the poker again, finding his shoulder. He cries out, staggering, and lurches at me, hands flailing in an attempt to grasp the weapon. I retreat a few steps, but only to find room to swing the poker with more vigour, and once again his head meets the iron shaft with a dull crack. He reels with exaggerated movements and sinks into the chair as I catch him again across his cheek and then the brow. He is blinded by blood and pain and whimpers and, I think, begs me to stop. But I am taken up by the hearty rhythm, and the straining of muscle and sinew as I swing again and again are regular and satisfying. I ignore the spits of blood and shards of bone which now erupt from the soft mass of his head and face, though the sight of a single tooth, yellow and bloody, lying upon the floor, strikes me as comical and I laugh aloud. Halls is pinned in his chair, unable to escape but still trying, and I simply continue until my arms ache and burn and his body slips to the floor and out of reach.

Breathing hard, I contemplate the no-face before me, a pulpy residue in a shining pool of pink and red and white. For some minutes the fingers futilely twitch and grasp the air, and the mucus bubbles and crackles in the scrawny throat. In the scullery, I wash the stickiness from my hands, and dab the same from my skirt. There are patterns of blood upon the wall and the tiles of the fireplace, and the floor is so dappled with dark droplets that it is impossible to avoid them. The hem of my skirt drags them into smears and the soles of my feet quickly become sticky with the residue.

Who would have thought the old man to have so much blood in him? I have heard that somewhere.

Upstairs, on the first landing, my room was as I had left it. The bed unslept in, the trunk still packed, standing in the middle of the floor. Still packed, but not undisturbed, for the straps were undone and the locks broken. There was no care, no subterfuge here. Either Halls had been telling the truth when he claimed that he was searching for information about my relatives or, more likely, he was desperate to find something, anything, of value. He was probably surprised, for there was little enough for him to take. A watch. Yates's leather boots. Some fine linen. But they were still there, if hurriedly and untidily jammed in. Helen's letters had gone, though. Their hiding place under the lining of the lid had been ripped apart. I was angry but reconciled, for Halls was dead – or on his way to that other place, for I had not waited until the end – and the letters, wherever he had secreted them, could do me no harm now.

How can I describe the pleasure, then, the intense pleasure of pulling on breeches and shirt, boots and gloves! The feeling of linen upon my skin, the smell of leather, even the crisp rustle of damask and silk as I buttoned the waistcoat snugly across my chest, were sensual delights. Unpinning the pieces and smoothing my own cropped hair was the final stage of preparation. I favoured macassar oil with its heady scent, and only the best, but it stained anything with which it came into contact, particularly the collars of my shirts, and so I reserved it for special occasions. I poured a small pale amber pool of it into my palms, carefully running it through and over my hair, and finishing with brush and comb so that it lay thick and shining. A dark cap of shining jet.

I stood before the mirror, and even though it was cracked and mildewed, James Yates stared out at me, proud and elegant. The childbed fever had left me thin and wasted and my chest and waist did not fill the clothes as they had done previously. Even my face was more angular, the line of my jaw and cheekbone more pronounced. But, I thought, as I considered the reflection, for the first time youthfulness had deserted me, I had grown and what looked out at me was a man, one who had seen the world, rather than hidden from it. From all angles I regarded myself, Yates. It was like being reacquainted with an old friend who had been away, out of the country perhaps, and though I had enjoyed the exciting sensation of putting on his skin, as it were, this contemplation was all the more exquisite for its pause. I was in no hurry and I took my time, savouring each tiny moment of pleasure, like a lover.

I stood outside Halls's Lodging House, Paradise-court. The sun was warm and there was a drowsy hum of flies flocking to the heaps of horse dung and rubbish that lay in the street. It was the only sound, and the only activity. So when I stepped on to the cobbles and strode briskly along, hands in pockets, a nonchalant air of a young man out upon business, I was playing to an empty house. A brief rehearsal for the real performance commencing shortly when I struck High-street, and then – for this was no jaunt, I knew exactly where I was headed – Lower Marlpool-street and Duchess-court.

## 15

*Visiting the Sick*

**James Yates – Lower Marlpool-street**

Mrs Strong went out every afternoon at two and returned at half past four. She washed pots and floors at the Great Turk public house and was paid fourpence for her labours (the landlord, Mr Minton, was a generous man). In the evening, at eight o'clock, she returned, washed more pots and floors, and remained until ten, receiving a further fourpence. Eightpence per day, six days per week. On the seventh she rested. Her daughter, taken very bad a while ago, was listened for by neighbours. If the weather was fine she sat out in the afternoon. If it was not, she sat in. She was put to bed early and never wakened. If anyone thought to, they called in and saw that she was not wanting.

It was easy to discover anything with a pocket full of pennies and a charming manner. So I lingered in the not-so-salubrious district of Lower Marlpool-street, keeping as inconspicuous as a gent could, until Mrs Strong's figure disappeared into the Great Turk. Then, trying not to seem in a hurry, I arrived in Duchess-court just as a cheerful little woman was coming out, and without any hesitation or even surprise, she pointed me to the right house and even offered to open the door! The sun struggled through a murky sky and there were a few drops of rain in the air as I rattled the latch and took off my hat, to dip under the lintel of a very low door.

If it was a shabby place without, once past the door the interior was surprising. There was a thick green curtain ready to be pulled across the door where there were gaps and holes in the wood. A plush cloth covered the table and, in the centre, stood a glass lamp ready to be lit. In the corner of the room, by the wall, was a bed with a substantial brass frame and a gay coverlet. There was bread on a board, and a tin for tea, a cheese dish, a meat safe. The coal scuttle was full, the grate black-leaded, the mantelpiece had requisite busts of Victoria and Albert. Mrs Strong's eightpence per day went a long way!

When I grew accustomed to the gloom of the small room – for the curtains were half drawn and the lamp not yet lit – it took little searching to discover my quarry, in a sturdy chair by the fire. She was carefully propped up with cushions, but to prevent her from falling out of it, a thick leather belt, extended by cords on each end, was around her waist and tied at the back of the chair. As helpless as a baby, she was strapped into her seat until Mrs Strong returned. Here was the beautiful Lucy Fitch, the toast of soldier heroes, widows and baby farmers the length and breadth of the country, reduced to a bundle of shawls and blankets!

She must have been sleeping when I opened the door, for the noise caused her to jump and, with an effort, she turned her head towards me. In the gloom she could not make me out, but I stepped, like the leading man I felt, into a little pool of sunlight for her benefit, and took in her reaction. Do I need to set it all down? The wide eyes; the constant mouthing suddenly arrested; the string of drool which shimmered like silver thread as it unwrapped itself from the corner of her mouth; the claw hands frozen in mid-tremor; the paddling feet stilled. It was as though she had been cast in stone, and only the delicate movement of strands of hair, caught in a draught, disclosed that she was flesh and blood.

But for my part, I too could have remained in that rapt pose for hours, so equally engrossing was the terrible change I had wrought upon her. I pulled out a chair, wiped it carefully with my handkerchief and sat down to contemplate my handiwork, not merely to revel in it. I wondered whether she could, if pressed, speak, but the painful moan that began to sound in her throat was all the evidence I needed. She was harmless. What could she possibly say or do, trapped as she was in her frozen body? How could she communicate? Even Mrs Strong, her closest confidante, could not decipher her grunts and moans beyond their raw emotion. That she was distressed was clear: tears began to well in her eyes and her chest heaved. Her hands clenched and unclenched and her feet drummed rhythmically. How shocking that her body should be reduced to such useless activity!

'I am sorry to see you like this, Lucy,' I said at last, 'for you know I had a deal of respect for your acuteness in the business of deception. Your games with the gullible were very smart, and even though the Captain Hawkers of this world deserve to be hoodwinked, you did it with great skill and invention. I will applaud you.' And indeed I did. I clapped until my hands began to sting.

Here was a speech worthy of Mr Macready, I thought, and I was of a mind to continue, since I had a captive audience. But then I reminded myself that the purpose of my errand was to be assured that Lucy Fitch was indeed as incapable as I had been told. Certainly, she was immobile, she was speechless and, who knows, an imbecile. But Sage's mission had not been to confirm whether she had made any disclosure of what she saw that afternoon in Burdon Oaks when she came upon me with James Yates's clothes. I was as certain looking at her shattered body as I had been looking into her surprised face that she had seen in that moment the murderer of Bessie Spooner. My task was to discover what she had done with her knowledge.

'You're a very clever young woman, Lucy Fitch,' I mused, thinking aloud, 'and I do wonder what you know and if you told anyone. I rather think you didn't, or I would have heard of it by now. But when we said our goodbyes outside the Live and Let Live at Burdon Oaks you were very eager to leave, so I think we both know what – who – you saw.'

Her eyes followed me, though her head lolled on one shoulder.

'But did you tell anyone? Your mother perhaps? Or your sister?'

Perhaps she attempted to speak, for she gargled and choked. I wondered how much she understood of what I said and whether she had some premonition of my intentions. For, I reasoned, even if she had not told Mrs Strong that Mrs Collette and James Yates were the same being, and that she had seen Yates murder her friend in the yard of the Constellation Concert Room, I could not believe that she had not told someone. Perhaps before she took the 'medicine' I had provided, or in the grips of it. She could have written it down, though I doubted her ability on that score given the unschooled quality of her letters to me, and anyway it seemed rather histrionic for such as her. Nevertheless I was caught in a dilemma here which detracted from my enjoyment of the moment.

It was an awkward silence, broken only by Lucy's involuntary noises and the tapping of her slipper against the leg of the chair. No conversation, no locking horns here. Not even the adversarial challenge presented by the odious Halls, who at least needed toppling from his presumptions. I was disappointed and struggled, for the first time, to know what to do, for Lucy was no contest. She was pliable. Even Tippy the pug-dog tried to save itself. But Lucy Fitch simply sat and slavered. And watched.

There was nothing more to be done, and I rose and opened the door. The draught blew in and a piece of paper fluttered down from the mantelshelf and came to rest at Lucy's feet. She saw it, as I did, watched it float to the floor and deliberately (if clumsily) covered it with her slippered foot. The action gave me pause, and I closed the door again and retrieved the note. In an uneducated hand was written:

> *Yor frend Corney Sage. Mind your eye, Lucy*
> *The Vine Concert Hall, New Clay*

So Corney Sage was not just a friend, but a good friend! One who visited and sat at this table and left his forwarding address! A confidant, perhaps. Now I realized that, of course, his report about visiting poor Lucy was guarded, incomplete, that he looked at me, Mrs Marsh, with very different eyes, that there was, there must have been, discussion about Yates. No matter that Lucy's mouth was stopped up, in their hugger-mugger meeting with Mrs Strong or sister Kitty, they had solved the puzzle of Yates, and even now the police were alerted, upon the doorstep even, with the red-haired comedian behind, smiling and pointing out the murderer of Bessie Spooner! I had been blind even to the most obvious dissembling! To have admired Lucy Fitch's consummate skills, when I was so easily taken in, displayed the worst kind of ignorance!

I brought my fist down upon the table with a bang that upset the lamp and sent it crashing to the floor. Lucy cried out. Not a thick and grizzling murmur, but a scream, dragged from her belly, that must surely alert her neighbours. I stopped her mouth quickly with my hand, and then saw, in slices of time, the locket she wore around her neck.

On a thin black ribbon.

A thin gold frame.

A picture of a golden-haired angel set against a blue background.

Helen. My Helen.

Hung around this whore's neck, warmed by her flesh.

She is clawing at my sleeves, but I am stronger and I wrench at the locket, snapping the ribbon as if it was thread. The picture tumbles through the air, glances off the hearth and breaks apart. Glass. Metal. Picture. A tiny scrap of paper. I am overcome, outraged at the blasphemy of my Helen slung about this creature's breast, and I grind my heel into the glass, the picture, everything, until it is utterly destroyed.

Lucy has stopped screaming, but her mouth still makes the shape, anticipating the next roar, so I step to the bed, grasp the pillow and press it down upon her face with all my weight. Her nails graze my cheeks and clutch at my hair, sliding through the sticky macassar oil and then grasping again. Her legs kick out feebly and her body, pinned fast by the belt and cords, writhes against me. Harder and harder I push the pillow into her face, feeling the dulled contours of brow and cheekbone beneath my hands. And still she fights, sinking back as if she has surrendered, and then summoning her strength again to clutch at me, to thrust me away.

There was no satisfaction in this and I wanted to have the business done and to be gone. I was worried that I might be disturbed, that neighbours might have heard her scream and come to investigate, and indeed a noise in the court was enough for me to drop the pillow and hurry away. No one challenged me, though, and the noise was perhaps a child playing or crying, or some domestic row, but I did not pause, not even to glance at myself in a shop window, until I was within yards of my new lodgings, courtesy of Roscius Soloman, showman and exhibitor of my Fairy Child.

# 16

## *A Fairy Child*

**Mrs Marsh – Birmingham**

It had become a matter of some urgency that I left the confines of the circus. As my health improved, Mr Chittick's plans became increasingly apparent. One morning he cornered me, told me I must leave the caravan for they were shortly moving on for the tenting season. He would take the kid, he said, but not me. He would give me five shillings for the kid, and a decent funeral, all paid, when it died. Which, he said, it would indeed.

I was no more prepared to share my fortunes (or my Fairy Child) with Mr Chittick than I had been with Mr Halls, and remembering a conversation with Corney Sage and his Negro friend about a showman and a penny exhibition, I threw caution away in favour of independence – and money. When I arrived with the child at the New-street establishment (a former undertaker's shop) and made the acquaintance of Mr Soloman, I think he was surprised, but not inclined to show it. If he had expressed any astonishment at my suddenly appearing on his doorstep, I would not have reproached him, for I was unannounced and had little luggage (only a bag containing some of Yates's clothes). But he made no comment, merely looked keenly at me and thus our unspoken agreement that explanations were not necessary was instituted.

# Walking in Pimlico

From the first, it was his businesslike detachment that impressed me, and I believe I impressed him with my attention to the detail of our contract, upon which we agreed within an hour of my arrival. One shilling per day, all found, the showman to provide shop and lodgings, a crib and stage for the child, and a wet-nurse on hand as required. Hearing its hungry cries, he immediately sent for a woman in a neighbouring show, one whose faculties were dulled by a lifetime of gin and exposure, but whose condition (like Blind Sally's from the workhouse) gave her a seemingly perpetual supply of milk.

Soloman was a smart fellow, with his bristling moustache and unblemished skin (suggesting a daily regime at the barber-shop), a man careful of his public appearance, and impenetrable. In all the time I was in his company, that quality of businesslike affability never changed. His bright blue eyes were at first startling, and a little disconcerting, giving an impression of deep interrogation, but our conversations were always to the point, and he never betrayed any emotion, nor gave any indication of what he might be thinking. When I held up the child to him, and he opened the blankets and scrutinized the creature within, his face was a perfect mask, displaying neither horror nor repulsion, nor even great interest. However, within the day, a large and many-coloured poster magically appeared outside the show depicting a tiny and beautiful child with gossamer wings flying above a field of flowers, and in his smart coat and top hat he was already spinning a fable about the Fairy Child of such alarming fantasy that I almost expected the assembled crowd to laugh and walk away. And, since the child's exhibition would not open until ten o'clock that evening, perhaps never to return! I misjudged him – and them – completely, for by nine o'clock the street was thronged with people waiting to see the show, and neighbouring shopkeepers were grumbling about the noise and confusion, while their trade trebled.

I surprised myself how quickly I adapted to the daily regime,

# A FAIRY CHILD

which was exhausting in its length and repetitiveness. Each day I told the same story (suggested by Soloman and embellished by myself) about the Fairy Child, discovered in a ditch, abandoned by its mother, fed water and chicken bones by an idiot woman, which regime alone accounted for its monstrous head and tiny limbs. Women gasped and some fainted and had to be removed outside, only to pay their penny again an hour later. Children laughed and pointed, some trying to squeeze its head, 'to see if it will bust', and pull its arms. It is said that the eyes are the windows of the soul. Here, then, were chasms of deep pain, as it struggled in its wide crib to avoid pokes and pinches, to sleep only to be woken again, and when it cried, with raw, dry misery that should have melted the hardest heart, the crowds were not silenced, nor moved, but instead laughed or shook their heads in disgust.

This was my child, flesh of mine, and though many times I wanted to abandon it, until necessity drove me there I could not. My circus friends advised against keeping the child, and suggested leaving it on the steps of the workhouse or convent. They thought only of the years ahead, they said, and reminded me that many such children lived into infancy, though few survived into adulthood, and that pain would be their constant companion. They told stories of 'monsters' that had come and gone in the circus, other 'fairy' children scarcely twelve inches high whose little lives were bound by their keeper's greed and public curiosity until they died from disease and rough treatment. Of giant men – and women – whose size belied weakness as their feet and knees and spines collapsed under the enormous weight. But mostly they spoke of the loneliness of the monster children, as if they had felt it themselves.

'For,' said little Mademoiselle Senga, as we sat in her caravan one morning, and I stitched away at the spangles on her costume, 'they can never be like your normal child. They must always be hidden away, never feeling the sunlight or the wind, and only seeing the

257

four walls, and so being imprisoned. Why? Well, for fear of being seen, of course. A monster is only useful if it is a paying monster, and not something anyone can see for free.'

Though they were tender-hearted, most circus folk spoke of the monster children with little emotion, and I quickly understood and adopted their detachment. Like an animal, a dog or a horse, that is to be sold, there is no profit in attachment, just pain, as I knew only too well. And so, rather than feed the child myself, I was recommended a wet-nurse at the workhouse who was simple and affectionate, which nature caused her to be constantly with child, and while she mourned their demise (for they were taken away from her immediately they entered the world), she had milk a-plenty, and when my hungry monster was brought yawling to her, she crooned at it softly, and tenderly stroked its swollen head as she laid it against her breast. So the arrangement with Soloman, though temporary, suited me, and allowed me some little interludes of leisure (while the wet-nurse was about her business).

And, living in that small corner of penny amusement, I was unable to avoid the ripples of horror and fascination that accompanied the demise of Mr Halls. To the illustrated newspapers it was a penny-spinner, and the crowds that gathered outside the stationers' shop windows (in which the front pages only of these garishly illustrated periodicals were displayed for public consumption) frequently overflowed into the public highway. Mr Soloman, who never passed up an opportunity to make an extra penny, immediately introduced into his shop a little waxwork scene depicting the murder victim, weltering in a pool of brilliant carmine, and the shadowy figure of the murderer lurking at the window.

'See the Paradise-court outrage!' he roared. 'Witness the bloody attack upon an old man! Only a penny! Just about to start!'

# 17

## Sorely Tried

**Corney Sage – Birmingham**

Here is a singular business and no mistake!
Oh, my!

Here I am, about my duties, tidying up around the ring and all, and of a sudden here are Brummagem's Best Blue Boys doing their liveliest to prevent me! So I put on my cockiest face and manner and run along the ring fence and kick up the tan, and try to draw a smile on and off, especially from the young 'uns.

I cry, 'Oh ho! Oh ho! Here we have, for the amusement of one and all, a crafty collection, a meddlesome medley, a fat and fortunate specimen of blue-backed, true-backed enforcers of Her Majesty's regs and ru-u-lations!'

I give 'em my best 'Potato' wheeze, including my good line where I stand on the back of Poney Cocking (or a tub if he is not handy) and say in my highest voice, 'Policemen they are blue potatoes – and very often turn out bad peelers.' This always gets a regular roar, even from the boys themselves.

Until now, for this bag of peelers will not be amused, though some haven't seen the inside of a circus before, or it was long ago when they was too young to remember. They gawp and look about them, and nudge each other, rough the tan about with their great plates, until I am beside myself with aggravation and give the ring fence a kick and another kick until it rattles. This brings out Chittick from the back where he is doing business with the knacker-man over one of the mares. He hears the commotion and comes out fighting, then quizzes the Sergeant hard about why his circus is being invaded by bluebottles (which, by-the-by, only he finds amusing). The Sergeant steps forward and acquaints him with the circumstances that concern me and Halls, of Paradise-court, who has been ''orribly done in'.

'This 'ere Merryman of yourn is spotted,' the Sergeant finishes, at which all the bluebottles bristle about and finger their persuaders and look hard at me. Now I have never been fond of Chittick, for he was always too chummy with his stick and my back, but for what he said that day I will forgive him every offence he ever gave me.

He laughs at the Sergeant, one of his wheezy efforts, and then, looking scornful at me, 'What, this pump-thunderer?' says he. 'He doesn't know his arse from his eye and can't find either without a picture!'

Even with this testament, I am still bounced around by the Sergeant as we inspect one of his loneliest cells (for he does not want to be interrupted), and this because I will not agree to having nobbled Halls. Perhaps I do not help my own cause, for I do say to the copper that I *applauded* the fellow who had clocked Halls. That fellow did the world a favour, in my opinion, for Halls was a piece of work about who you could say nothing good. His wife left him for a cat's-meat man, and even his children hated him, and if he could rob you or otherwise do you down, he would. But I would not have done for him (though I would think hard about going to his aid). I would not have smashed his head about, I say nor left him in his own back parlour to die alone.

In the end, like true pros, it was my circus friends who came forward and agreed with my story, for they could all say I had not left the circus for days, and Mrs Chittick quietly affirmed the nights, for I had been warming her feet while her master was away. (However, this was not a circumstance I wanted all the world to know, and Mr Chittick in particular I wanted to remain ignorant of how I plumped his pillow and drank his brandy and squeezed his wife.) But it was enough, and I breathed the fresh air with only a black eye.

I returned to my circus duties, thinking about the new shop I was going to and wishing I was going that moment, for it seemed to me that as fast as I ran, trouble caught up with me one way or another, so I ought to try to get a head start. Even my good turn to Mrs Marsh had left me contrary-wise, for she disappeared one day with her baby and not a word of thanks, and some few outstanding expenses that she had promised to cover and not made good. With this in mind as a church clock struck, I hove back to Halls's, thinking I might see if she had cleared out of that front room, and if there were something left behind that I might sell and take as my dues. With my eyes set on that nobby shop in New Clay, I wanted to pick up my bits of things – a pair of boots, a comforter (useful for winter mornings) and my gag-book, which I would be very sorry to lose. Not that I used it much at Chittick's, doing less talking and more tumbling as it worked out. But there were gags in there that had been given to me at other times when I had worked in circuses, and they were like remembrances of fellow professionals I had known. I had a song-book too, and here were songs given to me, and little notes of patter and the like. Very useful to write down when a song has gone well, and the words are fresh.

So I took myself off to Paradise-court with no great cheer but the sustaining thoughts of pastures new. It was not a pleasant place. Always gloomy, being at the dark end of a dark street and much closed in by warehouses and a brickyard. There was always a good deal of green about the bricks and a feeling of dampness which dragged along with you when you went inside Halls's estab., and clung still along the front passage and up the stairs. My room, number 3 at the back, was always cool and dark, even when the sun was shining and the ice-man doing a belter. Halls said (in the summer, of course) that number 3 was the coolest room in the house and he ought to charge me extra. In the winter he would have kept quiet, for like as not it would be colder in number 3 than outside.

So, going in the front door and standing in the passage and looking down that passage at the door to the back room where he was bashed about – well, here was a strange feeling and no mistake. It was the middle of the day and already it was dark in there, and there was a smell about the place – damp, of course, but something else, which might have been a perfume, so I didn't linger on it, fearing I would lose my nerve and run out and never return. I hastened up the stairs, noticing how heavy my boots seemed and how there were creaks and groans that I had never noticed before. Number 3 was down the passage, which had never seemed quite so long and narrow and gloomy. And the door to number 3 had never stuck before, but now I had to put my shoulder to it, bursting it open and rattling it hard.

It all looked as I left it, though it was some weeks since. My good coat still hanging on the back of the door, and the comforter over it. The gag-book and the song-book on the little table. I gathered them up, looked around once more, and pulled the door behind me. But it wouldn't shut, so I left it, standing ajar, like all the doors along the passage, including the one at the front, belonging to Mrs Marsh. Now I am not usually inclined to poke around in other people's property but I felt, since she owed me cash and wasn't forthcoming with it, entitled. I pushed the door open and went in.

The trunk was in the middle of the floor, sturdy and dark, with bands about it. And of course I recognized it as belonging to Mrs

Marsh, for didn't I arrange for it to be brung on my handcart, and hadn't Halls and I discussed it. Or, rather, Halls had, for he had a fancy that a quantity of jewels lay within. I recall that my cut of the operation was going to be books, which pleased me not at all. But now at least I would have the trunk. And if I had nothing much to put in it, I could always sell it.

This trunk should have been tight shut with a padlock, but it was not and sprung open like a tart's legs. In it – and it was a great surprise to me – were gents' clothes: a coat, trousers, a pair of boots and a shirt, a fancy waistcoat. And gents' bits and pieces – hair oil, macassar mostly, and a great waft of it greeted me when I opened the lid, and I realized that was what I had nosed downstairs. I have heard that the lining of trunks should always be searched for that is where jewellery is often put for safe-keeping. But Halls knew this too, for the lining was ripped to flinders and there was nothing left to be found. Here's a teaser, I thought, for why would Mrs Marsh want a box of gents' clothes, and certain it *was* her box, for I had carried it myself. There were no books, but no jewels neither, unless Halls had already searched them out. Just a box of duds, which I might get a few bob for. But I had no time nor inclination to pack them up and hawk them round.

Here was a turn-up. I sat on the edge of the bed and looked hard at the heap of stuff in the middle of the floor. I tried to think of why Mrs Marsh should have a box of men's clothes, good ones, well made, though none would do for me, for while they were small, they were also flashy. A young man's duds.

I sat there awhile, with the light getting dimmer and dimmer, and just a fly buzzing, listening to those creaks and shifts what empty houses make. Like they was a-talking to themselves. Squeaks and groans and every now and then a foot upon the stairs. I started to think of Halls and how someone – 'Person Unknown' the Sergeant called him – had done him to death for nothing. For unless

Halls had a secret pot of treasure that the murderer helped himself to, he'd been done in for nothing. Or one of those poor beggars who he'd done over came back to get him. So, I thought, as it seemed another footstep found its way up the stairs. Supposing the murderer came back, which they always say they do in the penny papers. Murderers, I thought, as I cast about me for a handy defender and found him in Brighton for the day, are said to be much inclined to visit the scene of their crime, the better to gloat over it, and have another taste of the deed they have done.

I sat good and still, till my legs ached and my feet felt like lumps of clay, and I stared hard at the doorknob till there was no light to see it by. Here was I, with no nerve and a weak bladder, in a murdered man's house with the murderer! For there were still creaks and scufflings outside the door, and on the stairs I heard the footsteps of fifty murderers traipsing up and down in their shifty way! Then bangs started, dull thuds at first, building up to thunderings, like the whole house was going to come down. And I fancied that the murderer had brought all his pals with him, rounded up every dark-visaged villain in Birmingham and had them all round for a shindig at the scene of his best misdeed, at Paradise-court. (This is how my fancy runs away with me! It is a sore trial and no mistake.) But then it seemed the noise was coming from a different place, and indeed I realized (and felt foolish) that here was the noise from the house next door, another lodging house in fact, and full of Paddys, who all wear big boots. Of course.

But so put about was I by now that it was a little comfort to know that there were other living beings nearby, and I resolved to make my exit quietly and quickly, thinking that if there were indeed villains now teeming around Halls's old house (looking for his money, no doubt) they might be distracted. I gathered up my coat and comforter and put the gag-book and song-book in my pocket. When I opened the door (and this could not be done silently, for it stuck and had to be pulled hard and clattered against the jamb), I half expected the passage to be crowded with villains, all waiting on me, and I had prepared a little speech, not very witty but with the option of gags, to get me along it and down the stairs. But it was not necessary. For here were shadows and dimness, and the long pale stream of light coming through the open door of the front room (which had been Mrs Marsh's), but no villains. Down the stairs and into the front hall, and a swift glance back down the passage where, strange, I had thought the door stood open to Halls's back parlour where all the horror took place, but now it was closed. I stopped for a moment and looked and listened, and it seemed to me, although my fancy was running wild, that there was someone in there, who didn't want to be seen. For I am certain I heard a shuffle or a rustle or a moving of feet.

Certain, but not as insistent as my bladder, which was giving me clear directions and I did not want to go agin it.

*An Unravelling*

**Corney Sage – New Clay**

I am on my way to the Vine Music Hall, my linen bag over my shoulder in which there is a pair of clogs and my little cloth to wipe them with. The tools of my trade. Indeed, there is much trade hereabouts, and New Clay is not at all the countrified place I thought it was going to be when I applied to Mr Bellmaker, landlord of the establishment. There might have been green fields here at one time, and, true to you, if I shin up the church tower and the smoke cleared for half an hour I could probably con some in a neighbouring county, but as a regular sight they are like virtuous women, hard to find. Here are brickmakers and nailmakers and ironmakers – and moneymakers, of course, for where you find poor people toiling hard and wearing their lives away for tuppence and starving to make a day of it, you will also discover fat old men keeping company with port and cigars and having a disregard for anything except a bag of money.

I am becoming cross-hatched, I believe, for I have seen too much misery of late, and still it comes on.

But I have reached the Vine, on my way passing a bill flapping on the foundry wall on which 'Mr Corney Sage, comic vocalist and champion clog-dancer' sits above 'the Sisters Delmar, vocalists and danseuses, Professor Bill Evemi, the prestidigitateur, and Mr Chapman with his sagacious canines, Brutus and Nero'. I pass the Quarry where the show folks are arriving with their living vans in readiness for the Wakes which will soon be setting up on the Market Place. The Vine might be seen from the Market Place, for it is a blaze of lamps, within and without, and warm and cheerful, in a tired kind of way.

I pick my way through the tables and chairs, nodding, for in New Clay cheery greetings and slaps on the back are not the order of the day. Indeed I wonder how it is that the music hall has any business at all, so downcast is the population, and certain Mr – or should I say Captain – Bellmaker does not ornament the company with good humour, but lays on it with bad grace. He is no more a captain than I am, but makes up for it by wearing a cocked hat, and being what is called a 'leading light' in the town. It is down to him that some working men have little gardens, though no bigger than a pocket handkercher it must be said, and grow potatoes and turnips from seeds bought specially at the Vine Public House. And he thought up the Working Man's Bicycling Club, weekly gallivants in the summer, returning for liquid refreshment at the Vine Public House. Where also are held the Penny Bank, and the Burial Club, and the Glee Club. In the street, people move aside to let Captain Bellmaker pass. He is large-whiskered and has been a ship's captain (hence his title), sailing the South China Seas with a crew of saints and sinners and he found God when, shipwrecked on an island and tortured by native tattooists (all women), he was saved by a plague of locusts arriving which ate everyone and everything except him.

It is an extraordinary day, though, for they mostly don't have much to distinguish them. Two things make it extraordinary. First, the news that Farmer Hardwood, a grim-faced young chap, who usually sits by the door like a statue with his glass of ale, has come into a fortune, and has left the farm, his aged mother, his cattle, pigs and turnips, even his best suit! It is rumoured he has gone to London, and this I make much of in my patter.

'I hear Farmer Hardwood's gone off to Lunnon town,' I say, 'where men of his size and girth – (*knowing wink*) – are much sought after by doctors and medical men. And ladies – (*another knowing wink*). In fact, a good friend of mine, who is something in the medical line, says Farmer Hardwood's reputation has gone before him. At least this much – (*gesture*) – before him!'

Some kids who have crept around the door snort and stuff their hands into their mouths, otherwise I am talking to the moon, and indeed I catch sight of myself as I clatter about for the clog dance in a large mirror recently installed. For a moment I don't recognize myself, and wonder who the little chap is with a short jacket like mine. And then I realize, it is me, and I wasn't expecting to see myself look so pale and my red hair, once a crowning glory, growing thin, and more grey than red. My hands look too big and my legs too long, and both are paining me these days with aches in the joints and stiffness in the damp weather. Mirrors tell secrets and lies of course. Like many things – and people – in life.

And while I am dancing (for I hardly have to think about it now) I consider the second thing that makes this Wednesday extraordinary – a letter delivered to my lodgings this morning and handed to me by Mrs Gumbs over my cup of tea. A letter from Mrs Strong, of Duchess-court, telling me that Lucy Fitch is dead. Sudden and not explainable, but perhaps another seizure, though a pillow on the floor is not accounted for. Nor the locket which had dropped from her neck and was smashed to flinders.

*I have been much put out, Corney, with doctors and police, and have had an inquest to attend and a funeral also. I thought I should write to you sooner only the note that you left with your address on I have mislaid, and have had to make enquiries. Indeed, it was Mr Minton at the Great Turk who told me where you are, for he is a great one for the Era, the Organ of the Profession, and reads it from front to back every Sunday.*

*Mr Shovelton has been a great help to me and asks me to say that, when we are straight here, he will visit you, for he has things to say to you. Perhaps the same as he has said to me.*

*I am glad you visited us and saw Lucy the last time, and I trust you will remember her as she used to be before she was taken bad, for she was always a good girl though headstrong. I am much alone now, dear Corney, so I had taken up my old work again, for I still have the skills and strength, scrubbing floors and moving barrels keeping me up to the mark. Kitty has left me too, and is dressing hats in London so I have nothing to keep me here.*

*Trusting you are well in your profession and life is being kind to you,*

> *Your friend and Lucy Fitch's grieving mother,*
> *Harriet Strong*

This news has put me in a strange take all day, and I have been walking about, instead of sleeping, and thinking about Bessie Spooner and Lucy, and wondering what Mr Shovelton might have to say to me that he would take the trouble to come all the way here.

Now the piano strikes up a jaunty tune and I'm off the stage as the Sisters Delmar prance on, and certain I am out of sorts, so I send a note to the Captain that I shall not do my second turn, feeling cheap, and will go to bed directly. The Delmars have done and squeeze past me, giggling and light-fingered, so I clutch my pockets where I am able.

'Here, Corney,' says one of them, 'this is our last night. We've got a nobby spot at Paul's in Brum and have to open tomorrow, so we're finishing here early.'

I say I'm right pleased for them, and wish them success and plenty of coin, and on the way back to my lodgings I wonder what Bellmaker will do tomorrow with a turn short. But it is not my concern, and certain I am so weary that I hardly know where I am and find myself outside Mrs Gumbs's door before I know it. That lady is early to bed as a rule, but as I go in she comes out of her sitting room, with her head full of rags and a look upon her face as would stop a saint in his tracks.

'When I took you on, you said nothing about letters and messages, and here are two in one day! I am not a messenger-service, Mr Sage,' she cries, 'and no matter how much you pay me, I will not take on those duties. I keep respectable lodgings. I am a widow and a paid-up member of the New Methodists and Dr Carroll's sick club, and how you, a jig-dancer in a public house, can expect me to carry notes and messages from persons unknown, well I . . .'

She ran out of outrage, and as I am eager that she does not fuel herself up again and have another go, I says as quickly and mildly as I can muster, 'I am very sorry to hear that you have been put out on my account, Mrs Gumbs, for no one knows better than me what a trying life it is for a respectable lady to keep herself from falling out of favour with the Methodys. As you will recall, my own grandmother, God bless her, had just that awkwardness to fret over when she took in a police constable as a favour. For, as you know, the police are called out all times of the day and night, and she was constantly answering her back door as well as her front, taking notes and messages for him. And this police constable never thanked her nor gave her so much as a penny for her trouble. She was very nearly out of the New Connexion in her part of Cottlingham. Which is near the fine city of Cambridge, as you know, Mrs Gumbs.'

I don't stop to draw breath until I have talked her down. I talk her down and round and back into her sitting room and into her tea caddy and a nice pot of tea. No malice intended, of course, just pleasant relations and getting on. So she is sweet enough when we get around to the message from a person unknown.

'A lady, I would say, Mr Sage, for I know a lady when I meet one. Well-spoken and quiet, but not so refined that she had brought paper with her. By no means, for she came in and sat in the hall at my little table and wrote with the stub of a pencil on the back of a scrap of paper she brung out the bottom of her bag! But she was very forceful about giving it to you as soon as you returned, which is why I have been a-sitting here waiting.'

I am much obliged, and weary also, so I ask for the note and the message and silently hope that another tale might not be attached to her parting with it.

The message, she says, is to read the note, taking it out of the drawer in the dresser where she keeps her hairpins and a ball of string. It is folded over and has my name upon it, 'Mr Corney Sage, comedian, care of Mrs Gumbs, Milk Street'. All very proper. And when I unfold it:

> *The Headless Woman Concert Hall*
> *New Clay*
>
> *My dear Mr Sage*
> *I wonder if you would be kind enough to call upon me at the above hostelry tomorrow at ten o'clock. I have recently arrived, having taken the position of Lady Pianiste, and would much value your re-acquaintance as I know no one in this town.*
> *Yours, very truly*
> *Phyllida Marweather (Miss)*

Who is this lady, Mrs Gumbs, do you know her? I ask, and she replies she has never seen her before, but that she gets out so little, being much occupied with cleaning and laundry, that it's a wonder she remembers who her children are. And then takes up where she left off about the New Methodists and being a messenger. I am on my beam-ends by this time and would like very much to be in my bed, even though it is narrower than a jacktar's berth and twice as damp. I turn the note over to fold it up and I am struck by my own name and my own writing.

> *Yor frend Corney Sage. Mind your eye, Lucy*
> *The Vine Concert Hall, New Clay*

It is my note, my very own, and I see myself writing it, at Mrs Strong's table with Lucy looking on and nodding. I turn it over and see the unknown lady's note to me, and back again to see my own note. And back again. I have done this before, sitting with Joe and turning a scrap from the *Era* back and forth and seeing my name and the Sisters Bellwood. What does it all mean? I say to myself and Mrs Gumbs and the world in general. Here I am, comfortable in Mrs Gumbs's warm parlour with a nobby shop for as long as I want it, and yet I feel the coldness of Mr Figgis's doorstep and the biting wind, and the nakedness that goes with knowing you are quite alone in the whole world, and not a fellow human being to call you kindly by your name. Mrs Gumbs stops gabbling for she realizes that I am not listening and am much taken with the note which I then pass to her, and since she is a-sitting there, with her rags and her nightgown, and now a big patched-up blanket about her shoulders and the fire poked up into life, I tell her about it, and how I came to be writing that note in the first place. It takes an hour or more, and Mrs Gumbs is obliged to set the kettle upon the fire again and give her tea caddy another excursion. I finish just as she is stirring the tea, which gives her a chance to get a word in.

'Does Miss Marweather know your friend? Is she an acquaintance perhaps?'

'I have never heard that name before,' I reply, and then straight away think that it's not completely true, because I *have* heard some of it before. Phyllida. Phyll. What bit of my memory has that come from? I reach into my coat pocket for my little screw of bacca to help me think and, like I expect to find it there as it was for so long, I remember Lucy's packet and the locket and the beautiful lady, and the tiny note which I last read with Mrs Strong and which, she tells me in her letter, is broken to pieces. But the note I do not need to see again, for I know that it is from 'Phyll' which is part of the same name on my message. I hear in my head my words to Mrs Strong about how rum it is that all these people are connected up somehow, but I don't know how – Bessie Spooner, and Helen Shovelton in the picture, her brother John who was thought to have murdered Bessie and was free because Lucy saw another face in the Constellation yard who *was* the murderer, who I had seen too. And now this 'Phyll'.

Mrs Gumbs is dozing and when her little chiming clock strikes again it is midnight. But I am not ready to climb the wooden hill yet. I tear off a piece of my handbill, and write, in the best hand I can muster with the stubby pencil, that I shall be pleased to attend upon Miss Marweather at the Headless Woman at ten o'clock, and looked forward to it, signing myself 'C. Sage (Mr), comedian and champ. clog-dancer'. I fold it up, put on my coat and muffler and slip out of the front door.

⁂

She is sitting at a table in the concert room, with a china cup and saucer and a plate of thin toast before her, and she smiles at me and beckons me over.

'Mr Sage, how pleasant it is to see you again! I did wonder if you would come, for as you see I am not Mrs Marsh here in New Clay. You should perhaps be more careful in agreeing to attend upon strange ladies!'

I think she is laughing at me though I can't be sure, and certain I can't be sure about anything to do with this lady, for here indeed is Mrs Marsh who is also Miss Marweather. And who knows who else!

'You are surprised, I should think, to find me here!' she is saying with a lot of breath and shaking of head. 'You must think Mrs Marsh is following you!'

I thought many things, and yes, I did think it was a rum thing to have this lady turn up in such a place, but I never had the idea she was following me. Why should she follow me? What am I to her, just an acquaintance? And sure, she should avoid me by rights, since she owes me money! She is talking about the baby and apologizing for doing a flit.

'It was sickly and weak as you know,' she goes on, stirring her tea, 'and someone told me of a Chinese herbalist who could help, and perhaps give it some special medicine. I thought it was the best thing at the time. And that is why I went. Straight away. As soon as I heard about it. But of course it did no good. The child died.'

I say I am sorry that her baby had died and hoped it was peaceful, and she never says anything, but just looks hard at me. For want of something to say, I said I have never heard of a herbalist, Chinee or otherwise, and wonder if it was parsley and thyme they give, being the only herbs I know? And arrowroot? Mrs Figgis swore by arrowroot.

And she laughs, loudly, throwing back her head, in a way that I thought was rum at the time, seeing as how we were talking about her dead baby. But now, of course, I think of it in quite a different way, if indeed I think of it at all. Which I try not to do.

I wonder what she is doing here and what this is all about. She is talking now about Mr Tipper and the Headless Woman Concert Room and did I think it was a refined place. It has a beautiful piano, she is saying, and Mr Tipper is a charming fellow and easy to impress, but she is not sure whether she wants to remain in New Clay or whether the career of Lady Pianiste in a concert room, however respectable, is to her taste. What do I think? I am more experienced in these matters than she. She would value my opinion.

She is talking fast, like she has too many words in her mouth and they all want to take the air at the same time. I say that the Headless Woman is a good hotel, and Mr Tipper a fair employer, so I have heard. But she is not listening at all, and is off again, talking ninety-nine to the dozen. She is asking me what I have been doing since last she saw me. How nice it is, she says, to meet old friends, and here is the Headless Woman, and what an old-fashioned place it is! But she is curious about me. What adventures have I had since she last saw me in Birmingham? Is Joe still with me? And Chittick? But without waiting for an answer, she is talking again. About the herbalist. Trains. Lodgings. The town and Mr Tipper. Anything and everything, but with her keen eyes upon me.

She talks to me like I am an old friend, as though we have known each other as kids or chewed the fat over a pint of ale, and although I had much sympathy for her and her difficulties, being took so bad, I feel ill at ease, perched on the edge of my chair turning my hat round and round. I am looking at her, but not listening to her. I am noticing the bits of hair on her neck, short and spiky coming through, like it has been cropped by a shickery barber's boy whose razor hadn't seen the strop in days. I think, That hair is not all one. Here are pins standing proud. Here are strands of a different colour, and some bits are thick and some thin. There, by her ear and by the other too, is a pad, a shinny, as Lucy used to call it. I've seen Lucy pin a pad to her head many times to give out that she had more hair than God gave her. And here is Mrs Marsh with loops and locks that are coarse, like they might have belonged to someone else, all over her head. And all put together in a hurry. I watch her mouth, and listen to her voice, like I would a vocaliste. But there is something wrong with her music too, though I cannot say what. She is off-key, I believe, singing too high or too low, and certainly something else in a hurry, but why I cannot say.

Then, it comes like a little explosion, taking me unawares so that I jolt like a puppet.

'Have you seen Lucy, Mr Sage?' she says, calm as a milk-bowl. 'Lucy Fitch, of the Sisters Bellwood? How is she? I do hope she is recovered, for you made mention of her sad calamity, and of course I was never able to visit her. And her sister, Kitty? And her mother? What *is* her name?'

'Mrs Strong,' I reply, and then the words shoot out before I have time to stop. 'But haven't you been to visit them in Duchess-court? Isn't that where you got my note? How you know I'm here, doing my job? Following my profession.'

Then I know, as if I had known all along.

Helen.

John Shovelton.

Bessie.

Lucy.

Halls, probably.

Corney Sage, certainly. What connects them all like a string of savage's beads is her, the woman sitting in front of me, drinking tea from a china cup, and eating thin toast. Phyll. Phyllida Marweather. Mrs Marsh.

And another. A young man. Short hair. Smooth skin. Flash. Trying hard.

I make an excuse, and stand up sharpish. The chair falls over, the table is rocked. I hurry to the door, and as I turn and fumble with the handle, she is still looking at me.

'Mind your eye, Corney,' she says. And smiles.

## 19

## 'Now We Come to It'

**Corney Sage – New Clay**

In the dramas by Mr Trimmer that I like to watch at the Pavilion Theatre, there is always a thrilling end for, come what may, Hector the dog will save his master from dying of cold in a snowstorm, and Nonsuch the native, with a string of lion teeth around his neck, will have a fearsome grapple with a vicious monkey to save Miss Barbara from certain mauling. When Susan or Ruth or Violetta are being drowned or taken advantage of by Mr Heavyman Villain, an agit. from the orchestra or a jolly romping tune brings on William or Charles and, one-two, one-two-three, one-two with his sword or his fists, and 'Oh, William, I knew you would come!', all is well.

Tableau.

Finis.

A fried fish supper and bed.

Yes. A good Pavilion finish-up would do me well now. It is noon and I am sitting in the Golden Bowl, by the window. This is not my usual crib, but I am very bad with the aches and shivers all night, and on my way from Mrs Gumbs's to the Vine, I come over very shivery-shaky and dip in here to find a quiet corner and ease my bones. All is not right with me, for as soon as I sit, I am away in slumber-country, and might have nodded for five minutes or five hours, I don't know, but in cert I am not inclined to shift.

For I am not myself. It is not just that I am tired to death and that even thinking makes my poor head pound. Nor that I am sore in every joint which also wears me to a shadow. No, I am tired of being Corney Sage, comedian, clown, clog-dancer, vocalist, fetcher and taker, runner and carrier, seeker-out and putter-down. I have been moving from town to city, concert hall to circus, street to lodgings without pause to wipe the other eye and, true to you, I have forgotten almost what my body feels like when it does not have to shift. Or when it is not tired from shifting. Why, I am always running, making haste to get to a place, or between shops, or to oblige. Or to get away. I have been running away from the blood and mess of a cold night, and now it has caught up with me and I cannot but think that it will not let me go.

It is very comfortable here in the window, and there is much to see. The Wakes have arrived in New Clay, and everywhere is bustling with newcomers. Under the arches of the Market Hall are the gingerbread sellers, stalls heaped high with spicy cakes, and next to them is Mr Pea-man, with his cry of 'Peas! Peas! Smoking hot!' from morn till night as he stirs his pan and ladles it up high for all to see and smell. We have the mummers in the Market Place too, and their outside show is a wonder to behold. There on the platform are Romans in short dresses and maids in velvet gowns, two Negroes chaffing each other and anyone else, and a midget clown running between their legs, all dancing and posing and singing for the delight of the crowd and to entice them in for the paying show, which is always 'Just about to begin!'. A feast for the eyes are the outside shows, whether it's the menagerie with its tame fox and crow, or the military tournament, which has soldiers doing their marching and parading. Even the strong man and woman, both alike with black hair and rosy cheeks, step out on to the platform to the sound of a trumpet, and heave mighty weights and show their girth.

I can see a deal from my corner crib, and as the sun has moved around to warm me, and the fire also is pleasant, I am not inclined to move, but just to sit and watch the comings and goings. I shift a little to ease myself in the chair, and I am overtaken by shivering, though sweating at the same time. This all-overishness has been coming on apace for the last few days, for my head is full of pains, my throat raw and I have been coughing hard. My adopted father, believing that everything was sent by the Almighty for our good, would have said we should not complain but consider all things, even a fever, as reminder that He is always about. It makes me smile to remember Mr Figgis and those gentle days of my childhood, and though I had an unfortunate beginning, my life has not been all bad, and much of that is due to him and his kindness. His Baptist God was everywhere and saw everything, and it has been sometimes a comfort to imagine Him looking into matters, and I wish fervently (and without disrespect) that He might look into my immediate difficulties, and the worries I have about Mrs Marsh. I am sorely tried, I say under my breath, and am inclined to take off and jump upon the next cart or coach away from this place, only I know that it will do no good, for Mrs Marsh or whoever she might be, having now fixed me in her sight, will surely come after me until she finds the opportunity to silence me once and for all. This is how it seems to me, and no matter how much I turn it about, it still comes out the same.

If I ever come to tell this story from its start to finish (though where I will start and how it will finish I do not know and cannot imagine), people will wonder why I haven't put on my good shoes, tidied myself up and nipped sharpish around to the Station House, and bent the ear of the kindly copper there. I have considered it, and even decided how my story might go when I have Mr Bluebottle's attention. I will say that I know of a lady, who is at this moment installed in the Headless Woman as a respectable Lady Pianiste, only she isn't a regular female at all, but one who dressed up as a young man and killed Bessie Spooner by stamping the life out of her in the yard of the Constellation Concert Rooms, Whitechapel. One person saw it happen, Lucy Fitch and she is dead, and I am sure now he (or she) had something to do with that business. Another person, yours truly, saw and knows too much also, and he too is counting his days, for this young man, Mrs Marsh, Miss Marweather, who, even as I speak, should be entertaining the customers at the Headless Woman, is come here to New Clay after me. For I saw him, like Lucy, and could finger him, and no mistake.

How do you know, asks the imaginary copper, stirring his tea. What does he look like, this young man? Where is your proof that he murdered Lucy Fitch? What makes you believe he means to do you harm? It all sounds very rum to me, and I am much inclined to lock you up for wasting my time. And for public safety.

I cannot blame him. What copper, who is mostly concerned with stray dogs and set-tos between man and wife, could make anything of this tale, so out of the way is it? All I can say is that where there is Mrs Marsh, there also is the young man. That I saw her trunk in Halls's lodgings and it was full of men's clothes. That she wears hairpieces to cover up her own, which is short in the neck. That she took the note I left Lucy, and wrote on it, and let me know by saying, 'Mind your eye, Corney,' and giving me a look like she did once before. Like one of Doré's angels. One that said, I'm on to you.

No, it would not hold water, and, like a punishment for even contemplating the notion, my head is suddenly full of thumping pain and my arms and legs ache like they've been racked, along with the shivers and shakes. But I am a pro and my thoughts turn to my pieces tonight, this being the first night of the new programme and the first day of the Wakes, when the Vine will be crowded out and everyone up to the mark. A man in my profession cannot take sick, and indeed that is why so many of us die in harness. I think, as I take some medicinal brandy and button my little coat up as far as it will go, of Bertie Bertram, whose arms and legs swelled enough to burst, but still did his two turns (he was fine ballad-vocalist and no mistake) and only died when he got to the wings, and then after taking an encore. But it is hard, and no mistake, to turn out when you feel so bad. The sweat stands out on my forehead as I plunge into the fair, and the smells of gingerbread and frying fish only make my stomach turn about whereas usually I would be feasting.

The shows are opening up properly now. Showpeople, still sleepy, are stumbling along the street, with their costume over their arm, or covered from head to toe in a heavy cloak to hide the splendours beneath. They shout to each other, jossing or complaining, and slap each other upon the back and shake hands, glad to be in familiar company. I am sorry not to be one of their number, for though I am acquainted with some showpeople, they are a race apart from the rest of us professionals, and like to keep it that way. They are their own family and have a strong feeling for family ties and the like. A show wedding is, I am told, a wonder to behold, with the wedding-feast taking place among waxwork figures or growling lions! But I am not a showman or even the friend of one, and though I have lived with circus people who are also travellers, they consider themselves a race apart and, like oil and water, do not mix with the showfolk. There is no ill-feeling between show and circus, but they are not family, so I understand.

I shiver awhile in front of Colonel Buxton's Military Show, where the soldiers are stripped to their undershirts, pumping and priming their muscles and calling to the girls to 'Step up and squeeze!'. The showfront is a picture, painted to look like the wall of a castle, with turrets and cannons (also painted) and a great flag fluttering on the pole. The door into the show proper is faked to look like it is a massive oak affair, with a knocker as big as your head and a smart soldier in blue and gold and bristling moustache to guard it. Colonel Buxton, tall and slender as a cat's elbow, is striding about and shouting to one and all to 'Look sharp!' and finding fault with everything. Next to the menagerie, which has a steam organ playing and scenes from tiger hunts painted on the front, the military show is the most elegant in the fair, and this is on account of the Colonel being so particular, for he will have everything and everyone up to the mark. There are no muddy costumes here, and all is neat but not gaudy. Now I am not acquainted with the Colonel, for he is somewhat standoffish, but I have enjoyed a glass in the Vine with his men, and they are regular fellows, who have seen much in the way of fighting for Queen and country and so regard the showlife as an easy shop. Two of my pals are on the platform and tip me a nod when they see me, which earns them a cut from their Gov, who then turns about and sees me.

'Here, you,' he bawls, in a voice like a steamer's whistle. 'Copper-Knob!'

I have not been called that since I was a kid, when I would fight to the ground anyone who dared say it. But in this present circumstance I decide to keep my fists in my pocket.

'I have a job for you,' he goes on, shouting when there is no need, for I am in front of him and not walking away. 'Take these bills and hand 'em out to your customers! Not two at a time, mind! One each. And bull it up.'

I am aching and cold and have no inclination to argue, so I take the bundle of bills with just a nod, and with that comes a wave of sweat and sickness which I struggle to keep down. The Colonel seems satisfied, for without another word to me, he takes a token from the tray and puts it into my hand.

'A free order, for I trust you,' he says, and turns away to bellow at the fellows just limbering up.

The bills announce, in large letters on a yellow ground and with figures striding across the top and bottom, that Colonel Buxton's Military Show is here for the duration of the Wakes, and inside the magnificent pavilion situated on the Market Square can be witnessed demonstrations of marching, swordsmanship, feats of strength and agility, as well as the Mysterious Herculine, who will perform the famous one-armed lifting exhibition on the hour. Don't miss it! It is well done, a natty piece of patter, flash and uncommonly neat. I fold the bills carefully and stuff them in my pocket, as another bout of shivering takes hold of me.

I am in haste to the Vine, already late and expecting a sour look upon the Bellmaker's face. But when I get there it is a pleasant surprise to find him with half a smile, and a full bar. In the concert room the one-legged pianist, Topper, is sober and all our company assembled, which also adds to his good humour. So while the ivory-feeler is running up and down his instrument with the Sisters Wallace (a girl and boy turn, and no great noise), and the bird-man Signor Papagenyo sorts out his pigeons, I find myself a quiet corner, wrap myself up in an old curtain and lie down behind the property baskets. I fall asleep almost straight away, and for the first time in some days am not troubled by bad dreams, but sleep like a baby.

I am woken suddenly by a rumble of thunder. Indeed, that is what at first it appears to be, but then I realize it is someone in the hall, knocking against the chairs and tables. I am hot and burning, the fever has picked up my limbs and wrenched them about, and my ears are singing, but not to a tune I know. I creep out of my hidey-hole (and even so small a movement has me shaking), and I peer between the stage curtains.

It is him.

I would know him anywhere though it is months since I set eyes on him in the Constellation.

He is dressed up to impress the girls, and I see his boots shine and his hair, licked down with macassar oil (which I sniff out straight away), shines also. He wears a natty coat and waistcoat, and carries a thin cane and gloves. He is looking about him, up and down, striding around the place and not caring who knows it. I hear him whistling a little tune, which I know very well, between his teeth.

It is my tune and Billy Ross's. 'Sam Hall'. About the man lining up for a stretching-match.

I try to keep very still, but it is hard since I am shaking enough to rattle the roof, and the cough also starts to rise in my throat. I am not eager to discover what he will do if he finds me, for I am sure that is why he is here. He is bold now, and desperate to keep himself from the law, and has come to deliver me up. But I am hot with fever and not at all in my sensible mind, and wonder if he might be talked around, and in certain the Devil (or someone) whispers in my ear that I might call him over, and shake his hand and say to him, in a friendly manner, that I would have no purpose in telling the law what I know, and that his secret is safe with me. I smile to myself, and fancy he might then clap me on the shoulder and say, 'Your word is good enough for me, Corney Sage. Go on your way. You will not see *me* again.'

But I know that will not happen, for when I see him, through the chink in the curtain, I think I see Mrs Marsh also, sitting before me, with her china cup and saucer, and saying with that smile upon her face, which is no smile at all, 'Mind your eye, Corney.'

The gent is still before me, listening hard, and looking around him like a beggar in a pantry. I am struggling hard now to keep the rattle down in my chest, and my eyes water and I swallow and swallow, but the fever is upon me and my mouth is as dry as a pot of feathers. I cannot help myself and cough like I was going to die.

How small a thing can be salvation? I am not certain, but sure as the young man spins round to find me, so the Sisters Wallace come out of the back, calling in unison, 'Who's there? Who's that? What d'yer want? Where are yer?' like they are reciting in Sunday School. And they find me straight off and cluck and twitter over me, so all I see of the young man is the shape of him standing at the back of the hall, watching. I am shaking and coughing and hot as a whore's pocket, but a true pro too, and after a brandy for my health and a lie down on their cot (with the Sisters still chirping away and bathing my head), I make myself ready for my turn.

The hall is packed with old and new faces, for the fair brings in throngs of hayseeds from far and wide to sell their sheep and marvel at the shows and drink themselves blind. They are easily spied, with their red faces and wide, stupid eyes. They laugh at anything and clap at everything, and make more noise than a Bedlam holiday. And they laugh at Corney Sage and his old jokes like they have never heard a funny story before. So I am almost finished, and in cert my voice has become a ghost of itself and is echoing in my head, so that I hear my own words like they were coming at me down a long tunnel, and the stageboards feel like they are made of sand which I am about to sink into. My little dance – a fast step-dance in clogs which are dead weights upon my feet – is encored, the hayseeds roaring me on again, but the Sisters Wallace are eager to ride my tide of approval and elbow themselves on, for which I am very glad.

I am out of breath and shaking and coughing and lean against the wall to recover when Toddy's head pops round the door. He is the pot-boy, small and thin, like a little stick on legs, and dressed in a waiter's coat and shirt so big for him he trips himself up.

'How now, Toddy?' I say, for I'm fond of him.

'Please, Mr Sage, sir, will you take a drink?'

Will I?!

'Who from, Tod?'

'Dunno, but he's flash.'

285

'Is he, by Jove! Then we'll have a glass with him. And two,' I say much too loudly, for the fever is making me reckless.

Toddy's watery eyes blink at me once, twice, and then he is suddenly bringing on the tray with the brandy bottle (not the best) and a water jug. Brandy has never been my drink, but I help myself, as they say, liberally. Very liberally, and after a fourth tumbler, my belly, which has been empty since my bread and butter at breakfast-time, gives a lurch. Another tumbler to settle it, I tell myself, and one to chase that one down, and all the time the fever is twisting my arms and legs, like the bones are trying to escape.

There is an urgent sensation in my belly that demands attention, and though the sweat stands out on my brow and I am shaking, I rattle to the back door, where the cold night wind slaps me and takes my breath away. I am not a drinking man, and will only take a glass of Butler's Cream of the Valley or Tolley's Old Gold to loosen my vocals before I go on, so I am obliged to lean for some minutes against the wall and breathe in deep, for the brandy has found its way into my legs also and as they go southwards, I am bound to follow, and slide down the wall and on to the damp yard. There are nasty goings-on in my gut, and my mouth is one moment dry, one moment watering itself by the bucket. The fever is coming on fierce, and I know this is a bad business, for my second turn is due. In cert, I am in a sorry way, sitting upon the wet ground, burning hot and freezing cold and trying to keep the gore down, when I hear a voice, then voices, on the other side of the wall. It is a lowish wall, separating the back yard of the concert room from the back yard of the public house. There is a little gate between the two, used by us pros to come and go to the bar without having to walk through the hall.

But these voices.

One of them is Bellmaker.

'I don't know where he is, sir,' he is saying in that voice he keeps especially for gents and nobs. 'Perhaps he's in the bar. We're busy tonight, with the Wakes and the extra customers. He's a popular performer. No doubt someone is standing him a drink.'

'But can you find him for me?' says the other. 'I need to speak to him and the matter is urgent.'

'I've sent the lad out to look for him,' came the reply from the boss.

'That won't do,' says the voice, with an edge to it. 'I want to see Mr Corney Sage now. It is a very grave matter. Are you sure you don't know where he is?'

I hear my name spoken by a voice I have heard before! It echoes round the yard and then around my head. I strain to hear what else is said, but I am hot as hell and the vomit suddenly races into my mouth at such a pace that I cannot hold it, and I turn my head only just in time to stop the contents of my guts dropping into my lap. It hits the stones with a sound like rain but, as I am thinking it will be heard and bring Bellmaker and the other fellow around, the door opens and a roar of laughter empties into the yard, followed by the pale face of Toddy who blinks two or three times and takes in the state of me.

'You've got to come now. The bird bloke's nearly done.'

The sounds of squawking and fluttering inside the hall are a sure sign that Signor Papagenyo has once again failed to prevent his pigeons from flying to the roof. It will take some few minutes to recover them, I think, and then Bellmaker will call an interval. I haul myself up on aching legs, with a belly that feels hard and sore, and start to follow Toddy inside. And it is then that I realize that there is someone still there, on the other side of the wall. For their boots rattle upon the stones, and they are walking swiftly towards the gate.

'Is that you, Corney Sage?' that someone calls out. 'Halloa! Hi! Wait! I want to see you!'

But I don't want to see that someone, for I am scared to know who it is. I cross the yard in two and vault the low gate like an acrobat over the ring fence, and I am once again running down the Row to the light with the familiar sound of footsteps coming after me.

## 20

### 'It Comes on Apace'

**Corney Sage – New Clay**

In the Market Place the Wakes are blazing, like a regular Bartlemy. Drums banging and trumpets blaring, each show trying to outdo the other with noise and flash. Indeed when the big drum is a-beating and the showman is giving it all at a rant all you can do is *watch* the goings-on, for nothing can be heard above the commotion.

Showmen are not the only ones going hell for leather, for the mild people of New Clay are turned for three days into madmen, every one of them drunk as a besom. I am tripped and jostled as I hurry into the crush, but I do not care, for I have it in my poor head that so long as I am closed about by people, even if they are stupid drunk and do not know me, I shall be safe from the one who is coming after me and is out to do me harm. My fever is very high, but I am certain I see his face coming at me in the crowd, and I am only just out of his reach. So I panic some and start to push and heave, but I am caught up in the crush of bodies all pushing and heaving down the avenues of shows and booths and stalls, and there is nothing for it but to stop trying to get through and let the crowd take me where it will.

Which I do. I shuffle along without knowing or caring where I am going. Certain, it is a strange feeling, but warming also, to be so cradled by my fellow men and women.

The crush ends, and I am once more in front of Colonel Buxton's Military Show. The platform is full of parading soldiers, uniformed in red and black, and marching all in step backward and forward until, when Buxton bawls a command, they stop smartly and dress. Then come forward some dapper fellows to tumble about and juggle clubs high into the night sky. Buxton is a great bellower, and promises a show within so rare, he says, that we can hardly imagine it, and which has, as its draw, the great one-armed lifting feat by the Mysterious Herculine which I have read about on the bill. Buxton is giving the patter his best greasing. Not only, says he, are these here fine fellows soldiers, they are h-athel-etes also. They are much admired by all the heads of Europe. The Derbaah of Rajerstan, he says, was particularly taken with the Mysterious Herculine and the one-armed lifting display. 'What does he lift? Skirts?' comes a voice out of the crowd, and before they are inclined to laugh, Buxton is back in there, quick as a rat. We will never find out, he says, if we do not pay our penny to see the show, which is just about to begin.

Some fellows push past me and on to the platform, where a grim-looking woman, a camp-follower perhaps, takes their pennies and lets them through. There is a buzz around me of people deciding what they will do. Where shall they spend their penny? Here? Or the mummers? Or on gingerbread? And then, above the voices, I hear another.

'Corney Sage! Corney Sage! Hoi! Wait! Wait there!'

The moment I move, a great wave of cold comes over me, like I have been doused with water, and I pull my little jacket around me and across my throat, to keep out the chill, but it does no good. Where that voice is coming from I cannot tell, and even as I search among the faces, the drum on the Military Show starts up again with a bang! bang! bang! and my head thuds along with it. Then, I think I see him coming, pushing through. I do see him, his hand aloft, and his pale face racing towards me, with an open mouth, black as a cavern, crying, 'Hoi! Hoi! Hoi! Corney Sage!' But, strange, then he seems to shrink and thin away, and I hear Lucy's voice, and, oh! I see her, in a crowd of young women, turning to wave to me, and smiling me on in that sleepy way she has.

I call out to her, 'Lucy! I thought you was dead!' and she laughs and laughs, with the sound getting louder and louder, when her face shifts and changes and it is not Lucy at all, but a woman mad with drink, shouting in my face to go to that other place and pushing me hard.

As I stumble against the steps and lose my legs, the world turns around and someone close by is saying, 'Look at him! Drunk as a piper! Disgusting!'

But I'm Corney Sage, I say, comedian and champion clog-dancer, sick with the ague. I'm a moderate man, I cry, never over the water-line, but they don't hear me, and continue to give me a wide berth. Above the noise, I hear someone shouting again, closer now.

'Corney Sage! Where are you?'

Lucy! It's Lucy again, and I turn about and search the crowd for her, but her face disappears among the great white moons of faces and lamps, and then comes at me again, out of the dark or the sky or a show-flash. And not Lucy, but her dead face, twisted and ter-rible, and the noise coming from her mouth now is – not Lucy but Bessie that's calling me, for *her* voice I couldn't mistake. I see her! There she is, a-pushing through the crowd, sometimes disappearing but always bobbing up again, waving her hands to me.

'Bessie, girl!' I cry. 'Oh, my eye, it *is* you! You aren't dead!'

Folks around me laugh and shake their heads. I lean against the steps and wipe my eye and laugh myself, for if Bessie's here then she can't be back there, lying in the yard of the Constellation Concert Rooms, Whitechapel, London, with her poor body tram-pled upon and her head smashed about. And none of this will have happened. It will not be real, but a tale told me by a pro one night, cosy by the fire. Or in a penny blood that I've read or a show seen in a gaff. Or on the front of the *Illustrated Police News*. Or sung about. Or shouted about.

But it won't be real.

It won't be real.

Not long now, I think, for Bessie's here and she's a good girl and will see me right! I feel warmed by the thought, and I don't wonder what Bessie is doing in New Clay, and why she has left Whitechapel and should be looking out for me. I am just glad as a fly that I see her sweet face. But I am brought up, coughing hard and have to gasp for breath, for there are pains like knives in my chest. Now that the brandy has worn off, all that is left is the ague, which gnaws at my joints and thunders in my head. My eyes, too, have mist about them, like I am now and then looking through a fog, and as I rub them I knock against a gang of lads outside a booth showing the Giant Girl, where the showman is crying, 'Hi! Hi! Here she is! Miss Rosie French, the biggest girl in the land!'

And he holds up, in his two hands, a huge pair of lady's down-belows, which makes the lads roar with laughter and point at them!

'Ladies and gentlemen, she has already grown out of these, her present undergarment being twice as large! Step right in! Only a penny to see the heaviest girl in the land!'

The lads push and shove each other and lark their way over, knocking off each other's hats, and jossing, and one shouts to me, 'Here you are, mester! Come and get an eyeful of this old girl!'

Then, from the middle of the avenue, I see *him* again, charging down upon me but from a long way away. He is sharp though all around me is misty, and racing towards me at a speed too fast to be right. I hear his heels cracking on the stones, and see his breath coming in clouds. I rub my eyes hard. The crowd parts, and no one seems to notice that this young man is tearing through them, for they just step aside whiles he comes on and on. The shiny black hair and the flash waistcoat are familiar, and I recognize the boots and coat that I saw in her trunk as if they were handed to me piece by piece. On he comes, faster and faster but he makes no gain upon me, though he is running powerful hard, for I see him bare his teeth with the effort of it, and his arms are driving at his sides. And as I stare, his face becomes hers and they melt together under the moon in the Constellation yard. They are the same.

I am roused by a sudden yell from nowhere, and turn around and about and, though I am powerfully struck with fear, force my legs to stumble up the steps of the Military Show though it is like a long march. On the empty platform, I look around and down and hope he and she are lost, but no, there he comes on, cutting through the throng, and growing larger now and closer. In a moment he will be in front of the show, another at the steps and another beside me. I do not know whether fear or fever makes me tremble so, and I reach in my pocket for a wipe with which to dry my head and hands, where my fingers close about a coin. No, not a coin but the token given to me by Colonel Buxton for the delivery of his bills. (To my knowledge, they still lie beneath the boards at the side of the platform in the Vine with the dust and the mice, where I thrust them!) In a moment it is whipped from my hand and I fall through the doors into the show.

The thick heat closes up my nose so perfectly it is as if Bendigo himself had clocked me and I struggle hard to breathe through my mouth, taking in great gulps of hot and smoky air which brings on my coughing again. Little wonder that people try to give me a wide berth, for if I had rung a bell and hung a legend around my neck reading, 'Avoid this man. He has the plague,' I could not have done better. Corney Sage, I say to myself as I stumble over feet and benches and apologize to both, you stand to lose the good favour of your fellow man if you carry on thuswise, and I am much inclined to laugh, and perhaps I do, though only I see the wit.

The show has just begun, and the booth is crowded to the rafters. There are seats up to the roof on three sides but no one sits, all preferring to stand instead to get a better view of the square, which is covered with white sand. The marching display has already begun. There is a side drum giving out a steady rhythm to eight guardsmen who parade, shoulder, dress and march out, and then in comes Colonel Buxton, in his red jacket jingling with medals and gold, holding a sabre above his head which flashes and glitters. It is a fine sight and no mistake, a regular triumph of clever parading, for they are never out of step and always to the mark. The Colonel roars an order and in troop more soldiers ready to show their skills in balancing and tumbling. So much activity and appreciation makes the booth very hot, for the crowd will hurrah every tumble and lift, and give chaff to each other as well as the muscle-grinders in the square, but in a regular, holiday way with no edge. They have left their pals outside and they call to them through canvas and shutters what they can see, and before long another good crowd is paid up and ready to come in. The Colonel hurries things along, for he wants to get to the meat of the show – the Mysterious Herculine and the one-armed lift – and get the next audience in. It is all showman's guff, and I know it well.

I am close to the front, pressed in on all three sides by hayseeds and tipsy boys and at the front by the square-fence, but though pressed and wanting air, I feel safe. The fever is now coming upon me in waves, and I scarcely know whether the side drum is beating or whether it is in my head, and likewise the figure of Colonel Buxton grows and shrinks before my eyes like a pantomime head, and his voice sings loud in my ears or makes me suppose I have come over deaf. I clutch the rail and hold myself steady, and close my eyes and wish that I was in a cool bed, and that my dear mother was beside me, to stroke my head. (I believe my mother does visit me in times of trial, for I have seen her twice – once when, only a little child, I was chased by a mad bull and had to hide in a haystack, and once when I fell in the Thames and was swept along in a mess of foul stuff and dead dogs until I was rescued by a waterman with a bill-hook. I had the fever for days after, owing to the quantity of Thames water I had swallowed, but my mother was by my bedside then, holding my hand, and talking to me about God and angels. Or it might have been a charity visitor.) The fellows around me are roaring again as the balancers and stretchers march away and Colonel Buxton, himself down to his underwear, is painting the air red, white and blue with the deeds of the Mysterious Herculine.

'Herculine's astonishin' strength comes of eatin' only good red meat!' (Cheers.) 'Herculine's astonishin' build comes of drinkin' only good English ale!' (Louder cheers!) 'Herculine's astonishin' . . .'

But I cannot hear any more, for the fellows have returned with dumb-bells and bellweights and the crowd around me cheers to see them. I am looking across the square, past Colonel Buxton's broad shoulders and glistening red neck, and the straining arms of the soldiers carrying on a heavy platform, to the cheering throng, who are hurroo-ing and waving their hats.

For there he is, opposite me, with his pale face and a smile which Mr Doré gave him, after he had done with the angels. The young man meets my eyes, nods, and lifts his hand, a little sign that he has seen me and knows who I am. All is misty around him, but he looks sharp and natty, not a sign that he lives from a trunk, packed up and packed away between towns. Between murders.

Do I run? Do I push my way through this crowd and out into the fair, down the steps, down the avenue, out on to the road that leads to Thendon one way and who-knows-where the other? Do I take off again, looking always over my shoulder, waiting for him and the blow that I know will come one day? If I am going to reach the door, I must go now, for he has moved, and is edging his way around the square.

I do beg your pardon.

Please excuse me.

May I come through.

I can read his lips from here. Soon he will reach me, and then what? A knife stuck under my ribs, perhaps? Quick and silent in a place as thronged as this, and then away. Who would know him? Or even see him.

I am still and everything around me goes quiet, though I can see Colonel Buxton's mouth opening and shutting, and faces laughing, and hands clapping. But I am tired to the very bone, and all of those bones feeling like they will not give me the time of day. And as if to confirm it, I sink to my knees and but for the rail and the press of the crowd around me, I would have fallen to the ground, and not cared who saw me, or whether they picked me up, just as long as they left me there to sleep. For the fever is so much upon me now that I am watching what happens in a dream.

A strapping red coat is pushing among the crowds and picking out, by tapping them on the shoulder, this body and that. Boys, mainly, and some smartish young men. I know what the fellow is about, for it is showman practice to line up volunteers in advance, rather than leave it to chance. My young man has disappeared into the crowd, and I crane around to see if he is behind me, but I am blocked on every side by bodies large and small, so if he is there, I cannot see him. He will come upon me like a thief in the night. As Mr Figgis used to say.

In the square, a rattle of drums and two lines of honour guard presenting arms bring on the Mysterious Herculine, and through the curtain at the back strides a tall masked figure, in white leggings, black laced boots, a white tunic with short sleeves and a broad black belt. A long black cloak lined with red and a close-fitting cap, and this black mask across the eyes complete the get-up. It is an odd costume, and no mistake, like a foreigner or a wizard, though more plain. But it pleases the crowd, which roars and claps and whoops, until my ears pound with the row. As the honour guard marches away, Herculine comes forward and flings off the cloak and strikes a pose, showing two arms not unlike Christmas hams, but broad and muscled nevertheless. A few more poses, then the customary lifting of the weights, and taking them slowly up, over the chest and over the head. A powerful youth, one of those nobbled by the red coat, is called into the square and begged to place a kettlebell in each of Herculine's hands when, of course, he struggles to lift one with both hands! The crowd roars and cheers and the youth is as red as a blacksmith's eye with shame.

All the time, the drum clatters and bangs, and Buxton keeps up a rattle about the skill of Herculine! The hours of practice Herculine has been forced to do! The agonies endured by Herculine from over-stretched muscles and limbs! It is a good show, and Herculine makes much of the applause, not being standoffish, but looking keenly around the audience and stepping up to the rail to shake hands and receive slaps upon the back.

Then the much billed one-armed lifting exhibition.

'Gentlemen! Your attention!' bawls the Colonel. 'Herculine will now perform the famous one-armed lift. A grown man lifted aloft with one arm.'

Herculine is preparing on the platform, pacing about and flexing. Then stopping still and staring into the crowd. Two or three times this happens, and when it does Herculine paces over, kicking up the white sand, and, going to the rail, puts a hand on a kid's head or fellow's shoulder and looks hard into the distance.

'Herculine draws strength using a magical method practised by H-eastern monks!' explains the Colonel. 'You might feel a little

297

weak about the head and neck when Herculine has done with you, but it will soon pass! You will soon recover, so don't come and complain. No money returned!'

Back on the platform, Buxton puts a round red cushion on the flat of Herculine's hand, 'for the volunteer to sit on and for his comfort', there is a rattle on the drum, and a little fellow is pushed into the ring, five or six years old and much inclined to weep. Herculine is not put out. The kid sits on the cushion, and with one easy movement he is hoisted up in the air. But he is not easy, for he begins to wriggle and squirm, and the crowd is just beginning to murmur when, with a swift toss, it is all done, for the child is up in the air and then caught safely, two strong arms cradling him like he was a baby. There is a gasp and a roar, and even I am taken up with the act, though I cannot breathe without coughing and my neighbours have so tumbled my condition that they are very anxious to remove elsewhere. But before they can escape, another boy is thrust into the square, older, longer, and not at all bashful. I glim the red coat press a coin into his hand, to parade and make a show, I expect, and sure enough he prances and preens, and ignores his friends until they pelt him with orange peel and he is obliged to knock one smartly upon the nose. Ever watchful for signs of trouble, the Colonel steps in and, none too gently, invites the lad to step up to the stool. Herculine repeats the show, with as much ease as the little chap before. Though he doesn't wriggle, this fellow soon loses his bravado, and on the way up to the stars he clings to the cushion, and is not easily persuaded to let go. But Herculine once more tosses the boy up, only to catch him again before his arms and legs start to grab the air, and gives him the baby treatment, which he much despises by the look of his face.

Boys are only boys, though, and I wonder how many more the crowd will wear before they tire of it. On the bills, it is a burly looking fellow who is raised up, shoulder-high, while Herculine is laughing and drinking from a foaming glass, and that is what they have paid their penny to see. Every showman knows that if they are disappointed, a holiday crowd might turn spiteful, but there is no opportunity for that here. Another rattle of the drum, another announcement by the Colonel – 'Here is our next brave young volunteer!' – and out into the square swaggers the young man. That young man. He is a good choice, and if I had been the showman, true to you, I would have chosen him. Small enough not to be too weighty. Handsome enough to bend the crowd's eye. But flashy and cocky, the sort of fellow that needs to be brought down and laughed at, have the stuffing taken out of him. He cuts a flash around the square, smiling and nodding, and shaking hands with the Colonel, who salutes him also. The crowd cheers, and he enjoys it, strutting like a cock pheasant, winking and chaffing. Then he turns upon his heel, and he strolls towards me across the square, peeling off his gloves. He reaches the rail before I can escape, and hands me the fine gloves.

'Please look after these for me, Mr Sage. I'll collect them from you after I've finished with this. Perhaps then we can continue our conversation.'

My hands shake, and I am hot and cold, and hot again, all within the time it takes him to hand me his stuff. It *is* him. And it *is* her, and as the fever rises again, I see them both. Both faces. I see how it is managed, and wonder how I could ever have been taken in and cleaned out.

But Herculine is ready. The crowd settles. The young man goes to the little platform. There is a ripple of clapping, and someone hoots, and a chorus of whistles follow. Herculine holds out a hand on which lies the round red cushion, and the young man, with a flourish to the crowd, sits upon it. The arm trembles a bit under the weight, for it must be considerable. Taking the strain, and steadying with the other hand planted just above the knee, there is a moment's pause when the masked face is turned out to the audience and then around to the young man. It is an awkward pose and, though I know nothing about it, I think it must hurt the back and neck. The drum rattles as the young man is raised, slowly, higher, higher, Herculine bracing the other arm against the knee, half kneeling, and shuddering with the effort of raising him. The muscles are hard in that arm and stand out in the neck and shoulders, as they strain to push up, for though he is light, he is no very small fry and the weight is all on Herculine's one hand.

And sure, the young man feels it too, for he is suddenly still and holding on, but when he reaches the shoulder and then above, and the elbow locks, and he can see the top of Herculine's cap, he holds out both arms, as though he has done something nobby, and the crowd cheers wildly. Indeed, he cuts a silly figure, with his legs dangling and looking around as though he owns the world and all in it. The drum rattles on, the Colonel marches up and down, and it seems the young man is up there for an age, waving and saluting, so that when, suddenly, he falls, there is surprise on his face. One moment he is perched up there, the next he is arms and legs and dropping, and landing awkwardly in Herculine's arms. I cannot see how he is caught, for Herculine is still half kneeling. But there is something wrong, for the young man has folded awkwardly, and cut not a sprightly flash figure at all, but one which looks for all the world like a doll. And not jumping up to take the crowd and the clapping, but lying, quite still. Herculine has his head upon one knee and the rest of his body drops, like a sack, and the heels of his boots clatter on the wooden platform.

The crowd roars, and then, to a man, falls silent. A crowd always knows when something is wrong, and it generally goes quiet first. It is strange to go from noise to silence in the time it takes to blink, but that is what happens. The silence wraps around the square, and as it does, everything moves as slow as a snail's gallop. Herculine looks

300

down at the figure, and then up, and with one movement pulls off mask and cap. There is a sound as though all the air is sucked out, as everyone gasps. Herculine's hair falls to the shoulder, the cheeks are smooth, the eyes are soft and blue. Herculine looks around the square and searches for me, Corney Sage, and, finding me, smiles. My legs give way, and I end up on the ground, peering through the railing at Herculine, who is still smiling, which smile belongs to Mrs Strong, Lucy's ma.

Then she looks at the young man. Mrs Marsh. Miss Marweather. Cradled in her arms is the young man who killed her Lucy. And Bessie. And was out for me. But that young man is saying nothing and his head is lying awkwardly upon Mrs Strong's knee and, when she releases her hold, that head rolls over and the eyes fix dead upon me.

The crowd gasps. Colonel Buxton is stunned, but only for a moment, and then rounds up all his forces to empty the show. All about me are legs and feet, and I am kicked and trodden upon and pressed until I think I shall die. But Mrs Strong is still there, on the platform, cradling the young man who is dead and his neck quite snapped, and I see tears rolling down her cheeks before the darkness washes over me like a warm tide.

## 21

*Safe at Last*

**Corney Sage – New Clay**

I am taken up by a pair of strong arms, which fold about me and put me in mind of my father, Mr Figgis, when I was just a little fellow. Though a Baptist, and not much given to affection when Mrs Figgis was hovering, when we were alone he would sometimes take me upon his knee, and tell me stories of giants and fairies and wrap me around with his arms if I got frightened, and when I fell and hurt myself, he would pick me up and hold me close to his chest. I remember the rough feel of his everyday coat against my cheek, which smelled of much wear and staleness, and the hairs upon his chin, and the round, pink mole hiding among them, which I longed to touch, but never dared. I am floating in these arms, out into the night, from heat into cold, and think I must be heading up to the stars, for in the black sky they seem very close and bright. If I am dead then it is not too bad, I think, for whoever has come to fetch me is careful with me, and I feel no pain at all, just the easy motion of someone walking in the dark and holding me in their strong arms.

That journey comes back many times, though I do not know who is carrying me and where they have taken me. But the bed is cool and soft, and there is a candle in the corner, and a fire in the grate,

302

and the light from both dances on the walls in a pleasing way that I like to watch. I know I am very sick, and have been so for some days, and the way in which the fever comes on, like a great army marching up and over my body and twisting my joints like they were tent-ropes, is very terrible. I think the doctor comes, and I say I have nothing to pay him with, but I cannot tell what he says, for though his mouth moves I can hear nothing except the army marching in my ears. He comes and goes a few times I think, but I cannot be sure, for the room is often full of people.

Here in this room are gathered people I have not seen for years, and true to you, some of them I know are dead and gone. My old master, Mr Halfpenny, who was swept away by a wave on the Lincolnshire coast thirty years ago, and his horse with him. Little Susie Wickenham, a tot, who died with her baby brother and their ma, all in one room, when a fire swept through a lodging house next door to mine. Old Roman, the hawker, with no roof to his mouth and only one eye, who was set upon by roughs for his savings which were said to be a fortune, but were only three shillings. He died in a ditch, all alone under the sky, lying there for four days before anyone came upon him. Rats, they said, had begun gnawing his fingers. And my father, Mr Figgis, who I have not seen since I left home when fifteen years old. He stands quiet in the corner of the room, and will not come over at first, and I am obliged to call him, when he does, but slowly. He takes my hands in his, and I am a child again, for I see his hands through my child's eyes, rough and thin, with their veins standing out like rivers on a map. Those hands held mine many a time, and they hold them now.

Finally, when the room is buckling and heaving, and the ceiling is streaming red, *she* comes. I know it is her. I have been calling for her and I know she will come, and I see her for the first time in all my life. She is as pretty as I knew she would be, with red hair like mine, and a smile that is sad and happy. She bends over me and kisses my cheek, and her hair falls across my face, when I smell lavender and clean linen and the fresh salt air. I think I must begin to cry, for she reaches out and wipes away my tears, and it is the softest touch I have ever felt.

I think my heart will break.

Is there an end to this? Certainly, for I must have one, otherwise my tales in the public will not be worth a clap on the back and a 'What will you have, Corney Sage?' I do produce the illustrated news-papers to prove my point, on which my face appears and that of the young man and Mrs Strong. And John Shovelton. He visits me often when I am getting better. Indeed it is he who has paid the doctor's bills, and sees that I have my old room back in the Old Pitcher at Springwell. It is a great comfort to see those yellow walls again, and to listen to the sound of the river through my window, and know that there is no one coming for me to do me harm. I have taken to visiting Mr Beeton in his box. We are great pals, and take a turn along the river to walk and talk about books that I have never read, but which doesn't seem to matter.

Yes, I am visited regular by Mr John Shovelton, and of course it was he who was asking for me in Springwell and looking out for me in New Clay, was quizzing Bellmaker of my whereabouts, and who carried me, in his arms, out of the Military Show. He it was who dis-covered Mrs Marsh's companion, Mrs Gifford, and a relative, an uncle, who were pleased to share their knowledge (which was very little) for a consideration (which was very great). He had not guessed who the murderer was, but had asked more questions than a lawyer and worked out something we had all missed – that who-ever killed Bessie also sent Lucy heavenward. He had sat with Mrs Strong and puzzled out with her that where Corney Sage was, there the murderer would be too. He had not expected Mrs Strong to do what she did, but she was powerful cut up over Lucy, and he thought that might explain much.

He finds me one day outside the Old Pitcher, with Mr Flynn's mastiff at my feet and a glass of Bunty's Best at my elbow. Mrs Flynn has put a shawl about my shoulders and a blanket across my knees, and though I would have generally pished at such softness, these days I am a changed man, and more accepting of kindness and gentle actions. We do not say much about the past, for it is my belief that there are things that need no more saying, and he seems to be of the same opinion. We have already put away the murders done by Mrs Marsh, or that young man who she pretended to be, and John has talked about his sister and whether murder was knocking at *her* door. Did it ever cross your mind, he says, that Mrs Marsh and Phyll Marweather and James Yates were all the same person? Even for a moment? I said no, not until the end, for I was never looking for him. When I saw Mrs Marsh, I saw Mrs Marsh, just as when I saw Herculine that is who I saw and not Mrs Strong. And the same for the young man. Did I ever think, Might this be a lady dressed up? No. Never.

All the same, when he left me, and a cool breeze came off the river and made me shiver, I turned over in my mind the strange adventure that had caught me up in it, like a tiddler in a child's net, and had trapped me there, unawares, until I was quite lost. And I wondered if I could ever again rub along with my fellows quite as cheerful in the world as I used to, and not be all the time looking over my shoulder and wondering if shadows are truly shadows, or someone walking behind me.

# ACKNOWLEDGEMENTS

*Walking in Pimlico* strode out of my lifelong fascination with the nineteenth century, but its peculiar gait originated in my academic work, and in particular a long research project on nineteenth-century popular entertainment at Royal Holloway, University of London. Two supporters must be acknowledged: the Arts and Humanities Research Council which provided the funding for the project, and Professor Jacky Bratton who guided the research and was Corney Sage's first admirer. Colleagues and friends in the Drama Department at the University of Manchester have been very generous with their support: Hayley Bradley, Maggie Gale and Viv Gardner. Jan Needle introduced me to Lucy Fawcett at Sheil Land Associates. She gave *Walking in Pimlico* the nod of approval, and for which kindness I shall always be grateful since there I met Gaia Banks, my wise, patient and talented literary agent. Jan has also been on the end of a telephone to boost my ever-failing confidence, as have many other good friends who read the manuscript in its different stages: Gilli Bush-Bailey, Helen Day-Mayer, Michael Eaton, Felicity Featherstone, Angela Read, Claire Richards, John Thesiger and Jane Traies. Amy Myers gave me sound, practical advice and showed me how to unravel the cat's cradle of a plot in which I became ensnared. Kate Parkin and Victoria Murray-Browne at John Murray made sound suggestions and positive noises, and guided this strange tale into print.

Finally, my wonderful family (James, mum and dad) have been constantly supportive in so many ways, from proofreading to supplying coffee and hugs – thank you.

# GLOSSARY

Extracts from *Murray's Dictionary of Slang, Cant and Flash Words and Phrases* (1857, 3rd edition)

**above the sawdust**: low down, though not at the bottom of, the hierarchy of entertainers
**berth**: place, employment
**blue boys**: police
**bluebottle**: policeman
**bull it up, to**: to exaggerate, embellish
**chaff, to**: to joke, banter
**clogs**: clog-dancing
**clucking and nodding**: acting in the correct manner, fitting in
**con a wheeze, to**: to learn a joke
**cove**: man, chap
**cross-hatched**: worried, anxious
**dollar**: coin
**duds**: clothes
**everyday**: daily wear
**fagged**: tired out, exhausted
**gamp**: umbrella
**hay-seed**: person from the countryside
**mardy**: grumpy, petulant

**more inclined to eel pie than potted shrimps**: cheap, unrefined

**nark**: spy, informant

**nobbler**: policeman

**nobby**: smart, upmarket

**peeler**: policeman

**physog**: face

**plates**: feet

**pod, to be in**: pregnant

**pump-thunderer**: blusterer

**ratting ken**: low dwellings used to host rat-fighting competitions

**refuse to go, to**: to go down badly with an audience

**rorty**: lively, jolly

**sea-William**: landlubber

**shickery**: incompetent, shabby

**shop**: job, employment

**slapping lime-and-litharge on your hairy lip of a Sunday**: the bandsman's practice of tending to his moustache, on a Sunday, to keep it dark and glossy

**swell**: smartly dressed gentleman

**tan**: sawdust used in the circus ring

**tell, to**: to go down well with an audience

**three-piecer**: a good tale

**under the stars**: alive

**weepers (abbreviation of Piccadilly weepers)**: long, flowing side-whiskers

# Read more . . .

## Beatrice Colin

### THE LUMINOUS LIFE OF LILLY APHRODITE

**Decadent, tantalizing Berlin in a Germany torn apart by war at the turn of the twentieth century**

The illegitimate, orphaned daughter of a cabaret dancer, Lilly Nelly Aphrodite's early life is one of reinvention. Transformed from maid to war bride via tingle-tangle nightclub girl, she lands in the heart of the glamorous motion picture world and quickly becomes one of Germany's leading silent film stars.

But when she falls in love with a Russian director, she has no idea that the affair will span decades, cross continents and may ultimately cost her everything.

'The storytelling is masterful and the language magical . . . a rich book, in both its prose and in the strength of its characters'
*Sunday Times*

'Full of suspense, this is an all-feeling novel, seductively and dramatically told' *Daily Mail*

'An exceptional novel' *Sunday Herald*

*Order your copy now by calling Bookpoint on 01235 827716 or visit your local bookshop quoting ISBN 978-1-84854-031-6*
*www.johnmurray.co.uk*